SELMA LAGERLÖF (a farm in Värmland, trained as a teacher and became, in her life-time, Sweden's most widely translated author ever. Novels such as *Gösta Berlings saga* (1891; *Gösta Berling's Saga*) and *Jerusalem* (1901-02) helped regenerate Swedish literature, and the school reader, *Nils Holgersson's Wonderful Journey through Sweden* (1906-07), has achieved enduring international fame and popularity. Two very different trilogies, the Löwensköld trilogy (1925-28) and the Mårbacka trilogy (1922-32), the latter often taken to be autobiographical, give some idea of the range and power of Lagerlöf's writing. Several of her texts inspired innovative films, among them *Herr Arnes pengar* (*Sir Arne's Treasure*), directed by Mauritz Stiller (1919) and based on *Herr Arnes penningar* (1903; *Lord Arne's Silver*), and *Körkarlen* (*The Phantom Carriage*), directed by Victor Sjöström (1921) and based on Lagerlöf's *Körkarlen* (1912). She was awarded the Nobel Prize for Literature, as the first woman ever, in 1909, and elected to the Swedish Academy, again as the first woman, in 1914. Having been able to buy back the farm of Mårbacka, which her family had lost as the result of bankruptcy, Lagerlöf spent the last three decades of her life combining her writing with the responsibilities for running a sizeable estate. Her work has been translated into close to 50 languages.

PETER GRAVES has translated works by Linnaeus, Jacob Wallenberg, August Strindberg, Selma Lagerlöf and Peter Englund, and he has been awarded a number of translation prizes. Before retiring he was Head of the School of Literatures, Languages and Cultures at the University of Edinburgh, where he taught Swedish.

Some other books from Norvik Press

Juhani Aho: *The Railroad* (translated by Owen Witesman)
Kjell Askildsen: *A Sudden Liberating Thought* (translated by Sverre Lyngstad)
Victoria Benedictsson: *Money* (translated by Sarah Death)
Hjalmar Bergman: *Memoirs of a Dead Man* (translated by Neil Smith)
Jens Bjørneboe: *Moment of Freedom* (translated by Esther Greenleaf Mürer)
Jens Bjørneboe: *Powderhouse* (translated by Esther Greenleaf Mürer)
Jens Bjørneboe: *The Silence* (translated by Esther Greenleaf Mürer)
Johan Borgen: *The Scapegoat* (translated by Elizabeth Rokkan)
Kerstin Ekman: *Witches' Rings* (translated by Linda Schenck)
Kerstin Ekman: *The Spring* (translated by Linda Schenck)
Kerstin Ekman: *The Angel House* (translated by Sarah Death)
Kerstin Ekman: *City of Light* (translated by Linda Schenck)
Arne Garborg: *The Making of Daniel Braut* (translated by Marie Wells)
Svava Jakobsdóttir: *Gunnlöth's Tale* (translated by Oliver Watts)
P. C. Jersild: *A Living Soul* (translated by Rika Lesser)
Selma Lagerlöf: *Lord Arne's Silver* (translated by Sarah Death)
Selma Lagerlöf: *The Löwensköld Ring* (translated by Linda Schenck)
Selma Lagerlöf: *The Phantom Carriage* (translated by Peter Graves)
Viivi Luik: *The Beauty of History* (translated by Hildi Hawkins)
Henry Parland: *To Pieces* (translated by Dinah Cannell)
Amalie Skram: *Lucie* (translated by Katherine Hanson and Judith Messick)
Amalie and Erik Skram: *Caught in the Enchanter's Net: Selected Letters* (edited and translated by Janet Garton)
August Strindberg: *Tschandala* (translated by Peter Graves)
August Strindberg: *The Red Room* (translated by Peter Graves)
Hjalmar Söderberg: *Martin Birck's Youth* (translated by Tom Ellett)
Hjalmar Söderberg: *Selected Stories* (translated by Carl Lofmark)
Anton Tammsaare: *The Misadventures of the New Satan* (translated by Olga Shartze and Christopher Moseley)
Elin Wägner: *Penwoman* (translated by Sarah Death)

Nils Holgersson's Wonderful Journey through Sweden

Volume 1

by

Selma Lagerlöf

Translated from the Swedish
and with an Afterword by
Peter Graves

Illustrations and Illustrator's Afterword by
Bea Bonafini

Series Preface by Helena Forsås-Scott

Norvik Press
2013

Originally published by Albert Bonniers förlag, Stockholm, under the title of *Nils Holgerssons underbara resa genom Sverige* (1906-07).

This translation and Translator's Afterword © Peter Graves 2013.
Series Preface © Helena Forsås-Scott 2013.
Illustrations and Illustrator's Afterword © Bea Bonafini 2013.
The translator's moral right to be identified as the translator of the work has been asserted.

Norvik Press Series B: English Translations of Scandinavian Literature, no. 56-1

A catalogue record for this book is available from the British Library.

ISBN: 978-1-870041-96-6

Norvik Press gratefully acknowledges the generous support of Svenska Akademien (The Swedish Academy) towards the publication of this translation.

Norvik Press
Department of Scandinavian Studies
University College London
Gower Street
London WC1E 6BT
United Kingdom
Website: www.norvikpress.com
E-mail address: norvik.press@ucl.ac.uk

Managing editors: Sarah Death, Helena Forsås-Scott, Janet Garton, C. Claire Thomson.

Illustrations: Bea Bonafini
Map of Sweden: Bea Bonafini
Cover design: Sture Pallarp
Cover illustration: based on *Photograph of writer Selma Lagerlöf*, taken in 1906 by A. Blomberg, Stockholm.
Layout: Marita Fraser

Printed in the UK by Lightning Source UK Ltd.

Contents

Nils Holgersson's Wonderful Journey through Sweden, Volume 1

Map of Sweden		7
Series Preface		9
I	The Boy	15
II	Akka from Kebnekaise	34
III	With the Wild Birds	54
IV	Glimmingehus	75
V	The Great Crane Dance on the Kullaberg	91
VI	Rainy Weather	103
VII	The Staircase with the Three Steps	110
VIII	By Ronneby River	115
IX	Karlskrona	127
X	The Journey to Öland	137
XI	The Southern Point of Öland	142
XII	The Big Butterfly	151
XIII	The Island of Lilla Karlsö	156
XIV	Two Towns	171
XV	The Legend of Småland	185
XVI	The Crows	191
XVII	The Old Peasant Woman	212
XVIII	From Taberg to Huskvarna	224
XIX	The Great Bird Lake	229
XX	The Prophecy	245
XXI	Homespun Cloth	251
XXII	The Saga of Karr and Greyfur	255
XXIII	The Beautiful Paradise Garden	292
XXIV	In Närke	306
XXV	The Ice Breaks Up	323
Notes		330
Translator's Afterword		332
Illustrator's Afterword		342
Photographic Credits		348

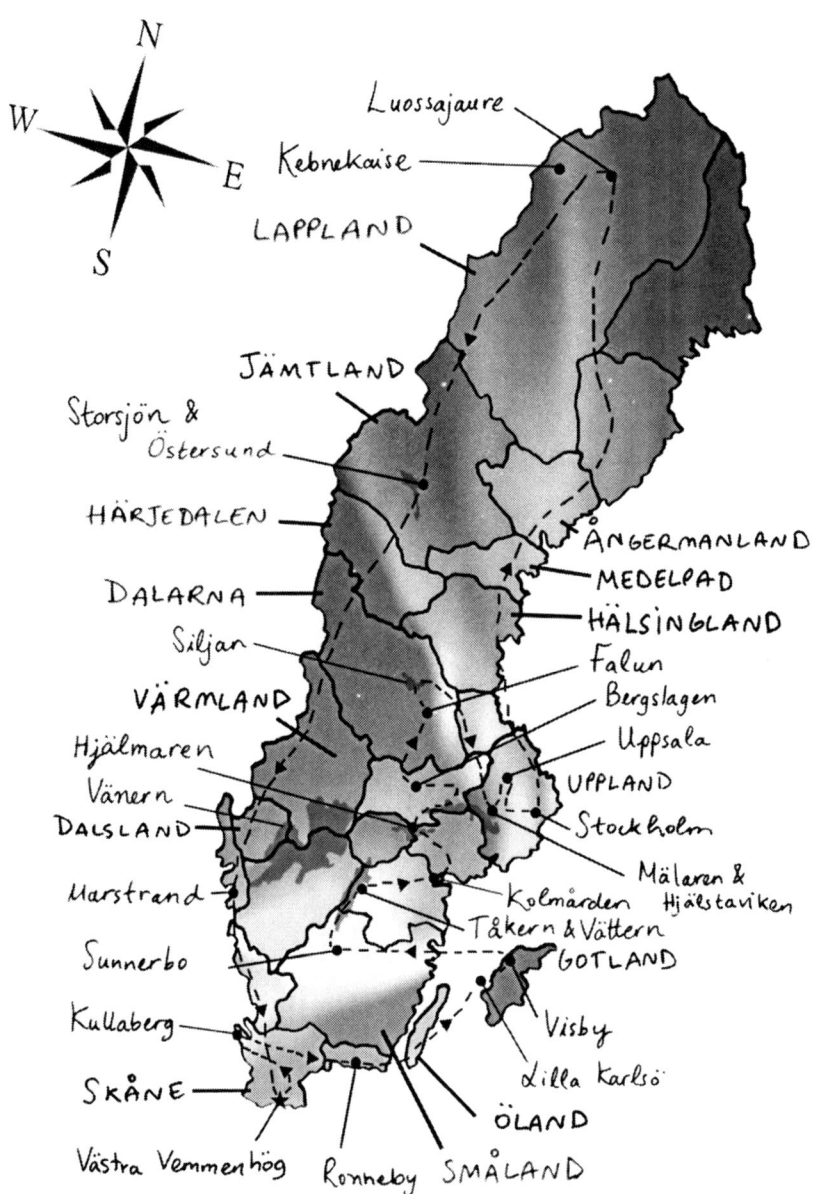

Series Preface

In the first comprehensive biography of the Swedish author Selma Lagerlöf (1858-1940), Elin Wägner has provided a snapshot of her at the age of 75 that gives some idea of the range of her achievements and duties. Sitting at her desk in the library at Mårbacka with its collection of classics from Homer to Ibsen, Lagerlöf is also able to view several shelves of translations of her books. Behind her she has not only her own works and studies of herself but also a number of wooden trays into which her mail is sorted. And the trays have labels like 'Baltic Countries, Belgium, Holland, Denmark, Norway, England, France, Italy, Finland, Germany, Sweden, Switzerland, the Slavic Countries, Austria-Hungary, Bonnier [her Swedish publisher], Langen [her German publisher], Swedish Academy, the Press, Relatives and Friends, Treasures, Mårbacka Oatmeal, Miscellaneous Duties'. Lagerlöf's statement, made to her biographer Elin Wägner a few years previously, that she had at least contributed to attracting tourists to her native province of Värmland, was clearly made tongue-in-cheek.

How could Selma Lagerlöf, a woman born into an upper-middle-class family in provincial Sweden around the middle of the nineteenth century, produce such an œuvre (sixteen novels, seven volumes of short stories) and achieve such status and fame in her lifetime?

Growing up on Mårbacka, a farm in the province of Värmland, at a time when the Swedish economy was predominantly agricultural, Selma Lagerlöf and her sisters learnt about the tasks necessary to keep the self-sufficient household ticking over, but their opportunities of getting an education beyond that which could be provided by their governess were close to non-existent. Selma Lagerlöf succeeded in borrowing money to spend three years in Stockholm training to become a teacher, one of the few professions open to women at the time, and after qualifying in 1885 she spent ten years teaching at a junior high school for girls in Landskrona, in the south of Sweden. Mårbacka had to be sold at auction in 1888, and Lagerlöf only resigned from her teaching post four years after the publication of her first novel, establishing herself as a writer in a Sweden quite different from the one in which she had grown up. Industrialisation in Sweden was late but swift, and Lagerlöf's texts found new readers among the urban working class.

Lagerlöf remained a prolific author well into the 1930s, publishing chiefly novels and short stories as well as a reader for school children, and she soon also gained recognition in the form of honours and prizes: an Honorary Doctorate at the University of Uppsala in 1907, the Nobel Prize for Literature, as the first woman, in 1909, and election to the Swedish Academy, again as the first woman, in 1914. Suffrage for women was only introduced in Sweden in 1919, and Lagerlöf became a considerable asset to the campaign. She was also able to repurchase Mårbacka, including the farm land, and from 1910 onwards she combined her work as a writer with the responsibility for a sizeable estate with a considerable number of employees.

To quote Lagerlöf's most recent biographer, Vivi Edström, she 'knew how to tell a story without ruining it'; but her innovative literary language with its close affinity with the spoken language required hard work and much experimentation. 'We authors', Lagerlöf wrote in a letter in 1908, 'regard a book as close to completion once we have found the style in which it allows itself to be written'.

Her first novel, *Gösta Berlings saga* (1891; *Gösta Berling's Saga*), was indeed a long time in the making as Lagerlöf experimented with genres and styles before settling for an exuberant and innovative form of prose fiction that is richly intertextual and frequently addresses the reader. Set in

Värmland in the 1820s with the young and talented Gösta Berling as the hero, the narrative celebrates the parties, balls and romantic adventures throughout 'the year of the cavaliers' at the iron foundry of Ekeby. But it does so against the backdrop of the expulsion of the Major's Wife who has been the benefactress of the cavaliers; and following her year-long pilgrimage and what has effectively been a year of misrule by the cavaliers, it is hard work and communal responsibility that emerge as the foundations of the future.

In *Drottningar i Kungahälla* (1899; *The Queens of Kungahälla*) Lagerlöf brought together a series of short stories and an epic poem set in Viking-age Kungälv, some distance north of Gothenburg, her aim being to explore some of the material covered by the medieval Icelandic author Snorri Sturluson in *Heimskringla*, but from the perspectives of the female characters. The terse narrative of *Herr Arnes penningar* (1903; *Lord Arne's Silver*), set in the sixteenth century in a context that highlights boundary crossings and ambivalences, has a plot revolving around murder and robbery, ghosts, love and eventual punishment. The slightly earlier short novel *En herrgårdssägen* (1899; *The Tale of a Manor*) similarly transcends boundaries as it explores music and dreams, madness and sanity, death and life in the context of the emerging relationship between a young woman and a man.

A few lines in a newspaper inspired Lagerlöf to her biggest literary project since *Gösta Berling's Saga*, the two-volume novel *Jerusalem* (1901-02), which also helped pave the way for her Nobel Prize later in the decade. The plot launches straight into the topic of emigration, prominent in Sweden since the 1860s, by exploring a farming community in the province of Dalarna and the emigration of part of the community to Jerusalem. The style was inspired by the medieval Icelandic sagas, but although the focus on emigration also establishes a thematic link with the sagas, the inversions of saga patterns such as bloody confrontations and family feuds become more prominent as the plot foregrounds peaceful achievements and international understanding. Yet this is first and foremost a narrative in which traditional structures of stability are torn apart, in which family relationships and relations between lovers are tried and often found wanting, and in which the eventual reconciliation between old and new comes at a considerable price.

Lagerlöf had been commissioned to write a school reader in 1901, but it was several years before she hit on the idea of presenting the geography, economy, history and culture of the provinces of Sweden through the narrative about a young boy criss-crossing the country on the back of a goose. While working on *Nils Holgerssons underbara resa genom Sverige* (1906-07; *Nils Holgersson's Wonderful Journey through Sweden*), Lagerlöf doubted that the text would find readers outside Sweden; paradoxically, however, *Nils Holgersson* was to become her greatest international success. Once perceived as an obstacle to the ambitions to award Lagerlöf the Nobel Prize for Literature, *Nils Holgersson* is nowadays read as a complex and innovative novel.

Körkarlen (1912; *The Phantom Carriage*) grew out of a request from The National Tuberculosis Society, and what was intended as a short story soon turned into a novel. The narrative about a victim of TB, whose death on New Year's Eve destines him to drive the death-cart throughout the following year and who only gains the respite to atone for his failures and omissions thanks to the affection and love of others, became the basis in 1921 for one of the best-known Swedish films of the silent era, with Victor Sjöström as the director (Sjöström also played the central character) and with groundbreaking cinematography by J. Julius (Julius Jaenzon).

The First World War was a difficult time for Lagerlöf. While many of her readers, in Sweden and abroad, were expecting powerful statements against the war, she felt that the political events were draining her creative powers. *Kejsarn av Portugallien* (1914; *The Emperor of Portugallia*) is not just a novel about the miracle of a newborn child and a father's love of his daughter; it is also a text about a fantasy world emerging in response to extreme external pressures, and about the insights and support this seemingly mad world can generate. Jan, the central character, develops for himself an outsider position similar to that occupied by Sven Elversson in Lagerlöf's more emphatically pacifist novel *Bannlyst* (1918; *Banished*), a position that allows for both critical and innovative perspectives on society.

Quite different from Lagerlöf's war-time texts, the trilogy consisting of *Löwensköldska ringen* (1925; *The Löwensköld Ring*), *Charlotte Löwensköld* (1925) and *Anna Svärd* (1928) is at once lighthearted and serious, a narrative *tour de force* playing on ambivalences and multiple interpretations to an extent that has the potential to destabilise, in retrospect, any hard and fast readings of Lagerlöf's œuvre. As the trilogy calls into question the ghost of the old warrior General Löwensköld and then traces the demise of Karl-Artur Ekenstedt, a promising young minister in the State Lutheran Church, while giving prominence to a series of strong and independent female characters, the texts explore and celebrate the capacity and power of narrative.

Lagerlöf wrote another trilogy late in her career, and one that has commonly been regarded as autobiographical: *Mårbacka* (1922), *Ett barns memoarer* (1930; *Memories of My Childhood*), and *Dagbok för Selma Ottilia Lovisa Lagerlöf* (1932; *The Diary of Selma Lagerlöf*). All three are told in the first person; and with their tales about the Lagerlöfs, relatives, friends, local characters and the activities that structured life at Mårbacka in the 1860s and 70s, the first two volumes can certainly be read as evoking storytelling in the family circle by the fire in the evening. The third volume, *Diary*, was initially taken to be the authentic diary of a fourteen-year-old Selma Lagerlöf. Birgitta Holm's psychoanalytical study of Lagerlöf's work (1984) read the Mårbacka trilogy in innovative terms and singled out *Diary* as providing the keys to Lagerlöf's œuvre. Ulla-Britta Lagerroth has interpreted the trilogy as a gradual unmasking of patriarchy; but with 'Selma Lagerlöf' at its centre, this work can also be read as a wide-ranging and playful exploration of gender, writing and fame.

With the publication over the past couple of decades of several volumes of letters by Lagerlöf, to her friend Sophie Elkan (1994), to her mother (1998), to her friend and assistant Valborg Olander (2006), and to her friends Anna Oom and Elise Malmros (2009-10), our understanding of Lagerlöf has undoubtedly become more complex. While the focus of much of the early research on Lagerlöf's work was biographical, several Swedish studies centring on the texts were published in connection with the centenary of her birth in 1958. A new wave of Lagerlöf scholarship began to emerge in Sweden in the late 1990s, exploring areas such narrative, gender, genre, and aesthetics; and in the 1990s the translation, reception and impact of Lagerlöf's texts abroad became an increasingly important field, investigated by scholars in for example the US, the UK and Japan as well as in Sweden. Current research is expanding into the interrelations between a range of media in Lagerlöf, performance studies, cultural transmissions, and archival studies. As yet there is no scholarly edition of Lagerlöf, but thanks to the newly established Selma Lagerlöf Archive (Selma Lagerlöf-arkivet, SLA) a scholarly edition in digitised form is underway.

By the time Lagerlöf turned 80, in 1938, she was the most widely translated Swedish writer ever, and the total number of languages into which her work has been translated is now close to 50. However, most of the translations into English were made soon after the appearance of the original Swedish texts, and unlike the original texts, translations soon become dated. Moreover, as Peter Graves has concluded in a study of Lagerlöf in Britain, Lagerlöf 'was not well-served by her translators [into English]'. The Norvik Press series 'Lagerlöf in English' aims to remedy this situation.

Helena Forsås-Scott

I

THE BOY

THE ELF   Sunday, 20 March

Once upon a time there was a boy of about fourteen years of age who was tall, gangling and flaxen-haired. His greatest pleasures were sleeping and eating, closely followed by making mischief. He was, in fact, good for more or less nothing.

It was Sunday morning and the boy's parents were getting ready to go to church. The boy, however, was sitting on the edge of the table in his shirtsleeves thinking how wonderful it was that both his father and his mother were going out. He would be able to do anything he liked for a couple of hours. 'I can take down father's gun and fire it without anyone interfering,' he said to himself.

It was almost as if his father guessed what was going through the boy's mind because he stopped in the doorway on his way out and turned round. 'Since you don't want to come to church with your mother and me,' he said, 'the least you can do is to read one of Luther's sermons at home. Will you promise to do that?'

'Yes,' said the boy, 'I don't mind doing that.' What he actually thought, of course, was that he would read just as much as suited him.

The boy had never seen his mother move so nimbly before; she was over by the bookshelf in a trice, took down Luther's Sermons, opened it at the sermon for the day and laid it on the table by the window. She also opened the prayer-book and set it alongside the Sermons before pulling the big armchair up to the table. They had bought the chair at the auction at the manse in Vemmenhög the year before and usually it was only his father who was allowed to sit in it.

The boy sat there thinking that his mother was going to far too much trouble laying out all these things when he had no intention of reading more than one or two pages. But then, for the second time, his father seemed to read his thoughts. He went over to the boy and said in a stern voice: 'And remember to read it properly! When we come back I am going to test you on every page and woe betide you if you have skipped any of them.'

To add insult to injury, his mother said: 'The sermon is fourteen and a half pages. You'll have to start reading straightaway if you hope to get through it.'

At last they left, and as the boy stood in the doorway watching them go, he thought he was trapped. 'There they go now, and I'm sure they'll be congratulating themselves on having fixed things so I'll have to spend all my time on that sermon while they're out,' he thought.

His father and mother, however, were far from congratulating themselves, in fact, they were more than a little downhearted. They were poor smallholders and their holding was not much bigger than a garden plot. When they had first moved there, it could not support more than one pig and a couple of hens but now, since they were an exceptionally capable and hard-working couple, they had both cows and geese. Things had gone very well for them and, had it not been for their son, they would have been two pleased and happy people walking to church that beautiful morning. As it was, however, the boy's father complained that not only was his son slothful and lazy, he did not want to learn anything in school and he was so useless you hardly dared let him tend the geese. His mother did not deny the truth of any of this, but what concerned her most was that he was unruly and spiteful, unkind to the animals and nasty to people. 'May God put a stop to his wickedness and give him a change of character!' his mother said. 'Otherwise he will bring misfortune on himself and on us.'

The boy stood there for a long time wondering whether he should bother to read the sermon or not. Then he decided that it would be best to be obedient on this occasion, so he sat in the manse armchair and started to read. After gabbling through the words half aloud for a while, they began to send him to sleep and he felt himself nodding off.

The weather outside was spring at its most beautiful. It was only 20 March and the year was still young, but in the far south of Skåne, in the parish of Västra Vemmenhög where the boy lived, spring had already arrived in full force. There was no greenery yet, but everything was fresh and in bud. The ditches were full of water and coltsfoot was in flower along their edges. All the shrubs growing on the stone walls had turned brown and shiny. The beechwood in the far distance seemed to be swelling and growing thicker with every moment that passed and the sky was clear and bright blue. The trilling of the larks could be heard through the half-open door of the cottage. The hens and the geese had already been let out into the open and even the cows in their stalls were welcoming the spring air with an occasional moo.

The boy was still reading but his head was nodding as he fought against sleep. 'I don't want to go to sleep,' he thought, 'because then it will take all morning and I still won't get all this out of the way.'

But he fell asleep anyway.

He did not know how long he had been asleep when a slight noise behind him woke him up.

There was a small mirror on the window ledge in front of him and in it he could see almost all of the room. As he lifted his head from his doze he happened to look in the mirror and he noticed that the lid of his mother's chest was open.

His mother owned a big iron-bound oak chest and she was the only one allowed to open it. In it she stored everything she had inherited from her own mother and wanted to keep really safe. There were several old-fashioned peasant dresses made of red woollen homespun, with short bodices and pleated skirts and pearls stitched on the breast panels. There were starched white kerchiefs and heavy silver buckles and chains. No one wants to wear clothes like that these days and mother had often thought of getting rid of these old things but did not have the heart to do so.

Looking in the mirror the boy could see that the lid was open but he could not understand how it had happened since she had closed the chest before leaving the house. She would certainly not have left the chest open with him at home on his own.

He felt very uneasy and was afraid that a thief had come into the cottage. Frightened to move, he sat still and stared into the mirror.

While he sat there waiting for the thief to show himself he began to wonder about a black shadow on the edge of the chest. He stared and stared and could not believe his eyes. What at first had seemed to be a shadow became more and more solid and he could soon see that it was something real. Without a shadow of doubt, there was an elf sitting astride the edge of the chest.

The boy had heard of elves but he had never imagined they could be so small. This elf, the one sitting there on the edge of the chest, was no taller than the breadth of a hand. His face was old, wrinkled and beardless and he was wearing a black frock-coat, knee breeches and a black hat with a broad brim. He was very trim and elegant, with white lace at his neck and wrists, buckles on his shoes and rosettes on his garters. He had taken an embroidered breast panel out of the chest and was studying the old-fashioned handiwork with such veneration that he failed to notice that the boy was awake.

The boy was more than a little surprised to see the elf but he was certainly not afraid. How could anyone be afraid of someone so small? And since the elf was so engrossed in what he was doing that he was deaf and blind to everything around him, the boy thought it would be fun to play a prank on him – push him down into the chest and shut the lid on him, or something like that.

He was not brave enough to touch the elf with his hands so

he looked around the cottage for something he could prod him with. He ran his eyes from the settle to the leaf-table, from the leaf-table to the stove. He looked at the saucepans and the coffee pot, which were on a shelf by the stove, at the pail by the door, at the knives and forks and ladles and dishes and plates that could be seen through the half-open cupboard door. He looked up at his father's gun hanging on the wall alongside the portrait of the Danish royal family and he looked at the geraniums and fuchsias flowering on the window-sill. And last of all his eyes came to rest on an old net for catching flies that was hanging up on the window frame.

No sooner did he catch sight of the net than he jumped up, grabbed it and swept it along the edge of the chest. Even he was surprised at his luck for, scarcely knowing how he had managed it, he caught the elf. The poor little fellow was now upside down in the bottom of the net and unable to climb out.

At first the boy had no idea at all what to do with his prisoner. He was careful, however, to swing the net to and fro so that the elf had no opportunity to climb out.

The elf began to speak, pleading to be set free. He had brought them good luck for many years, he said, and deserved to be treated better than this. If the boy released him he would give him a valuable old coin, a silver spoon and a golden penny as big as his father's silver watch-case.

The boy did not consider the offer to be particularly generous but now that he had trapped the elf he felt rather afraid of him. He knew he had become involved with something uncanny and mysterious, something that was no part of his world. He would be only too happy to be rid of this strange creature.

So he immediately agreed to the deal and held the net still so the elf could crawl out of it. When the elf was almost out of the net, however, it struck the boy that he ought to have bargained for great wealth and all kinds of good things. He ought at least to have stipulated that the elf cast a spell that would fix the whole sermon in his head. 'How stupid of me to set him free!' the boy thought, and began shaking the net so that the elf would fall back into it.

But the moment the boy did this something boxed his ear so violently that he thought his head would split. He crashed first against one wall and then against the other before finally collapsing to the floor and lying there senseless.

When he woke he was alone in the cottage. There was no sign of the elf, the lid of his mother's chest was closed, and the fly net was hanging in its usual place in the window. If it had not been for the way his right cheek was still stinging from the blow he had received, he would have been tempted to believe it had all been a dream. 'That's what mother and father are going to say anyway,' he thought. 'They aren't likely to make any allowances about the sermon because of an elf. I had better sit down and get on with the reading.'

But as he was walking over to the table he noticed something very strange. The cottage could surely not have grown bigger, could it, so why was it taking him so many more steps than usual to reach the table? And what had happened to the chair? It did not look any bigger than before but he had to get up onto the slats between the legs and then climb to reach the seat. And it was the same with the table. He could not see up over the tabletop without clambering on the arms of the chair.

'What on earth is going on?' the boy said. 'That elf must have been messing about with the chair and the table and the rest of the cottage.'

The book of sermons was still lying on the table and appeared to be unchanged, but there must have been something wrong with it because he could not read a word without actually standing on the book.

He read a few lines and then happened to look up and catch sight of the mirror. 'Look! There's another one of them!' he shouted quite loudly.

There, in the mirror in front of him, he could clearly see a tiny little boy dressed in a pointed hat and leather breeches.

'That boy's dressed just like me!' the boy said, clapping his hands in amazement. And then he saw that the little boy in the mirror was doing exactly the same thing.

So he began to pull his hair, pinch his arms and spin round, and as he did so, the boy in the mirror immediately did whatever he did.

The boy ran in circles round the mirror a couple of times to see if there was some little creature hidden behind it, but no one was there. That is when he began to feel so afraid that he began to tremble. Because now he understood that the elf had put a spell on him and that the tiny little boy whose image he could see in the mirror was not someone else, it was him.

THE WILD GEESE
The boy simply could not bring himself to believe that he had been turned into an elf. 'It's just a dream, or my imagination,' he thought. 'If I wait a little while I'll become a human being again.'

He stood in front of the mirror and closed his eyes. He waited for a few minutes before he opened them again, expecting that it would all be over. But it was not – there he was still, just as small. In every other respect he was the same as he had always been, the same flaxen hair, the same freckles on his nose, the same patches on his breeches, the same darns in his socks. Everything was as before, except that everything had been shrunk.

Well, he could see there was no point in standing around waiting. He would have to try something else, and the very best thing he could do, he thought, was to get hold of that elf and make peace with him.

He jumped down onto the floor and began his search. He looked behind the chairs and the cupboard, under the sofa and in the baking oven. He even crawled down a couple of rat holes, but nowhere was there any sign of the elf.

And as he searched he wept and pleaded and promised everything he could think of. Never again would he break a promise, never again would he be nasty, never again would he fall asleep during the sermon. If only he could be human again he would become the best and the kindest and the most obedient boy imaginable. But nothing helped: however much he promised, it simply did not help.

Suddenly he remembered hearing his mother say that the little people usually lived in cowsheds, so he decided to go to the cowshed as quickly as possible to see if he could find the elf there. Fortunately for him the door was ajar and he was able to go out unhindered, since he would never have been able to reach up to the latch to open it.

Inside the house he had, of course, been going around in his stockinged soles but once out in the hall he looked round for his clogs. He wondered how he was going to manage with his big clumsy clogs, but at that very moment he saw a pair of tiny clogs lying by the door. The fact that the elf had been thoughtful enough to shrink his clogs made the boy even more anxious. It suggested that this dreadful state of affairs was intended to last for a long time.

A house-sparrow was hopping around on the old oak plank outside the front door. No sooner had he caught sight of the boy than he began to call: 'Tweet! Tweet! Look at Nils the goosey boy! Look at Thummitot! Nils Holgersson Thummitot!'

All the geese and hens turned round to look at the boy and immediately set up a horrendous cackling. 'Cock-adoodle-do,' the cock crowed, 'serves him right. Cock-adoodle-do, he pulled my comb.' 'Cluckety-cluck, serves him right,' went the hens, and kept it up endlessly. The geese clustered up close, put their heads together and asked: 'Who can have done that to him? Who can have done that?'

The strangest thing of all, however, was that the boy could understand what they were saying. He was so surprised that he came to a halt on the doorstep and listened. 'It must be because I've been turned into an elf,' he said. 'That must be why I can understand bird talk.'

Finding it intolerable that the hens would not stop saying 'Serves him right,' he threw a stone at them and shouted: 'Cut the cackling, you lot!'

It had not occurred to him, however, that the hens no longer needed to be afraid of someone his size. The whole flock rushed up and surrounded him, yelling: 'Cluckety-cluck, serves you right! Cluckety-cluck, serves you right!'

He tried to escape but the hens ran after him, shouting and making a deafening noise. He would never have got away from them if the family cat had not arrived at that moment, and as soon as the hens saw the cat they pretended that their only concern was scratching at the ground to find worms.

The boy ran quickly up to the cat. 'Dear sweet Puss,' he said, 'you know every corner and hidey-hole in the garden, don't you? Please, please tell me where I can find the elf.'

The cat did not answer at once. He sat down, carefully curled his tail around his front legs and stared at the boy. He was a big black cat with a white bib. His fur was smooth and gleamed in the sunshine. His claws were drawn in and his eyes were grey but with a small narrow strip across the middle. He looked thoroughly good-natured.

'Indeed I do know where the elf lives,' the cat said in a silky voice, 'but that doesn't mean I'm going to tell you.'

'Dear Puss, you have to help me,' the boy said. 'Can't you see he's put a spell on me?'

The cat's eyes widened slightly and a malicious green gleam became visible in them. He purred and purred with smug satisfaction before answering at last: 'Why should I help you when you've pulled my tail so often?'

That made the boy angry and he completely forgot how small and powerless he had become. 'And I'll see to it that you get your tail pulled again, I will,' he said, jumping at the cat.

The next moment such a change came over the cat that the boy could scarcely believe it was the same animal. Every hair on its body stood on end, its back arched, its legs stretched, its claws ripped at the ground, its tail became short and thick, its ears went back, its mouth hissed and its eyes opened wide and shone a fiery red.

Not willing to be scared by a cat, the boy took another step forward, at which the cat sprang, landed on top of him and knocked him over. Then it stood over him, front paws on his chest and its jaws open at his throat.

The boy felt its claws cutting into his skin through his shirt and waistcoat and he sensed its sharp eye-teeth toying with his throat. He screamed for help as loudly as he could.

No one came and he was sure his last hour had arrived. Then he felt the cat folding its claws and letting go of his throat.

'That will be enough for now,' the cat said. 'I'm going to let you off this time for the sake of your mother, who feeds me. I just wanted you to know which of us two has the power now.'

At which the cat walked away, looking just as smooth and pious as when it had arrived a few minutes earlier. The boy was so ashamed that he could not speak; he just hurried on to the cowshed to search for the elf.

They only owned three cows, but when the boy entered there was enough mooing and bellowing to make anyone think there were at least thirty of them.

'Moo, moo, moo!' bellowed May Rose. 'It's good to see that there is justice in this world.'

'Moo, moo, moo!' the others joined in, but he could not hear what they were saying because they were all bellowing at the same time.

The boy wanted to ask them about the elf but he was unable to make himself heard because the cows were making so much noise. They were behaving in the way they had usually behaved when the boy let a strange dog into the cowshed – kicking out their hindlegs, shaking the chains around their necks, turning their heads to the side and threatening with their horns.

'You dare come near me,' May Rose said, 'and you'll get a kick you won't forget in a hurry.'

'You dare come near me,' Gold Lily said, 'and I'll have you dancing on my horns.'

'You dare come near me,' Star roared, 'and you'll find out what it felt like when you threw clogs at me as you did all last summer.'

'You dare come near me,' Gold Lily bellowed, 'and I'll get my own back for the wasp you put in my ear.'

May Rose was the oldest and most sensible of them and she was the angriest of the three. 'You dare come near me,' she said, 'and I'll pay you back for all the times you pulled the milking-stool from under your mother, and for all the times you tripped her up when she was carrying a pail of milk, and for all the tears she has wept in here because of you.'

The boy wanted to tell them that he regretted being nasty to them and that he would always be kind from now on if only they would tell him where to find the elf. But the cows would not listen. They were struggling so much he was afraid one of them might break free, so he thought the wisest thing to do was to creep out of the cowshed.

Once he was back outside he felt thoroughly downhearted. He realised that no one on the farm was prepared to help him find the elf and it looked as if it would not be much use even if he did find him.

He crawled up onto the broad stone wall that ran round the whole croft. It was overgrown with briars and brambles but he found a seat and sat down to think what it would be like if he were never to become human again. When mother and father came home from church they were in for a shock, no doubt about that. Indeed, it would be a shock for the whole country, with people coming from Östra Vemmenhög and from Torp and from Skurup and from everywhere in the neighbourhood just to look at him. Father and mother might even put him on show at the market at Kivik.

It was all too dreadful to contemplate. What he wanted most of all was simply not to be seen. By anyone!

He was so unhappy, so terribly unhappy. There was no one in the whole world unhappier than he was. He was no longer human, he was a freak.

He was slowly beginning to understand what it meant not to be human any more. He was cut off from everything: he could no longer play with other boys, he would not be able to take over the croft after his parents, and he certainly would not find a girl willing to marry him.

He sat there looking at his home – a small, whitewashed, half-timbered house that looked as if it was being pressed into the ground by its steep, high thatched roof. The outbuildings were small, too, and the fields were so narrow there was hardly room for the horse to turn with the plough. But however small and poor the place was, it was far too good for him now. The best he could expect from now on was a hole under the stable floor.

The weather was almost unbelievably beautiful. There was the drip, drip, drip of meltwater and everything around him was in bud or buzzing or twittering, whereas he was sunk in the deepest sorrow. Nothing was ever going to make him happy again.

He had never seen the sky so blue as it was on that day. And the migrating birds were on the wing. Coming from overseas, they were flying in over the Baltic Sea and aiming straight for Smygehuk, the southern point of Sweden, before continuing their journey north. There were all kinds of birds, of course, but the only ones he could recognise were the wild geese that were flying along in two long rows in the shape of a 'v'.

Many skeins of wild geese had already passed over, flying at a great height, but he had still heard them calling: 'We're off to the mountains! We're off to the mountains!'

When the wild geese saw the tame geese down in the farmyard, they flew closer to the ground and called: 'Are you coming too? Are you coming too? We're off to the mountains!'

The tame geese could not help stretching their heads up and listening, but they answered very sensibly: 'We're fine where we are! We're fine where we are!'

It was, as we have said, an utterly beautiful day and the air was so fresh and light that it must have been a real joy to fly through it. With every flock of wild geese that flew by, the tame geese became more and more restless. Sometimes they flapped their wings as if they would have liked to join the wild geese, but whenever that happened an old mother goose would say: 'Don't be silly now! That lot will have to put up with hunger and with cold.'

There was one young gander, however, in whom the call of the wild geese stirred a passionate desire to travel. 'If another skein comes over, I'll go with them,' he said.

And a new skein did come, calling as the others had done, and the young gander answered: 'Wait! Wait! I'm coming!'

He spread his wings and took off, but he was so unused to flying that he crashed to earth again.

But the wild geese must have heard his calls and they turned and flew slowly back to see if he would join them.

'Wait! Wait!' he called and tried again to fly.

The boy, who was lying on the wall, heard all this. 'It would be a great loss,' he thought, 'if that big gander flew off. If he is gone when father and mother get back from church, they will be really sorry.'

While he was thinking this, he forgot yet again that he was small and powerless. He jumped down off the wall into the middle of the flock of farmyard geese and threw his arms around the gander's neck. 'Hey you, don't you dare think of flying away!' he shouted.

At that very moment, however, the gander worked out what he needed to do to take off. He could not stop to shake off the boy and Nils had to go with him up into the air.

They gained height so quickly that it took the boy's breath away. He had no time to think of letting go of the gander's neck before he was so far off the ground that the fall would have killed him.

The only thing he could do to improve his situation was to try to climb up onto the gander's back, so he wriggled his way up, though not without the greatest difficulty. Nor was it easy to hang on to the gander's smooth back as his wings beat up and down. The boy had to take a firm grip with both hands deep in the feathers to stop himself tumbling back to earth.

THE CHECKED CLOTH
The boy was so confused by it all that it took a long time for him to come to his senses. The air whined and whistled past

him, the wings beat and the feathers swished as if there was a full storm blowing. There were thirteen geese, all uttering their honking calls as they flew on each side of him. Everything was dancing before his eyes and roaring in his ears. He had no idea whether they were flying high or low, nor in which direction they were heading.

At last he came to sufficiently to realise that he ought to pay attention to where the geese were taking him. That was easier said than done given that, first of all, he had to find the courage to look down. He was absolutely sure that any attempt to do so would make him giddy.

The wild geese were not flying very high because their new companion was not used to breathing in the thinnest air. And, for his sake, they were also flying a little slower than usual.

Finally the boy forced himself to turn his eyes down to the earth beneath. What he saw looked like a huge cloth spread out below him, a cloth that was divided into an unbelievable number of large and small checks.

'Where in heaven's name am I?' he wondered.

He could see nothing but check after check. Some of them were slanting, some were long and narrow, but they all had corners and straight edges. None of them was circular and none of them crooked.

'What is that big checked cloth I'm looking at?' the boy said, not expecting anyone to answer.

But the wild geese flying around him immediately began honking: 'Fields and meadows. Fields and meadows.'

Then he realised that this great piece of checked cloth was the flat plain of Skåne passing below him. And he began to understand why it was so checkered and why it was so many different colours. He recognised the bright green checks first – they were the fields of autumn-sown rye which had stayed green under the snow. The greyish-yellow checks were the stubble fields, where corn grew last year; the brownish checks were old clover fields, and the black were empty sugar-beet fields or ploughed fields lying fallow. The checks that were brown with yellow edges must be beech woods, because

the big trees in the middle of the wood lose all their leaves in winter whereas the small beeches around the edge of the wood retain their dry yellow leaves right through to the spring. There were also dark checks, with grey in the middle of them: these were the big farms, with buildings roofed with blackened thatch placed in a square around a paved yard. And then there were checks that were green in the middle and brown round the edges: they were gardens, where the lawns were beginning to turn green while the bushes and trees around them were still bare and bark-coloured.

The boy could not stop himself laughing at just how checkered everything was.

When the wild geese heard him laugh, they called out, as if reprimanding him: 'Good and fertile land. Good and fertile land.'

But the boy had already become serious again. 'How can you laugh,' he thought, 'when what has happened to you is the most terrifying thing that can happen to a human being?'

His serious mood remained for a while, but he soon began laughing again.

As he gradually became so used to the ride and the speed that he could risk thinking of other things besides hanging on to the gander's back, he began to notice that the sky was full of birds and all the flocks were flying north. There was much shouting and calling between the flocks.

'So you came over today?' some of them yelled.

'Yes, we did,' the geese answered. 'How do you think the spring is going?'

'Not a leaf on the trees and cold water in the lakes,' came the answer.

When the geese flew over a place where domestic fowl were pecking around outside, they would call down, 'What's the name of the farm? What's the name of the farm?' Then the cockerel down there would raise his head and shout: 'It's called Lillgärde this year – same as last year, same as last year!'

As is usual in Skåne, most of the cottages were probably named after their owners, but instead of answering that this was Per Matsson's place or Ola Bosson's place, the cocks would come up with names they thought suited the place. If they lived on poor crofts or smallholdings, they shouted: 'This farm is called Grainless.' Those living on the poorest places of all would call: 'This farm is called Too-Little-To-Eat, Too-Little-To-Eat.'

The cocks gave splendid names to the big, well-to-do farms, calling them things like Luckyacre, Egghill and Pennyrich.

But the cocks at the manor houses were too snooty to come up with anything funny. One of them crowed with all his might, as if he wanted his voice to carry all the way to the sun: 'This is Dybeck Manor this year – same as last year, same as last year!'

And a little farther on there was a cock that crowed: 'This is Svaneholm. Surely the whole world knows that!'

The boy noticed that the geese were not flying in a direct line, they were meandering hither and thither across the Söderslätt plain as if they were happy to be back in Skåne and wanted to visit every single farm.

They came to a place with tall, solid buildings and high chimneys. It was surrounded by a mass of smaller houses. 'This is Jordberga Sugar Refinery,' the cocks crowed. 'This is Jordberga Sugar Refinery.'

Up there on the gander's back, the boy jumped – he should have recognised that place. It was not far from home and he had worked there as goose-boy the summer before. But then it seemed unlikely that anything would look the same when you saw it from above.

Oh my, oh my! Remember Åsa the goose-girl and Little Mats, who had been his friends there last year! The boy would have liked to know if they were still there. What would they say if they knew he was flying past high above their heads?

Jordberga passed out of sight and they travelled towards Svedala and the manor house at Skabersjö, then back over the castles of Börringekloster and Häckeberga. The boy was seeing more of Skåne in one day than he had seen in all the years of his life.

The best fun of all was when the wild geese met tame geese. They would pass overhead very slowly, calling down: 'We're off to the mountains. Are you coming too? Are you coming too?'

But the tame geese replied: 'Winter is still with us. You are too early. Go back! Go back!'

At which the wild geese would fly lower so that they could be heard better and they would call: 'Come with us and we'll teach you to fly and to swim.'

That annoyed the tame geese so much that they refused to utter a single cackle in response.

But then the wild geese would fly even lower, their wings almost brushing the ground, before gaining height as quick as lightning as though something had suddenly terrified them. 'Oh, oh, oh!' they honked. 'Not geese! Just sheep! Just sheep!'

Which made the geese on the ground livid with rage. 'Hope you're shot! The lot of you! The lot of you!' they shrieked.

The boy laughed when he heard all this banter. Then he remembered how bad he had made things for himself and he wept instead, but after a little while he started laughing again.

Never before had he travelled at such a speed, although he had always enjoyed riding fast and recklessly. Of course, he had never imagined anything could feel as fresh as it did up here in the sky while, at the same time, a pleasant scent of soil and resin rose up from the earth below. Nor had he ever thought what it would be like to travel at such a height: it was like flying away from all the troubles and sorrows and vexations imaginable.

II

AKKA FROM KEBNEKAISE

THE EVENING

The big tame gander that had followed the wild geese into the air felt very proud to be flying back and forth across the Söderslätt plain in the company of the wild geese while making fun of the tame birds. But however happy he was, it was inevitable that he began to feel tired as the afternoon wore on. He tried taking deeper breaths and beating his wings faster but, despite that, he was falling several goose-lengths behind the others.

As soon as the wild geese flying at the back of the skein noticed that the tame goose could not keep up, they called to the goose who was leading them at the front of the formation: 'Akka from Kebnekaise! Akka from Kebnekaise!'

'What is it you want?' asked the leading goose.

'The white one's falling behind. The white one's falling behind.'

'Tell him that it's easier to fly fast than slow!' the leading goose called, racing on as before.

The tame gander tried hard to follow the advice and speed up but became so exhausted that he sank right down almost to the level of the pollarded willows that lined the fields and meadows.

'Akka, Akka, Akka from Kebnekaise!' the geese at the rear called again, seeing the difficulties the gander was in.

'What is it you want now?' the lead goose asked, sounding extremely annoyed.

'The white one is sinking to the ground. The white one is sinking to the ground.'

'Tell him that it's easier to fly high than low!' the lead goose called, racing on as before without slackening her pace.

The gander again tried to follow her advice but when he tried to gain height he became so breathless that his chest almost burst.

'Akka, Akka!' the geese at the rear called again.

'Can't you let me fly in peace?' the lead goose said, sounding even more impatient than she had been before.

'The white one is going to crash. The white one is going to crash.'

'Tell him that anyone who can't keep up with the flock must turn and go home!' said the lead goose, and she raced on as before, with no thought of slackening her pace.

'So that's the way of it, is it?' the gander thought. He suddenly understood that the wild geese had never intended to take him to Lapland with them and they had lured him away from home for fun.

He was annoyed to find that his strength was failing and stopping him showing these vagabonds that a tame goose was not to be sneezed at. What made it particularly mortifying was that he had fallen in with Akka from Kebnekaise. Even a tame goose like him had heard of a lead goose called Akka, who was more than a hundred years old and had a reputation so great that the very best wild geese used to join her flock. But no other geese looked down on tame geese with as much scorn as Akka and her flock did, and the gander really wanted to show them that he was their equal.

He flew along slowly behind the others, wondering whether he should turn back or continue. Then suddenly the tiny little boy on his back spoke up: 'Dear Mårten Gander, don't you realise it's impossible for you to follow the wild geese up to Lapland. You've never flown before. Why don't you turn back before you kill yourself?'

As far as the gander was concerned there was nothing in the world worse than that crofter's boy and no sooner did he realise that the wretched boy thought him incapable of making the journey than he decided to stick with it. 'If you dare say another word about it, I'll drop you in the next marlpit we fly over,' he said, and his anger lent him enough strength to start flying almost as well as the others.

It is unlikely he would have been able to carry on very far, but it proved unnecessary anyway because the sun was going down and just as the sun set the geese made their descent. Before the boy and the gander knew anything about it, they found themselves on the shore of a lake called Vombsjön.

'This must be where we're intending to spend the night, I suppose,' the boy thought before jumping down from the gander's back.

He was standing on a narrow strip of sandy beach with a good-sized lake in front of him. It was not a very pleasant sight since it was almost completely covered with a dirty and uneven crust of ice that was full of cracks and holes, as is usually the case with spring ice. The ice here would not last much longer, however. It had already shrunk away from the shore, leaving a wide belt of gleaming black water all the way round. But the ice was still there just now and it spread its chill and sinister winteriness over the surrounding area.

The country on the other side of the lake seemed to be open and light. Where the geese had landed, however, there was a large plantation of pine-trees and the pines seemed to have the power to hold the winter fast. The ground was clear of snow everywhere else, but snow still lay under the scrubby branches and it had melted and frozen, melted and frozen, so often that it was as hard as ice.

The boy thought the geese had brought him to a winter wilderness and he was so anxious he felt like crying his eyes out.

He was hungry, too, not having had anything to eat all day. But where was he to find food? There is nothing edible growing either in the ground or on the trees in March.

So where was he to get food, and who would give him house-room, and who would make his bed, and who would light a fire to keep him warm, and who would protect him from wild animals? The sun had gone down and the chill of the lake was spreading all round. The dark of night was falling from the sky, terrors were creeping out in the wake of the deepening dusk and the sounds of rustling and pattering could already be heard in the forest. There was nothing left now of the happy courage the boy had felt while he was in the air and he began to look round anxiously for his travelling companions. Now he had no one but them to cling to.

Then he noticed that the gander was in an even worse state than he was. He was lying in the same place he had landed and he looked as if he was dying. His neck was stretched out along the ground, his eyes were shut and his breathing was no more than a weak rasp.

'Dear Mårten Gander,' the boy said, 'try to have a drink of water at least. You are only a couple of steps from the lake.'

But the gander did not move.

It was true that the boy had been unkind to the gander and all the other animals in the past, but now he thought that the gander was the only support he had and he was terribly afraid of losing him. He began to push and heave the bird to move him to the waterside. The gander was big and heavy, so it was hard work for the boy, but at last he succeeded.

The gander reached the lake head first. For a moment he lay motionless in the mud but then he quickly raised his beak, shook the water out of his eyes, sneezed and swam proudly out into the reeds and bulrushes.

The wild geese were already on the lake. They had hurried into the water without stopping to look round for either the tame goose or his rider. They had bathed and preened their feathers and were now swimming round sucking up the half rotted pondweed and bogbean.

The white gander had the good fortune to catch sight of a small perch, which he quickly snapped up before swimming to the shore and putting it down in front of the boy. 'This is for you,' he said, 'to thank you for helping me get to the water.'

That was the first time all day anyone had said a kind word to the boy. He was so happy he would have liked to throw his arms around the gander's neck but he could not bring himself to do so. He was also happy about the gift, although at first, of course, he thought it would be impossible to eat raw fish, but he made up his mind to give it a try.

He felt at his waist to see if he still had his sheath-knife and fortunately it was still there, buttoned to the back of his breeches. It was now shorter than a matchstick but still fine for scaling and cleaning fish. In no time at all, he had eaten the fish.

No sooner was the boy's belly full than he began to feel ashamed of having eaten something raw. 'That shows that I'm a real elf and not human any more,' he thought.

The whole time the boy was eating, the gander stood beside him in silence, but once the boy had swallowed the last piece of fish the gander said in a quiet voice:

'We've obviously fallen in with a stuck-up bunch of geese here and they have no time at all for tame birds.'

'Yes, I've noticed that, too,' the boy said.

'It would be a real feather in my cap if I could stick with them all the way to Lapland and show them what a tame goose is capable of.'

'Mm, yes,' the boy said a little hesitantly, for he was not convinced that the gander was up to it but did not want to contradict him.

'But I don't think I could manage a journey like that on my own,' the gander said, 'and I was going to ask whether you would come along too and help me.'

Until then, of course, the boy's only thought had been about how to get home as soon as possible and he was so surprised by the gander's suggestion that he was not sure what to say. 'I thought we were enemies, you and me?' he said. The gander, however, seemed to have completely forgotten that and only remembered that the boy had just saved his life.

'I really ought to be going home to father and mother,' the boy said.

'Of course, and I'd definitely take you back to them by the start of autumn,' the gander said. 'I won't leave you until I can put you down on your own front doorstep.'

The boy thought it might be a good idea not to face his parents for a while and he was inclined to go along with the suggestion. He was about to say that he agreed when he heard a loud crashing and splashing behind him. The wild geese had come out of the lake all at the same time and were shaking themselves dry. Then they formed up in a long line, lead goose at the front, and walked up to the boy and the gander.

When the white gander looked at the wild geese he felt ill at ease. He had expected them to be more like tame geese and thought he would have felt a closer kinship with them. But they were much smaller than he was and not one of them was white – they were a grey colour with brown mottling. He found their eyes rather frightening – all yellow and gleaming as if there was fire behind them. The gander had been taught that a genteel goose should walk slowly and with a rolling motion, but these wild geese did not walk, they half ran. What worried him most, however, was their feet. They were big, and their soles were ragged and torn. It was obvious that the wild geese were quite unconcerned about what they walked on and did not bother to walk around things. In every other respect they were tidy and well-preened, but you could see from their feet that they were poor creatures of the wilderness.

Before the geese arrived, the gander only had time to whisper to the boy: 'Speak up for yourself now, but don't tell them who you are.'

The wild geese came to a halt in front of them and proceeded to nod their necks many times and the gander did the same, bobbing his neck even more than they did. And once enough nodding and greeting had been done, the lead goose spoke: 'The time has come for you to tell us something about yourselves.'

'Not a great deal to say about me,' the gander said. 'I was born in Skanör last spring. Last autumn I was sold to Holger Nilsson in Västra Vemmenhög and that's where I've been ever since.'

'You don't seem to have much of a pedigree to boast of,' said the lead goose, 'so what makes you arrogant enough to want to join the wild geese?'

'I suppose it's because I want to show you wild geese that even tame geese have their merits.'

'Yes, it would be good if you could show us that,' the lead goose answered. 'We've already seen the standard of your flying. Is there perhaps some other skill in which you are a bit more competent? Are you any good at long-distance swimming, for instance?'

'No, I can't pretend I've got anything to boast about there either,' the gander said. He suspected that the lead goose had already made up her mind to send him home so he did not really care what he answered. 'I've never swum farther than across a marlpit,' he continued.

'Well, in that case, I assume you must be a champion runner,' said the lead goose.

'Can't say I've ever seen a tame goose run,' the gander said, making things out to be worse than they were, 'and I've certainly never done so myself.'

The big white gander was now certain that the lead goose would say that she could not take him with her. He was very surprised when she said:

'You've given some bold answers to my questions and a gander who is bold might make a good companion on our travels even if he is ignorant at the start. What do you say to staying with us for a couple of days and we'll see how you get on?'

'I would be quite happy with that,' the gander said, feeling very pleased.

Then the lead goose pointed her beak and said: 'And who is this you have with you? I've never seen anything like him before.'

'He is my friend,' said the gander. 'He's been a goose-boy all his life and he could well be useful to have with us on the journey.'

'Could be useful to a tame goose, I suppose,' the wild goose said. 'What do you call him?'

'He has several names,' the gander said hesitantly, not sure what to come up with on the spur of the moment as he did not want to reveal the boy's human name. Finally he said: 'He's called Thummitot, actually.'

'Is he one of the elfin folk?' the lead goose asked.

'What time do you wild geese settle down to sleep?' the gander asked quickly, trying to avoid answering the last question. 'I can't keep my eyes open much longer.'

It was quite obvious that the lead goose, who was doing the talking, was very old. All her plumage was ice-grey, with no sign of darker streaks. Her head was bigger, her legs thicker and her feet even more ragged than the rest of them. Her feathers were stiff, her shoulders knobbly and her neck thin. All this was the work of old age. But time had failed to quench the light in her eyes, which had a brighter and more youthful gleam than those of any of the other geese.

She turned back to the gander and began to speak in a very haughty voice: 'Know this, young gander: I am Akka from Kebnekaise and the goose who flies closest on my right is Yksi from Vassijaure, and the one on my left is Kaksi from Nuolja! Know, too, that the second goose to my right is Kolme from Sarjektjåkko, and the second goose to the left is Neljä from Svappavaara, and behind them fly Viisi from Oviksfjällen and Kuusi from Sjangeli!* And know this, too, that they – like the six goslings who fly at the rear, three to the right and three to the left – are all high mountain geese of the very best pedigree! Do not imagine that we are vagrants who will keep company with anyone and everyone, and do not imagine that we will let anyone share our roosting places unless he is prepared to tell us his kin.'

On hearing Akka talk in this way, the boy quickly stepped forward. He had found it distressing to listen to the gander speaking up boldly on his own behalf but giving such evasive answers about him. 'I have no wish to keep secret who I am,' he said. 'My name is Nils Holgersson and I am the son of a smallholder. Until this very day I was a human being but this morning ...'

The boy did not get any farther than that. As soon as he said he was human the lead goose took three steps back and the other geese withdrew even further. Then they all stretched out their necks and began hissing furiously at him.

'Just what I suspected ever since I first saw you on the shore,' Akka said. 'Be off with you at once! We will not tolerate human beings among us.'

'It hardly seems possible,' the gander said in a conciliatory tone, 'that you wild geese could be afraid of someone so small. Surely you could send him off home tomorrow, but you should let him stay here with us for tonight. None of us could take the responsibility for leaving such a pitiful little creature to fend for himself among foxes and weasels at night.'

Akka came closer but it was quite clear that she was finding it difficult to overcome her fear. 'I have been taught to be afraid of anything to do with human beings, whether they are big or small,' she said. 'But if you are prepared to guarantee that he will do us no harm then he can stay with us tonight. I don't think, though, that our sleeping quarters will suit either you or him since we intend to sleep out on the ice surrounded by water.'

She obviously expected the gander to have second thoughts when he heard that, but he did not let it put him off and said: 'It's very clever of you to choose such a safe roost.'

'Remember you are the one responsible for seeing that he sets off home tomorrow,' Akka said. 'In that case, I shall have to leave you too,' the gander said, 'since I have promised not to desert him.' 'You are free to fly wherever you like,' the lead goose answered.

With that she opened her wings and flew out onto the ice and one by one the other geese followed her.

The boy felt miserable that he could no longer look forward to his Lapland trip and, what's more, he was very worried about their cold sleeping quarters. 'Things are getting worse and worse, gander,' he said. 'And we are going to freeze to death out on the ice for a start.'

But the gander was now in good spirits. 'No danger of that,' he said. 'What I would ask you to do, as quickly as possible now, is to collect as much grass and straw as you can carry.'

Once the boy had his arms full of dry grass, the gander took a firm hold of his shirt with his beak and flew out onto the ice, where the wild geese were already asleep with their heads under their wings.

'Spread the grass out on the ice so that I have something to stand on to stop me freezing to it. You help me, and I'll help you!' the gander said.

The boy did as he was told and when he was finished the gander once again picked him up by his shirt and tucked him under his wing. 'I think you'll be fine and warm there,' he said and closed his wing over him.

The boy was so well-wrapped in down that he could not answer, but he was certainly fine and warm and, tired as he was, he fell asleep a moment later.

THE NIGHT
It is a truth that ice is always treacherous and is not a thing to be trusted. In the middle of the night the icy crust on the lake drifted so that it came to rest against the bank at one point. Smirre Fox, who was living at that time in the park of Övedskloster Manor on the eastern side of the lake, noticed the ice against the bank when he was out on his nightly hunt. Smirre had seen the wild geese earlier and he had not dared hope that he would be able to get at them. Now, however, he immediately set off over the ice.

When Smirre was quite close to the geese he slipped and his claws scraped on the ice, waking the geese. The geese flapped their wings in an attempt to hurl themselves into the air, but Smirre was too fast. He charged forward as fast as if someone had thrown him, grabbed one goose by the wing and rushed back towards the bank.

On this particular night, however, the wild geese were not alone out on the ice, they had a human being with them, however small he was. The boy was shaken awake by the gander beating his wings. He fell down onto the ice and sat there half-awake with no idea what the fuss was about until he saw a small short-legged dog running away across the ice with a goose in its mouth.

The boy immediately raced after it in order to take the goose from the dog. He could hear the gander shouting after him: 'Take care, Thummitot, take care!' But the boy did not think he had any reason to be afraid of such a small dog and so he stormed after the animal.

The wild goose that Smirre Fox was dragging along could hear the clatter of the boy's clogs on the ice and she could hardly believe her ears. 'Can that tiny fellow be intending to save me from the fox,' she wondered, and as wretched as her situation was, a happy cackle started deep in her throat almost as if she was laughing.

'The first thing that will happen to him is that he'll fall down a crack in the ice,' she thought.

Dark as the night was, however, the boy could see all the cracks and holes in the ice and leapt over them in a series of daring bounds. The fact was, he now had the good night-eyes of an elf and could see in the dark. Both the lake and its banks were as clearly visible to him as if it had been broad daylight.

Smirre Fox left the ice where it had drifted against the bank and as he was making his way up the slope the boy shouted at him: 'Put the goose down, you scoundrel!' Smirre had no idea who was shouting and, wasting no time by turning to look, he speeded up.

The fox ran into a wood of large and magnificent beech trees and the boy followed him without stopping to think of the risk he was running. He was, however, thinking the whole time of the scornful reception he had been given by the wild geese the evening before and he was very keen to show them that, when all is said and done, a human being is a little superior to the rest of creation.

He shouted at the dog time after time ordering him to let go of his prey. 'What kind of dog are you? You should be ashamed of yourself stealing a whole goose! Put her down at once, or wait and see the beating you get! Put her down, or I'll tell your master what you have done!'

When Smirre Fox realised he was being taken for a dog afraid of a beating, he thought it was so funny that he almost dropped the goose. Smirre was a rapacious raider and, not satisfied with hunting rats and voles in the fields, he would also venture into farmyards to steal hens and geese. He knew that he was feared across the whole district and he had never heard anything as ridiculous as this since he was a little cub.

The boy was running so quickly that the huge beech trees seemed to be flowing backwards past him. He was catching up on Smirre and eventually he was so close that he could grab the fox's brush. 'Now I'll have that goose from you!' he shouted, heaving back as hard as he could. But he did not have the strength to stop Smirre and the fox dragged him along with dry beech leaves spinning up all round him.

Now, at last, it seemed to have dawned on Smirre quite how harmless his pursuer actually was. He stopped, laid the goose down on the ground and placed his front paws on her so that she could not fly away. He was about to sink his teeth into her throat but could not resist the temptation to taunt that little wretch first. 'Away with you and tell the farmer that I'm about to bite the head off this goose!' he said.

No one could have been more surprised than the boy when he saw the pointed snout and heard the hoarse and angry voice of the dog he had been chasing. But he was so enraged by the fox making a fool of him that it did not occur to him to be afraid. He took a tighter grip on the fox's brush, dug his feet in against the root of a beech tree and, just as the fox opened his jaws to bite the goose's throat, he tugged with every ounce of strength in his body. Smirre was so taken by surprise that he fell back a couple of steps and let go the goose. She managed to take to the air clumsily, though one wing was so damaged she could hardly use it. Moreover, unable to see anything in the darkness of the night and the wood, she was as good as blind and could do nothing to help the boy. She struggled up through a gap in the branches overhead and flew back to the lake.

Smirre, however, hurled himself at the boy. 'If I can't have one, I'll have the other,' he said, and you could hear from his voice how angry he was.

'Don't you believe it!' the boy said, beside himself with excitement at having saved the goose. He still had a firm grip on the fox's brush and whichever way the fox turned the boy swung in the opposite direction.

What a dance they led through the wood, beech leaves spinning all round them! Smirre twisted and turned round and round but his brush twisted and turned too, with the boy holding on tight and the fox unable to grab him.

At first the boy was so exhilarated by his victory that he laughed merrily and made fun of the fox, but Smirre was tenacious, as old hunters often are, and the boy began to fear he would eventually be caught.

Then his eye fell on a beech sapling which was as slender as a stick but had shot up tall in order to reach the fresh air and light above the canopy of the old beech trees. He quickly let go of the fox's brush and climbed the sapling. Smirre, however, was so over-excited that he continued dancing around chasing his tail for some time, until the boy said: 'There's no need for you to carry on dancing round, you know!'

But Smirre could not bear the ignominy of failing to get the better of such a little creature and he lay down at the foot of the tree to keep guard and wait until the boy was tired out.

Things were not looking too good for the boy sitting up there astride a weak branch. The sapling did not reach right up to the high canopy, so there was no way for him to climb across to a different tree and he could not risk returning to the ground.

He was so cold he was beginning to get stiff and lose his grip on the branch, and although he was dreadfully tired, he could not risk going to sleep for fear of falling off.

He could not believe how creepy it was being out in the woods at night. He had never really appreciated before what night was: it was as if the whole world had turned to stone and would never come to life again.

At last it began to grow light and the boy was happy to see things returning to their familiar forms, though the cold became even sharper than it had been earlier in the night.

When the sun rose at last, it was red rather than gold. The boy thought it looked angry and wondered what it was angry about. Perhaps it was because the night had made everything so cold and dismal while the sun had been away.

Great clusters of sunbeams streamed down to see what night had been getting up to, and everything blushed red as if it had a bad conscience. The clouds in the sky, the silky smooth trunks of the beech trees, the small plaited branches up in the canopy, the rime that covered the beech leaves on the ground – everything lit up and shone red.

More and more sunbeams chased through the air until at last all the horrors of night had been driven away. No longer turned to stone, the earth came to life and was filled with living things. A black woodpecker with its red nape began hammering a tree-trunk with its beak; a squirrel scuttled out of its drey with a nut, which it sat on a branch to shell; a starling flew past carrying a piece of root, and a chaffinch sang in the tree-tops.

Then the boy understood that the sun had spoken to all these small creatures, saying: 'Wake up and come out of your nests! I am here now, and you no longer need to be afraid of anything.'

The calls of the wild geese could be heard from the lake as they prepared for departure. And then all fourteen geese came flying over the forest. The boy tried to shout to them but they were flying too high for his voice to reach them. They must think that the fox had eaten him hours ago and they did not even bother to look for him.

He came close to tears of anxiety, but the sun was shining now, glorious and golden-yellow in the sky and giving the world courage. 'There is no reason for worrying and being troubled by things as long as I am here,' the sun said.

GOOSE-PLAY   Monday, 21 March

Everything in the forest remained unchanged for about as long as it takes a goose to eat breakfast, but just as dawn was moving into morning a solitary wild goose came flying along beneath the dense canopy of trees. She was picking her way hesitantly between the branches and trunks and flying very slowly. As soon as Smirre Fox saw her he left his post at the foot of the sapling and crept towards her. The wild goose made no effort to avoid the fox and flew very close to him. Smirre made a great leap but missed her and she flew on towards the lake.

It was not long before another wild goose came flying along. She followed the same path as the first goose but she was flying even lower and more slowly. She, too, passed close to Smirre Fox and he leapt so high that his ears brushed her feet, but she escaped and continued as silently as a shadow on her way to the lake.

A short time passed and yet another goose came flying along. She was flying lower still and even more slowly and she seemed to be finding it even more difficult to pick a line between the beech trees. Smirre made a mighty bound and came within a hair's breadth of catching her, but this goose too made her escape.

No sooner had she disappeared than a fourth goose arrived. She was flying so slowly and so badly that Smirre thought he would catch her without any great difficulty, but by now he was afraid of failing so he decided to let her fly past unmolested. She took the same path as the others and when she was right above Smirre she came down so low that he was unable to resist leaping at her. He jumped high enough to touch her with his paw, but she flipped quickly to one side and saved herself.

Before Smirre had got his breath back three geese came into sight, flying in a row. They flew along the same path and in the same way as the others, but even though Smirre made great leaps at each of them he failed to catch any of the three.

Next came five geese, flying better than the earlier ones. They, too, appeared to be trying to tempt Smirre to jump, but he withstood the temptation.

Quite some time passed before a solitary goose came flying along. This was the thirteenth goose and she was so old that she was grey all over, without a single dark patch on her body. She appeared to be unable to use one wing properly, so she was lopsided and flew so badly she almost brushed the ground. Smirre not only leapt at her, he ran jumping and chasing after her all the way to the lake but, just as before, his efforts went unrewarded.

When the fourteenth goose came, it was a beautiful sight because it was white and the beat of its great wings made a bright gleam in the dark forest. When Smirre saw it, he summoned up all his strength and leapt halfway up to the canopy but, like all the others, the white bird went on its way unharmed.

Everything was quiet for a while under the beech trees. The whole flock of wild geese seemed to have departed.

And then, suddenly, Smirre remembered his prisoner and raised his eyes to look at the sapling. Just as might be expected, that tiny wretch had disappeared.

Smirre did not have very long to think about him because the first goose now returned from the lake and once again flew slowly through the trees. In spite of all his bad luck, Smirre was pleased to see her come back and he rushed after her, taking great leaps. But he was in too much of a hurry and had not given himself enough time to aim his leap properly, so he jumped to one side of her.

Then, following this goose, came a second and a third and a fourth and a fifth, the whole flock one after the other, finishing with the old ice-grey goose and the big white gander. All of them flew slowly and low, and as they passed over Smirre they swooped even lower, as if inviting him to catch them. Smirre rushed after them, leaping six feet in the air, but still quite unable to grab a single one of them.

It was the most awful day of Smirre's life. The geese kept

flying ceaselessly over his head, coming and going, coming and going. Big, splendid geese that had eaten themselves fat on the fields and heaths of Germany swept backwards and forwards through the forest all day, coming so close to him that he often touched them – and yet he was unable to catch one of them to appease his hunger.

Winter was scarcely over and Smirre could recall days and nights when he had been forced to roam around aimlessly with no prey to hunt, when the migratory birds had flown south, when the rats were hiding beneath the frozen earth and the hens were all shut in. But even the hunger of winter had not been so hard to endure as this day's failures.

Smirre was not a young fox. Many was the time the hounds had been on his heels and bullets whined round his ears. He had lain hidden deep in his den when the dachshunds were crawling into his tunnels and close to finding him. But the anguish he had felt in the heat of the hunt could not compare with what he felt every time he failed to catch one of the wild geese.

In the morning, when this game began, the geese had been amazed at how handsome a fox he was. Smirre loved to be grand – his coat was bright red, his breast was white, his snout was black and his brush as fluffy as a plume. By the evening of that day Smirre's coat was tousled, he was sodden with sweat, his eyes were dull, his tongue hung out of his panting jaws, and he was foaming at the mouth.

Come the afternoon Smirre was so tired that he became delirious. He saw nothing but geese flying before his eyes and he began pouncing on patches of sunlight he saw on the ground and leaping at a poor little tortoiseshell butterfly that had emerged from its pupa too early.

The wild geese continued flying tirelessly, oh, so tirelessly. They spent the whole day tormenting Smirre, showing no sympathy even now that he was broken, overwrought and out of his mind. They showed no mercy even though they knew he could hardly see them and that he was jumping at shadows.

Only when Smirre Fox finally sank down on a pile of dried leaves, exhausted, drained and almost at death's door, did they stop taunting him.

'Now you know, fox, what happens to those who cross swords with Akka from Kebnekaise,' they shouted in his ear, and then they left him in peace.

III

WITH THE WILD BIRDS

THE FARM Thursday, 24 March

At the same time as all this was going on, an event occurred in Skåne that caused a great deal of discussion and even reached the newspapers. Since they were unable to explain it, however, many people thought it was just a tall story.

What happened was that a doe squirrel was trapped in a hazel thicket on the banks of the Vombsjön lake and taken to a nearby farm. All the people at the farm, both young and old, were very taken with the pretty little animal with her big tail, clever inquisitive eyes and neat little feet. They thought they could look forward to the pleasure of watching her nimble movements, her skilful way of shelling nuts and her jolly games for the whole summer. They immediately tidied and mended an old squirrel cage with a little green house and a wire wheel. The idea was that she would use the little house – which had both a door and windows – as her dining room and bedroom, so they put in a bed of leaves and a bowl of milk and some nuts. The wheel was to be her playroom, where she could climb, run and spin.

The people on the farm thought that they had set things up very nicely for her and were surprised when she did not appear to be happy. In fact, she simply sat in one corner of her room, cross, despondent and continually uttering a shrill cry of complaint. She did not touch her food and she did not spin in the wheel, not even once.

'It must be because she's afraid,' the people said, 'and tomorrow, when she feels at home here, she'll eat and play.'

Now it happened that the women on the farm were busy

preparing for a feast and on the day the squirrel was trapped they were doing a big bake. Either they had been unlucky and the dough had not risen, or they had been slow, so they were still working long after darkness had fallen.

Everyone in the kitchen was bustling about busily and eagerly and it seems likely that no one had any time to wonder how the squirrel was getting on. There was, however, one old woman, the granny of the house, who was too ancient to help out with the baking. She knew this, but she did not like to be left out of things so, feeling a little miserable, she sat by the window in the living room and looked out rather than go to bed. Because of the heat in the kitchen they had left the door open and a bright strip of light fell across the yard outside. The yard was surrounded by buildings and the light from the kitchen door lit them up so well that the old woman could see the cracks and holes in the plaster on the wall opposite. She could also see the squirrel cage, which was hanging up just where the light was brightest, and she noticed that the squirrel was running from the room to the wheel and from the wheel to the room the whole time, without resting for a moment. She felt there was something strange about how restless the animal was, but then she thought it must, of course, be the bright light that was keeping the doe awake.

The entrance to this particular farm was a wide arched gateway between the cowshed and the stable and the light fell in such a way that it, too, was lit up. As the night was drawing on, the old woman suddenly saw a tiny little fellow, no more than a hand's breadth in height and wearing clogs and leather breeches just like any other workman, slip quietly and cautiously through the arch into the yard. She realised at once that he was an elf and she was not in the least afraid. She had always heard that they had one living there although she had never seen him before. And she knew that elves brought good fortune wherever they turned up.

Once the elf was in the cobbled yard, he ran straight to the squirrel cage and since it was hanging too high for him to reach, he went to the tool-shed, fetched a piece of cane, leant it against the cage and swung himself up just as a sailor climbs a rope. Once up, he hurried to the door of the little green house as if intending to open it. But the old woman was unconcerned: she knew that the children had put a padlock on the door because they were worried that the boys on the neighbouring farm would try to steal the squirrel. She watched the squirrel come out into the wheel when the elf was unable to open the door and she saw the squirrel and the elf having a lengthy discussion. When the elf had listened to everything the captive squirrel had to say, he slid down the cane to the ground and ran out through the gate.

The old woman did not expect to see any more of the elf that night but she stayed by the window anyway. After a while, however, the elf did return and he was in such a hurry that his feet scarcely seemed to touch the ground. He rushed up to the cage. The old woman, who was long-sighted, saw him clearly and could see he was carrying things in his hands, though she could not work out what they were. Whatever it was he had in his left hand, he placed it down on the paving stones while he carried the thing in his right hand up to the cage, used his clog to smash the glass in the little window and passed what he was carrying through to the squirrel. Then he shinned down again, picked up the thing he had left on the ground and climbed up to the cage with that too. After which he rushed off at such a speed that the old woman's eyes could scarcely keep pace with him.

Now it was the old granny's turn to move. Unable to sit still in the cottage any longer, she walked very slowly out into the yard and stood hidden in the shadow of the pump waiting for the elf to return. Someone else had noticed him too and was becoming inquisitive. That someone was the house cat, who crept slowly forward and took up position by the wall, just a couple of paces outside the bright strip of light.

They stood there waiting for quite some time in the cold air of the March night and the old woman was just wondering whether to go back in when she heard the clatter of clogs on the paving stones and saw the tiny little elf trudging back yet again. As before, he was carrying something in each of his hands and whatever those somethings were they were squealing and wriggling. It suddenly dawned on the old granny what the elf was doing – he was running back and forth to the hazel bushes fetching the squirrel's babies and bringing them to her so they would not starve to death.

The woman remained very still so as not to disturb him and the elf did not appear to have noticed her. He was about to put one of the baby squirrels down on the ground in order to clamber up to the cage with the other one when he saw the glint of the cat's green eyes right in front of him. He stood there with a squirrel in each hand, at a complete loss as to what to do next.

He turned round and looked in every direction, and then he saw the old granny. Without any hesitation he walked up to her and handed her one of the baby squirrels.

Not wanting to show herself unworthy of his trust, the old woman bent down, took the squirrel and held it until he had climbed up to the cage with the first one and returned to collect the one he had entrusted to her.

When the people of the farm gathered for breakfast the following morning, the old woman simply had to tell them what she had witnessed during the night. Of course, they all laughed at her and said she must have dreamt it all. And anyway, there weren't any baby squirrels this early in the year.

She stuck to her story, however, and asked them to take a look in the squirrel's cage. They did so and, sure enough, lying there on a bed of leaves in the living room of the cage were four small half-naked and half-blind baby squirrels at least a couple of days old.

As soon as the farmer saw the squirrels, he said: 'Whichever way we look at this, whether we see it from the point of view of people or of animals, it is clear we should be ashamed of what we have done.' Having said that, he picked up the squirrel and all her babies, laid them in the old woman's apron and said: 'Take them out to the hazel bushes and give them back their freedom.'

This was the event that caused so much talk that it even found its way into the newspapers, although most people refused to believe the story simply because they were unable to explain how it could have happened.

VITTSKÖVLE   Saturday, 26 March
Yet another strange event occurred a couple of days later. One morning a flock of wild geese arrived and landed on a field over in the east of Skåne, not far from the great manor at Vittskövle. The flock had thirteen geese of the usual grey colour and a white gander which was carrying on his back a tiny little fellow dressed in yellow leather breeches, a green waistcoat and a white pointed hat.

They were now very close to the Baltic Sea and the soil in the field in which they had landed was very sandy, as it usually is on the coast. It looked as if there had been shifting sands in the district at one time and in order to fix the sands several large pine-woods had been planted at various points.

After the geese had been grazing for a while, some children came walking along the edge of the field. The goose who had been acting as look-out immediately took off, clapping her wings loudly so that the whole flock would hear that danger was approaching. All the wild geese took off but the white gander remained on the ground and was quite unconcerned. Seeing the others take flight, he raised his head and called after them: 'No need to fly away from them! They're just a couple of children.'

The little fellow who had been riding on the gander's back was sitting on a tussock at the edge of the wood pulling a pine-cone to pieces to get at the seeds. The children were so close to him that he could not risk running across the field to the white gander, so he quickly hid under a big dry thistle leaf and gave a warning shout.

The gander had clearly decided not to let himself be scared off. He carried on grazing out on the field and did not even bother to watch where the children were going.

They, however, had turned off the path and were walking

across the field towards the gander. When he did look up at last they were almost on top of him and in his confusion he forgot that he could fly and tried to escape by running away from them. The children followed him, chased him into a ditch and caught him. The biggest of the children then tucked him under his arm and off they went.

The little fellow lying under his thistle leaf saw what was happening and leapt up with the intention of taking the gander from the children. But then he must have remembered how small and weak he was, because he threw himself down on the tussock and furiously beat the ground with his fists.

Meanwhile the gander was yelling for help at the top of his voice: 'Thummitot, come and help me! Thummitot come and help me!' In spite of his distress, the boy could not help laughing. 'Me? What me? A fine one to help anyone, I am!'

He got to his feet and followed the gander anyway. 'I may not be able to help him,' he said to himself, 'but I can at least see what they are going to do with him.'

The children had a good start on him but he had no difficulty keeping them in sight until he reached a hollow through which flowed a brook filled with rushing meltwater. It was not that deep or that powerful but he still had to run along the bank until he found a place he could jump across.

By the time he came up out of the hollow the children had disappeared, but he could see their footprints on a narrow path leading into the woods. He continued following them.

After a little while he came to a place where paths crossed and the children must have split up there because there were now footprints going in two directions. The little fellow was at a complete loss as to what to do.

Then, suddenly, he saw a small white downy feather on a tuft of heather and realised that the gander had dropped it at the roadside in order to show which way he was being taken. So the boy set off again and followed the children right through the wood. He still could not see the gander, but wherever there was any danger of him taking a wrong turning, he would find a little piece of white down showing him the right way.

Thummitot faithfully followed the pieces of down and they led him out of the wood, across a couple of ploughed fields, up onto a road, and finally along an avenue of trees leading to a manor house. At the end of the avenue he caught a glimpse of some gables and towers built of red brick and decorated with lighter coloured edging and ornamentation. As soon as the boy saw the manor house he thought he knew what must have happened to the gander. 'I'm sure the children have taken the gander to the manor and sold him. He's probably been slaughtered by now,' he said to himself. Not satisfied, however, until he was really sure what had happened, he hurried on even more impatiently than before. He did not meet a single soul anywhere along the avenue, which was just as well because creatures of his sort are usually wary of being seen by people.

Vittskövle, the manor house he was approaching, was a splendid old building consisting of four wings ranged around a courtyard. On the eastern side there was a high arched gateway leading through to the courtyard. The little fellow ran up to it without any hesitation but once he got there he came to a halt. He did not dare go any farther and stood wondering what to do.

He was still standing there deep in thought with his finger on his nose when he heard footsteps behind him and, on turning round, he saw a whole crowd of people walking along the avenue towards him. As quickly as he could, he hid behind a water-butt that happened to be standing by the gateway.

The people turned out to be twenty or so young men from a folk high school out on a walking tour. They were accompanied by a teacher and when they came to the gateway the teacher told them to wait there while he went in and asked whether they might look round the fortified old manor house.

The newcomers were hot and tired, as if they had walked a long way. One of them was so thirsty that he went up to the water-butt and bent down to drink. Obviously thinking that the botanical collecting box hanging round his neck would get in the way, he took it off and threw it down on the ground. The lid burst open and revealed the spring flowers he had been collecting.

The tin box landed right in front of the tiny boy and it must have occurred to him that this could provide him with the perfect opportunity to get inside the manor house and discover what had happened to the gander. He slipped quickly into the box and concealed himself as well as he could among the anemones and coltsfoot that were already in there.

No sooner had he done so than the young man picked up the box, hung it back around his neck and slammed the lid shut.

The teacher returned and told them they had been given permission to go into the manor house. He started by taking them as far as the courtyard, where he stopped and began to tell them about the old building.

He reminded them that the very first people who lived in this country had lived in caves and holes in the ground, in tents made of animal hides and shelters made of brushwood. A long time passed before they learnt how to construct houses from tree trunks. And there was a very long period of toil and struggle indeed before they moved on from building one-roomed log cabins and reached the stage of erecting a fortress like Vittskövle with its hundred rooms or more!

It was some three hundred and fifty years ago that rich and powerful people built fortified manor houses like this, the teacher told them. It was easy to see that Vittskövle was built at a time when war and raiders still made Skåne a dangerous place. There was a water-filled moat all round, and there had once been a drawbridge that could be wound up with chains. The watchtower over the gateway still existed and there were walkways for sentries along the sides of the fortress. Solid towers with walls three feet thick stood at the corners. Even so, this fortress had not been built in the most warlike period and Jens Brahe, the man who built it, had been at pains to make it an elegant and richly ornamented building. Once they had seen the great solid stone castle at Glimminge – built just a generation earlier – they would realise at once that its builder Jens Holgersen Ulfstand had only been interested in building big and solid and strong and had not given a thought to beauty and comfort. On the other hand, when they looked at great houses like Marsvinsholm and Svenstorp and Övedskloster, built a century or two after Vittskövle, they would see that times had become more peaceful. The gentlemen who built these places had not fortified them at all and all their efforts had been concentrated on building themselves great and splendid homes.

The teacher talked at great length and in considerable detail and the tiny boy shut in the collecting box became more than a little impatient, but he must have kept very still because the owner of the box had no idea at all that he was carrying him.

At last the group moved on into the manor house itself, but if the boy had been hoping to have a chance to slip out of the collecting box he was disappointed, because the student carried it with him through all the rooms and the boy had no choice but to go with him.

It was a slow tour. The teacher stopped time after time to explain things and impart information.

There was an old fireplace in one room and the teacher stopped in front of it to talk about the different kinds of fireplaces people had used through the ages. The first indoor fireplace had been a slab of stone in the middle of the cottage floor with a smoke-hole in the roof that let in both the wind and the rain. That had been followed by big stone-built fireplaces, still without chimneys, so cottages would certainly have been warm enough but they would also have been full of smoke and fumes. By the time the house at Vittskövle was built, people had got round to building open fireplaces with a wide chimney for the smoke, but most of the warmth disappeared up the chimney as well.

However impatient and impulsive the tiny boy may have been in the past, he was now getting plenty of practice at being patient. He must have been lying motionless in the collecting box for at least an hour.

In the next room the teacher stopped in front of an old four-poster bed with rich curtains and a canopy high above it. He immediately began giving them an account of the beds and bedsteads of past ages.

The teacher was in no hurry. He did not know, of course, that there was a poor little mite shut in a collecting box waiting for him to finish. In a room with gilded leather wall coverings he talked about how people had dressed their walls from the very earliest times; in front of an old family portrait he held forth about the many changes there had been in styles of dress; and in the banqueting rooms he described how weddings and funerals had been celebrated in the olden days.

After that the teacher talked a little about the many outstanding men and women who had lived in this manor house; about the ancient Brahe family and the ancient Barnekow family; about Kristian Barnekow who gave up his horse to help the king escape; about Margareta Ascheberg who was married to Kjell Barnekow and had managed the estates and the whole district for fifty-three years after she was widowed; about the banker Hagerman, who was the son of a Vittskövle crofter but made so much money that he bought the whole estate; and about the Stjernsvärd family who had introduced better ploughs for the people of Skåne so that they could give up those ridiculous old wooden ploughs that even three pairs of oxen had trouble in dragging.

The little fellow kept still through all this. The teacher went on and on for hours and the boy now learnt how his mother and father must have felt when, in one of his fits of naughtiness, he had locked the cellar door on them.

At last the teacher led them back out into the courtyard, where he started talking about the long human struggle to acquire tools and weapons, clothes and houses, furnishings and ornaments. He told them that an old manor house like Vittskövle was a milestone along the way and it allowed them to see how far people had progressed three hundred and fifty years ago. They could judge for themselves whether things had moved on or moved back since then.

The boy was spared this lecture, however, since the student carrying him felt thirsty again and crept off to the kitchen to ask for a drink of water. Once he was in the kitchen, the little boy must have decided to have a look round for the gander. He began to move and accidentally pushed too hard on the lid of the collecting box, which burst open. The lids of collecting boxes have a habit of bursting open, so the student thought no more of it and simply closed it again. But then the cook asked him whether he had a snake in the box.

'No, just a few plants,' the student answered.

'I'm sure I saw something move in there,' the cook insisted.

The student opened the lid to show her she was mistaken. 'See for yourself …'

He got no farther than that because the little fellow did not dare stay in the collecting box any longer. He leapt down to the floor and rushed out. Although the kitchen maids hardly had time to see what it was, they ran after him anyway.

The teacher was still holding forth in the courtyard when he was interrupted by loud shouts. 'Catch him! Catch him!' the maids yelled as they ran out of the kitchen, at which all the young men began chasing the boy, who was scuttling off faster than a rat. They tried to head him off in the gateway, but it was not easy to catch someone so small and he made it out into the open.

The little fellow could not take the risk of running down the open avenue and he turned off in a different direction. He rushed through the garden into the backyard, chased the whole time by laughing and shouting people. The poor boy fled as fast as he could but it looked as if the people were catching up with him.

As he hurried past a small workman's cottage he heard the cackle of a goose and saw a piece of white down lying on the steps. There, there was the gander! He had been following a false trail. He forgot about the serving maids and students chasing him and he climbed up the steps to the porch but was unable to proceed any farther because the cottage door was locked. He could hear the gander screaming and moaning inside but there was no way he could get the door open. All the hunters chasing him were coming nearer and the gander in the house was yelling more and more pitifully. Finally, in his dire need, he summoned up all his courage and pounded on the door as hard as he was able.

The door was opened by a child and the little fellow looked into the room. There, in the middle of the floor, sat a woman holding the gander in a firm grip in order to cut off his quill feathers. Her children were the ones who had found him and she had no intention of doing him any harm. She was planning to release him among her own geese once she had clipped his wings so that he could not fly away. But the gander could not imagine a worse fate, which was why he was yelling and complaining with all his might.

It was fortunate that the woman had not started her clipping sooner and her scissors had only cut two quills when the door opened to reveal the little fellow on the threshold. The woman had never seen anything like him before and was convinced that it was none other than Goa-Nisse, the elf-king himself. In her horror she dropped her scissors, clapped her hands together and forgot to hang on to the gander.

As soon as the gander felt her let go, he ran for the door. Without stopping he grabbed the little fellow by the collar as he passed and took him with him. Once out on the steps he opened his wings and rose into the air while, at the same time, making a showy sweep with his neck and placing the boy on his downy back.

And so they sailed off up into the air with the whole of Vittskövle standing gazing up at them.

IN ÖVEDSKLOSTER PARK
The whole day the geese had spent playing their tricks on the fox, the boy had been asleep in a deserted squirrel's drey and when he woke towards evening he was very worried. 'They're

going to send me home soon and I'll have no choice but to face father and mother,' he thought.

But when he went and found the geese, who were swimming around on the Vombsjön lake, none of them said a word about him leaving. 'Perhaps they think the white gander is too tired to fly home with me tonight,' the boy thought.

The following morning the geese were awake at first light, long before the sun had come up. Now the boy felt certain that he would have to go home but, curiously enough, both he and the white gander were allowed to join the wild geese on their morning trip. The boy was quite unable to work out the cause of the delay, but he came to the conclusion that the wild geese did not want to send the gander on such a long journey before giving him time to eat his fill. Whatever the reason might be, the boy was more than happy for every hour that postponed a meeting with his parents.

The wild geese flew over Övedskloster Manor, which lay in the middle of a wonderful park east of the lake. It looked so splendid with its grand manor house, its beautiful paved courtyard surrounded by low walls and pavilions, its fine old-fashioned garden with clipped hedges, leafy tunnels, ponds, water features, magnificent trees and regular lawns, their borders a colourful motley of spring flowers.

There was no sign of human life when the wild geese passed over in the early morning light and once they had made quite sure of this, the geese descended towards the dog's kennel calling, 'What kind of little hut is this? What kind of little hut is this?'

The chained dog leapt out of his kennel, barking up into the air in a furious rage.

'So you call this a hut, do you, you vagrants, you? Can't you see that it's a tall stone manor house? Can't you see the beautiful walls, can't you see all the windows and the huge doors and the beautiful terrace? Bow-wow! So you call this a hut, do you? Can't you see the courtyard, can't you see the garden, can't you see the conservatories, can't you see the marble statues? So you call this a hut, do you? Do huts have a park with beech woods and hazel copses and parkland and groves of oak-trees and spruce woods and a deer park full of roe-deer? Bow-wow! So you call this a hut, do you? Have you ever seen huts with so many outhouses that they look like a whole village? I suppose you know plenty of huts that have their own churches and their own manses, that rule over lordly estates and farms and tenancies and labourers' cottages? Bow-wow! So you call this a hut, do you? This hut owns the biggest estate in Skåne, you beggars! There is not a single piece of the land you can see from up there in the sky that is not ruled by this hut! Bow-wow!'

The dog managed to shout all that in one breath and the geese flew back and forth over the estate listening to him until he had to stop for breath. But then they yelled back:

'What are you getting so worked up about? We weren't talking about the manor house, we were talking about your kennel.'

At first the boy laughed when he heard them joking in this way but then he was struck by a thought that suddenly made him feel serious.

'Just think of all the amusing things you would hear if the wild geese let you go the whole length of the country with them, all the way up to Lapland!' he said to himself. 'Since your life is in such a mess, a trip like that would be just about the best thing you could find to do.'

The wild geese flew off to one of the big open fields east of the manor house in order to graze on the grass. They stayed there for hours and while they were there the boy wandered off looking for hazelnut bushes in the great park that bordered the field. He started by searching the bushes for any nuts left over from the autumn, but as he walked in the park the thought of that long journey came into his mind time after time. He pictured to himself what a wonderful time he would have if he went with the wild geese. He had no doubt that he would often go hungry and feel cold but, in return for that, he would escape both farm work and school work.

While he was walking around, the old grey lead goose

came up to him and asked whether he had found anything to eat. No, he had not, he told her, and so she tried to help him. She had no more luck than him when it came to nuts but she did find several rosehips hanging on a wild rose bush. The boy ate them with relish and he wondered what his mother would have said if she knew he was living on raw fish and old rosehips that had survived the winter.

After the wild geese had finally eaten their fill, they went back to the lake and enjoyed themselves playing about until it was almost midday. They challenged the white gander to all sorts of competitions – swimming races, running races and flying races. Even though the tame gander did his best, he was always beaten by the nimble wild geese. The boy sat on the gander's back, cheering him on the whole time and he had just as much fun as everyone else. There was so much yelling and laughing and cackling that it was amazing that the people on the estate did not hear them.

When the wild geese were tired of playing games, they went out on the ice and rested for some hours. Then they passed the afternoon in more or less the same way as the morning: first a couple of hours grazing, followed by bathing and playing in the water at the edge of the ice until sunset, after which they immediately settled down to sleep.

'This is the life for me!' the boy thought as he slipped in under the gander's wing. 'But I suppose they'll send me home tomorrow.'

Before falling asleep he lay awake thinking that if the geese allowed him to go with them he would no longer have to put up with being scolded for laziness. He would be able to laze around all day and his only worry would be finding things to eat. Not that it was likely to be much trouble since he needed so little these days.

And he imagined all the things he would see and all the adventures he would be part of. Oh, how different it would be from the dreary round of work and drudgery at home!

'If only I can make this journey with the wild geese,' he thought, 'I won't be in the least bothered about having had a spell put on me.'

The only thing he was afraid of was being sent home, but Wednesday came and still the geese said nothing about him going back. That day was spent in the same way as Tuesday and the boy was finding this wilderness life more and more to his taste. He felt as if he had the secluded park at Övedskloster all to himself – and it was the size of a forest! He had no desire at all to return to the confinement of the cottage and the small fields at home.

All day Wednesday he thought the wild geese were intending to keep him with them, but on Thursday he lost all hope again.

Thursday began in the same way as the other days. The geese fed on the wide fields and the boy looked for things to eat in the park. Akka came up to him after a while and asked if he had found anything to eat. No, he hadn't, so she found him a dry caraway plant which still had all its small seeds hanging on it.

Once the boy had eaten, Akka told him that she thought the way he was running around the park was far too reckless. She wondered if he had any idea how many enemies he needed to watch out for, given how small he was. No, he had no idea at all, so Akka began to list them for him.

He should be on his guard against foxes and pine martens when he was walking in the park, she said; on the shores of the lake he should think about otters; if he was sitting up on a stone wall, he should not forget that weasels can creep through the smallest of holes; if he was going to sleep in a pile of leaves, he should always check that an adder was not using the same leaves for its winter hibernation. As soon as he went out onto an open field he should keep his eyes peeled for hawks and buzzards, for eagles and falcons, hovering in the sky above him. Among the hazel bushes a sparrowhawk could pounce upon him, and there were magpies and crows everywhere – and they were not to be trusted. As soon as dusk fell, he must keep his ears open for the big owls, whose wing-beats were so silent that they could be on him before he was aware of them.

When the boy heard that there were so many creatures after his life, he thought he had very little chance of surviving. He was not particularly afraid to die but he did not like the idea of being eaten up, so he asked Akka what he could do to protect himself against these predators.

Akka told him at once that he must try to make friends with the small animals of the forests and the fields, with the squirrel folk and the hare folk, with the finches and the tits and the woodpeckers and the larks. If he became their friend, they would warn him of danger, find hiding places for him and, when danger was at its worst, they would flock together and protect him.

Later that day, however, when the boy tried to follow Akka's advice by approaching Sirle the squirrel and asking for his support, Sirle did not want to help him. 'Don't think for one moment you can expect any help from me and the other small animals,' Sirle said. 'Do you think we don't know that you are Nils Goose-boy who only last year tore down swallows' nests, smashed starlings' eggs, threw crow chicks into the marlpit, snared thrushes and put squirrels in cages? You'll have to look after yourself as well as you can, and you can think yourself lucky that we don't all gang together and chase you back to where you came from.'

The boy would not have let that sort of answer go unpunished in the past when he was still Nils Goose-boy, but now he was simply afraid that the wild geese might have learnt how nasty he could be. He had been so worried that the geese would not let him stay with them that he had not risked getting up to any mischief at all since joining their company. It is true, of course, that being as small as he now was he would have been incapable of doing anything very bad, though he could certainly have destroyed many birds' nests and smashed plenty of eggs had he wanted to do so. But he had been good the whole time: he had not so much as plucked a feather from a goose's wing or given a cheeky answer to anyone, and every time he said good morning to

Akka he doffed his cap and bowed.

All day Thursday he went round thinking that it must be his past naughtiness that was making the wild geese reluctant to take him up to Lapland. So when he heard in the evening that Sirle Squirrel's wife had been captured and his children were starving to death, he decided to help them – and we have already heard how successful he was.

When he went out into the park on Friday he could hear the chaffinches in every thicket cheeping about how Sirle's wife had been snatched away from her little ones by cruel robbers and how Nils Goose-boy had been brave enough to go among the humans in order to take her squirrel babies to her.

'Who is the toast of Övedskloster Park?' the chaffinches sang. 'Thummitot is! Thummitot, who everyone was afraid of in the days when he was Nils Goose-boy! Sirle Squirrel will give him nuts, the poor hares will play with him, the roe-deer will take him on their backs and flee when Smirre Fox approaches, the tits will warn him about the sparrowhawk, and the larks and finches will sing of his heroic deed.'

The boy was sure that Akka and the other wild geese heard all this but still Friday passed without them saying a word about him being allowed to stay with them.

Smirre Fox left the geese to graze the fields around Öved undisturbed until Saturday. But when they came out onto the fields on Saturday morning, he was lying in wait and he stalked them from one field to the next so they had no peace to feed. Akka realised that the fox was not intending to leave them alone and, coming to a quick decision, she took off and led her flock over the plains of Färs-härad and the juniper-covered hills of the Linderöd ridge. They flew for twenty-five miles and did not land until they came to the neighbourhood of Vittskövle.

We have already heard how the gander was taken captive at Vittskövle and how, if it had not been for the boy doing everything in his power to help, things would never have been set right.

When the boy returned to Vombsjön with the gander on Saturday evening he thought he had done a good day's work and wondered what Akka and the wild geese would have to say. And the wild geese were certainly not sparing with their praise, but they did not say the words he was longing to hear.

Sunday came round again. A whole week had passed since the elf had put a spell on the boy, who was still as tiny as ever.

He did not, however, appear to be greatly concerned. On the Sunday afternoon he was sitting crouched among the withies of a big bushy osier by the side of the lake, blowing a reed pipe. There were as many tits and chaffinches and starlings perched around him as the bush could hold and all of them were twittering songs that he was trying to learn to play. But the boy was far from mastering the art and the notes he blew were so out of tune that the feathers on all his tiny teachers stood on end and they shrilled and flapped their wings in despair. The boy laughed at their excitement so much that he dropped his pipe.

He started again but it went just as badly as before and all the small birds lamented: 'Your playing is even worse today than it usually is, Thummitot. You can't play a single note in tune. What's on your mind, Thummitot?'

'My thoughts are elsewhere,' the boy said, and it was true. He was wondering how long he would be allowed to stay with the wild geese or whether they were going to send him home – perhaps even today.

The boy suddenly threw away his pipe and jumped down from the bush. He had seen Akka and all the other geese approaching him in a long line. They were walking so slowly and solemnly – quite unlike their usual walk – that it seemed to him that they were coming to tell him what they intended to do about him.

When, at last, they came to a halt, Akka spoke: 'You have every reason to wonder, Thummitot, why I haven't thanked you for saving me from Smirre Fox. But I'm the sort that prefers to show my gratitude with deeds rather than words. Now, Thummitot, I believe I have succeeded in doing you a great service. I sent a message to the elf who put a spell on you. At first he wouldn't hear of lifting the spell, but I have sent him message after message telling him how well you have behaved among us. So he has now asked us to tell you that you will become human again as soon as you go home.'

But would you believe it! When the goose finished speaking the boy was as sad as he had been happy when she started! He said nothing, just turned away and wept.

'What on earth is this?' Akka said. 'It appears you were expecting more from me than I have offered.'

But the boy was thinking of the carefree days and happy fun, of the adventures and the freedom and the journeys high above the earth, all of which he was going to lose, and he howled in misery.

'I don't care about becoming human,' he said. 'I want to come to Lapland with you.'

Akka spoke again: 'I'll tell you something. That elf is very quick-tempered and I'm afraid that if you don't accept his offer now, it will be very difficult to persuade him a second time.'

The peculiar thing about the boy was that as long as he had lived he had never really cared for anyone. He had not cared for his father and mother, nor for his schoolteacher, nor for his schoolmates, nor for the boys on the neighbouring farms. Everything they had wanted him to do, whether work or play, had always seemed boring. So there was no one he missed and no one he longed to be with.

The only people he had ever seen more or less eye to eye with had been Åsa Goose-girl and Little Mats, the two children who, like him, had tended the geese out in the fields. But he did not really feel close to them even. Far from it.

'I don't want to be human,' the boy howled. 'I want to come to Lapland with you. That's why I've been good all week.'

'I'm not going to refuse to take you with us as far as you want to go,' Akka said, 'but think hard now whether you wouldn't prefer to return home. There may well come a day when you will regret that you didn't.'

'No,' said the boy, 'there is nothing to regret. Things have never been so good as since I've been with you.'

'In that case,' Akka said, 'why shouldn't your wish come true?'

'Thank you!' the boy said and was so happy that he wept tears of joy, just as earlier he had been weeping tears of sorrow.

IV

GLIMMINGEHUS

BLACK RATS AND GREY RATS

In south-eastern Skåne, not far from the sea, there is an old castle called Glimmingehus. It consists of a single tall and solid stone building, visible across the plain for miles around. It is no more than four storeys high but it is so massive that an ordinary house that stands alongside it looks as tiny as a play house.

The outer and inner walls and vaulted ceilings of this great stone structure are so thick that there is scarcely room inside it for anything but its thick walls. The stairways are narrow, the passages small and there are few rooms. To keep the walls as strong as possible, there are only a small number of windows in the upper floors and the lower floors have nothing but narrow slits to let in a little light. In the old days people were as glad to be able to creep into massive and strong buildings like this during times of war as they are these days to slip into their fur-coats in the depths of winter. Once good and peaceful times arrived, however, they no longer wanted to live in the dark and cold rooms of this ancient fortress. The mighty Glimmingehus Castle was abandoned long ago and people moved into houses built to let in light and air.

At the time Nils Holgersson was travelling with the wild geese there were no people living in Glimmingehus, which did not mean that the castle was short of residents. A pair of storks nested every summer in a great nest up on the roof, a pair of tawny owls occupied the attic, bats hung in the secret passages, an old cat lived in the fireplace in the kitchen and down in the cellar were several hundred old black rats.

Rats are not usually held in high regard by other animals, but the black rats at Glimmingehus were an exception. They were spoken of with respect, because they had shown much courage in fighting their enemies and great endurance in the face of the many misfortunes that had afflicted their tribe. For they belonged to a race of rats that had once been powerful and numerous but was now dying out. The black rats had held sway over Skåne and, indeed, the whole country for very many years. They had lived in every cellar, every loft, in barns and byres, in storehouses and bakeries, in cowsheds and stables, in churches and castles, in breweries and mills, in every building erected by man – but now they had been driven out from everywhere and were almost extinct. It was only in the occasional lonely old place that they were still to be found and it was only at Glimmingehus that they survived in any numbers.

When a race of animals dies out, it is usually the fault of human beings, but not in this case. People had certainly waged war on the black rats but had not succeeded in doing them any damage worth mentioning. No, the black rats had been defeated by a tribe of their own kind – they had been defeated by grey rats.

The grey rats had not been resident in this country from time immemorial as the black rats had. They were the descendants of a couple of poor immigrants who had come ashore from a Lübeck cog in Malmö a hundred years or so before. These poor starving homeless beasts remained in the harbour, swimming around among the piles that supported the wharves and eating any refuse thrown into the water. They did not risk moving up into the town itself, which was left in the possession of the black rats.

Gradually, however, as the grey rats grew in number, they became bolder. First they moved into some old houses that were empty and condemned and had been deserted by the black rats. They scavenged for food in the gutters and rubbish heaps and were prepared to put up with all the garbage that black rats did not deign to touch. They were hardy, easily satisfied and fearless and within a few years they had become so powerful that they set about driving the black rats out of Malmö. They took over their attics and their cellars and their warehouses, they starved them out or bit them to death, for they certainly were not afraid to fight.

Once they had taken Malmö they moved on, sometimes in small bands, sometimes in great hosts, to conquer the whole country. It is almost impossible to understand why the black rats failed to gather together and mount a great united campaign to annihilate the grey rats while their numbers were still small, but the blacks were probably so certain of their power that they did not believe they could lose. They stayed quietly on their estates while the grey rats took over farm after farm, village after village and town after town. And so the black rats starved, were pushed out and exterminated; Glimmingehus was the only place in the whole of Skåne where they had managed to hang on and survive.

The walls of the old stone castle were so solid and so few rat-runs penetrated through them that the black rats had been able to defend the castle successfully and prevent the grey rats from forcing their way in. The battle between the attackers and the defenders had gone on night after night, year after year, but the black rats had remained loyal and true, fighting with no regard for their own lives and, thanks to the magnificent old castle, they had always been victorious.

It has to be admitted that as long as the black rats were in power every other living creature detested them as much as they now detested the grey rats. And with justification. They had pounced on poor shackled prisoners and tormented them, gorged on corpses, stolen the last turnip in the cellars of the poor, bitten the feet of sleeping geese, stolen eggs and chicks from the hens and committed a thousand crimes. But all this seemed to have been forgotten once misfortune befell them, and everyone felt forced to admire these last survivors for holding out against their enemies for so long.

The grey rats living on the Glimminge estate and in the surrounding district kept up their campaign and were forever on the watch for any opportunity that would allow them to conquer the castle. Anyone would think that, having taken over the whole of the rest of the country, they could have left the little company of black rats to occupy Glimmingehus in peace, but that, quite clearly, did not occur to them. They used to say that the defeat of the black rats was a matter of honour as far as they were concerned, but anyone who knew the grey rats understood that the real reason the grey rats would not rest until they had taken the castle was that people were using Glimmingehus as a grain store.

THE STORK   Monday, 28 March
Early one morning while the wild geese were still asleep on the ice of the Vombsjön lake, they were woken by loud cries in the sky above them. 'Trirop! Trirop!' came the call. 'Trianut the crane sends greetings to Akka the wild goose and her flock. Tomorrow is the day of the great crane dance on the Kullaberg.'
Akka immediately lifted her head and stretched her neck and answered: 'Pass on our greetings and thanks! Greetings and thanks!'

Then the cranes flew off, but the wild geese could still hear them far away as they called out over every field and every wood: 'Trianut sends greetings! Tomorrow is the day of the great crane dance on the Kullaberg.'

The news filled the wild geese with joy. 'You are so lucky,' they said to the white gander, 'to be given the chance to witness the great crane dance.'

'Is it that unusual to see cranes dancing?' the gander asked.

'It is a sight such as you have never dreamt of,' the wild geese answered.

'Now we shall have to think of what to do with Thummitot, to keep him out of harm's way while we are at the Kullaberg,' Akka said.

'Thummitot won't have to be left on his own,' the gander said. 'If the cranes won't allow him to see their dance, then I shall stay with him.'

'No human being has yet been allowed to be present at the meeting of the animals on the Kullaberg,' Akka said, 'and I daren't take Thummitot with me. But we can talk about that later in the day. First and foremost we need to think about getting a bite to eat.'

Akka gave the signal for them to set off and, because of Smirre Fox, they once again chose distant pastures, not landing until they reached the marshy meadows a little to the south of Glimmingehus.

The boy spent the whole of that day sitting on the bank of a little pond blowing on reed pipes. He was in a bad mood because he was not to be allowed to see the crane dance and neither the gander nor any of the others could get a word out of him.

He took it very hard that Akka still did not trust him. When a boy has given up being a human being in order to travel with some poor old wild geese, you would have thought they would have understood that he had no wish to betray them. And since he had sacrificed so much to be with them, they really ought to understand that it was their duty to let him witness all the remarkable things they could show him along the way.

'I am really going to have to speak my mind,' he thought, but hour after hour went by and he still could not bring himself to do so. Amazing as it may sound, the boy had actually come to have a measure of respect for the old lead goose. And he realised it was not easy to oppose her wishes.

A broad stone wall ran along one side of the marshy meadowland where the geese were grazing and, towards evening, as the boy finally raised his head and prepared to speak to Akka, his gaze fell on this wall. He gave a sudden little cry of surprise and all the geese immediately looked up and began staring in the same direction as the boy. At first both the boy and the geese thought that all the grey cobbles the wall was built of had sprouted legs and begun to run, but they quickly realised that what they were seeing was a great host of rats running over it. They were moving very quickly, rushing forward tightly packed, rank after rank of them, and in such numbers that the wall was completely hidden by them for some time.

Even when he had been a big strong fellow the boy had always been afraid of rats, so it is not difficult to imagine what he must have been feeling now that he was so small that two or three of them could easily get the better of him. Shivers ran up and down his spine as he stood there watching them.

The strange thing was that the geese seemed to share his loathing for rats. They did not speak to them and once they had passed by the geese shook themselves as if dirt had got into their feathers.

'So many grey rats out and about!' Yksi from Vassijaure said. 'Not a good sign!'

The boy was just about to speak to Akka and to say that he thought they should let him accompany them to the Kullaberg when he was prevented yet again, this time by a large bird that suddenly landed in the middle of the flock of geese.

From the look of this bird, anyone would think it had borrowed its body, neck and head from a small white goose. But then it had added huge black wings, long red legs and a long stout beak, which was too big for its small head and which weighed it down and caused the bird to have a rather sad and worried appearance.

Akka quickly smoothed down her wing coverts and walked towards the stork, bowing her head up and down many times. She was not particularly surprised to see him in Skåne this early in the spring because she knew that male storks usually migrate back in good time to check whether their nests have been damaged during the winter and before the females go to the bother of flying across the Baltic Sea. But she did wonder why he had sought her out, since storks tend to stick to those of their own kind.

'There surely can't be anything the matter with your residence, Herr Ermenrich?' Akka said.

The old saying that a stork cannot open its beak without

complaining now proved to be true. What made the stork's news even more dreary than it might otherwise have been was the fact that he had such difficulty in getting the words out. For some time he just stood there clapping his beak and then he spoke in a voice that was weak and hoarse. He complained about everything imaginable: his nest, which was right up on the ridge of the roof of Glimmingehus, had been completely ruined by winter storms, added to which it was impossible for him to find food in Skåne these days. The people of Skåne were taking over all his property, draining his marshlands and bringing his mosses into cultivation. He was intending to leave this country and never return.

While the stork grumbled on and on, Akka the wild goose, who owned neither a shelter nor a refuge, could not help thinking: 'If life was as comfortable for me as it is for you, Herr Ermenrich, I should feel myself above complaining. You have remained a wild and free bird and yet you are on such good terms with humankind that no one wants to shoot you or to steal eggs from your nest.' But she kept all this to herself. All she said to the stork was that she could not believe that he wanted to move away from a house where storks had nested ever since it was built.

Then the stork quickly asked whether the geese had seen all those grey rats marching on Glimmingehus, and when Akka replied that she had indeed seen the pests, he went on to tell her about the brave black rats who had been defending the castle for so many years. 'But tonight,' the stork said with a sigh, 'Glimmingehus is going to fall to the grey rats.'

'Why tonight, Herr Ermenrich?' Akka asked.

'Well, you see, it's because almost all the black rats set off for the Kullaberg last night,' the stork said. 'They are counting on all the other animals going there too, but the grey rats are staying at home. Tonight they have gathered their forces to mount an attack on the fortress while its only defenders are a few poor old black rats who were not up to making the journey to the Kullaberg with the others. I've no doubt they will achieve their end, but I have lived on good neighbourly terms with the black rats for so many years that I have no desire to live alongside their enemies.'

Akka understood now that the behaviour of the grey rats had angered the stork so much that he had come to her with his complaints. But, given the nature of storks, he would undoubtedly have done nothing at all to forestall the disaster.

'Have you sent a message to the black rats, Herr Ermenrich?' she asked.

'No,' answered the stork, 'there was no point. The castle will be captured before the others have time to return.'

'Don't be so sure of that, Herr Ermenrich,' Akka replied. 'I know one old wild goose who would be only too pleased to prevent such a foul deed.'

While Akka was saying this, the stork lifted his head and looked at her wide-eyed. Which is hardly surprising since old Akka had neither claws nor a sharp beak to use in a fight. What is more, she was a day bird who fell helplessly asleep as soon as darkness fell, whereas rats were night fighters.

But Akka had obviously decided to support the black rats. She called Yksi from Vassijaure to her and ordered him to lead the geese up to Vombsjön, and when the geese objected, she said in an authoritative voice: 'I think it will be best for all of us if you obey me. I need to fly up to the great stone castle and if you follow me, the people on the estate are bound to see us and shoot us down. The only one I am taking with me on this journey is Thummitot. He will be a great help to me because he has sharp eyes and can stay awake at night.'

The boy, however, was in one of his awkward moods that day and when he heard what Akka said he stretched up to make himself as big as he could, stepped forward with his hands behind his back and his nose in the air and was about to say that he most certainly did not want to be involved in a fight with the grey rats. If she wanted help, she would have to look elsewhere.

The moment the boy came into view, however, the stork began to move. Until then he had been standing, as is the way with storks, with his head bowed and his bill pressed against his neck. Suddenly there was a gurgle deep in his throat, as if he was laughing. Quick as a flash he lowered his bill, grabbed the boy and tossed him ten feet in the air. He then repeated this trick seven times, with the boy yelling and the geese shouting, 'What do you think you're doing, Herr Ermenrich? That's not a frog, that's a human being, Herr Ermenrich.'

At last the stork put the boy down completely unharmed. Then he said to Akka: 'I'm now going to fly back to Glimmingehus, Mother Akka. Everyone living there was very anxious when I left. You can imagine how happy they'll be when I tell them that Akka the wild goose and Thummitot the human midget will be coming to rescue them!'

At which the stork stretched out his neck, opened his wings and shot off like an arrow fired from a fully drawn bow. Akka realised he had been making fun of her but she did not allow it to affect her. She waited until the boy had found his clogs, which had been shaken off by the stork, and then she put him on her back and set off after the stork. For his part, the boy offered no resistance and said nothing about not wanting to go with her. The stork had made him so angry that he was snorting with rage. So that gangly redlegs thought he was good for nothing just because he was small, did he? But he'd soon show him what Nils Holgersson from Västra Vemmenhög was made of!

In no time at all Akka was standing on the stork's nest on top of Glimmingehus, and a big and splendid nest it was too. The nest had a cartwheel as its foundation, on top of which lay several layers of twigs and tufts of grass. The nest was so old that numerous shrubs and plants had taken root, and when the mother stork laid her eggs in the round hollow in the middle of the nest, she could not only enjoy a glorious view over much of Skåne but she also had her own dog-roses and houseleeks to look at.

Akka and the boy saw at once that something was going on here that turned the natural order of things upside down. There were two tawny owls sitting on the edge of the nest and alongside them sat an old greying cat and a dozen ancient rats with overgrown teeth and runny eyes. They were hardly the kind of animals normally found together peacefully in one place.

None of them turned round to look at Akka or to welcome her. Their thoughts and their eyes were fixed on several long grey lines they could glimpse moving forward here and there across the bare winter fields.

All the black rats remained silent. You could see they were filled with despair and knew only too well that they were incapable of defending either the castle or their lives. The two owls sat there rolling their big eyes, twitching their facial discs and talking in strange sharp voices about how cruel the grey rats were and how they would have to move away because they had heard that the rats would spare neither their eggs nor their chicks. The old cat, all streaked with grey, was sure the rats would bite him to death once the hordes of them had broken into the castle. He grumbled incessantly at the black rats: 'How could you be so stupid as to let all your best warriors go away? How could you be so stupid as to trust the grey rats? It's absolutely unforgiveable.'

The twelve black rats did not say a word but the stork, despite his gloomy nature, could not resist teasing the cat: 'No need to worry, Måns,' he said. 'Not now that Mother Akka and Thummitot have come to save the castle! You can feel certain they'll succeed! I'm going to sleep peacefully tonight in the sure knowledge that when I wake they won't have let a single grey rat into Glimmingehus!'

The boy winked at Akka and made a sign that he would push the stork off his perch since the bird was standing on the edge of the nest on one leg with the other tucked up. Akka restrained him, but without looking the least bit angry at the idea. Instead she said in a confident tone of voice: 'It would be a pretty poor thing, wouldn't it, if someone as old as me couldn't find a way out of worse difficulties than these. If the owl and his wife, who are able to stay awake all night, will agree to flying off on my behalf with a couple of messages, I think everything can be sorted out.'

The tawny owls were willing, so Akka asked the male owl to fly and find the black rats who were away on their travels to the Kullaberg and to advise them to hurry home at once. The female owl was to visit Flammea, the barn owl who lived in the cathedral in Lund, and to entrust her with a mission so secret that Akka could not risk confiding it except in a whisper.

THE RATCATCHER

Midnight was approaching when the grey rats, after much searching, at last managed to find an air-vent open in the cellar. It was quite high on the wall but, by standing on one another's shoulders, it did not take long for the boldest rat to enter the vent and be ready to invade Glimmingehus, before whose walls so many of her forefathers had met their deaths.

The grey rat in the vent sat still for a while, expecting to be attacked. She knew that the main force of defenders was away but she assumed that the black rats remaining in the castle would not give up without a fight. She sat with her heart pounding and listened for the slightest noise, but everything remained silent. Then the leader of the grey rats plucked up her courage and jumped down into the coal-black cellar.

One after another the grey rats followed their leader. They all kept very quiet and they all expected to be ambushed by the black rats. Not until so many of them had forced their way in that there was no space left on the cellar floor did they dare move on.

Although they had never been inside the fortress before they had no difficulty in finding their way. Very soon they found the passageways in the walls which the black rats used to reach the upper floors. Before beginning to climb these steep and narrow passages, they listened again very carefully. They felt far more frightened by the fact that the black rats were staying out of sight than if they had met them in open battle, and they could hardly believe their luck when they reached the first floor without misfortune striking.

From the moment they entered, the grey rats were met by the smell of the grain stored in huge bins on the floor. But it was not yet time for them to enjoy the fruits of victory. First of all, taking great care, they made their way through the bare and gloomy rooms. They jumped up into the fireplace in the middle of the floor of the old castle kitchen, and they very nearly tumbled down the well in the inner room. They inspected every single one of the narrow slits that let in the light, but still they found no sign of any black rats. Once they were in full possession of that floor they moved on as cautiously as before to take control of the floor above. Once again they had to risk the perilous and laborious climb through the walls, holding their breath in anxious expectation of an enemy attack at any moment. Although they were tempted by that wonderful smell from the grain bins, they forced themselves to be thoroughly methodical and inspect the vaulted quarters in which the men-at-arms had lived in olden times, to check the stone table and the hearth and the deep window embrasures and the hole in the floor, constructed so that boiling pitch could be poured down on any enemy trying to get in.

And still there was no sign of the black rats. The grey rats worked their way up to the third floor, where the great banqueting hall of the lords of the castle stood as empty and cold as all the other rooms in the ancient house, and then they moved on up to the top floor, which consisted of one big empty space. The only place they did not think of inspecting was the stork's nest on the roof where, at that very moment, the female owl was waking Akka and informing her that Flammea, the barn owl, had approved of her proposal and sent her what she had asked for.

Once the grey rats had inspected the whole castle conscientiously, they felt more relaxed. They realised that the black rats had fled and had no intention of putting up any resistance. So, with joy in their hearts, they leapt up into the grain bins.

The grey rats had scarcely had time to swallow the first grains when the sound of a shrill little pipe could be heard down in the courtyard. The grey rats raised their heads from

the grain, listened uneasily, hopped a few steps as if they were about to leave the bin, but then began eating again.

The pipe sounded again, a powerful tone that cut through the air. Then something remarkable began to happen. First one rat, then two, then a whole swarm, stopped eating, jumped out of the bin and hurried by the shortest route down to the cellar in order to leave the building. Many grey rats remained, however. Thinking of the toil and effort they had put in to the conquest of Glimmingehus, they did not want to leave. But the notes of the pipe reached them once more and they had no choice but to obey them. In a fit of wild excitement they hurled themselves out of the bins and rushed down through the narrow holes in the walls, tumbling over one another in their eagerness to get out.

There, in the middle of the courtyard, stood a tiny little fellow playing a pipe. He already had a whole circle of rats around him and more were joining them at every moment. Amazed and enchanted, they listened to his playing. Once, however, when he took his pipe away from his lips just for a second to thumb his nose at the rats, it looked as if they wanted to hurl themselves at him and bite him to death, but as soon as he blew the pipe, they were back in his power.

When the little fellow had played all the grey rats out of the castle building, he began walking slowly out of the courtyard of Glimmingehus on to the high road, and so sweet did the tones of the pipe sound to the rats that, unable to resist them, they followed him.

The little fellow walked in front of them and lured them along the road towards Vallby. He led them through all sorts of bends and turns and zig-zags, through hedges and down into ditches, and wherever he led they had to follow. And all the time he kept blowing his pipe, which looked as if it was made from the horn of an animal, though the horn was so small that there are no animals in our times from whose forehead it could have been taken. Nor did anyone know who had made it. Flammea the barn owl had found it in a niche in the tower of Lund Cathedral. She had shown it to Bataki the raven, and they had worked out between them that it was the kind of instrument that used to be made in times past by those who wanted to gain power over rats and mice. The raven was a friend of Akka and it was from him she had heard that Flammea possessed such a precious thing.

And it was true that rats found the pipe irresistible. The boy marched in front, playing for as long as the starlight lasted and the rats followed him. He played as the day broke and he played as the sun rose and the whole army of grey rats followed him as he lured them farther and farther away from the great grain stores at Glimmingehus.

V

THE GREAT CRANE DANCE ON THE KULLABERG

Tuesday, 29 March

Many magnificent buildings have been built in Skåne but it has to be said that there is not one of them that can boast of walls as beautiful as the ancient Kullaberg.

Far from being a great and mighty mountain, the Kullaberg is a long and low ridge. There are woods and ploughlands and one or two heaths up on its broad summit, and here and there heather-covered rocky knolls and bare outcrops of rock poke up. None of it is outstandingly beautiful and, in fact, it looks just like all the other high ground in Skåne.

A traveller passing along the high road that runs along the ridge of the Kullaberg cannot help feeling a little disappointed. But should the traveller leave the road, walk out to the sides of the ridge and look down the steep slopes, he will suddenly find so much that is worth seeing that he will be hard-pressed to know how to fit it all in. For, unlike other hills, the Kullaberg is not surrounded by land and plains and valleys, it juts far far out into the sea. There is not even a narrow strip of land at the foot of the hill to protect it from the sea, so waves wash right up against the cliffs, eroding and shaping them at will.

It is the sea, assisted by its trusty helper the wind, which has moulded these cliffs into such richly ornamented forms. It has carved sheer-sided ravines deep into the sides of the hill and left spits of black rock polished smooth by the constant lashing of the wind. Solitary pillars of rock rear up from the waters, and there are dark caves with narrow entrances. Here the precipices of bare rock are vertical, there the slopes are gentle and cloaked in vegetation. There are small headlands and small bays and pebbles that rustle as they are washed back and forth, back and forth by every breaking wave. There are stately rock arches that vault high over the water, and there are sharp boulders, some of them constantly sprayed by white foam while others see their reflections mirrored in still and unchanging dark-green waters. There are giant cauldrons bored into the rock and great crevices that entice the wanderer to venture deep into the hill to Kullamannen's Cavern.*

And up and over and around all these crevices and cliffs grow creepers and tendrils. There are trees growing there, but the force of the wind is such that they, too, are forced to turn themselves into creepers in order to cling to the steep slopes. Oak-trees hug the ground, lying prostrate with their foliage forming a shallow arch over them, and beech trees with stunted trunks poke out of the crevices like great leafy tents.

These remarkable cliffs, with the wide blue sea around them and the shimmering clear air above, are what make the Kullaberg so popular that crowds of people are drawn there every day as long as summer lasts. It is more difficult to say what makes it so attractive to the animals that they gather there every year for their great meeting. But it is a custom they have followed faithfully since ancient times and we would have had to be present when the first wave smashed and foamed against the shore in order to explain why they chose the Kullaberg as their meeting place rather than anywhere else.

When it is time for the meeting, the red deer, roe-deer, hares, foxes and all the other wild mammals make the journey to the Kullaberg at night so as not to be seen by human beings. Immediately before the sun rises, they all march to the games field, which is a heath to the left of the road, not far from the outermost point of the headland.

The field is surrounded on all sides by rounded rocky knolls which conceal it from all but those who come right up to it, and in the month of March it is very unlikely that anyone will be out walking and will stray in that direction. Many months ago the storms of autumn drove away all the visitors who at other times of the year wander around these knolls and climb these hillsides. And the lighthouse keeper out on the point, the old woman at Kullagården, and the local farmer and his household, all stick to their usual paths and would not be running around out on the deserted heathland.

When all the four-legged creatures have arrived at the field, they take their places on the rocky knolls. Each species sticks to its own kind even though it is understood that on a day like today peace will reign and no one need fear being attacked. On a day like this a young leveret could wander across the foxes' knoll without losing as much as one of his long ears. In spite of that, however, the animals keep to their own. That is the ancient custom.

Once they have all taken their places, the animals begin to look round for the birds. The weather on this special day is usually beautiful – the cranes are excellent weather forecasters and would not have summoned the animals together if rain was expected. But although the sky is clear and there is nothing to obstruct the view, there is no sign of the birds. Which is strange, for the sun is high in the sky and the birds should already be on their way.

What the animals do see, however, are one or two small dark clouds advancing slowly across the plain. And then, all of a sudden, one of these clouds turns and veers along the coast of the Öresund towards the Kullaberg. When the cloud is right over the field, it stops and all at once the whole cloud begins to chirp and twitter as if it was composed of nothing but musical notes. It rises and falls, rises and falls, still chirping and twittering the whole time, before descending – the whole cloud at once – on to one of the knolls. And the next moment the knoll becomes invisible beneath a host of grey larks, elegant red, grey and white chaffinches, speckled starlings and greenish-yellow tits.

And then, immediately, another cloud crosses the plain. As it passes, it hovers over every estate, every labourer's cottage and manor house, every village and town, every farm and railway station, every fishing station and sugar refinery. Each time it stops, it sucks up a small whirling spiral of tiny grey specks from the earth beneath and the cloud grows and grows. By the time the cloud has finally gathered and turned for the Kullaberg, it is no longer a small puff, it is now a great billowing cloud, so big that the shadow it casts on the ground stretches all the way from Höganäs to Mölle and when it comes to a halt over the gathering field it obscures the sun. And even when this host of house sparrows begins to rain down on to one of the hillocks, it still takes a long time before the birds flying in the densest part of the cloud are at last able to see the light of day.

But the largest of these clouds of birds is the one that appears next. It is formed of flocks that have flown in from all directions and then joined together. It is so dense and blue-grey that not a single ray of sunshine can penetrate it. It is as sombre and frightening as a thundercloud and it makes the most horrific din – dreadful screams and mocking laughter and croaks that bode misfortune. All the animals on the gathering field feel a sense of relief when the cloud dissolves into a shower of flapping and squawking crows and jackdaws and ravens and rooks.

Then the sky fills not only with puffy clouds but with all kinds of signs and symbols. Straight, dotted lines can be seen in the east and north-east: they are the black grouse and capercaillie, forest birds from the Göinge area, flying in long lines with a couple of yards between each bird. And then the waterfowl from Måkläppen, the sandy spit on the Falsterbo peninsula, come swinging in across the Öresund in all kinds of strange formations – triangles and long curves, crooked hooks and half-moons.

The year that Akka and her flock of wild geese had Nils Holgersson with them, they arrived at the great meeting later than all the other animals, which is scarcely to be wondered at since they had to fly across the whole of Skåne to reach the Kullaberg. In addition to which, once awake, Akka had needed to fly and find out where Thummitot had got to as he marched along playing the pipe and luring the grey rats far away from Glimmingehus. The tawny owl had returned with the news that the black rats would be home again shortly after sunrise and it would now be safe to let the barn owl's pipe fall silent and allow the grey rats to go wherever they wanted.

But it was Herr Ermenrich the stork, not Akka, who located the boy marching at the head of the long procession of rats. Herr Ermenrich swooped quickly down, seized the boy with his beak and swept back up into the air with him. Herr Ermenrich had not only set out to find him but, once he had carried him back to the stork's nest, he apologised for having treated him so disrespectfully the evening before.

This really pleased the boy and he and the stork became good friends. Akka, too, was very friendly, stroking his arm several times with her old head and praising him for helping those who were in distress.

And it is to the boy's credit that he did not want to accept praise he did not feel he had earned. 'No, Mother Akka,' he said, 'you mustn't think I lured the grey rats away to help the black ones. I just wanted to show Herr Ermenrich that I was useful for something.'

No sooner had the boy said this than Akka turned to the stork and asked whether he thought it advisable to take Thummitot to the Kullaberg with them. 'I think we can rely on him as much as on ourselves,' she said.

The stork was quick to agree that the boy should be allowed to accompany them. 'Of course Thummitot should come with us to the Kullaberg, Mother Akka,' he said. 'We are fortunate to be able to reward him for everything he endured for our sakes. And since I am still embarrassed about the improper way I treated him yesterday evening, let me be the one to carry him all the way to the gathering field on my back.'

There are few things that taste better than praise that comes from those who are clever and capable and the boy had never felt so happy as when he heard the wild goose and the stork talking about him in this way.

So he made the journey to the Kullaberg riding on the stork's back. Although he was aware how great an honour this was, it nevertheless caused him a good deal of anxiety: Herr Ermenrich was a flying ace and set off at a very different speed to the wild geese. Whereas Akka flew in a straight line with steady wing-beats, the stork enjoyed performing aerial acrobatics. At one moment he would hover motionless at a dizzying height without moving his wings, at the next he would hurl himself downwards at such a speed that it seemed inevitable that he was going to crash into the ground like a stone, but then he would ascend again and fly round Akka in small and large circles like a whirlwind. The boy had never experienced anything like it and in spite of his permanent state of terror he had to admit that this was the first time he had really understood the meaning of good flying.

They only made one stop during their journey and that was when Akka was reunited with her flock at the lake at Vombsjön. She called to them that the grey rats had been defeated and then all the travellers took the direct route to the Kullaberg.

There they landed on top of the hillock reserved for wild geese. As the boy's eyes swept from hillock to hillock, he saw the many-pronged antlers of the red deer towering above one of them, the crested necks of the grey herons rising above another; one hillock was red with foxes, another black and white with seabirds, another grey with rats; one was occupied by black ravens with their constant croaking, another by larks which, quite unable to keep still, constantly rose into the air singing joyfully.

As has always been the custom at the Kullaberg, it was the crows who led off the fun and games of the day with their flying dance. They divided into two flocks, which then flew towards one another, met, turned back and performed the same thing again. This figure was repeated many times and the spectators – those who were not experts at the rules, anyway – thought it was much too monotonous. The crows, however, were very proud of their dance, though all the other animals were only too glad when it finished. They thought it just about as gloomy and pointless as the way snow-flakes dance about in the wind of a winter storm. Just watching it made them depressed and they waited eagerly for something that would be rather more joyful.

They did not wait in vain, for as soon as the crows had finished, in jumped the hares. They streamed forward in a long line, in no particular order. Some came in single file, others ran three or four abreast, but all of them had risen up on their hind legs and were running at such a speed that their long ears swung this way and that. And as they ran, they spun round, leapt high into the air and beat their chests with their front paws so hard that the thumping was audible. Some of them performed a series of somersaults, others curled up and rolled along like wheels, one stood on one leg and spun round, another walked on his front paws alone. There was no kind of order about the hares' games but there was a great deal of fun, and all the many animals watching them began to breathe faster. Spring had arrived, bringing joy and pleasure with it. Winter was over. Summer was coming. Soon life itself would be playful.

When the hares had run their course and exhausted themselves, it was time for the great forest birds to perform. A hundred cock capercaillie with their gleaming dark-brown plumage and bright red eyebrows swarmed up into a great oak tree that stood in the middle of the gathering field. The one on the topmost branch puffed up his feathers, dropped his wings and raised his tail so that the white under-coverts could be seen. Then he stretched his neck and uttered a couple of deep notes from his thick throat: 'Tjeck, tjeck, tjeck.' More than that he could not manage, though there were several gurgles and clunks deep in his throat. Finally he closed his eyes and whispered: 'Sis, sis, sis! Hear how pretty! Sis sis, sis!' Which made him feel so ecstatic that he was no longer aware what was happening around him.

While the first capercaillie continued his sissing, the three who were perched immediately below him began their song, and before they had finished, the ten below them started, and so it went on downwards branch by branch until there were a hundred cock capercaillie all singing and gurgling and sissing. As they sang, they all fell into the same ecstatic state and this seemed to transport all the other animals into an infectious trance. Their blood, which had been pulsing bright and cheerful a moment before, became heavy and hot. 'Yes, spring has truly come,' all the animals thought. 'The chill of winter has disappeared and the fire of spring is spreading across the earth.'

When the black grouse saw the success the capercaillie were enjoying, they could no longer keep quiet. Since there was no tree for them to occupy, they rushed out on to the field, where the heather grew so deep that only their beautiful lyre-shaped tail feathers and their thick beaks were visible. They began singing: 'Orr, orr, orr.'

Just as the black grouse were beginning to compete with the capercaillie, something utterly dreadful occurred. While all the animals had eyes for nothing but the capercaillies' performance, a fox was creeping slowly towards the knoll occupied by the wild geese. He was moving with the utmost caution and had already climbed well up the hillock before anyone noticed him. Suddenly, however, a goose caught sight of him, and since she found it impossible to imagine that a fox would be among the geese unless he had mischief in mind, she began shouting: 'Beware, wild geese, beware!' Mainly to silence her, perhaps, the fox grabbed her by the throat, but the wild geese had already heard her call and they all rose into the air. Once the geese had taken off, the rest of the animals could see Smirre Fox standing on the knoll with a dead goose in his jaws.

For breaking the peace of the games' day, Smirre Fox was punished so severely that he would regret to his dying day that he had been unable to control his thirst for revenge on Akka and her flock. Now he suddenly found himself surrounded by a great crowd of foxes and according to the ancient custom he was condemned to outlawry. Not a single fox argued for a

more lenient punishment, for they all knew that if they tried to do so they, too, would be driven from the gathering field and never permitted to return. So Smirre's banishment was pronounced without a voice being raised in his favour. He was forbidden to reside in Skåne and he was banished from his wife and his kin, his hunting grounds and his home, his resting places and his lairs, from everything that had been his until now. He would have to seek his fortune in foreign lands, and so that all the foxes in Skåne might know that Smirre was an outlaw, the oldest of the foxes bit off the tip of his right ear. As soon as this was done, all the young foxes began to howl with blood-lust and to attack Smirre. He had no choice but to flee, and with all the young foxes snapping at his heels he scurried away from the Kullaberg.

While all this was going on, the capercaillie and the black grouse simply carried on lekking. These birds become so lost in their song that they neither see nor hear anything else, and they had not allowed anything to disturb them.

No sooner was the contest of forest birds at an end than the red deer from Häckeberga stepped forward to show off their fighting game. Several pairs of stags fought at the same time, charging one another with all their strength, clashing horns so the points became entangled, and trying to push each other back. Their hooves ripped up the heather, their breath hung in the air like smoke, they uttered horrendous roars from deep in their throats and their shoulders dripped with foam.

A breathless silence reigned on all the hillocks while the battle-hardened stags clashed. New emotions were stirred among the spectators and each and every one of the animals felt strong and brave, invigorated by renewed strength, reborn by the arrival of spring, eager and ready for all kinds of adventures. They felt no animosity towards one another, but everywhere wings were opened, neck feathers raised and claws sharpened. If the Häckeberga stags had carried on a moment longer, a wild battle would have erupted among the hillocks, for all the animals were seized by a burning desire to show that they too were full of life, that strength was surging through their bodies and the weakness of winter was over.

But the stags stopped fighting at just the right moment and a whisper ran quickly from hillock to hillock: 'Now it's time for the cranes.'

And so the great dusky-grey birds, long-legged and slim-necked, with plumes on their wings and decorative red feathers on the crowns of their small heads, came gliding down from their hillock in a state of mysterious abandon. As they slid forward, they swung this way and that, half flying, half dancing. Lifting their wings gracefully, they moved at an unbelievable speed. There was something strange and uncanny about their dance. It was as if grey shadows were playing a game that the eye could scarcely follow, as if they had learnt their dance from the mists that hang above lonely marshlands and mosses. There was magic in it, and all those who had never been at the Kullaberg before understood why the whole gathering was named after the dance of the cranes. There was wildness in it too, but the feeling it aroused was nevertheless one of harmonious yearning. No one was thinking of strife now; instead, all of them, those with wings and those with no wings, wanted to rise for evermore, to rise above the clouds and seek what lay beyond, to be released from the encumbering bodies that chained them to the earth and to soar up and away into the ether.

This longing for the unattainable, for the mysteries beyond this life, came to the animals only once a year, and that was on the day they witnessed the great crane dance.

VI

RAINY WEATHER

Wednesday, 30 March

It was the first rainy day of their journey. As long as the wild geese had remained in the vicinity of Vombsjön, they had enjoyed wonderful weather, but the day they set out on their journey north it began to rain and for hour after hour the boy sat on the gander's back soaked to the skin and shivering with cold.

Everything had been calm and clear when they set off in the morning. The wild geese had flown high in the sky, steady and unhurried, in strict order with Akka in the lead and the others in two diagonal lines behind her. They did not even give themselves time to shout mischievous remarks down to the animals on the ground although, incapable of staying really quiet, they kept up their ceaseless, come-hither chant in time with their wing-beats: 'Where are you? Here I am! Where are you? Here I am!'

All of them joined in this constant calling and the only time they stopped was to point out to the white gander the landmarks they were using to set their course. On this part of the journey the landmarks were the barren slopes of the Linderöd ridge, Ovesholm House, the church tower in Kristianstad, the royal estate at Bäckaskog situated on the narrow neck of land between two lakes – Oppmannasjön and Ivösjön – and finally the steep slopes of the Ryssberg.

It had been a monotonous journey and when the rain clouds began to appear, the boy found them entertaining. In the past, only seeing rain clouds from below, he had always thought of them as grey and boring, but being up among them was a different matter altogether. Now he could clearly see that the clouds were enormous wagons, piled high with the great loads they carried across the sky; some of them were laden with huge grey sacks, others with casks big enough to contain a whole lake, and others again with great containers and bottles stacked up to a frightening height. And as soon as so many wagons had driven past that it seemed that the whole sky was full of them, it was as if someone gave a signal and all at once these containers, barrels, bottles and sacks released a deluge of water over the earth beneath.

As soon as the first spring showers began to patter on the earth, all the small birds in the fields and copses set up such cries of joy that the air echoed with them and made the boy jump on the gander's back. 'Here comes the rain and the rain brings spring, and spring gives us flowers and green leaves, and green leaves and flowers give us larvae and insects, and larvae and insects give us food! Good food and plenty of it is the best thing in the world!' the small birds sang.

And the wild geese, too, were happy at the arrival of the rain, which would wake the plants from their winter sleep and make holes in the ice covering the lakes. The serious mood they had shown so far began to grow lighter and they shouted down cheerfully to the places they were passing over.

As they flew over the big bare and black potato fields, of which there are so many around Kristianstad, they yelled: 'Wake up and do something useful! Here comes the rain to wake you up. You've been lying there idle quite long enough.'

When they saw people hurrying to take shelter from the rain, they shouted down words of encouragement: 'What's the hurry? Can't you see that it's raining loaves and cakes, loaves and cakes?'

There was a big dense cloud moving quickly north and apparently following the geese. The geese seemed to think they were towing the cloud along and when there were gardens immediately below them they would shout proudly down: 'Here we come with anemones, here we come with roses, here we come with apple blossom and cherry blossom, here we come with peas and beans and turnips and cabbage. If you want it, come and get it! If you want it, come and get it!'

That is what they said during the first showers of rain, when they were all still pleased that rain was falling. But when it carried on raining the whole afternoon, the geese lost their patience and began shouting to the dry forests around Ivösjön: 'Haven't you had enough yet? Haven't you had enough yet?'

Greyness spread across the whole sky and the sun was so well hidden that no one could work out where it was. The rain fell more and more heavily, hammering hard against the wings of the geese and penetrating through the oily outer feathers to the skin. The earth beneath was cloaked in a veil of rain, and lakes, hills and forests merged together into an indistinct blur. It was no longer possible to pick out landmarks and the flight of the geese became slower and slower. The happy calls fell silent and the boy could feel the cold biting more sharply.

In spite of all this, his spirits did not fail him as long as they were flying through the air. Even in the afternoon, after they had landed under a stunted little pine out in the middle of a great moss where everything was wet and everything was cold and where there were still hummocks covered in snow and others that stuck up from pools of half-melted ice, even then he did not feel dejected and ran around in good spirits hunting for cranberries and frozen cowberries. But then evening came, bringing darkness so impenetrable that even eyes as sharp as the boy's could see nothing, and now the wilderness became eerie and frightening. The boy lay tucked in under the gander's wing but even there he was too cold and wet to be able to sleep. All around he could hear rustling and rattling and stealthy footsteps and threatening voices and he was so afraid that he did not know what to do with himself. But he knew he must find somewhere where there was fire and light, otherwise he was going to die of fright.

'I wonder if I dare go back among human beings for just one night?' the boy thought. 'Just so that I can sit by a fire for a while and have a bite to eat. I can always come back to the wild geese before sunrise.'

He crept out from under the wing and slid down to the ground. Without waking the gander or any of the other geese, he slipped away silently and unobserved across the moss.

He did not really have much idea where on earth he was, whether he was still in Skåne or whether he was now in Småland or Blekinge. But just before they landed on the moss, he had caught a glimpse of a large village and that is what he aimed for. Before very long he came to a road, which soon led to a long, tree-lined village street with house after house along each side.

The boy had arrived at one of the large church villages that are so common up-country but are not to be found at all down on the plain.

The dwelling-houses were built of wood and were neat and pretty. The gables and frontispieces of most of them were edged with fretwork eaves and they had glazed verandas with the occasional pane of coloured glass. The walls were painted with light-coloured oil paints and the doors and window-frames were bright blue or green or even red. As the boy walked along the street looking at the houses, he could hear the people talking and laughing in the warmth of their living rooms. He could not pick out the words but he thought it was lovely to hear human voices. 'I wonder what they would say if I knocked on the door and asked to be let in?' he thought.

That is what he had intended to do. But his fear of the darkness had left him as soon as he saw all the lighted windows and been replaced by the shyness that always afflicted him in the proximity of human beings. 'I'll have a look around the village for a while longer,' he thought, 'before I ask someone to let me in.'

One of the houses had a balcony and just as the boy was passing the balcony doors were thrown open and yellow light poured out through the elegant light curtains. A beautiful young woman came out on the balcony and leaned over the rail: 'Ah, it's raining. Spring will soon be with us now,' she said. The sight of her made the boy feel strangely emotional, almost tearful. For the very first time he felt apprehensive about having shut himself off from humankind.

A moment later he walked past a merchant's store, outside which stood a red seed-drill. He stopped, looked at it and climbed up and sat on the driver's seat. Once there, he smacked his lips and pretended to be the driver. He thought how much fun it must be to drive such a smart machine across a ploughed field. For a moment he forgot what he was like now, but then it came back to him and he jumped down from the drill. He was feeling more and more troubled. There were certainly many things he was going to miss by spending his life among the animals and there could be no doubt that human beings were clever and remarkable creatures.

He walked past the post office and thought of the newspapers that arrive every day with news from every corner of the globe. He looked at the chemist's shop and the doctor's surgery and he thought about how great was the power of humankind in the struggle against disease and death. He came to the church and he thought about the fact that human beings had built it so that they could hear of a world beyond the world in which they lived, hear about God and resurrection and eternal life. And the more he walked round, the fonder he became of his own kind.

That's the way it is with children – they cannot see beyond the end of their own noses. No sooner do they see something than they want it, without any thought as to what it might cost them. Nils Holgersson had, of course, had no idea what he was losing when he chose to remain an elf, but now he was dreadfully afraid that he might never be able to return to his real form.

What on earth did he have to do in order to become a human being? He really did want to know the answer.

He crawled up onto a step and sat there thinking in the pouring rain. He sat there for an hour, for two hours, his brow furrowed in thought. But he was none the wiser for all that and his thoughts just went round and round in circles. The longer he sat there, the more unlikely it seemed that he would find a solution.

'This is all too difficult for someone who has learnt as little as I have,' he thought at last. 'There's no doubt I'll have to go back to human beings anyway. Then I'll have to ask the parson and the doctor and the teacher and other learned people who might know what the cure is for something like this.'

So that is what he decided to do – and to do it at once. He stood up and shook himself, because he was as wet as a dog that has rolled in a puddle.

At that very moment, however, he saw a large owl fly over and settle in one of the trees that lined the village street. And immediately after that a tawny owl that was sitting under the eaves of a house began moving and calling: 'Too-whit, too-whoo! Is that you home again, short-eared owl? How were things abroad?'

'Thank you, tawny owl, thank you! Everything went well,' the short-eared owl answered. 'Has anything special happened here while I was away?'

'Not here in Blekinge,' the tawny owl said. 'But a boy in Skåne has been changed into an elf. He's as small as a squirrel now and he has gone off to Lapland with a tame goose.'

'That's a remarkable piece of news, a remarkable piece of news. Will he ever be human again? Will he ever be human again?'

'It's a secret, short-eared owl – but I'll tell you anyway. The elf has said that if the boy watches over the tame gander and sees to it that he comes home again unharmed …'

'And what else, tawny owl? What else? What else?'

'Come and fly up to the church tower with me,' the tawny owl said, 'and I'll tell you everything. I'm afraid someone may overhear us down here on the village street.'

And with that the two owls flew off, but the boy threw his cap high in the air: 'As long as I look after the gander and bring him home unharmed, I can be a human being again! Hurrah! Hurrah! I can be a human being again!'

He shouted hurrah so much that it is amazing that the

people in the houses did not hear him. But they did not, and he hurried back to the wild geese out on the wet moss as fast as his legs could carry him.

VII

THE STAIRCASE WITH THE THREE STEPS

Thursday, 31 March

The next day the geese were intending to travel north through the district of Allbo in the province of Småland. They sent Yksi and Kaksi on in advance to scout out the land and when they returned they said that the lakes were still frozen and the ground snow-covered. 'Let's stay where we are,' the wild geese said. 'We can't travel over country where there is neither water nor grazing.' But Akka said: 'If we stay where we are, we might have to wait a whole month. It will be better to fly east through Blekinge and try to pass over Småland through the Möre area, which lies close to the coast and has an early spring.'

So the following day the boy found himself flying over Blekinge. Now that it was daylight he was back in his usual mood and could not understand what had got into him the night before. There was no way he wanted to give up this journey and his life in the wilderness now.

Blekinge was blanketed in a thick mist and the boy was unable to see what it looked like. 'I wonder whether the land I'm riding over is good or bad?' he thought and tried to dig into his memory for what he had learnt about the province in school. But he knew there was really not much point in thinking about it since he had never bothered to pay attention to his lessons.

All of a sudden a picture of school came back to him. The children were sitting at their small desks and putting up their hands, the teacher was sitting at his big desk looking displeased, and Nils himself was standing in front of the map trying to answer a question about Blekinge and unable to say a word. The teacher's face was growing darker with every second that passed and the boy thought that the teacher was much more demanding about their knowledge of geography than about any other subject. Finally the teacher came down from his desk, took the pointer from the boy's hand and sent him back to his seat. 'This is going to end badly,' the boy had thought.

But the teacher had walked over to the window, stood there looking out for a while and then whistled for a bit. Then he went back up to his desk and said he would tell them something about the province of Blekinge. And what he told them had been so amusing that even Nils had listened. Once he stopped to think about it, he could remember every word.

'Småland is like a tall building with spruce trees on the roof,' the teacher said. 'And in front of it is a wide staircase with three big steps – that staircase is called Blekinge.

'It's a staircase on a grand scale. It stretches for forty-eight miles along the front of the building that is Småland, and anyone who walks down the whole staircase to the Baltic Sea will have a walk of twenty-four miles.

'A very long time has passed since that staircase was constructed. Countless days and years have passed since the first steps were carved out of the rock and laid smoothly and evenly to make a comfortable route between Småland and the Baltic.

'Since the staircase is so ancient, it's easy to see why it no longer looks the way it did when it was new. I don't know how much they worried about such things in those days but the staircase was so big there probably weren't any brushes big enough to keep it clean. After a couple of years moss and lichen began to grow on it, dry grass and dry leaves were blown down over it in autumn, and stones and gravel tumbled down and covered it in spring. And since all this was just left to lie there and rot, the staircase was eventually covered in enough soil for plants and grass and even bushes and big trees to take root.

'At the same time, however, we can see big differences between the three steps. The top step, the one closest to Småland, is mainly covered with poor soil and small stones and just about the only trees that will grow there are downy birch and bird cherry and spruce, which can tolerate the cold on the high ground and need little by way of sustenance. You only have to look at the tiny patches of arable land hacked out of the forest, at the small size of the cottages people have built for themselves, and at the long distances between the churches, to come to a proper understanding of how poor and meagre conditions are up there.

'The soil on the middle step is better and the land is not subject to such severe cold. You can see this at once, because the trees are both taller and of finer species, such as maple and oak, lime and silver birch and hazel. And there are hardly any conifers at all. What makes the improvement even more obvious is the large area of cultivated land and the fact that people have built such big and beautiful houses. There are many churches on this middle step and large villages have grown up around them. In fact, everything looks better and grander in every way than on the top step.

'But it's on the bottom step that things are best. That step is covered with an abundance of fertile soil, and where the land runs down and bathes in the sea there is not even a whisper left of the cold of Småland. Beech trees and chestnut trees and walnut trees flourish down there, and they grow so tall that they tower above the roofs of the churches. There, too, lie the biggest arable fields, but the people have more than just forestry and farming to support them, they also have fishing and trade and seafaring. Which is why the most luxurious houses and most beautiful churches are down there, and why the villages have grown into towns and boroughs.

'That's not the end of the story of the three steps. We must remember that when it rains up on the roof of the great house that is Småland, or when the snow up there melts, the water has to go somewhere and, naturally enough, some of it pours down this great staircase. In the beginning it probably used to flow across the whole width of the staircase, broad as it was, but then cracks began to appear in the staircase and the water took to flowing along a few well-worn furrows. Water is water, when all is said and done, and it never rests. In one spot it digs and erodes and washes away, and at another spot it adds and builds. The water excavated furrows and created valleys and it covered the walls of these valleys with soil, to which bushes and vines and trees cling in such richness and profusion that they almost hide the watercourse that flows along the valley floor. When the rivers come to the drops between the three steps, however, they have to hurl themselves down and the water builds up sufficient speed and strength to be capable of driving the watermills and machinery people have built beside every waterfall.

'And this is still not the end of the story of the land with the three steps. Once upon a time, up in the great house that is Småland, there lived a giant. He had grown old and, given his great age, he found it tiring to have to go all the way down this long staircase in order to fish for salmon in the sea. He thought it would be far more convenient if the salmon were to come up to where he lived. So he went up on to the roof of his great house and stood there hurling huge boulders down into the Baltic Sea. He threw them so hard that they flew across the whole of Blekinge and landed in the sea. When the boulders crashed down, the salmon were so terrified that they left the sea and fled up the rivers of Blekinge, ran the rapids, hurled themselves in huge leaps up the waterfalls and did not stop until they were right up in Småland, the home of the old giant.

'All the islands and skerries that lie off the coast of Blekinge prove the truth of this story – they are quite simply the huge boulders thrown by that giant.

'Another mark of its truth is that salmon still run up the rivers of Blekinge and work their way through rapids and calm waters all the way to Småland.

'The people of Blekinge owe that giant a debt of gratitude and honour, for salmon fishing in the rivers and stone-cutting on the islands still provide a living for many of them even today.'

VIII

BY RONNEBY RIVER

Friday, 1 April

Neither the wild geese nor Smirre Fox had imagined they would ever meet again once they had left Skåne. But now it turned out that the wild geese took the route across Blekinge, which is where Smirre Fox had gone. Up until now he had remained in the northern part of the province, where he had seen no sign of any great estates or parklands full of roe-deer and tasty roe-deer calves. He was, in fact, thoroughly disgruntled.

One afternoon, as Smirre was roaming around a desolate stretch of forest in Mellanbygden, not far from Ronneby River, he caught sight of a flock of wild geese flying across the sky. He noticed that one of the geese was white and, of course, he realised at once which geese he was dealing with.

Smirre immediately began stalking the geese, as much because he wanted a good meal as for revenge for all the trouble they had caused him. He saw them fly eastwards until they came to the river, where they changed direction and followed the river south. He knew they must be looking for night quarters somewhere along the banks of the river and he thought he would be able to grab a couple of them without too much difficulty.

But when Smirre finally caught sight of the place where the geese had landed, he saw they had chosen such a well-protected spot that he would be unable to get at them.

Ronneby River can hardly claim to be a big or powerful watercourse but it is nevertheless well-known for the beauty of its banks. There are several places where the river threads its way between steep rocky walls that rise vertically from the water and are completely overgrown with honeysuckle and bird cherry, with hawthorn and alder, with rowan and willow. There are few greater pleasures than rowing along this dark little river on a beautiful summer's day and gazing up at all the soft lush greenery that clings to the rough rocks.

Now, however, at the time Smirre and the wild geese came to the river, the weather was still the bleak and cold weather between winter and spring; all the trees were bare and it is unlikely that anyone was sparing a thought for whether the banks were pretty or ugly. The wild geese praised their good fortune in finding, tucked below a steep cliff, a strip of sandbank with just enough room for all of them. The river roared past in front of them, fast and strong because of the melting snow, an unclimbable cliff rose behind them, and overhanging branches sheltered them. They could not have found a better place.

The geese fell asleep instantly but the boy found it impossible to get a wink of sleep. As soon as the sun disappeared, his fear of the dark of the wilderness returned and he longed to be among people. Lying tucked in under the gander's wing, he could see nothing and hear little and the thought occurred to him that if anything was to threaten the gander he was in no position to save him. He could hear rustling all round and he became so uneasy that he crept out from under the wing and sat on the ground beside the goose.

Smirre was standing up on the clifftop and his face fell when he looked down at the wild geese. 'You may as well give up the chase now,' he said to himself. 'You can't climb down a vertical cliff, you can't swim across such wild water, and at the foot of the cliff there isn't even a narrow strip of land leading to where the geese are sleeping. These geese are too clever for you. You may as well give up any idea of hunting them.'

But, like all foxes, Smirre found it hard to give up a task once he had started it, so he lay down right on the edge of the clifftop and did not take his eyes off the geese. And while he lay there watching them he thought of all the trouble they had caused him. It was their fault, wasn't it, that he had been outlawed from Skåne and been forced to move to this poverty-stricken part of Blekinge. He lay there and worked himself up to such a pitch that he wanted to see those geese dead, even if there was no chance of eating them himself.

When Smirre's bitterness was at its height, he heard a scratching and scraping in a large pine tree close beside him and he saw a squirrel coming down the tree with a pine marten in hot pursuit. Neither of them noticed Smirre and he kept still and watched the chase go from tree to tree. He saw the squirrel moving among the branches so nimbly that it almost seemed to fly. He saw the marten – not quite so skilled a climber as the squirrel, but still able to run up and down the trunks of the trees as securely as if they had been smooth paths through the forest. 'If I could climb half as well as those two, those geese down there wouldn't be sleeping so peacefully,' he thought.

As soon as the squirrel was caught and the hunt over, Smirre went up to the pine marten but stopped two paces away as a sign that he had no intention of stealing the marten's prey. He greeted the marten in a very friendly way and congratulated him on his success. Smirre had a way with words, as foxes do. The marten, on the other hand, in spite of being a little miracle of beauty with his long slim body, his neat head, his soft fur and his pale-brown bib, was actually a crude forest type and he hardly bothered to answer. 'I find it surprising,' Smirre said, 'that a hunter as good as you are would be satisfied with hunting squirrels when much better game is in reach.' He paused at this point, but when the marten just grinned at him insolently he continued: 'Perhaps you haven't noticed the wild geese sleeping at the bottom of the cliff? Or perhaps it's just that you aren't a good enough climber to get down to them?'

Smirre did not have to wait for an answer this time. The pine marten rushed towards him, his back arched and his fur bristling. 'Have you seen some wild geese?' he snarled. 'Where are they? Tell me at once – or I'll rip your throat out!'

'I think you should mind your manners and remember that I'm twice as big as you,' Smirre said. 'But there's nothing I'd like better than to show you the wild geese.'

A moment later the pine marten was on his way down the cliff and, as Smirre watched the way his slim body snaked from branch to branch, he thought: 'That pretty little tree-hunter has the cruellest heart in the forest. The geese are going to have me to thank for a very bloody awakening.'

But just when Smirre was expecting to hear the death screams of the geese, he saw the marten fall off a branch and plummet down into the river with a great splash that sent the water high in the air. That was followed immediately by the sound of loud hard wing-beats as all the geese took off in a great hurry.

Smirre thought about rushing off after the geese but he was so curious to know what had saved them that he waited until the pine marten had climbed back up the cliff. The wretched animal was sodden and stopped every now and then to rub his head with his front paws. 'I might have known that you were a clumsy so-and-so who would go and fall in the river,' Smirre said scornfully.

'I wasn't clumsy. There's no need to go on at me,' the marten said. 'I had already reached the bottom branches and was thinking how to set about tearing a whole lot of geese to pieces when a tiny little fellow – no bigger than a squirrel – rushed up and threw a stone that hit me in the head so hard that I fell in the river and before I managed to get out …'

The pine marten did not need to say any more. He had lost his audience. Smirre was already far away, off after the geese.

Meanwhile Akka had flown southwards, looking for a new place to sleep. There was still a little daylight and that, together with the half-moon that was high in the sky, gave her just enough light to see. And, fortunately, she was familiar with this district because the wind had more than once driven her to Blekinge when she crossed the Baltic Sea in spring.

She followed the river for as long as she could see it winding its way like a gleaming black snake through the

moonlit countryside. In this way she followed it all the way to Djupafors, where the river first of all hides in a subterranean channel and then emerges clear and transparent as glass before plunging down into a narrow gorge and shattering into glittering drops and spinning foam. Below the white falls there are rocks in the riverbed and the water roars between them as a wild set of rapids. It was there that Akka landed. This was a good place to sleep, especially this late in the evening when there were no people around. The geese would not have been able to land there at sunset because Djupafors is not out in wild country – there is a pulp mill on one side of the waterfall and on the opposite bank, which is steep and wooded, lies Djupadal Park, in which there are always people wandering around on the steep, slippery paths to enjoy the wild, whirling waterfall crashing down into the gorge.

Just as at their previous resting place, none of the travellers gave a thought to the fact that they were at a famous beauty spot. They thought rather that it was strange and dangerous to be standing and sleeping on slippery wet rocks in the middle of roaring rapids. But they were happy to put up with it as long as they were safe from predators.

The geese fell asleep at once but, once again, the boy was too worried to sleep and sat down beside them in order to keep watch over the gander.

After a while Smirre came running along the riverbank. He immediately caught sight of the geese out there surrounded by foaming whirlpools and he realised yet again that he would never be able to reach them. But he still could not bring himself to give up, so he sat on the bank and watched them. He felt utterly humiliated and thought that his whole reputation as a hunter was at stake.

Then all of a sudden he saw an otter sliding up out of the rapids with a fish in its mouth. Smirre went up to him but stopped two paces away as a sign that he had no intention of stealing his catch. 'You're a strange one, you are, satisfied with catching fish when the rocks out there are alive with wild geese,' Smirre said. He was so eager that he did not take the time to choose his words as carefully as he usually did. The otter did not even turn his head to look out to the rocks. Like all otters, he was a nomad and had often fished in the Vombsjön lake, so he knew Smirre Fox all too well.

'I know exactly how you go about tricking others out of a sea-trout, Smirre,' the otter said.

'Oh, it's you is it, Gripe,' Smirre said, happy to see him because he knew that Gripe was a bold and skilful swimmer. 'I can understand why you're showing no interest in the geese. After all, you can't get to them anyway.'

But the otter, who had webbed toes, a stiff tail that was as good as an oar and fur that was impermeable to water, was not about to let anyone suggest there was such a thing as a set of rapids he could not handle. He turned round and, catching sight of the wild geese, tossed the fish aside and stormed down the steep bank into the river.

If it had been later in the spring after the nightingales had returned to Djupadal Park, the birds would have spent many a night singing about Gripe's battle with the rapids. The waves snatched at the otter time after time and dragged him downstream, but he repeatedly fought his way upstream again. Where there was dead water he swam, otherwise he crawled over the rocks and gradually approached the geese. It was a dangerous journey and would certainly have been worthy of the nightingales' song.

Smirre watched the otter's progress as well as he could. He saw the otter climbing up on to the rocks where the geese were, but then there came a shrill scream and the otter tumbled backwards into the water and was washed downstream as if he was a blind kitten. Immediately after that, Smirre heard the loud clapping of the geese's wings as they took off to find somewhere else to sleep.

The otter soon managed to reach the bank and, without saying a word, began to lick one of his front paws. When Smirre began to make fun of him for not succeeding, the otter snapped: 'There's nothing the matter with my swimming, Smirre. I had got right up to the geese and was about to climb onto the rocks when a tiny little fellow ran up and stabbed my paw with a sharp piece of iron. It hurt so much that I lost my grip and the rapids washed me away.'

There was no need for him to say any more. Smirre was already far away, off after the geese.

So once again Akka and her flock were forced to fly at night. Fortunately the moon had not set and, helped by its light, she managed to find another of the sleeping places she knew in that district. They followed the gleaming river south, flying on over Djupadal Manor and the white waterfalls and dark roofs of the town of Ronneby without landing. A little south of the town and not far from the sea lies Ronneby Spa with its baths and its pump-rooms, its big hotels and its summer-houses for those who have come to take the waters. All the birds are well aware that the spa is empty the whole winter and many a flock has sought shelter in stormy weather on the deserted verandas and balconies of these buildings.

Here the wild geese landed on a balcony and, as usual, immediately fell asleep. The boy could not sleep, however, and did not want to slip in beneath the gander's wing.

The balcony faced south and the boy had a view out to sea. Since he was unable to sleep, he sat there admiring the beauty of the meeting of the land and the sea in Blekinge.

There are, you see, many different ways in which land and sea can meet. There are places where the land comes down to the sea in the form of flat tussocky meadows and the sea greets the land with windblown sand piled up in dunes and drifts. It is as if they dislike each other so much that they are only willing to reveal their worst sides. And there are other places where the land erects a wall of rock as if the sea is something dangerous, and then the sea reacts with angry breakers that pound and lash the cliffs as if wanting to tear them down.

But the meeting between the land and the sea in Blekinge is quite different. Here the land shatters into headlands and islands and skerries, while the sea splits into bays and sounds and firths. Which is perhaps why the sea and the land here seem to meet in joy and harmony.

Take the sea for a start! Far, far out, it is vast and desolate and empty and has nothing else to do but to roll its grey waves. As it moves closer to the land, it comes into contact with the first skerry, which it immediately overwhelms, stripping off anything green that is trying to grow there and making the skerry as bare and grey as the sea itself. Then it meets another skerry and the same thing happens. And another, and the same thing happens again – it is stripped and plundered as if it had fallen into the hands of robbers. But then the skerries occur more and more frequently and the sea seems to understand that the land is sending out the smallest of its offspring to soften its heart. And the farther inshore it washes, the kinder the sea becomes, its waves less high, its storms less violent. It begins to leave green growth in the cracks and clefts, divides itself up into many small sounds and inlets, and finally, close to the shore, becomes so safe that even small boats can venture upon it. It has become so bright and friendly that it hardly knows itself.

And then there is the land! It lies there apparently uniform and more or less the same everywhere, made up of flat ploughed fields interspersed with the odd copse of birches or long forested ridges. It looks as if it has nothing on its mind but oats and turnips and potatoes and pines and spruces. But then comes an inlet, cutting far inland. The land pays no attention to it, simply places a fringe of birches and alders along its shores as if it were an ordinary freshwater lake. Then there is another inlet, and the land still ignores it, just putting the same fringe of trees as before. But then the inlets begin to broaden out and to separate off fields and woods – and now the land cannot avoid paying attention to them. 'I do believe that's the sea coming in there, the sea,' the land says, and begins to primp and prettify itself, crowning itself with flowers, moulding itself into hills and vales and throwing islands out into the sea. It wants nothing more to do with pines and spruces and, tossing them aside like everyday old clothes, it dresses instead in the finery of grand oaks and linden trees and chestnut trees set in flower-filled meadows. It becomes as magnificent as the park of a great house and is so transformed by the time it meets the sea that it, too, cannot recognise itself.

Of course, none of that is really apparent until summer comes, but the boy could see how mild and gentle nature had become and he felt much calmer than he had earlier that night. And then, all of a sudden, he heard a loud and sinister howl coming from the park around the spa, and when he stood up he saw a fox standing in the white moonlight below the balcony. Smirre had followed the geese yet again, but once he discovered where they had landed, he realised it was impossible to find a way of approaching them and he could not stop himself howling in frustration.

At the sound of a fox howling, old Akka the lead goose woke up and thought she recognised the voice even though she could hardly see a thing.

'Is that you Smirre, out there in the night?' she said.

'Yes, it is,' Smirre answered, 'it's me, and I'd like to know what you think of the night I've put you through.'

'Are you telling me that it was you who set the pine marten and the otter on us?' Akka asked.

'A good deed should never be denied!' Smirre said. 'You played goosey games with me and now I've begun playing foxy games with you, and I have no intention of stopping as long as one of you is left alive – even if I have to follow you the whole length of the country.'

'Smirre,' said Akka, 'you are armed with teeth and claws. How fair do you think it is to persecute those of us who are defenceless?'

Smirre thought that Akka was sounding afraid and he quickly said: 'Well then, Akka, if you will just throw that Thummitot fellow down to me I promise to make peace and will never persecute you or any of your kind again. But he has defied me all too often!'

'I can't hand over Thummitot,' Akka said. 'Every one of us, from the youngest to the oldest, would happily sacrifice our lives for him.'

'If you love him that much,' Smirre answered, 'I can promise you that he'll be the first I take revenge on.'

Akka did not answer and, after Smirre had done a bit more howling, silence fell. The boy, however, was still awake, and what was keeping him awake now was Akka's words to the fox. The boy would never have believed that he would hear anything so wonderful as the fact that someone was prepared to risk their life for him. From that moment on, it would have been impossible for anyone to claim that Nils Holgersson did not take care of others.

IX

KARLSKRONA

Saturday, 2 April

It was a moonlight night in Karlskrona. The weather was calm and fine, although it had been so stormy and wet all day that people seemed to think the weather was still bad and so there was hardly a soul to be seen in the streets.

With the town lying there quiet and deserted beneath them, Akka and her flock of wild geese came flying in over the islands of Vämmön and Pantarholmen. They were out this late looking for a safe place to sleep among the islands because they could not risk staying on the mainland where Smirre Fox was persecuting them wherever they landed.

Riding along high in the air and looking down at the sea and the islands spread out below him, everything seemed strange and ghost-like to the boy. The sky was no longer blue but arched above him like a dome of green glass. The sea looked milky white, its small white waves topped with a touch of silver and rippling away as far as the eye could see. In the midst of all this whiteness the many islands of the archipelago stood out as black as coal – all of them equally black, irrespective of whether they were large or small, whether they were made up of smooth flat fields or rocky cliffs. Even the houses, the churches and the windmills, which are usually white or red, looked black against this green sky. It seemed to the boy that the earth beneath him had been transformed, as if he had entered a different world.

He was just thinking that tonight he would be brave, tonight he would not be afraid, when he caught sight of something that really frightened him. It was a high rocky island, covered with huge angular blocks but with patches of brightly shimmering gold shining between the blocks. He could not help thinking of the enormous Maglesten boulder at Trolle-Ljungby Castle, which the trolls sometimes raised on tall gold pillars so that they could hold parties under it.* The boy wondered whether he was looking at something similar.

If it had only been the great blocks and the glints of gold, everything would have been fine, but there were so many horrifying objects in the water around the island. They looked like whales and sharks and other great sea creatures, but the boy took them to be sea-trolls gathering around the island ready to crawl ashore and do battle with the land-trolls who lived there. And the trolls on shore were undoubtedly afraid, because the boy could see a great giant standing at the highest point of the island with his arms raised as if in despair at the calamity that was about to engulf him and his island.

The boy was more than a little frightened when he realised that Akka was beginning to descend towards that very island. 'For Heaven's sake! We're not going to land there, are we?' he said.

But the geese continued to descend and in no time at all the boy was amazed at how wrong he had been. The huge blocks of stone turned out to be houses and the whole island was a town, the bright patches of gold simply being the streetlamps and rows of lighted windows. The giant standing over the town with uplifted arms was a church with two towers and all the sea-trolls and monsters he had imagined he was seeing were ships and boats of all kinds anchored all round the island. On the side of the island that lay closest to the mainland they were mostly rowing boats, sailing boats and small coastal steamers, but on the side facing the open sea lay ironclad warships, some of them broad across the beam and with enormous sloping funnels, others long and slim and designed to cut through the water like fish.

What sort of town could this be? Given all the warships, the boy had quickly worked out where he was. All his life he had been fascinated by ships, although the only thing he had

had to do with them were the little galleys he had sailed in the ditch that ran alongside the road at home. He was quite certain that this town, with all these warships, could only be Karlskrona.

The boy's grandfather had been an old navy man and, while he was alive, not a day had passed without him talking about Karlskrona with its great naval dockyard and all the other sights to be seen in the town. So the boy felt completely at home here and was really happy to see all these things he had heard so much about.

But he only had time for a quick glimpse of the many buildings in the dockyard and of the towers and fortifications guarding the harbour entrance before Akka landed on the flat roof of one of the church towers.

It was without doubt a good place for anyone wanting to be safe from foxes and the boy wondered whether he could risk creeping in under the gander's wing for one night anyway. Surely he could risk it, and it would be good to get some proper sleep. He would try to see a bit more of the ships and the dockyard once it was light.

*

But Nils found it strange that he was unable to remain where he was and wait until morning to see the ships. He had probably not been asleep more than five minutes before he slipped out from under the gander's wing and climbed down the lightning conductor and drainpipes to the ground.

There he found himself standing on a large square in front of the church. The square was paved with rounded cobbles, which made walking as difficult for him as crossing a tussocky meadow is for ordinary-sized people. Those who spend most of their time in the wilderness or who live right out in the country are always nervous when they come into a town where the houses stand rigidly in straight lines and the streets are so open that everyone can see anyone walking along them. That is how the boy felt. Standing there on the square in Karlskrona and looking at the German Church and the Town Hall and the Great Church, from which he had just climbed down, he desired nothing more than to be back up on the church tower with the geese.

Fortunately the square was completely empty and not a soul was to be seen unless you count a statue that was standing there on a high plinth. The boy looked long and hard at the statue and wondered who it was supposed to be: it portrayed a big heavily-built man wearing a three-cornered hat, a long coat, breeches and heavy shoes. He was holding a long staff in his hand and he looked as if he knew how to use it, for the expression on his face was unbelievably stern and he had a hooked nose and an ugly mouth.

'What's that long-faced misery supposed to be doing?' the boy said at last. He had never felt so small and pathetic as he felt that evening so he was trying to cheer himself up by being cheeky. Then he put the statue out of his mind and turned into a wide street that led down towards the sea.

He had not gone far before he heard someone coming after him. Whoever it was behind him was tramping on the cobbles with heavy boots and striking the ground with an iron-shod staff. In fact, it sounded exactly as if the big bronze statue back on the square had decided to take a walk.

As he ran down the street the boy listened to the steps and became more and more convinced that it was the bronze statue. The ground shook and the houses trembled. No one but the statue could be walking that heavily and, remembering what he had just said, the boy became frightened and could not bring himself to look back to see if it really was the statue.

'Perhaps he is out for a walk for pleasure,' the boy thought. 'Surely he can't be angry with me just because of what I said. I didn't really mean any harm by it.'

Instead of carrying straight on and trying to reach the dockyard, the boy turned off along a street that ran east. More than anything else he wanted to escape whoever it was who was following him. But no sooner had he changed direction than he heard the bronze man turn into the same street and the boy became so afraid that he did not know which way to turn: finding somewhere to hide in a town where all the doors were locked was very difficult! Then, over to his right, he saw an old wooden church set back from the street in the middle of a large shrubbery. Without stopping to think, he rushed towards the church: 'If I can get there,' he thought, 'I'll be protected from all evil, won't I?'

As he was running he suddenly caught sight of a man standing on the sandy path and beckoning to him. 'That must be someone who wants to help me,' the boy thought, hurrying towards the man with a sense of relief. He was actually so frightened that his heart was pounding.

But when he reached the man, who was standing on a small dais at the edge of the sandy path, he was utterly dismayed. 'That can't be the man who waved to me,' he thought, realising that this figure was made of wood.

He stood and gazed at the wooden man – a thick-set fellow with short legs and a broad ruddy face, gleaming black hair and a full black beard. He was wearing a black wooden hat on his head, a brown wooden coat with a black wooden belt around the waist, wide grey wooden breeches with wooden stockings up to his knees, and black wooden shoes on his feet. He had recently been re-painted and re-varnished so that he gleamed in the moonlight, and this no doubt added to his good-natured appearance and made the boy feel he could trust him.

In his left hand the man was holding a wooden board on which the boy could read the following words:

> I beg you most humbly
> Though a voice I may lack,
> Please drop in a penny
> By lifting my hat!

Oh well, the figure was nothing but a poor-box and the boy felt really disappointed. He had expected it to be something really remarkable. But then he remembered that his grandfather had talked about the wooden man in Karlskrona and about how all the children in the town had been so

Selma Lagerlöf

fond of him. And true enough, he was finding it difficult to say goodbye to the wooden man. There was something so old-fashioned about him that you could easily take him to be hundreds of years old, and he looked so strong and self-assured and full of the joys of life that it was easy to imagine that people had been like that in the past.

The boy was so taken with the wooden man that he completely forgot the one he was running away from. But now he could hear him again, turning off the street and coming into the churchyard. He was even following him here! What was the boy to do?

At that moment he saw the wooden man bend down towards him and reach out his big, broad hand. It was impossible to think anything but good of him, so the boy jumped up on to his hand and the wooden man lifted him up to his hat and tucked him in under it.

No sooner was the boy hidden and the wooden man's arm back down by his side than the bronze figure came to a halt in front of him and struck the ground so hard with his staff that the wooden man shook on his platform. Then the bronze man spoke in a strong and ringing voice: 'And who might you be?'

The wooden man's arm shot upwards so fast that the old wood creaked as he touched the brim of his hat before answering: 'Rosenbom, if you please, Your Majesty! Formerly bosun on the ship of the line Audacity, then, after completing my naval service, sexton of the Admiralty church, before finally being carved in wood and set up in the churchyard as a poor-box.'

The boy gave a jump when he heard the wooden man say 'Your Majesty!' Because now that he thought about it he knew that the statue on the square was that of the man who had founded the town. The man he had met was no less a person than Karl XI himself.*

'You give a good account of yourself,' the bronze statue said. 'Perhaps you can also tell me whether you've seen a tiny boy running around the town tonight. A cheeky little devil and if I get hold of him I'll teach him some manners.' And he thumped the ground with his staff yet again and looked frightfully angry.

'By your leave, Your Majesty, I have indeed seen him,' the wooden man said, at which the boy was so frightened that he began to tremble in his hiding place under the wooden man's hat, from where he could see the bronze statue through a crack in the wood. But he calmed down when he heard the wooden man continue: 'Your Majesty is on the wrong track! That boy was obviously intending to run into the dockyard and hide there.'

'So that's the way of it, is it, Rosenbom? Well, don't just stand there on your platform – come along and help me find him! Four eyes are better than two, Rosenbom!'

But the wooden man responded in a mournful voice: 'I must humbly request permission to remain where I am. Thanks to being repainted I may look bright and healthy but I'm actually old and rotten and can't risk moving around.'

The bronze figure was clearly a man who did not brook contradiction: 'What sort of attitude is that? Just come along, Rosenbom!' And he raised his staff and delivered a resounding blow to the wooden man's shoulder. 'See, you didn't fall to pieces, Rosenbom, did you?'

So, big and powerful as they were, the two of them set off along the streets of Karlskrona until they came to a high gate that led into the dockyard. A sailor was marching up and down on guard outside, but the bronze figure simply strode past him and kicked open the gate while the sailor pretended not even to notice.

Once in the dockyard an extensive harbour opened up before them, divided up by pile-bridges. Warships, looking bigger and more terrifying close up than they had looked when the boy had seen them from above, were anchored in the various basins. 'I wasn't so silly when I took them for sea-trolls,' Nils thought.

'And where do you think is the most suitable place for us to start our search, Rosenbom?' the bronze man said.

'I should think the easiest place for someone like him

to hide would be in the hall of models,' the wooden man answered.

A row of old buildings ran along a narrow strip of land that stretched the whole length of the harbour to the right of the gate. The bronze man walked up to one of the buildings, which had low walls, small windows and an extensive roof. He struck the door so hard with his staff that it burst open and then he marched in and up a staircase with worn steps. They entered a large hall completely filled with fully-rigged miniature vessels and, without anyone telling him, the boy realised that these were all models of ships that had been built for the Swedish navy.

There were vessels of many different kinds. There were old ships of the line with high structures fore and aft and their sides bristling with cannon, their masts heavy with a jumble of sails and ropes. There were small inshore vessels with benches along the sides for the oarsmen, and there were undecked gunboats and richly gilded frigates – models of the ships the kings had used on their voyages. And then, finally, there were the wide-beamed, heavily armoured ships in use today, with their guns and gun-turrets on deck, and with them were narrow, gleaming torpedo boats that looked like long slim fish.

The boy could hardly believe his eyes as he was carried around all these ships. 'Who would have believed that such big and splendid ships could have been built here in Sweden!' he thought to himself.

He had plenty of time to look at everything in the hall because as soon as the bronze man caught sight of the models he forgot about everything else. He looked at every one of them from the first to the last and he asked questions about them. Rosenbom, bosun on The Audacity, told him everything he knew about the men who had built the ships, about the men who had commanded them, and about the fate they had met. He told him about the shipbuilder Chapman and the heroes Puke and Trolle and the battles of Hogland and Svensksund* – about everything, in fact, right up to 1809, after which date Rosenbom had no longer been present.

Both the wooden man and the bronze man talked mostly about the fine old wooden warships. They did not really seem to understand the modern ironclads.

'I can tell that you don't know anything about these new-fangled things, Rosenbom,' the bronze man said. 'So let's go and look at something else. I'm enjoying myself, Rosenbom.'

He had clearly given up searching for the boy, who was now feeling safe and secure under the wooden hat.

The two men walked through the whole of the great establishment, through the sailmakers' shop and the anchor foundry, the machine shops and the carpenters' shops. They looked at the masting cranes and at the docks, at the great storehouses, the arsenal, the artillery depot, the long ropewalk and the great deserted dock that had been blasted out of the solid rock. They walked out on the pile-bridges where the warships were moored, went aboard and inspected them like two old sea-dogs, admiring or criticising, approving or disapproving.

Safe and sound under the wooden hat the boy listened to them talking about the toil and struggle involved in equipping the fleets that had sailed from here. He heard of the risk to life and limb, how every last penny had been sacrificed to build the warships, how men of genius had dedicated all their talents to perfecting these vessels for the defence of the fatherland. Listening to all this, there were times when the boy's eyes filled with tears and he was glad to hear the whole story.

Finally they went out into an open yard where all the figureheads from old ships of the line were arrayed. The boy had never seen a stranger sight – all of the figureheads had such incredibly powerful and terrifying faces. They were big, bold and wild, full of the same proud spirit that had imbued the great ships. They came from a different age to the age he lived in and the mere sight of them made him feel small.

When they reached this part, the bronze figure said to the

wooden man: 'Remove your hat, Rosenbom, out of respect for all of them. Every one of them has been into battle for the fatherland.'

Rosenbom, like the bronze man, had forgotten why they had undertaken their walk in the first place. Without thinking he raised his wooden hat from his head and called out: 'I raise my hat to the man who selected this harbour and founded the dockyard and rebuilt the navy! I raise my hat to the king who brought all this to life.'

'I thank you, Rosenbom, that was well said! You are a splendid fellow! But what on earth is that?'

For Nils Holgersson was now standing upright on Rosenbom's bald head. No longer afraid, he raised his white cap and shouted: 'Hurrah, hurrah, to you with your long face!'

The bronze figure pounded his staff hard against the ground, but the boy never did find out what he was intending to do because just then the sun rose and all of sudden both the bronze man and the wooden man disappeared as if made of mist. And while Nils was still standing there, the wild geese rose from the church tower and flew back and forth over the town. Suddenly they caught sight of Nils and the big white gander swooped down from the sky and picked him up.

X

THE JOURNEY TO ÖLAND

Sunday, 3 April

The wild geese flew out to one of the islands in the archipelago to feed and there they met some greylag geese who were surprised to see them since they knew that the wild geese usually preferred to travel inland. They were quite unbelievably nosy and were not satisfied until the geese told them how they were being persecuted by Smirre Fox. When they had finished, one of the greylag – who seemed to be as old and wise as Akka – spoke: 'It was a grave misfortune for you that the fox was outlawed from his home province. He will undoubtedly keep his word and follow you all the way up to Lapland. If I were you, instead of flying north over Småland, I would take the outside route to Öland so that he loses track of you. To be really sure of putting him off the track you should spend a couple of days at the southern point of Öland, where there is plenty of food and plenty of company. You won't regret it if you go that way.'

This was a really good piece of advice and the wild geese decided to follow it. As soon as they had eaten their fill, they set off on the journey to Öland. None of them had ever been there before but the greylag had provided them with good waymarks: all they had to do was to fly due south until they encountered the great migration route that ran parallel to the coast of Blekinge. All the birds which spent the winter out by the western seas and were now returning to Finland and Russia would be following that route and, in passing, all of them would land on Öland to rest. The wild geese should have no difficulty in finding guides.

The day was as still and warm as a summer's day, the very best weather for a journey over the sea, apart from the fact that the sky was grey and hazy rather than clear. Here and there great banks of cloud reached right down to sea level and obscured the view.

Once the travellers had got out beyond the islands, the sea spread out below them so smooth and mirror-like that when the boy looked down it seemed as if the water had disappeared. The earth was no longer beneath him and there was nothing but sky and clouds around him. It all made him feel quite dizzy and he clung to the gander even more anxiously than the very first time he had sat on his back. It felt as though it was impossible for him to hang on, as though one way or another he was bound to fall off.

Things became even worse once they reached the great migration route the greylag had told them about. Flock after flock, all flying in the same direction, flew past as if following a signposted route. There were duck and greylag, velvet scoter and guillemot, divers and long-tailed duck, mergansers and grebes, oystercatchers and common scoter. When the boy leaned forward and looked towards where the sea should be, he could see the whole procession of birds mirrored in the water. He was so dizzy and he could not understand why, but all the birds seemed to be flying belly up. Still, he did not puzzle his mind about this for long, because he really had no idea what was up and what was down.

The birds were exhausted and impatient to arrive. None of them uttered a peep or made a joke and that, too, made everything seem strangely unreal.

'What if we have travelled away from the earth?' Nils said to himself. 'What if we are now travelling all the way up to heaven?'

He could see nothing but clouds and birds around him and he began to think it was quite probable that they were heading for heaven. The thought made him happy and he wondered what he would see up there. He no longer felt giddy and he became quite ecstatic at the thought that he was leaving the earth and going up to heaven.

At that very moment, however, he heard the crack of shots and saw two thin white columns of smoke rising.

This caused consternation among the birds. 'Wildfowlers! Wildfowlers! Wildfowlers in boats!' they called. 'Fly high! Fly away!'

Now the boy saw that they were still flying over the sea, not flying up to heaven. And below them was a long line of small boats filled with wildfowlers who were firing shot after shot. The flocks at the front had failed to notice them in time and had been flying too low. A number of dark bodies fell towards the sea and, as each of them fell, loud cries of lamentation rose from those left alive.

For someone who had recently thought he was in heaven it was strange to wake to such terror and anguish. Akka gained height as quickly as possible and she and her flock made off as quickly as they could. The wild geese escaped unharmed but the boy could not get over his amazement that anyone would want to shoot at Akka and Yksi and Kaksi and the gander and all the others? Human beings had no understanding of what they were doing.

And so the birds flew on through the still air and once again everything was as silent as before apart from a few exhausted birds who called: 'Will we soon be there? Are you sure we're going the right way?' To which those flying in the lead would answer: 'We're flying straight towards Öland, straight towards Öland.'

The mallard were tiring and the divers overtook them. 'Don't be in such a hurry!' the ducks called. 'You'll have eaten up all the food before we get there.' 'There'll be plenty both for you and for us,' the divers answered.

Well before Öland had come into sight, they were met by a gentle wind, which carried with it what seemed to be huge clouds of white smoke, just as if there was an enormous fire somewhere.

On seeing the first curls of white, the birds became anxious and increased their pace. The smoke-like billows of white grew denser until the birds were completely surrounded. But there was no smell, and the billows were not dark and dry like smoke but damp and white. The boy suddenly realised that it was fog, not smoke, they were encountering.

When the fog became so dense that they could not see a goose-length in front of them, the birds began to behave like mad things. Whereas earlier they had all been flying in good order, they now began to play in the fog, flying hither and thither to lead each other astray. 'Watch out!' they called. 'You're just going round in circles! For heaven's sake, turn round! You won't get to Öland that way.'

Every one of them knew very well where the island was but they did their best to confuse each other. 'Just look at those long-tailed duck – they're heading back to the North Sea!' said a voice in the fog. 'Watch out, greylag!' came a shout from a different direction. 'If you carry on the way you are going you'll end up on the island of Rügen.'

There was, of course, no danger that the birds which habitually followed this route would let themselves be tricked into taking the wrong route. But it was difficult for the wild geese. The mischief-makers noticed how uncertain of the route they were and did all they could to send them astray.

'Where are you good folk heading?' a swan called, coming right up to Akka with a sympathetic and serious expression.

'We're going to Öland but we've never been there before,' Akka said, thinking this was a bird she could rely on.

'Too bad!' the swan said. 'They've sent you off on the wrong route. You're on the way to Blekinge. Come with me and I'll show you the right way.'

And so he set off leading them, but when he had led them as far away from the migration route as possible – so far that they could not hear the cries of the other birds – the swan disappeared into the fog.

For a while the geese were all at sixes and sevens until they managed to find their way back to the migrating birds. No sooner were they there than a duck came up to them and said: 'Best thing for you would be to settle on the water until the fog passes. It's quite obvious that you are not used to looking after yourselves on journeys like this.'

It reached the point where the combination of all of these rogues succeeded in making Akka utterly confused and as far as the boy could tell the geese spent a long time flying in circles.

'Watch out! Can't you see that you're flying upside down?' a diver shouted as he stormed past. The boy spontaneously wrapped his arms tightly round the gander's neck – turning upside down was something he had always been frightened of.

It is impossible to say how long it would have taken them to get there if they had not heard the dull rumble of a cannon in the distance.

At the sound of the shot Akka stretched her neck, beat hard with her wings and set off at full speed. Now she had something to guide her. The greylag had told her not to descend at the very southernmost point of Öland because there was a cannon there that people used to fire at the fog. So now Akka knew the direction to take and no one was going to lead her astray.

XI

THE SOUTHERN POINT OF ÖLAND

3-6 April

In the southernmost part of Öland lies an old royal estate called Ottenby. It is a very large estate that stretches right across the island from shore to shore and what makes it remarkable is that it has always harboured large numbers of animals. In the seventeenth century, when the kings used to go to Öland to hunt, the whole estate was a great deer-park. In the eighteenth century there was a stud there for the breeding of thoroughbred horses and a sheep-run that supported many hundreds of sheep. Today, however, you will find neither sheep nor thoroughbreds at Ottenby, instead you will find great herds of young horses ready to provide mounts for our cavalry regiments.

There is no doubt that there is no other estate in the whole country that provides such an excellent haunt for animals. What used to be sheep pasture, a mile and a half long and the biggest meadow on the whole of Öland, lies along the east coast and animals are as free to graze and roam and play there as if they were in the wild. And then there is Ottenby Wood, famous for its hundred-year-old oak-trees that provide shade from the sun and shelter from the strong Öland wind. Nor should we forget Ottenby Wall, which is so long that it runs right across the island from shore to shore and cuts Ottenby off from the rest of the island. It provides the animals with a marker of the boundary of the old royal estate and warns them against straying onto lands where they will not be so well protected.

Tame animals are not the only ones to thrive at Ottenby. It is almost as if the wild animals came to feel that they too, like the tame animals, could count on shelter and protection on this ancient royal land, which is why they flock there in such huge numbers. Not only are red deer of the old race still resident, and hares and shelduck and partridges love to live there, but it also provides a resting place for many thousands of migrating birds in spring and late summer. The migrating birds settle to feed and rest mainly on the marshy eastern shore below the sheep meadow.

When Nils Holgersson and the wild geese finally reached Öland, they landed on the shore below the sheep meadow like all the other birds. The fog was as dense on the shore as it had been out at sea. But the boy was still utterly astounded by all the birds he could see just on the small section of the beach visible to him.

It was a low sandy beach with stones and pools and piles of washed-up seaweed. Given the choice, the boy would probably never have considered landing there but the birds seemed to think it was paradise. Ducks and greylag walked around grazing on the meadow, sandpipers and other shore birds ran around closer to the water, and out on the water itself the divers were fishing. The busiest places of all, however, were the long banks of seaweed, on which birds were packed shoulder to shoulder, pecking away at the bugs and grubs that were there in such limitless quantities that no one could complain of a shortage of food.

Almost all the birds were going to travel onward and had only landed here for a rest. As soon as the leader of a flock thought his companions were sufficiently rested he would say: 'If you are ready, we'll be on our way.'

'No, wait, wait! We haven't eaten anything like enough yet,' his companions would plead.

'You don't imagine I'm going to let you eat so much that you can't move, do you?' the leader would say, clapping his wings and setting off. But it was not unknown for him to have to turn back because he had been unable to convince the others to accompany him.

A flock of swans was drifting out beyond the outermost bank of seaweed. They did not bother to go ashore and rested by rocking and floating on the water. Now and then they plunged their necks down into the water and picked up food from the sea bottom. If they found something particularly tasty they gave loud calls that sounded just like blasts on a trumpet.

As soon as the boy heard there were swans in the shallows, he hurried out on the banks of seaweed. He had never seen wild swans at such close quarters before and he was lucky enough to be able to approach them closely.

The boy was not the only one to have heard the swans. The wild geese and the greylag and the ducks and the divers all swam out between the banks of weed, formed a circle around the swans and gazed at them. The swans, meanwhile, puffed up their feathers, lifted their wings like sails and raised their necks high in the air. Now and again one of them would swim up to a goose or a black-throated diver or a diving duck and say a few words; when this happened the birds they spoke to looked as if they hardly dared raise their beaks to answer.

There was, however, one red-throated diver, a little bundle of mischief who could not be doing with all this pomposity. He suddenly dived and disappeared beneath the surface of the water and a moment later one of the swans squawked and swam away so fast that the water foamed. Then the swan stopped and began looking majestic again; meanwhile, however, a second swan squawked just as the first had done, and then a third did the same.

The red-throated diver could not stay underwater any longer and had to surface. The swans rushed towards him, but when they saw what a tiny wretch he was – small, dark and mischievous – they quickly turned away, as if they thought it beneath their dignity to squabble with him. So the diver submerged again and nipped their feet, which were sore, although the worst part was that it made it impossible for them to retain their dignified poise. All at once, they made up their minds. They began to beat the air noisily with their wings and rushed forward as if running on the water for quite a distance until they finally got enough air under their wings to take off.

Once the swans had gone, everyone missed them, and all those who had been enjoying the diver's pranks a moment before now started criticising him for his impertinence.

The boy walked back to the shore and stood watching the way the sandpipers behaved. They resembled tiny little cranes with their small bodies, long legs and necks and light, flitting movements – though they were brown rather than grey. They stood in a long line on the part of the beach washed by the waves. As soon as a wave rolled in, the whole line quickly retreated, and as soon as the wave receded, they followed it out. They carried on like this for hours.

The shelduck were the showiest of the birds there. They were, of course, related to the ordinary ducks with their heavy bodies, broad bills and webbed feet, but their appearance was so much more splendid. Their plumage was white but with a broad chestnut belt around the neck, their speculum shone green and red and black, their wing-tips were black, and their heads were a blackish-green colour that shimmered and shifted like silk.

The moment one of them appeared on the beach, the other birds would say: 'Just look at them! Talk about overdressing!' 'If they weren't so flashy they wouldn't have to bury their nests in the ground, they'd be able to nest up on the surface like the rest of us,' said one dull brown female mallard. 'They can try as much as they like, but they are going to get nowhere with noses like that!' said a greylag. And it was true: the shelduck had a big knob at the base of their bill, and it ruined their appearance.

Just offshore, gulls and terns swooped over the water fishing. 'What kind of fish are you catching?' one of the geese asked. 'Sticklebacks! Öland sticklebacks! The best sticklebacks in the world!' a gull answered. 'Here, do you want to taste?' he said, flying towards the goose and offering her a mouthful of small fish. 'Ugh! Do you think I want to eat horrid things like that?' the goose said.

It was still just as foggy the following morning when the wild geese were up on the meadow grazing and the boy had gone down to the shore to collect mussels, of which there were plenty. It occurred to him that the following day they might be somewhere where there was no food available, so he decided to try to make himself a small bag that he could fill with mussels. Up on the meadow he found some old sedge that was strong and tough and he started to weave himself a knapsack. He worked at this for several hours and he was really pleased with it when he finished.

Around midday all the wild geese came rushing up and asked whether he had seen the white gander. 'No, he hasn't been with me,' the boy said. Akka said: 'He was with us until a short time ago but now we don't know where he is.'

The boy leapt up, filled with fear. He asked whether any foxes or eagles had been seen or whether any human beings had been noticed in the vicinity. But no one had seen anything dangerous: the gander had probably simply got lost in the fog.

Whatever the reason for the white gander's disappearance, it was a great misfortune for the boy and he immediately set off to look for him. The fog gave him cover and he could run wherever he liked without being seen, but it also prevented him from seeing anything. He ran along the coast all the way to the lighthouse and the fog cannon on the southernmost point of the island. Wherever he went there were crowds of birds but no sign of the gander. He even took the risk of approaching Ottenby Manor and searching every one of the hollow old oaks in Ottenby Wood, but he could find no trace of the gander.

He carried on searching until it began to get dark, when it was time to set off back to the east coast of the island. He walked with heavy steps and was feeling thoroughly gloomy. He had no idea what was to become of him if he could not find the gander. He needed the gander more than anything else in the world.

But as he walked across the meadow, who should he see coming towards him in the fog but the big white gander, completely unharmed and very happy to have found his way back to the others at last. The fog had confused him so much, or so he said, that he had been going in circles round the big meadow all day. The boy threw his arms around his neck in joy and begged him to take care of himself and not wander away from the others. The gander promised that he would never do it again: 'No, never again!'

But when the boy went down to the shore the following morning to look for mussels, the wild geese came running to him again asking whether he had seen the gander.

No, he had not seen him. So the gander was gone again. No doubt he was lost in the fog just like the day before.

Once again the boy ran off in great dismay and began searching. He found a place where the Ottenby Wall had fallen down and where he could climb over it. Then he searched around both down on the shore, which gradually widened out and became big enough for fields and meadows and farms, and up on the flat plateau that occupied the centre of the island, where the only buildings were windmills and where the ground vegetation was so thin that the white limestone showed through.

But still he could not find the gander, and when evening came and the boy had to return to the shore, he was convinced that his travelling companion was lost. He was so depressed that he did not know where to turn.

He had just climbed back over Ottenby Wall when he heard a stone falling down close by. Turning round to see what it was, he thought he saw something moving on a heap of rocks that lay against the wall. He crept closer and saw the white gander struggling up this heap with his beak full of long roots. The gander did not see the boy and the boy did not call to him, knowing that this was his chance to find out why the gander kept disappearing.

And he soon discovered the reason. There was a young

greylag lying on the pile of rocks and she uttered cries of joy on seeing the gander. The boy crept closer so he could hear what they said and he discovered that the greylag had an injured wing and was unable to fly; the rest of her flock had travelled on, leaving her alone here. She had been close to dying of hunger when the gander had heard her calling the day before. Since then he had been bringing her food and they both hoped her wing would heal before he left the island, though as yet she was still unable to fly or walk. She was very distressed but the gander comforted her by saying that he would not be moving on for a long time. Finally he bade her goodnight and promised to return the following day.

The boy let the gander go and as soon as he had disappeared he crept up to the pile of rocks himself. He was angry that he had been tricked and he wanted to tell the greylag that the gander was his property – he was going to take the boy to Lapland so there was no question of him remaining here for her sake. But once he saw the young greylag close up he understood both why the gander had been bringing her food for two days and why he had not wanted to tell anyone he was helping her. She had the prettiest little head, her plumage was as soft as silk and her eyes were gentle and pleading.

When she saw the boy she wanted to run away, but her left wing was dislocated and dragged on the ground and prevented her from moving.

'You mustn't be afraid of me,' the boy said, not looking anything like as fierce as he had intended to be. 'I am Thummitot and I am Mårten Gander's travelling companion,' he continued, after which he just stood there not knowing what it was he wanted to say.

There is sometimes a strange quality about animals that makes one wonder what kind of creatures they really are, a quality that makes one almost afraid that they might be human beings who have undergone a transformation. There was something of that about the greylag. As soon as Thummitot had said who he was, she bowed her head and neck to him in a very sweet way and spoke in a voice so beautiful the boy could hardly believe it was a goose speaking: 'I am so glad you have come to help me. The white gander has told me that there is no one as wise and kind as you.'

She said this with such dignity that it made the boy feel really shy. 'This can't be a bird,' he thought. 'It must surely be a princess on whom someone has put a spell.'

He was seized by a desire to help her and he put his small hands in under her feathers and felt along the wing bone. The bone was not broken but there was something wrong about the joint. He moved his finger into an empty socket. 'Careful how you go now!' he said, took a firm grip of the bone and slotted it back into its proper place. He did it quickly and well considering it was the first time he had done anything of the kind, but it must have been very painful for the greylag because the young goose uttered a shrill scream before sinking back on the stones without any sign of life.

The boy was dreadfully afraid. He had wanted to help her but now she was dead. He leapt down from the pile of rocks and ran away. He felt just as if he had killed a human being.

By the following morning the fog had cleared and Akka said that they should be on their way. All the others were willing to leave but the white gander raised objections. The boy understood that he did not want to leave the greylag, but Akka paid no attention to him and set off.

Nils jumped up on the gander's back and, slowly and reluctantly, the white gander followed the flock. The boy was thoroughly glad that they were leaving the island. His conscience was troubling him about the greylag and he did not want to tell the gander what had happened when he tried to cure her. He thought it would be best if Mårten Gander never found out what had happened. But at the same time he wondered how the gander had the heart to leave the greylag.

And then suddenly the gander turned back – the thought of the young greylag had become more than he could bear. The Lapland trip was neither here nor there, he simply could not go with the others when he knew that she was lying there alone and sick and doomed to starve to death.

With just a few wing-beats the gander was back at the heap of rocks, but there was no young greylag lying among the stones. 'Finedown! Finedown! Where are you?' the gander called.

'She must have been taken by a fox,' the boy thought. But at that moment he heard a pretty voice answering the gander: 'I am here, gander, I am here! I have just been having a morning bathe.' And the little greylag surfaced on the water fresh and healthy and told how Thummitot had put her wing back into joint. Now everything was fine and she was ready to accompany them on their journey.

The droplets of water hung like pearls on her shimmering silky feathers and Thummitot thought yet again that she really was a princess.

XII

THE BIG BUTTERFLY

Wednesday, 6 April

The geese flew the whole length of the long island, which was now clearly visible below them. Nils felt happy and light-hearted during the journey – he was as pleased and well-satisfied as he had been gloomy and depressed the day before while roaming around the island trying to find the gander.

He could see now that the interior of the island consisted of a barren plateau surrounded by a wide fringe of good fertile land along the coasts, and he now began to understand the meaning of something he had heard the evening before.

He had sat down to rest by one of the many windmills to be found up on the plateau when a couple of shepherds accompanied by their dogs and a large flock of sheep came along. The boy had not been worried because he was well-hidden under the windmill staircase but, as luck would have it, the shepherds came and sat on the staircase, which left the boy with no choice but to stay there and keep still.

One of the shepherds was young and looked no different from most other people; his companion, however, was a funny-looking old fellow. His body was big and gnarled but his head was small and his face had a mild and gentle expression. It was as if his body and his head did not really belong together.

For a while he rested there silently staring into the fog with a look of indescribable weariness on his face. Then he began talking to the younger man, who took some bread and cheese from his bag in order to have his supper. The young shepherd said little or nothing in response, but he listened very patiently, as if he was thinking, 'I'll let you have the pleasure of talking for a while.'

'Let me tell you something, Erik,' the older shepherd said. 'I've come to the conclusion that in the old days, when human beings and animals were much bigger than they are now, butterflies must also have been enormous. Once upon a time there was a butterfly that was many miles in length and had wings as wide as any lake. These wings were blue and shone like silver and they were so magnificent that when the butterfly was flying all the other animals stood still and gazed at it.

'There was, of course, a problem, which was that the butterfly was too big. The wings found it hard to keep it aloft, which would not have been a problem if it had been clever enough only to fly over the land. But it wasn't that clever and it set out over the Baltic Sea. It hadn't gone far before a storm blew up and started to tear at the wings. Well, you can easily imagine, can't you Erik, what will happen when a Baltic storm starts playing its rough games with delicate butterfly wings? In no time at all they were torn off and blown away and then, of course, the poor butterfly fell into the sea. At first it was tossed backwards and forwards by the waves and then it ran aground on some rocky shallows off Småland. And that's where it stayed, big and long as it was.

'The way I see it, Erik, is that if the butterfly had been lying on the ground it would have quickly rotted and fallen to pieces, but since it fell in the sea it was impregnated with lime and became as hard as rock. You know how we've found stones on the beach that are actually calcified worms – well, I believe that the same thing happened to the body of that big butterfly. I believe it turned into a long, narrow rock where it lay out in the Baltic. Don't you think that is what happened?'

He stopped and waited for an answer until the other shepherd nodded to him and said: 'Carry on with what you are saying, now, so I can see where you are going with it.'

'Well, Erik, the thing is that this island of Öland that you and I live on is no more and no less than the body of that old butterfly. The moment you stop and think about it, you can see that the island is a butterfly. In the north you can see the narrow thorax and round head, and in the south you can see the abdomen, which widens out at first before becoming narrower and ending in a sharp point.'

Here he stopped once more and looked at his companion, as if anxious about how he would take what had been said. But the young man calmly carried on eating and nodded to him to continue.

'As soon as the butterfly had been transformed into limestone, the seeds of many kinds of plants and trees were carried out on the wind and tried to take root. But they found it difficult to gain a hold on the smooth bare rock and it was a long time before anything but sedge could grow. Then came sheep's fescue and briars and sea buckthorn. Even today there is not enough vegetation up on the limestone pavement of the Great Alvar to really cover the underlying rock and it still shines through here and there.* And ploughing and sowing is out of the question up here because the soil cover is so thin.

'But if you accept that the Great Alvar and the rock structures that surround it were formed from the body of the butterfly, you still need to ask where the land that lies below those rocks came from.'

'Yes, exactly, I really should like to know that,' said the shepherd who was eating his supper.

'Well, you have to bear in mind that Öland has been lying in the sea for very many years and during that time all kinds of things – seaweed and sand and molluscs and things that get tossed around by the waves – collected around it and stayed there. In addition to that, stones and gravel from the rock formations on the east and west sides tumbled down, and all this has given the island a wide shoreline on which grain and flowers and trees can grow.

'Up here on the hard back of the butterfly there is only grazing for sheep and cows and small horses; nothing but lapwings and golden plovers live up here, and the only buildings are windmills and the few miserable stone-huts into which we shepherds crawl. Down on the shores, however, there are big villages and churches and manses and fishing settlements and even a whole town.'

He looked questioningly at his companion, who had finished eating and was in the process of tying up his food bag. 'I wonder where you are going with all this,' the younger man said.

'Well, the one thing I would like to know is this,' the shepherd said, lowering his voice almost to a whisper and staring into the fog with his small eyes, which seemed exhausted by seeking for everything that does not exist. 'What I would like to know is this: do the farmers living in their square-built farms down below the rocky zone, or the fishermen who catch the herring in the sea, or the merchants in Borgholm, or the visitors who come here to bathe every summer, or the tourists who wander around the castle ruins in Borgholm, or the hunters who come every autumn to shoot partridges, or the painters who come up here on the Great Alvar to paint the sheep and the windmills – do any of them realise that this island used to be a butterfly which flew around on great shining wings, that's what I'd like to know?'

'Ah now!' the younger shepherd said suddenly. 'It must surely have occurred to some of them as they sat on the edge of the rocky outcrops of an evening listening to the nightingales singing in the wooded meadows below and looking out over the Sound of Kalmar, that this island cannot possibly have originated in the same way as all the others.'

'I would like to ask,' the older man continued, 'whether anyone has ever thought of fitting the windmills with such large sails that they touched the sky and were strong enough to lift the whole island up out of the sea and make it fly like a butterfly among butterflies.'

'There might be something in what you're saying,' the younger man said. 'On summer nights when the sky above is a high open vault I have sometimes thought the island was trying to rise from the sea and fly away.'

Now that the old man had finally got the young one to talk,

however, he did not pay much attention to him. 'I should really like to know,' the older man said in an even quieter voice, 'if anyone can explain why there is such a sense of longing up here on the Alvar. I have felt it every day of my life and I imagine it preys on everyone who has to spend time up here. I'd like to know whether anyone else has understood that it is the result of the whole island being a butterfly – a butterfly which is longing for the return of its wings.'

XIII

THE ISLAND OF LILLA KARLSÖ

THE STORM   Friday, 8 April

The wild geese had spent the night on the northern point of Öland and were now on their way towards the mainland. There was a strong south wind blowing over the Kalmar Sound so the geese were being pushed northwards, in spite of which they were still managing to work their way towards land at a good speed. As they were approaching the first skerries however, they heard a terrific noise as if a great crowd of birds with powerful wings was approaching and the water beneath them suddenly grew completely black. Akka slowed down so quickly that she almost hung motionless in the air, and then she descended in order to settle on the sea. Even before the geese could reach the water, they were hit by the storm from the west which, already driving dust clouds, salt foam and small birds before it, now dragged the wild geese along, turning them back and pushing them further from the mainland.

It was a ferocious storm. Time after time the geese attempted to turn, but they were unable to and were driven farther out into the Baltic Sea instead. The storm had already driven them past Öland and now the open sea lay before them, empty and desolate. They had no choice but to run before the wind.

As soon as Akka recognised that it was impossible for them to fly against the wind, she decided there was no point in allowing the storm to drive them right across the Baltic and she descended and landed on the water. The swell was already violent and was increasing every minute.

Great green waves surged forward with white foam at their crests, each rising higher than the one before. It was as if they were competing to see which could be highest, which could produce the wildest spray. But the wild geese were not afraid of the surging swell – quite the opposite, they seemed to be thoroughly enjoying it. They did not exert themselves by swimming, they simply let the waves wash them up to the crest and down into the hollow, and they enjoyed it as much as a child enjoys a swing. Their only worry was that the flock would be split up. Meanwhile the poor land birds which were being driven past them by the storm called out enviously: 'It's easy for you – you can swim!'

But there was danger for the wild geese, too. In the first place, all the swaying made them hopelessly sleepy and they kept wanting to turn their heads, tuck them under their wings and go to sleep. Nothing could be more dangerous than falling asleep like that and Akka was continually shouting: 'Geese, geese, don't fall asleep! Anyone who falls asleep will get separated from the flock. Anyone separated from the flock is lost!'

In spite of all their efforts to resist, one after the other of them fell asleep. Akka herself was close to succumbing when she suddenly saw something round and dark appear above a wave. 'Seals! Seals! Seals!' Akka shouted in a piercing voice and took off, her wings clapping hard. And it was only just in time – before the last of the wild geese had managed to take off from the water, the seals were so close that they were snapping at her feet.

So the geese were once again up in the storm and it drove them even farther out to sea. The storm did not rest, nor did it give them any rest, and there was no sign of land, just the wild and empty sea.

The geese settled on the water again as soon as they dared. But after a while the rocking of the waves made them sleepy again, and as soon as they fell asleep the seals swam up once more. If old Akka had not been so watchful, not a single one of them would have escaped alive.

All day long the storm continued, causing havoc and devastation among the host of birds migrating north at this time of year. Some of them were driven off course to distant lands where they died of hunger; others were so exhausted that they dropped into the sea and drowned; many of them were smashed against the rocky walls of cliffs, and many fell prey to the seals.

All day long the storm continued and Akka began at last to wonder whether she and her flock were doomed to disaster. They were now dead tired and she could see nowhere safe to rest. As evening approached she no longer dared settle on the sea because it was now filling with great ice-floes that piled up against each other and made her fearful they would all be crushed. On several occasions the geese tried to settle on the ice-floes but the wild storm swept them down into the water or the merciless seals came slithering up onto the ice.

At sunset the geese were once again in the air, flying onwards but becoming anxious about the night. Darkness seemed to be overtaking them all too quickly this evening – an evening full of dangers.

There was still no sign of land and they dreaded the thought of being forced to spend all night at sea, where they would either be crushed by ice-floes or bitten to death by seals or separated from one another by the storm.

The sky was shrouded with clouds, the moon remained hidden and darkness came on quickly. Nature itself seemed so strange and uncanny that even the bravest hearts quailed. The calls of birds in distress had been ringing out over the sea all day without anyone paying attention to them, but the cries sounded even more mournful and frightening now that it was impossible to see those who were calling. The ice-floes drifting on the sea crashed into each other with a thunderous roar and the seals joined in with their wild hunting songs. It was as if heaven and earth were foundering and collapsing.

THE SHEEP

The boy had been staring down at the sea for some time when suddenly he sensed that its roar was becoming even louder than before. He looked up and right in front of him, no more than a few yards away, loomed a bare craggy cliff at the foot of which the pounding waves hurled foam high into the air. The geese were flying straight at the cliff and the boy could not see how they could avoid smashing into it.

He scarcely had time to wonder why Akka had not noticed this danger before they reached the cliff. But then he saw the semi-circular mouth of a cave open up in front of them. The geese steered their way in and the next moment they were in safety.

The first thing the travellers did before taking the time to celebrate their salvation was to check that all of their companions were safe. Akka was there and Yksi, Kolme, Neljä, Viisi, Kuusi, all six goslings, the white gander, Finedown and Thummitot were all there, but Kaksi from Nuolja – the first goose on the left – had disappeared and no one knew what had become of her.

When the geese realised it was Kaksi who had become separated from the flock, they were not too worried. Kaksi was old and wise, she knew all their routes and all their habits and would no doubt know how to find her way back to them.

Then the wild geese began to inspect the cavern. There was enough light coming in through the opening for them to see that it was both deep and wide. They were pleased to have discovered such a splendid refuge for the night until one of them caught sight of two green spots glowing over in a dark corner.

'Those are eyes,' Akka said, 'there are some big animals in here.' They all began rushing to the entrance until Thummitot, who could see in the dark better than the geese, shouted to them: 'You don't need to run away! It's just some sheep lying along the wall of the cave.'

Once the wild geese had become accustomed to the gloomy light in the cave, they could see the sheep without any difficulty. There were roughly as many adult sheep as there were geese but there were also a number of little lambs. A big ram with long twisted horns seemed to be the leader of the flock and the wild geese approached him with much bowing and scraping: 'Well met in the wilderness,' they said, but the ram just lay there without offering a word of welcome.

At first the geese thought the sheep must be annoyed that they had come into the cave. 'It may be inconvenient that we have come into your place like this,' Akka said, 'but we can't help it. We have been driven by the wind and we have been travelling in the storm all day, so it would be really good to be able to stay here for the night.'

It was some time before any of the sheep said a word in response – on the other hand, several of them could be heard drawing deep sighs. Akka was quite familiar with the fact that sheep are always shy and a bit peculiar, but these animals seemed to have no idea at all how to behave. Finally an old ewe with a long and mournful face and a plaintive voice spoke: 'It's not that any of us would want to turn you away, but this is a house of mourning and we cannot receive guests as we used to.'

'You don't have to worry about that,' Akka said. 'If you had any idea what we have been through today, you would understand that we are quite satisfied just to get a safe place to sleep.'

After Akka said this, the old ewe got up and said: 'I do believe it would be better to be flying around in the most violent of storms than to stay here. But we certainly won't let you leave without offering the best hospitality the house can provide.' She showed them a hollow in the ground, which was full of water, and alongside it there was a pile of chaff and husks, which she told them to help themselves to.

'We had a severe winter this year, with heavy snow on the island,' she said. 'The farmers who own us came over with hay and oat-straw so that we wouldn't starve to death. These scraps are all that's left.'

The geese threw themselves on the food at once. They

thought everything had turned out well and they were in the best of moods. They could not fail to notice, however, how nervous the sheep were, but knowing how easily frightened sheep tend to be they did not think there was any real danger for them to worry about. As soon as they had eaten they were ready – as usual – to settle down to sleep, but the big ram stood up at that point and walked over to them. The geese could not remember ever having seen a sheep with such long and heavy horns, and he was remarkable in other ways, too: he had a large rounded forehead, intelligent eyes and a good bearing, as though he was a proud and brave animal.

'I cannot take the responsibility of letting you go to sleep without telling you that this is not a safe place,' he said. 'We can no longer take in guests for the night.'

Akka at last began to realise that something serious must be going on. 'We shall, of course, be on our way if you absolutely want us to,' she said. 'But won't you tell us first what it is that is troubling you? We have no idea what it is all about. We don't even know where we are.'

'This island is called Lilla Karlsö,' the ram said. 'It lies off Gotland and nothing but sheep and seabirds live here.'

'You must be wild sheep, then,' Akka said.

'Not far from it,' the ram answered. 'We don't have much to do with people. There is an old agreement between us and the farmers on a farm on Gotland that they will provide us with fodder in snowy winters and in exchange they can take some of us away when we become too numerous. This is a small island and it can't feed too many of us. Otherwise we look after ourselves all year and we live in caves like this rather than in buildings with doors and locks.'

'Do you stay out here the whole winter as well, then?' Akka asked, surprised.

'Yes, we do,' the ram answered. 'There's good grazing all year round up on the hill.'

'It sounds to me as if though things are better for you than for most sheep,' Akka said. 'So what is the misfortune that has befallen you?'

'The cold was extreme last winter and the sea froze over, with the result that three foxes came across the ice and have stayed here ever since. Apart from them there are no other dangerous predators on the island.'

'Ah, I see. But do foxes dare attack animals like you?'

'Not in the day, they don't, because then I can defend myself and my flock,' the ram said, shaking his horns. 'But they creep up on us at night when we are asleep in the caves. We try to stay awake – but we have to sleep at some point, of course, and that is when they attack. They have already killed all the sheep in the other caves, and there were flocks just as big as mine.'

'It's not very pleasant to have to admit how helpless we are,' the old ewe said. 'But we can't look after ourselves much better than tame sheep can.'

'Do you think the foxes will come tonight?' Akka asked.

'We can't expect anything else,' the old ewe answered. 'They came last night and they stole one of our lambs. They'll keep on coming as long as any of us are alive – that's what they did in the other places.'

'If it goes on like this you will all be wiped out,' Akka said.

'Yes, it won't be long before there are no sheep left on Lilla Karlsö,' the ewe said.

Akka stood and wondered what to do. The thought of going back out into the storm was not a pleasant one, but nor was it good to remain in a place where visitors like foxes were to be expected. After pondering for a while, she turned to Thummitot.

'I wonder if you would help us as you've done so many times before?' she said.

Yes, of course he would, the boy replied.

'It's a pity that you won't get any sleep,' the goose said. 'But I wonder if you can manage to stay awake until the foxes come and then wake us so we can fly away?'

The boy was not particularly pleased at the thought but anything was better than going back out into the storm, so he promised to stay awake. He went to the mouth of the cave, crept in behind a rock for shelter from the storm and sat there on guard.

After he had been sitting there for a while, the storm seemed to be easing off. The sky grew clear and moonlight began to play on the waves. The boy went right to the lip of the cave to look out and he saw that it was situated quite high up the hillside. Only a steep narrow path led up to it and that was certainly the way the foxes would come.

He could not see any foxes yet but he did see something that, at first sight, he was much more afraid of. Down on the strip of beach below the rocks stood some giants ... or stone trolls ... or perhaps they were people? At first he thought he was dreaming, but he was quite sure he had not fallen asleep. He could see the huge figures so clearly that they could not be an illusion. Some of them stood right out on the edge of the beach, others were close in to the cliff, just as if they were intending to climb it. Some of them had great big heads, others had no heads at all. Some of them were one-armed, others had humps on their backs and on their chests. He had never seen anything so extraordinary.

The boy stood there, working himself up into such a state of fear about the trolls that he almost forgot to keep his eyes open for foxes. But suddenly he heard the sound of claws scraping on a stone and he saw three foxes coming up the steep slope. As soon as he knew that he had something real to deal with, he calmed down and was not in the least afraid. And he thought what a pity it would be just to wake the geese and leave the sheep to their fate, and so he came up with a different way of dealing with the problem.

He hurried into the cave, shook the big ram by the horns so that he woke up, and at the same time he swung himself up onto the ram's back. 'Get a move on now, Grandad, and we'll see if we can give those foxes a bit of a fright!' the boy said.

He had tried to be as quiet as possible but the foxes must have heard something because when they reached the mouth of the cave they stopped and deliberated.

'One of that lot in there must have moved,' said one of the

foxes. 'I wonder if they are awake?'

'Oh, come on, let's just get at them! They can't do anything to us, anyway,' said another.

After moving a little farther into the cave they stopped and sniffed the air.

'Which of them are we going to take tonight?' whispered the fox at the front.

'Tonight we'll take the big ram,' said the one at the back. 'Then it will be an easy job for us to finish off all the rest.'

Nils sat there on the old ram's back and watched them creeping forward. 'Butt straight in front of you now!' he whispered, and the ram butted, hurling the first fox head over heels back towards the mouth of the cave. 'Now butt to the left!' the boy said, turning the ram's great head in the right direction. The ram aimed a ferocious blow that hit the second fox in the side. He rolled over time after time before he was able to get to his feet and flee. The boy would really have liked to see the third fox receive his due, too, but he had already made his escape.

'I think they have probably had enough for tonight,' Nils said.

'I agree with you there,' the big ram said. 'Lie down on my back and creep in under the wool. You deserve some comfort and warmth after the storm you have been out in.'

HELL'S HOLE   Saturday, 9 April
The following day the ram carried the boy around on his back and showed him the island. It was really just one enormous rock, like a big house with vertical sides and a flat roof. First of all the ram took the boy up on the roof of the rock to show him the good grazing up there, and Nils had to admit that the island seemed to be ideal for sheep. There was little else growing up there other than sheep's fescue and other small dry herb-scented plants of the kind sheep like.

But there was much more than pasture-land to be seen by anyone who climbed the steep slopes to the top. In the first place there was the sea all round: a smooth shining swell, blue

and sunlit – only here and there around the headlands was there any sign of spray. The long unbroken coast of Gotland lay due east, and to the south-west was the slightly bigger island of Stora Karlsö, similar in form to Lilla Karlsö. When the ram went right to the edge of the roof so that the boy could look down the rocky precipices, he could see that they were crowded with birds' nests, and the blue sea below was alive and lovely with scoter and eider and kittiwake and guillemot and razorbill peacefully fishing for herring.

'It truly is a promised land,' the boy said. 'You live in a beautiful place.'

'It certainly is beautiful,' the ram said, looking as if he wanted to say more but falling silent and sighing instead. 'But if you are walking alone here,' he continued after a while, 'you need to beware of all the cracks and crevasses in the rock.' It was a useful warning because the surface was broken up by many deep and wide fissures. The biggest of these was called Hell's Hole – a crevasse many fathoms deep and almost a fathom wide. 'If anyone were to fall down there, it would be the end of them,' the ram said, and the boy thought that it sounded as if there was some special meaning hidden in his words.

Then the ram carried the boy down to the beach for him to see at close quarters all the giants he had found so frightening the night before. They turned out to be no more than eroded pillars of rock, which the ram called 'raukar'. The boy was utterly fascinated by them, and he thought that if there ever had been trolls who were turned to stone, this was exactly how they would have looked.

Although it was beautiful down on the shore, the boy still preferred the roof of the rocky island. It was gruesome down on the shore because that was where the foxes had eaten their meals and there were dead sheep lying everywhere. Some of them were skeletons stripped bare, but there were also half-eaten bodies and others lying virtually untouched. It was heartbreaking to see that the wild beasts had attacked the sheep just for fun, just for the pleasure of hunting and savaging them.

The ram did not stop at the dead animals, he walked calmly past them. The boy, however, could not avoid seeing all the horrors.

They went back up to the top of the island and when they were there the ram stopped and said: 'If someone who really knew what they were doing could see the misery we are suffering, I don't think he would rest until those foxes had got what they deserve.'

'But foxes have to live, too, don't they?' the boy said.

'Yes,' said the ram, 'of course they have to live – as long as they don't savage more animals than they need in order to survive. But this lot are criminals.'

'The farmers who own the island could surely come over and help you, couldn't they?' the boy wondered.

'They have rowed over several times,' the ram said, 'but the foxes have always hidden in caves and crevasses so that the farmers have been unable to shoot them.'

'You surely don't imagine that a poor little fellow like me can deal with them when you and the farmers haven't been able to manage it?'

'Someone who is small and cunning can put many things right,' the ram said.

They talked no more about it and the boy went and sat with the wild geese, who were feeding up on the high pasture. Although he had not wanted to let the ram see it, the boy was very upset by the plight of the sheep and he would have liked to help them.

'I need to talk to Akka and Mårten Gander about this,' he thought. 'Perhaps they can advise me as to what's best to do.'

A little while later the white gander put Nils on his back and walked across the flat pasture towards Hell's Hole.

He walked carelessly across the open ground without appearing to give any thought to how big and white he was, and he walked quite openly without seeking cover behind tussocks and mounds. It was strange that he was not more careful since he seemed to have had a rough time in yesterday's storm – he was limping with his right leg and his left wing was hanging down and dragging as if broken.

In spite of all that he was behaving as though there was no danger, plucking a blade of grass here and another there, without bothering to look round in any direction. The boy was lying outstretched on the gander's back, looking up at the blue sky. By now he was so used to riding on the gander that he could either stand up or lie down on his back.

The boy and the gander were being so careless that inevitably they failed to notice the three foxes coming out onto the pasture. At first, knowing it was almost impossible to approach a goose in the open, the foxes did not bother to chase the gander. But having nothing else to do, they eventually went down into one of the long fissures and tried to creep up on him. They went about this so cautiously that the gander did not see any sign of them.

They succeeded in getting close to him before the gander made any attempt to take off. He opened his wings but failed to get off the ground. The foxes assumed from this that he was unable to fly and they hurried forward with greater interest. No longer staying hidden in the crevasse, they crossed the open ground, taking cover as best they could behind tussocks and rocky outcrops. They were getting closer and closer to the gander without him even seeming to realise he was being hunted. At last they were close enough to dig in their claws for the final bound and all three of them at once hurled themselves in a great leap at the gander.

At the very last moment the gander must have noticed something and jumped aside so that the foxes missed him. Not that this meant much, since the gander only had a few yards advantage and he was limping. The poor bird ran on anyway, as fast as he was able.

The boy was sitting backwards on the gander's back, shouting and screaming at the foxes: 'You've got so fat from eating mutton that you can't even catch up with a goose.' He goaded them so much that they were reduced to a blind fury with only one thought in mind – to charge forward.

The white gander was running straight for the huge crevasse and when he reached it he gave a quick flap of his wings and crossed it. At that point the foxes were right on his heels.

On the other side of Hell's Hole the gander continued at the same speed. He had only run a few yards, however, when Nils tapped him on the neck and said: 'You can stop now, Mårten Gander.'

And at that moment they heard wild howls and scraping claws and the thud of falling bodies. But there was no sign of the foxes any longer.

The following morning the lighthouse keeper on Stora Karlsö found a piece of bark stuck under his front door. On it, scratched in angular slanting letters, were the words: 'The foxes on Lilla Karlsö have fallen into Hell's Hole. Take care of them!'

And that is just what the lighthouse keeper did!

XIV

TWO TOWNS

THE TOWN AT THE BOTTOM OF THE SEA   Saturday, 9 April

It was a calm and clear night. The wild geese had not bothered to seek shelter in any of the caves but were asleep up on the roof of the island and the boy was asleep beside the geese on the short dry grass.

The moonlight was very bright that night, so bright that Nils had trouble getting to sleep. He lay thinking about how long he had been away from home and he worked out that it was three weeks now since he had set out on this journey. He also remembered that tonight was Easter Eve.

'Tonight's the night all the witches return from Blåkulla,' he thought, laughing to himself.* Because although he was a little afraid of water-sprites and elves, he did not believe at all in witches.

And if there had been any witches out that night, he would certainly have seen them. The sky was so bright and clear that he would have noticed even the smallest black dot moving across it.

As he lay there thinking these thoughts, he found himself gazing up at a beautiful sight. The disk of the moon was full and round and quite high in the sky and a large bird was flying in front of it. It did not fly past the moon, it flew in such a way that it looked as though it had flown out of the moon. The bird looked black against the bright background and its wings stretched across the full moon from rim to rim. It was flying along so smoothly in the same direction as the moon that the boy thought it must have been drawn on the surface of the moon. Its body was small, its neck long and slim, and its legs hung down long and thin. It could only be a stork.

A few moments later Herr Ermenrich the stork landed beside Nils, bent over him and poked him with his beak to wake him up.

Nils sat up at once. 'I'm not asleep, Herr Ermenrich. What brings you out in the middle of the night? And how are things at Glimmingehus? Do you want to speak to Mother Akka?'

'It's too light to sleep tonight,' Herr Ermenrich answered, 'so I decided to fly over to Karlsö and call on my friend Thummitot. A seagull told me you were here tonight. And I haven't moved over to Glimmingehus yet, I'm still living in Pomerania.'

The boy was overjoyed that Herr Ermenrich had come to visit him. They talked about everything possible, as old friends do, and finally the stork asked whether he would like to come and ride around for a while since it was such a lovely night.

Nils was more than happy to do so as long as the stork would ensure that he was back with the geese before dawn. The stork gave his promise and so they set off.

Once again Herr Ermenrich flew straight towards the moon. They flew higher and higher and the sea sank far below them, but the flight was so extraordinarily light that it almost felt as if they were lying motionless in the air.

Nils thought the flight was over far too soon when Herr Ermenrich began to lose height ready to land.

They landed on a deserted beach covered with fine, even-grained sand. A long line of sand-dunes with lyme-grass growing on top of them ran along the coast and although they were not very high they prevented the boy seeing anything of the interior beyond them.

Herr Ermenrich stood on a sand-dune, tucked up one leg and bent his neck back to put his head under his wing. 'You can wander around on the beach a bit while I have a rest,' he said to Thummitot. 'But don't go any farther than you can find your way back to me!'

The first thing the boy intended to do was to climb up one of the dunes to see what it looked like inland, but he had taken no more than a few steps when the toe of his clog struck something hard. He bent down and saw that there was a small copper coin lying on the sand. It was so eaten away by verdigris that it was almost transparent and, in fact, it was in such a bad condition that he simply kicked it away without bothering to pick it up.

When he stood upright again he was completely astonished for, just two steps in front of him, there was a high dark wall with a big turreted gateway in it.

When he had bent down a moment before it had been the sea that lay before him bright and glittering, but now it was hidden by a long wall with battlements and towers. And right in front of him, where there had been nothing but some piles of seaweed, there stood a big open gate.

The boy understood well enough that this was all some kind of illusion but he did not think it was anything to be frightened of. It had nothing to do with dangerous trolls and all the other evils he was always afraid of meeting at night. Both the wall and the gate were built so magnificently that he wanted to see what could lie behind them. 'I just have to find out what's there!' he thought and proceeded through the gate.

Guards were sitting in the deep archway playing dice and they were dressed in brightly coloured clothes with puffed sleeves. They had their long-shafted halberds beside them but, interested only in their game, they paid no attention to the boy, who quickly slipped past them.

Once inside he came to an open area paved with large smooth stones, and magnificent tall houses stood on every side with long narrow streets running between them.

The space inside the gate was swarming with people. The men were wearing long capes edged with fur, beneath which their clothes were made of silk. They were also wearing plumed berets at a jaunty angle on their heads and they had magnificent chains hanging on their chests. They were all so splendidly dressed that they could easily have been kings.

The women wore tall conical headdresses, long skirts and tight-fitting sleeves. They, too, were wonderfully dressed but their splendour came nowhere near that of the men.

All in all it was just like the book of old fairy tales his mother had sometimes taken out of her chest and shown him. Nils could not believe his eyes.

What was even more remarkable than the men and women was the town itself. Every house was built with its gable-end turned to the street and these gables were decorated so expertly that it looked as if they were competing with each other to see which could put on the most beautiful show.

When you see so many new things all at the same time, it is impossible to retain them all in your memory. Nevertheless the boy could remember later that he had seen stepped gables with pictures of Christ and his apostles on the different steps, gables where the images stood in niche after niche all the way up the wall, gables that were inlaid with pieces of glass of many different colours, gables that were striped or checked with black and white marble.

For a while he stood there in wonderment, but then he was seized by a terrible sense of urgency. 'My eyes have never seen anything like this before, and they will never see anything like it again,' he said to himself. And he began running around the town, up and down the streets.

The streets were narrow and constricted but they were not empty and gloomy as they were in the towns he knew. There were people everywhere. Old women sat in the doorways spinning, using just the distaff, without a spinning wheel. The shops were open to the street like market stalls. All the craftsmen worked outdoors: in one place fish-oil was being boiled, in another hides were being tanned, and in a third there was a long ropewalk.

Given enough time Nils could have learnt how to manufacture all kinds of things. He saw how the armourers hammered out thin breastplates, how the goldsmiths mounted precious stones in rings and armbands, how turners used their lathes, how shoemakers soled soft red shoes, how the gold-wire drawers twisted their gold thread and how the weavers wove silk and gold into their work.

But the boy had no time to stand and stare. He rushed on in order to see as much as possible before it all disappeared again.

The high wall ran around the whole town, enclosing it as a fence encloses a field. The wall with its battlements and towers could be seen at the end of every street and up on the wall men-at-arms in shining armour and helmets were on patrol.

When he had run right across the town, Nils came to another gate in the wall, beyond which lay the harbour and the sea. He saw old-fashioned ships with benches for oarsmen amidships and high structures at the prow and stern. Some were loading cargo, others were dropping anchor. Porters and merchants were rushing hither and thither and the whole scene was one of hustle and bustle.

But he did not allow himself time to linger even here. He hurried back into the town and came to the Great Square, where he saw the cathedral with its three high towers and deep arched doorways decorated with images. The stonemasons had carved the walls so much that there was scarcely a stone left without ornamentation. And through the open door he caught a glimpse of the splendour inside – gilded crosses, altars inlaid with gold and priests in golden vestments. Right opposite the cathedral stood a building with battlements on its roof and a single slim tower that reached for the heavens. It was presumably the Town Hall, and around the whole square between the cathedral and the Town Hall ran a series of those beautiful gable-ends with their endless variety of decorations.

By now the boy was hot and tired from all his running. Believing that he had already seen the most remarkable things, he began to walk more slowly. The street he turned into next was obviously where the citizens bought their magnificent clothes. Crowds of people were standing in front of small shops, on the counters of which the merchants were laying out floral-patterned brocade, heavy gold cloth, shimmering velvet, light gauze cloths and lace as fine as spiders' webs.

Earlier, when he had been running around so quickly, no one had paid any attention to him. People had probably assumed he was just a little grey rat scuttling past. But now that he was walking quite slowly, one of the merchants caught sight of him and beckoned him over.

At first Nils was nervous and wanted to hurry away, but the merchant just beckoned and smiled and spread out a piece of gorgeous damask on the counter as if to tempt him.

The boy shook his head. 'I'll never be rich enough to afford a yard of that material,' he thought.

But now everyone in every shop along the street had seen him and wherever he looked there were shopkeepers beckoning him to come over. They were deserting their rich customers and thinking only of him. He saw them hurrying back into the deepest recesses of their shops to fetch the very best wares they had to offer and their hands trembled with haste and eagerness as they set things out on the counter.

When the boy just carried on walking past, one of the merchants leapt over his counter, ran and caught him up and laid before him silver-threaded cloth and tapestries woven in the brightest colours. Nils could only laugh – surely the shopkeeper must realise that a poor fellow like him could not buy things of that kind? He stopped and held out his empty hands to make them understand that he owned nothing at all and they should leave him in peace.

But the merchant simply held up one finger, nodded and pushed the whole pile of wonderful things towards Nils.

'Can he really mean that he'll sell all of this for one gold piece?' the boy wondered.

Then the merchant took out one small worn and damaged coin, so small you could hardly see it, and showed it to him. And so eager was he to make a sale that he added a pair of big heavy silver goblets to the pile.

Nils began to dig in his pockets. He knew that he really did not have a single penny but he could not stop himself feeling for one.

All the other merchants stood there watching to see whether the sale would come off, and when they saw the boy start to dig around in his pockets, they too leapt over their counters, picked up handfuls of gold and silver jewellery and offered them to him. And all of them showed him that the only payment they were asking for was just one small coin.

The boy turned his waistcoat and trouser pockets inside out so that they could see that he did not have as much as a penny. Then their eyes filled with tears, all of these grand merchants, all of them so much richer than him. They all looked so distressed that Nils was moved and wondered what he could do to help them. And his thoughts went back to that discoloured coin he had seen on the beach earlier.

He set off running along the street and fortune was on his side because he came to the same gate as he had found at the start. He charged through the gate and began to look for the little verdigris-coated copper coin which had been lying on the beach.

He found it without too much trouble, but when he picked it up and was about to hurry back into the town with it, all he could see in front of him was the sea. Nothing else was to be seen: no town wall, no gate, no men-at-arms, no streets, no houses – just the sea.

His eyes filled with tears – he could not help it. He had forgotten that he had believed at first that this was all an illusion: all he could think of was how beautiful everything had been. He was overwhelmed by deep sorrow that the town had disappeared.

Just then Herr Ermenrich woke up and came over to him. Nils did not hear him coming and the stork had to poke him with his beak to get his attention. 'I believe you are standing here sleeping, just as I was,' Herr Ermenrich said.

'Oh, Herr Ermenrich!' the boy said. 'What was that town that I saw here a moment ago?'

'Did you see a town? As I said, you must have been asleep and dreaming,' the stork said.

'No, I haven't been dreaming,' Nils said, and he told the

stork everything he had seen and done.

'Well, Thummitot, for my part I believe you fell asleep on the beach and dreamt all this,' said Herr Ermenrich. 'But I won't hide the fact that Bataki the raven, who is the most learned of all birds, told me that long, long ago there used to be a town called Vineta on the shore here. It was so wealthy and happy that there has never been a more magnificent town, but unfortunately the people who lived there fell into arrogance and a love of display. As a punishment for that, according to Bataki, the town of Vineta was inundated by a great flood and sank below the waves. But its inhabitants cannot die and the town cannot be destroyed. And one night every hundred years the town rises from the sea in all its splendour and remains on the surface for exactly one hour.'*

'That must be true,' Nils said, 'for that is what I have seen.'

'When that hour has passed, it sinks back into the sea unless one of the merchants of Vineta has managed to sell something to a living creature. Thummitot, if you had possessed even the smallest coin to pay the merchant, Vineta would have remained on the shore and its people would have been permitted to live and die like ordinary folk.'

'Now I understand why you came and fetched me in the middle of the night, Herr Ermenrich,' the boy said. 'It was because you believed that I could save that ancient town. I am so sorry that things did not work out as you wanted them to.'

He put his hands over his eyes and wept, and it was not easy to say which of the two of them, Nils or Herr Ermenrich, looked more sorrowful.

THE LIVING TOWN　　　　　　　　　　　Monday, 11 April
In the afternoon of Easter Monday Thummitot and the wild geese were once again on the wing and flying over Gotland.

The great island lay flat and smooth beneath them and, just as in Skåne, the ground was checkered and there were many churches and farms. There were some differences, however, in that the fields here were interspersed with wooded meadows and the farms were not built in a square around a yard. Nor were there any great estates with turreted old castles and extensive parklands.

The wild geese had taken the Gotland route for the sake of Thummitot. For the last two days he had been quite unlike his usual self and had not said a single cheerful word. He could not get that town out of his mind. It had been revealed to him in such a remarkable way and he had never seen anything so splendid and beautiful. He could not reconcile himself to the fact that he had failed to save it. He was not usually so soft-hearted, but now he was filled with grief for those beautiful buildings and all the elegant people.

Both Akka and the gander had tried to convince him that it had all been a dream or an illusion, but the boy would have none of it. He was so utterly certain that he had seen what he had seen that no one could shake his conviction. He went around in such a state of despondency that his companions were worried about him.

Just when the boy was at his most depressed, old Kaksi returned to the flock. She had been driven towards Gotland and had flown across the whole island before some crows informed her that her travelling companions were on Lilla Karlsö. As soon as Kaksi heard that Thummitot was in low spirits, she said quickly:

'If Thummitot is grieving about an ancient town, we can soon console him. Follow me and I'll take you to a place I saw yesterday. He won't stay miserable for long.'

So the geese had said goodbye to the sheep and were now on their way to the place Kaksi wanted to show Thummitot. And however upset he was, he could not help looking down as usual at the countryside he was travelling over.

He thought the whole island looked as if it must have started as a steep, high rock like Karlsö, although much bigger, of course. But then it had somehow been flattened. Someone had taken an enormous rolling-pin and rolled it out as if it were a piece of dough. Not that it had become completely flat and smooth everywhere: it certainly had not, and as they were flying along the coast he saw high limestone walls with caves and rock pillars in several places, but in most places these things had been levelled out and the shore ran undramatically down to the sea.

They had a pleasant and peaceful holiday afternoon on Gotland. It was warm spring weather, the buds on the trees were swelling, the meadows were bedecked with spring flowers, long thin catkins hung and swayed on the poplar trees, and the gooseberry bushes were all green in the small gardens that were attached to every cottage.

The spring warmth and the budding plants had tempted people outdoors and wherever a few of them were gathered together they were playing. It was not only the children, the adults were playing too. They were hurling stones at targets and throwing balls so high into the air that they almost reached the geese. It was such a jolly sight to see grown-ups playing and the boy would have been really happy if only he had been able to forget how vexed he was at not being able to save the old town.

But in spite of everything, he had to admit that this was a pretty journey. The air was filled with sounds and singing and down below little children were dancing round dances. The Salvation Army was out and he could see a large group of people in red and black sitting on a wooded knoll playing their guitars and brass instruments. A great crowd of people were walking along a road: they were Good Templars of the temperance movement, who had been out on an excursion. Nils could recognise them by the great gold-embroidered banners that waved above their heads. And they sang song after song for as long as they were within earshot.

Ever after, whenever Nils thought of Gotland, he thought of games and songs.

For a long time he had been sitting looking straight down, but now he happened to lift his eyes and it is impossible to describe his surprise. He had not noticed that the geese had left the interior of the island and were flying westwards towards the coast. The wide blue sea lay in front of him, but it was not the sea that was so remarkable, it was a town situated on the shore.

The boy was approaching it from the east and the sun had started to sink in the west. As he approached the town, all of its walls and towers and high-gabled houses and churches stood out black against the light evening sky. Because of this, he could not really see what they were like and for a few moments he thought that this town was as wonderful as the one he had seen on Easter Eve.

When they came right up to the town, however, he saw that it was both like and unlike the town from the bottom of the sea. It was the same kind of difference as between seeing a man dressed in purple splendour and jewels one day and seeing the same man reduced to wearing rags the next day.

But surely this town must once have been like the one he had been thinking about? This town, too, was surrounded by a wall with towers and gates, but in this town, which the sea had not swallowed, the towers were roofless, hollow and empty, the gateways lacked their gates and the guards and men-at-arms were gone. All the gleaming splendour had disappeared and what was left was just a bare carcass of grey stone.

As they flew in close above the town, Nils saw that most of it consisted of low little houses, although here and there tall gabled houses and churches remained from the old days. The walls of their gable ends were whitewashed and carried no decorations at all but, having seen the sunken town so recently, he was sure that these must once have been decorated, some of them with statues and others with black and white marble. And the old churches were in the same state as the towers – most were roofless and their interiors were bare. The windows had no glass, grass grew on the floors and ivy climbed the walls. But now Nils knew how they once had looked, knew that they had been covered with statuary and paintings, knew that the sanctuaries had contained decorated altars and golden crosses and that the priests in them had been resplendent in golden vestments.

The boy could also see the narrow streets, almost empty

today because of the holiday afternoon. But now he knew what a stream of magnificently dressed people had once filled these streets, and he knew what great workshops there had been, full of workmen of every kind.

But what Nils Holgersson did not see was that this town was still beautiful and remarkable. He did not see the sweet cottages with their black walls, white-painted corners and red pelargoniums behind windows in which the glass gleamed; nor did he see the lovely gardens and avenues, nor the beauty of the overgrown ruins. His eyes were so blinded by the splendour of the past that he failed to see anything good about the present.

The wild geese passed back and forth across the town several times so that Thummitot could get a really good view of everything. Finally they descended and landed on the grassy floor of a ruined church in order to spend the night there.

When they had settled down to sleep, Thummitot remained awake staring up at the pale-red of the evening sky through the ruined vault of the roof. After sitting there for a while he decided he would not worry any more that he had been unable to save the sunken town.

Having seen this town, he would not want to have saved the other. If the town he had seen had not sunk back to the bottom of the sea, it would probably have fallen into the same kind of decay as this town. It would have been unable to resist time and corruption and soon been left with roofless churches and houses without decoration and empty streets. It was better, then, for it to retain all its splendour even though it was hidden.

'Best that things happened as they happened,' he thought. 'If I had the power to save that town now I don't think I'd use it.' After which he no longer grieved about the matter.

No doubt many young people think the same way. But those who are old and whom life has taught to be satisfied with little are happier with the Visby that exists than with a magnificent Vineta at the bottom of the sea.

XV

THE LEGEND OF SMÅLAND

Tuesday, 12 April

The wild geese had a good journey across the sea and landed in the district of Tjust in northern Småland. It was the kind of place that had found it impossible to decide whether it wanted to be land or sea. Inlets and firths cut into the land, dividing it into islands and peninsulas, headlands and isthmuses. The sea was so dominant that only hills and ridges could rise above it, any lower ground being hidden below the surface of the water.

It was evening when the geese flew in from the sea and the landscape of small hills between shining firths looked beautiful. Here and there on the islands the boy could see cabins and cottages, and the farther inland they flew, the bigger and better the houses became until eventually they became big white manor houses. The shores were mostly fringed with trees, behind which lay a patchwork of fields and then, up on the small hills, the trees took over again. He could not help thinking of Blekinge. This, too, was a place where the land and the sea met each other prettily and peacefully, as if desiring to show only their best and most beautiful sides.

The wild geese landed on a treeless island far up the Gåsfjärd Firth. The moment they looked at the shores of the firth they could see that spring had made great progress during the time they had been out on the islands in the Baltic. The fine trees were still not in leaf but the ground beneath them was a motley of wood anemone, yellow star-of-Bethlehem and hepatica.

When they saw the carpet of flowers the geese were afraid

they had lingered too long in the southern part of the country. Akka immediately said that there was no time for them to visit any of their usual stopping places in Småland and they would have to fly north over Östergötland the very next morning.

So the boy would not see anything of Småland, and that grieved him. There was no other province that he had heard so much about and he wanted to see it with his own eyes.

He had spent the summer before working as a goose-boy for a farmer near Jordberga and almost every day he had met two poor Småland children, who were also tending geese. He had found the two children really irritating because they talked about Småland all the time.

It was perhaps unfair to say that the goose-girl Åsa annoyed him – she was much too wise for that. But her brother, Little Mats, that boy really knew how to be annoying!

'You've heard what happened when Småland and Skåne were created, haven't you, Nils Goose-boy?' he would ask. And when Nils answered no, he would immediately start telling the old story.

'It was at the time when Our Lord was creating the world. While he was working away as hard as he could along came St Peter, who stopped and watched and asked whether it was difficult work. "It's not actually that easy," Our Lord answered. St Peter stood there for a while and when he saw how easy it seemed to be to lay out one country after the other, he wanted to have a try himself. "Perhaps it's time you took a rest," St Peter said, "and I could look after your work for a while." Our Lord was reluctant: "I'm not sure that you really have enough of the tricks of the trade for me to trust you to take over where I leave off." That made St Peter angry and he said he thought he was capable of creating places every bit as good as Our Lord's.

'Now Our Lord just happened to be creating Småland at that point. It wasn't even half finished but it already looked as if it was going to be an amazingly fertile and beautiful province. Our Lord found it hard to refuse St Peter – apart from which, he no doubt thought that no one could ruin something that had been given such a good start. So he said: "If you like, we can put it to the test and see which of us best understands this kind of work. Since you are a beginner, you can continue with what I've already started and I'll create a new province." Peter immediately agreed and so each of them set about his work.

'Our Lord moved a little south and there he began creating Skåne. It did not take him long and then he asked whether St Peter had finished and would like to come and take a look at his work. "I had mine finished ages ago," St Peter said, and you could hear from his voice how pleased he was with what he had achieved.

'When St Peter saw Skåne he had to admit that there was nothing but good to be said about the province. It was fertile land with wide flat areas, easy to cultivate and hardly any sign of hills. It was obvious that Our Lord had given much thought to making it a pleasant place for people to live. "Yes, that is certainly a good province," St Peter said, "but I think mine is better." "Let's go and take a look at it, then," said Our Lord.

'The north and the east of the province had already been finished when St Peter took over the work, but he had created the southern, western and inland parts on his own. When Our Lord arrived where St Peter had been working he was so horrified that he stopped short and said: "What on earth have you done with this province, St Peter?"

'St Peter stood there looking round in surprise. His idea had been that it would be best to create a warm district, so he had dragged together an enormous heap of rocks and stones and built them up as high as possible in order to get closer to the sun and thus gain more of its heat. He had spread a thin layer of topsoil on top of these stones and thought that would do the trick.

'But while he had been away looking at Skåne there had been a couple of heavy showers of rain and that was all it took to show how little his work was worth. By the time Our Lord came to look at it all the topsoil had been washed away and bare rock was showing through everywhere. At best, there was clay and heavy gravel lying on top of the rocky slabs, but it all looked of such poor quality that it was difficult to see how anything apart from spruce and juniper and moss and heather was ever going to grow there. But one thing there was plenty of was water. All the cracks and crevices in the underlying rock were filled with it and there were lakes and rivers and streams everywhere – not to mention the bogs and mosses that covered large areas. And the most annoying thing of all was that while some parts had too much water, other parts were so short of it that there were great tracts of dry heath from which clouds of sand and soil whirled into the air at the slightest hint of a breeze.

'"What on earth were you thinking of when you created a province like this?" said Our Lord and St Peter made his excuses and told him how he had wanted to build the land up so high that it would receive plenty of warmth from the sun. "But that also means that it will get plenty of cold at night," Our Lord said, "since that also comes from the sky. I'm very much afraid that the little that can grow here will be killed off by frost anyway."

'That was something St Peter had not thought about, of course.

'"I'm afraid this is going to be a poor and frost-ridden district, no question about it," Our Lord said.'

When Little Mats reached this point in his story, Åsa the goose-girl interrupted him and said: 'I can't bear it when you say how miserable everything is in Småland, Little Mats. You are forgetting all the good land there is. Just think of the Möre district over by the Sound of Kalmar – I doubt if you will find better land anywhere for growing corn. There is field after field there, just as there is here in Skåne, and the soil is so fertile I don't know anything that won't grow there.'

'I can't help it,' Mats said. 'I'm just telling it the way others have told it before me.'

'And I've heard people say,' Åsa said, 'that you won't find anywhere more beautiful than the coast around Tjust. Think of all the bays and islands and manor houses and woods there.'

'Yes, that's certainly true enough,' Little Mats conceded.

'And don't you remember,' Åsa continued, 'how our teacher told us that there is nowhere in Sweden so pretty and busy as the part of Småland just south of Lake Vättern? Think of the beautiful lake and the yellow hills along its shores, think of Gränna and Jönköping with its match factory, think of Munksjö and think of Huskvarna and all the big workshops there.'

'Yes, that's certainly true,' Mats repeated.

'And remember Visingsö, Little Mats, with its ruins and oak-woods and legends! Think of the valley through which the Emån flows, with all its villages, its mills and pulp mills and saws and timber-yards.'

'Yes, that's all true,' Mats agreed, looking more than a little troubled. And then suddenly he looked up. 'Now we are being really stupid,' he said. 'All those places are in Our Lord's part of Småland, the part that was finished before St Peter took over the work. And, of course, it's only to be expected that everything would be fine and beautiful there. But in St Peter's part of Småland, everything is just as it says in the story. No wonder Our Lord was sad when he saw it.'

Mats took up the tale again. 'St Peter did not lose heart, however, and he tried to comfort Our Lord. "Don't take it too hard," he said. "Wait until I've managed to create the kind of people who can cultivate bogs and clear fields on stony slopes."

'That is the point at which Our Lord lost patience and said: "No! You go down to Skåne, which I created as a fertile and easily cared-for province, and create Skåne people, but I will create the Smålanders myself." And so Our Lord created the Smålanders and he made them quick-witted and contented and happy and hard-working and enterprising and so clever that they would be able to make a living out of their poor land.'

Little Mats left it at that and everything would have been fine if Nils Holgersson had been prepared to do the same, but he simply could not refrain from asking how St Peter had got on when creating the people of Skåne.

'Well, what do you think?' Mats said with such a scornful look on his face that Nils Holgersson rushed at him to give him a thrashing. Mats was just a tiny lad, however, and Åsa the goose-girl, who was a year older, immediately rushed to his assistance. Good-natured as she was, she behaved like a lion if anyone dared touch her brother. And since Nils Holgersson did not want to fight a girl, he turned his back on them and refused to have any more to do with the Småland children for the rest of the day.

XVI

THE CROWS

THE EARTHENWARE POT

There is a district called Sunnerbo in the south-western corner of Småland. The landscape there is fairly flat and smooth and a visitor seeing it in the snow of winter might assume that, as usual in flat country, the snow is covering fields lying fallow, green rye-fields and fields of cut clover. But when the snow finally melts in Sunnerbo at the beginning of April, what emerges turns out to be dry sandy heath, slabs of bare rock and great boggy mosses. There are occasional cultivated fields here and there, but they are so insignificant as to be hardly noticeable; there are some small grey or red farm cottages, too, frequently hidden away in copses of birch trees almost as if they were afraid to show themselves.

Where Sunnerbo meets the border of the province of Halland there is a sandy heath so extensive that a traveller standing on one side of it cannot see across to the opposite side. Nothing but heather grows on the heath, nor would it be an easy task to get other plants to thrive there. First of all, it would be necessary to eradicate the heather because, although heather only has a stunted little stem, small stunted branches and dry stunted foliage, it imagines that it is a tree. The result is that it behaves as real trees do – it spreads over wide areas, sticks loyally together and causes any other plants that encroach on its domain to die out.

The only part of the heath on which heather is not completely dominant is a low stony ridge that cuts right across the middle of it. On this ridge there is juniper, rowan and some beautiful big birch trees. At the time Nils Holgersson was travelling with the geese there was also a small cottage there with a little bit of cleared ground, but the people who had once lived there had moved away for some reason or other. So the little cottage was empty and the field uncultivated.

When the people moved out of the cottage they shut the damper in the chimney, shut the window catches and locked the door. But they had forgotten that one of the window panes was broken and a rag had been stuffed in it to block the hole. The rains of a couple of summers had rotted and shrunk the rag and eventually a crow had managed to push it out.

Since it was home to a large population of crows, this ridge up on the heath was by no means as deserted as might be imagined. The crows obviously did not live there all year round. In the winter they moved abroad and during the autumn they moved from one cornfield to another across the whole of Götaland pecking up the grain.* In the summer they spread out across the farms in the Sunnerbo area and lived on eggs, berries and young birds; when it was spring, however, and time to nest and lay their eggs, they moved back to the heath.

The crow who had pushed the rag out of the window was a cock-bird by the name of Garm Whitefeather, but he was never called anything other than Fumble or Bumble or, indeed, Fumble-Bumble, because he always behaved so stupidly and clumsily that it was impossible not to make fun of him. Fumble-Bumble was bigger and stronger than any of the other crows but that was of no help to him – he was and he remained a laughing-stock. The fact that he came from a good family was of no help either; in fact, if everything had gone as it should have done, he ought really to have been the leader of the whole flock since that distinction had belonged to the eldest of the Whitefeathers since time immemorial. But the power had passed from his family long before Fumble-Bumble was born and was now held by a savage and cruel crow called Windgust.

This transfer of power was the result of the crows on Crow Ridge wanting to change their way of life. There may well be many people who believe that all crows live in the same manner, but that is quite incorrect. There are whole tribes of crows which lead decent lives – which is to say, they only eat seeds, worms, maggots and animals that are already dead. But there are others who live like pirates, attacking leverets and chicks and robbing every nest they catch sight of.

The old Whitefeather clan had been strict and moderate and as long as they had been leaders of the flock they had compelled the crows to behave in a way that gave the other birds no cause to speak ill of them. But the crows were numerous and there was a good deal of poverty among them. They were not in the long term prepared to adhere to such a strict code of conduct and eventually they rebelled against the Whitefeathers and gave the power instead to Windgust, who was the worst nest-robber and thief imaginable – though his wife Windpuff may well have been even worse. Under their rule the crows had started living in a way that made them more feared even than goshawks and eagle owls.

Fumble-Bumble, of course, had no influence at all in the flock. They were all agreed that he had not inherited any of the blood of his forefathers and that he was in no way fit to be the leader. Indeed, his name would never have been mentioned had he not continually been committing new blunders. Some of the really wise birds pointed out that it was probably lucky for Fumble-Bumble that he was such a pathetic incompetent, otherwise Windgust and Windpuff would hardly have allowed him, as a member of the old ruling family, to remain with the flock.

As it was, however, they were quite friendly towards him and were happy to take him along on their hunting trips: it gave everyone a chance to see how much bolder and more skilful they were than him.

None of the other crows knew that Fumble-Bumble had pecked the rag out of the window and they would have been very surprised to hear that he had done so. They would never have believed him daring enough to approach a human dwelling and he was very careful to say nothing about it – and he had his own good reasons not to. Gust and Puff might treat him well during the day when the other crows were present but one dark night, when all the others were roosting, he had been attacked by two crows and almost murdered. Every evening since then, as soon as darkness fell, he would leave his usual sleeping perch and move into the empty cottage.

One afternoon after the crows had put their nests in order on Crow Ridge, they happened to make a remarkable discovery. Windgust, Fumble-Bumble and a couple of others had flown down into a hollow at one corner of the heath. The hollow was actually just a gravel pit but the crows were not satisfied with such a simple explanation and they flew down into it time after time, turning over every grain of sand trying to work out why human beings had dug the pit. While the crows were messing about there, a great pile of gravel fell down on one side of the pit. They hurried to the spot and among the fallen debris of stones and grass they discovered a good-sized earthenware pot sealed with a wooden lid. Naturally enough, they wanted to find out if there was anything in it and they tried to peck holes in the pot or to force open the lid. Neither method was successful.

They were standing there staring at the pot and at a loss as to what to do when they heard someone say: 'Hello there, crows, do you want me to come down and help you?' They quickly looked up and saw a fox sitting on the edge of the pit staring down at them. He was one of the most handsome foxes they had ever seen, both as to his colour and his build. He only had one fault, which was that he had one ear missing.

'If you are offering to do us a favour, we aren't going to refuse,' said Windgust, and he and the other crows flew up out of the hollow. The fox jumped down and began biting at the pot and pulling at the lid but he could not open it either.

'Can you work out what's in it?' Windgust said. The fox rolled the pot backwards and forwards and listened carefully.

'It can't be anything other than silver coins,' the fox said.

This was more than the crows had dared expect. 'Do you really think it's silver?' they asked, their eyes almost popping out of their heads with greed; for strange as it may sound, there is nothing in the world that crows love more than silver coins.

'Listen to how they rattle!' the fox said as he rolled the pot around once more. 'But I don't know how we are going to get at them.'

'No, it certainly looks to be impossible,' the crows said, while the fox stood there scratching his head with his left leg and thinking. With the crows' help this was perhaps his chance of getting the better of that little wretch who was always managing to escape him.

'I'm sure I know the very person to open that pot for you,' the fox said.

'Tell us who, tell us who!' the crows cried and became so eager that they fluttered back down into the pit.

'I will, but only if you promise to agree to my conditions,' the fox said.

The fox then told the crows about Thummitot and told them that he would certainly be able to open the pot if they could find a way of bringing him to the heath. But as a reward for giving them this advice the fox demanded that they hand Thummitot over to him as soon as he had opened the pot of silver coins. Having no reason to show any mercy to Thummitot, the crows immediately agreed to his condition.

It was easy for them to come to this agreement but it was more difficult to find out where Thummitot and the wild geese actually were. Windgust himself set off accompanied by fifty crows and said he would soon be back, but one day after another passed and the crows on Crow Ridge saw no sign of him.

KIDNAPPED BY CROWS   Wednesday, 13 April

The wild geese were up at first light in order to have time for a bite to eat before setting off for Östergötland. The island they had slept on in the firth was small and bare but the water around it had enough plants for them to eat their fill. It was worse for the boy, however, since he could not find anything edible.

He was standing there hungry and cold in the morning air looking round this way and that when he caught sight of a couple of squirrels playing on a tree-covered headland right opposite the rocky island. He wondered whether the squirrels still had any of their winter stores left and he asked the gander to take him over to the headland so that he could beg a few hazel-nuts from them.

The big white gander swam across the water carrying the boy but unfortunately the squirrels were having so much fun chasing each other from tree to tree that they could not be bothered to listen to the boy. In fact, they went deeper and deeper into the thicket and the boy hurried after them, soon losing sight of the white gander, who remained on the beach.

The boy was wading his way through some patches of wood-anemones that came up to his chin when he felt someone grab him from behind and try to lift him up. When he turned round he saw that a crow had caught hold of the neckband of his shirt. He tried to jerk himself free but before he succeeded another crow hurried forward, grabbed hold of him by one of his stockings and tripped him up.

If Nils had immediately shouted for help there is no doubt that the gander would have been able to rescue him but the boy obviously thought that he could deal with a couple of crows on his own. He kicked and punched but the crows would not let go and they managed to take off carrying him. In fact, they were so careless that his head struck a branch and the blow was so hard that he was knocked unconscious and everything went black.

He slowly regained his senses and when he opened his eyes again he found himself high above the ground, although at first he neither knew where he was nor what he was seeing. When he looked down he thought he saw an enormous woollen carpet spread out beneath him. It was woven in big irregular patterns of greens and browns. The carpet was thick and splendid but Nils thought it was a pity it was in such bad condition. It was really quite ragged, with long tears running across it and, in some places even, quite large patches torn away. The most remarkable thing of all, however, was that it appeared to have been spread over a mirror and the glass sparkled and gleamed through wherever there were holes and rips.

What the boy noticed next was that as the sun rose in the sky the glass in the mirror immediately began to shine red and gold through the holes and tears in the carpet. It looked wonderful and the boy was entranced by the changing colours although he did not really understand what it was he was seeing. But now the crows began to descend and he realised at once that the great carpet beneath him was the earth, which was all cloaked in bare brown deciduous trees and green conifers, while the holes and the tears were gleaming inlets and small lakes.

He remembered thinking that the landscape of Skåne looked like a piece of checked cloth when he first saw it from the air. What sort of countryside could this be, given that it looked like a torn carpet?

He began asking himself all sorts of questions. Why was he not sitting on the gander's back? Why was there a big flock of crows flying around him? Why was he being pushed and pulled around so much that he felt he was coming to pieces?

All at once it all became clear to him. He had been abducted by a couple of crows. The white gander would still be waiting on the shore and the wild geese would be travelling on to Östergötland today. He, however, was being taken southwest – he knew that because the disc of the sun was behind him. And the great forest carpet below him must surely be Småland?

'What's going to happen to the white gander now that I can no longer look after him?' the boy thought and began shouting at the crows to take him back to the wild geese at once. He was not in the least concerned on his own account since he believed that it was pure mischievousness that had led the crows to carry him off.

The crows, however, paid no attention at all to his

protestations and flew on as fast as they could. After a while one of them clapped his wings, giving the signal that means 'Danger! Watch out!', at which they all dived down among the spruce trees and pushed their way through the twiggy branches right down to ground level. There they put the boy under a thick spruce tree, where he was so well hidden that not even a falcon could have spotted him.

Fifty crows then took up position around him, all on guard and all with their beaks pointing at him. 'Now perhaps you'll be good enough to tell me what you mean by kidnapping me,' the boy said. He had hardly finished before a big crow snarled at him: 'Just you keep quiet! Otherwise I'll peck your eyes out!'

It was obvious the crow meant what she said and the boy had no choice but to obey. So he sat there staring at the crows while the crows for their part stared back at him.

The longer he looked the less he liked them. Their plumage was in a dreadful state, all dusty and badly looked after, as if they had never heard of bathing and oiling themselves. Their toes and claws were filthy and covered in dried mud, and they had bits of food stuck in the corners of their mouths. They were a very different kind of bird to the wild geese, he could see that. They had, he thought, the kind of cruel, avaricious, watchful and brazen look that rogues and vagrants have.

'It seems I've fallen foul of a real gang of pirates,' he thought.

Just then he heard the wild geese calling above him: 'Where are you? Here I am. Where are you? Here I am.'

He realised that Akka and the others had come looking for him, but before he had time to answer them, the big crow – who seemed to be leader of the gang – hissed in his ear: 'Think of your eyes!' And he had no choice but to stay silent.

The wild geese could not have known he was so close. They must have flown over this wood by chance and he heard them calling a few more times before their calls died away. 'You're just going to have to look after yourself now, Nils Holgersson,' he said to himself. 'You'll have to show the world what you have learnt during these weeks in the wilderness.'

A little while later the crows began preparing to move on. Since they appeared to be intending to carry him with one crow holding on to the neckband of his shirt and another holding his stocking, the boy said to them: 'Isn't there one of you strong enough to carry me on his back? You've already pulled me around so much that I feel as if I'm coming apart. Let me ride! I promise you I shan't hurl myself down from the crow's back.'

'Don't imagine for one second that we care whether you're comfortable or not!' the leader said.

But then the biggest of the crows stepped forward, a scruffy and clumsy bird with a white feather in his wing, and said: 'It would be better for all of us, Windgust, if we deliver Thummitot all in one piece. I'll try to carry him on my back.'

'I've got nothing against it if you can manage, Fumble-Bumble,' said Windgust. 'But don't lose him!'

This was an important victory for the boy and he felt very pleased. 'No point in letting things get me down just because I've been kidnapped by crows,' he thought. 'I'm sure I'll come up with some way of dealing with these wretched birds.'

The crows continued flying in a south-westerly direction across Småland. It was a wonderful morning, sunny and calm, and the birds down below them were all singing their courtship songs. At the top of a spruce-tree in a tall dark wood sat a thrush, his wings drooping and his throat thick as he sang time after time: 'How pretty you are! How pretty you are! How pretty you are! No one is so pretty! No one is so pretty! No one is so pretty!' As soon as he had finished his song, he would start it again.

The boy was passing over the wood at that point and when he had heard the song repeated time after time he realised that it was the only one the thrush knew, so he put his hands in front of his mouth like a trumpet and shouted down: 'We've heard that one before! We've heard that one before!'

'Who's that? Who's that? Who's that? Who's making fun of me?' the thrush called, trying to catch sight of whomever it was who was shouting at him.

'It's me, Kidnapped-by-Crows, who's making fun of your song,' the boy answered.

On hearing what he said, the chieftain of the crows turned to him and said: 'You'd better watch out for your eyes, Thummitot!'

'I'm not going to worry about that,' the boy thought. 'I'm going to show you that I'm not afraid of you.'

They flew farther and farther inland, with forests and lakes everywhere beneath them. A wood pigeon was sitting on a bare branch in a clump of birch trees and the cock bird was standing in front of her. He puffed up his feathers, bent his neck and raised and lowered his body so that his breast feathers rustled against the branch. And all the time he was cooing: 'You, you, you are the most beautiful one in the forest. No one in the forest is so beautiful as you, you, you.'

But as the boy passed above them, he heard what the cock bird said and could not resist calling: 'Don't believe him! Don't believe him!'

'Who, who, who's that telling lies about me?' the pigeon cooed, trying to catch sight of whoever had shouted at him.

'It's me, Abducted-by-Crows, who is telling lies about you,' the boy answered, and once again Windgust looked at him and ordered him to keep quiet.

But Fumble-Bumble who was carrying the boy said: 'Let him talk. The small birds will think that we crows have become witty and funny birds!'

'They couldn't possibly be that stupid,' Windgust said, but the idea appealed to him anyway and he let the boy shout as much as he wanted to after that.

Forest and more forest passed beneath them for most of the time but there were also churches and villages and small cabins at the edge of the forest. At one place they saw a pretty old manor house lying there with the forest behind it and a lake in front; its walls were red and its roof curbed and there were great maple trees all round the courtyard and big scrubby gooseberry bushes growing in the garden. Right at the very top of the weathervane sat a cock starling, singing loudly enough for every note to be heard by the hen, who was sitting on their eggs in the nest-box in the pear tree. 'We have four pretty little eggs,' the starling sang. 'We have four pretty, round little eggs. Our whole nest is full of lovely eggs.'

The starling was singing the same song for the thousandth time as the boy flew over the estate. He cupped his hands into a tube in front of his mouth and shouted: 'The magpie will take them. The magpie will take them.'

'Who's that who is trying to frighten me?' the starling asked, flapping his wings uneasily.

'It's me, Captured-by-Crows, who is frightening you,' the boy said. This time the chief of the crows did not try to silence him – in fact, he and the rest of the flock thought it was so funny that they crowed with satisfaction.

The farther inland they flew, the bigger the lakes became and the more islands and headlands they contained. On one beach they saw a drake mallard bowing and scraping to his duck. 'I shall be faithful to you all the days of my life. I shall be faithful to you all the days of my life,' the drake said.

'Won't last the summer!' the boy shouted as he travelled past.

'And who are you?' the drake called.

'I am called Stolen-by-Crows,' the boy yelled.

When it was time for dinner the crows landed in a pasture field. They walked around feeding themselves but none of them thought of giving the boy anything. Then Fumble-Bumble went up to the chieftain carrying a twig from a thorn bush, on which there were some red rose-hips. 'This is for you, Windgust,' he said. 'Lovely food, and just right for you!'

'Do you think I want to eat dry old rose-hips?' Windgust snorted scornfully.

'Oh well, there was me thinking you'd like them,' said Fumble-Bumble and threw away the twig disconsolately. But it landed right in front of the boy and he was quick to grab it and eat his fill.

Once the crows had eaten they began to talk. 'What's on

your mind, Windgust? You are very quiet today,' one of them said to their leader.

'I'm thinking about a hen that used to live in this area. She was really fond of her mistress and in order to please her she laid a clutch of eggs that she kept hidden under the floor of the barn. All the time she was sitting on the eggs she thought how pleased the chicks would make her mistress and that thought made her very happy. Her mistress, of course, wondered where the hen was all this time. She looked for her but couldn't find her. Can you guess who found her and the eggs, Longbeak?'

'I think I can guess, Windgust, but since you've mentioned it, let me tell you about something similar. Do you remember that big black cat at the manse in Hinneryd? She was annoyed because they always took away her new-born kittens and drowned them. Only once did she manage to keep them hidden, which was when she had put them in a haystack out in the fields. Oh, how pleased she was with those kittens – but I do believe that I got more pleasure from them than she did!'

Now the crows became so eager to join in that they all talked at once. 'Where's the skill in stealing eggs and chicks?' one of them said. 'I once chased a hare that was almost fully grown. I had to follow him from thicket to thicket.'

She got no farther than that before another crow interrupted. 'Annoying hens and cats may be great fun but it's much more special when a crow can upset a human being. I once stole a silver spoon and ...'

By this point Nils could not bring himself to sit listening to this kind of talk any longer. 'Now listen here, you crows,' he said. 'You should be ashamed to boast about all your wicked deeds. I have been living among wild geese for three weeks and not once have I heard or seen anything but good things. You must have a bad leader if he lets you rob and murder as you do. You had better start living differently because I can tell you that human beings have grown so sick of your evil ways that they are doing their best to exterminate you. We are more than likely to see the last of you soon.'

When Windgust and the other crows heard this they became so angry that they were about to attack the boy and tear him to shreds. But Fumble-Bumble laughed and croaked and stood in front of him. 'No, no, no,' he said, apparently in abject terror. 'What do you think Windpuff is going to say if you tear Thummitot to pieces before he's got us the silver coins?'

'It's just like you to be afraid of females, Fumble-Bumble,' Windgust said, but both he and the other crows left Thummitot in peace.

A little while later the crows continued their journey. Up to this point the boy had been thinking that Småland was not such a poor province as he had heard. There were certainly plenty of forests and hilly ridges but there were also cultivated fields beside the rivers and lakes and he had not encountered any real desolation. But the deeper into the province they moved, the fewer became the villages and dwellings until eventually he thought he was flying over a wilderness in which he could see nothing but bogs and heaths and juniper-covered slopes.

The sun had set but it was still broad daylight when the crows reached the big heath. Windgust sent a bird on in advance to inform the other crows that he had been successful and on hearing the news Windpuff and several hundred crows rose from Crow Ridge to greet the arrivals. Under cover of the deafening cawing made by the crows that came to meet them, Fumble-Bumble said to the boy: 'You have been so jolly and cheerful during this journey that I've come to like you. So I'm going to give you some good advice. The moment we land you will be asked to carry out a task which may seem very easy to you. Beware about doing it!'

Soon afterwards Fumble-Bumble set Nils Holgersson down at the bottom of a sandy pit. The boy threw himself to the ground and lay there as if he was utterly worn-out and weary. So many crows were flapping around him that the air roared as if in a storm, but he did not look up.

'Get up now, Thummitot,' said Windgust. 'You have to help

us with something that should be very easy for you.'

But the boy pretended to be asleep and did not move. Then Windgust took him by the arm and dragged him across the sand to an old-fashioned earthenware pot that stood in the middle of the pit.

'Get up, Thummitot, and open this pot!'

'Why can't you let me sleep?' the boy said. 'I'm too tired to do anything tonight. Wait until tomorrow.'

'Open the pot!' said Windgust, shaking him.

The boy sat up, studied the pot closely and said: 'How is a poor child like me supposed to be able to open a pot like that? It's as big as I am.'

'Open it!' Windgust commanded once again. 'Or it will be the worse for you!'

The boy got to his feet, staggered over to the pot, fumbled with the lid and let his arms fall to his sides. 'I'm not usually this weak,' he said. 'If you will just let me sleep until the morning, I think I'll be able to deal with that lid.'

But Windgust was impatient and he rushed up and pecked the boy's leg. The boy was not going to put up with that sort of treatment from a crow. He quickly jerked himself free, jumped back a couple of steps, pulled his knife from its sheath and held it straight out in front of him. 'You be careful!' he shouted at Windgust.

But the crow was so incensed that he paid no attention to the danger. He rushed blindly at the boy and ran straight onto the knife so that it went through his eye and penetrated his brain. Nils quickly pulled the knife out but Windgust just flapped his wings and then sank down dead.

'Windgust is dead! The stranger has killed our chieftain Windgust!' yelled the crows who were standing closest, and then a horrendous uproar broke out. Some of them wailed, some of them called for vengeance, and all of them ran or flapped towards the boy – with Fumble-Bumble in the lead. But the latter, as usual, did the wrong thing, just flapping and spreading his wings over the boy and preventing the others from reaching him and stabbing him with their beaks.

Things were certainly not looking good for him, Nils could see that! There was no way he could run away from the crows and there was nowhere he could hide. Then he thought of the earthenware pot. He took a firm hold of the lid and jerked it loose, after which he jumped in and hid inside. It was a poor hiding-place because it was full almost to the brim with small thin silver coins and the boy could not get down deep enough, so he bent down and began throwing out the coins.

Up until then the crows had been flapping around pecking at him in a dense swarm, but the moment he began throwing out the coins they forgot their desire for revenge and hurried to collect them instead. He threw out fistfuls of money and all the crows, even Windpuff, collected it, and anyone lucky enough to get hold of a coin rushed off in great haste to hide it.

When the boy had thrown all the silver money out of the pot he looked up and saw that there was only one crow left in the sandpit. It was Fumble-Bumble, the bird with the white wing feather, the bird who had carried him. 'Thummitot, you've done me a bigger favour than you can possibly imagine,' the crow said in a very different voice and a quite different tone than before. 'Now I will save your life. Sit on my back and I'll take you to a hiding place where you will be safe for the night. Tomorrow I'll arrange for you to rejoin the wild geese.'

THE COTTAGE   Thursday, 14 April

When the boy woke the following morning, he was lying on a bed. Seeing that he was indoors, with four walls around him and a roof over his head, he thought he was back at home. 'I wonder if mother will bring the coffee soon?' he muttered as he lay there half asleep. But then he remembered that he was in a deserted cottage on Crow Ridge and that Fumble-Bumble, the crow with the white feather, had carried him there the evening before.

The boy's body was tender all over after the journey he had made the day before and he thought it was nice to be able to lie still while he waited for Fumble-Bumble, who had promised to come and fetch him.

Checked cotton curtains hung in front of the bed and Nils pushed them aside in order to look out into the cottage. He realised at once that he had never seen anything like this building. The walls consisted of no more than a couple of rows of logs before the roof took over, and since there was no ceiling he could see right up to the ridge of the roof. The whole cottage was so small that it looked as if it had been built for someone like him rather than for real people, although the stove and the fireplace were so big that he could not remember ever having seen bigger. The cottage door was in the gable wall alongside the stove and it was so narrow that it looked more like a slit than a door. In the other gable wall there was a wide, low window with many small panes. Hardly any of the furniture in the cottage was moveable. The bench along one long wall and the table under the window were fixed, as were the painted cupboard on the wall and the big bed in which he was lying.

Nils could not help wondering who owned the cottage and why it was deserted. It certainly looked as if the people who had lived there had been intending to return. The coffee pot and the porridge pan were still on the stove and there was some firewood ready for use. A fire-rake and a bread-spade stood in the corner, the spinning-wheel had been put up on a bench and on a shelf above the window lay tow and flax, a couple of skeins of yarn, a tallow candle and a bundle of matches.

Yes, it certainly looked as if the people who owned the cottage had intended to come back. There were bedclothes on the bed and on the wall there were long cloth hangings on which three men on horseback – Caspar, Melchior and Balthasar – were painted.* The same horses and the same riders were depicted repeatedly. They rode round the whole cottage and even continued their journey up on the beams in the roof.

But then, hanging from the roof, the boy caught sight of

something that brought him to his feet like a shot. A couple of dry rounds of flat bread were hanging there on a spit and, old and mouldy as they might prove to be, they were still bread. He hit them with the bread-spade and a piece fell to the floor. He ate some and then filled his bag – it was quite incredible how good bread tasted.

He looked around the cottage once more to check whether there was anything else that might be useful for him to take. 'I can surely take what I need,' he thought, 'since no one else seems bothered about it.' But most of the things there were too big and heavy and the only things he might manage were some of the matches.

He climbed up on to the table and with the help of the curtains swung himself up to the window-sill. While he was standing there tucking the matches into his bag, the crow with the white feather came in through the window.

'Here I am then,' Fumble-Bumble said and landed on the table. 'I couldn't come earlier because we crows have been choosing a new chieftain to succeed Windgust.'

'And who have you chosen?' the boy asked.

'We have chosen someone who will not permit piracy and injustice, that's what we've done. We have chosen Garm Whitefeather, who was formerly known as Fumble-Bumble,' he answered, drawing himself up to his full height so that he looked quite majestic.

'That was a good choice,' the boy said and congratulated him.

'And you may well need to wish me luck,' Garm said before telling Nils the kind of life Windgust and Windpuff had led in the past.

While this was going on the boy heard a voice outside the window and thought he recognised it. 'Is this where he is?' he heard the voice of Smirre Fox asking.

'Yes, he's hiding in there,' a crow's voice answered.

'Take care, Thummitot!' Garm shouted. 'That's Windpuff out there with the fox who wants to eat you.' That was all he had time to say because Smirre leapt at the window, and the window-frames, being old and rotten, gave way. The next moment Smirre was standing there on the table and Garm Whitefeather had no time to fly away before Smirre bit him to death. He then jumped down to the floor and began looking for the boy.

Nils tried to hide behind a big tow winder but Smirre had already seen him and crouched ready to pounce. Given how small and low the cottage was, the boy knew the fox could reach him without any difficulty. But the boy was not without a weapon to defend himself. He quickly struck one of the matches, held it to some pieces of tow and when they flared up he threw them down at Smirre Fox. Smirre, terrified out of his mind by the flames, gave no more thought to the boy and fled headlong out of the cottage.

But it looked as if the boy had jumped out of the frying pan only to land in the fire, for the flames spread from the piece of tow he had thrown at Smirre to the bed curtains. Nils jumped down and tried to smother them but they were flaring up too vigorously and the cottage was quickly filling with smoke. Smirre Fox, who had stopped outside the window, saw how things were going inside. 'Well, Thummitot,' he shouted, 'which are you going to choose: to fry in there or to come out here to me? I would prefer the chance to eat you but I'll be happy to see you die whichever way you meet your death.'

It looked as if the fox was going to be proved right. The fire was spreading at a frightening speed, the whole of the bed was already alight, smoke was beginning to rise from the floor and the flames were creeping along the painted hangings from one rider to the next. The boy had jumped up on the stove and was trying to open the door of the baking oven when he heard someone putting a key in the lock and slowly turning it. There must be people coming and, given the distress and danger in which he found himself, the boy was happy and relieved rather than frightened. He had already rushed over to the threshold by the time the door opened. He saw two children standing in front of him but, not stopping to look at the expression on their faces when they saw the cottage on fire, he ran past them out into the fresh air.

He did not dare run too far. He was only too well aware that Smirre Fox was lying in wait for him and he realised he had to stay close to the children. He turned round to see what kind of people they were and no sooner did he see them than he began hurrying towards them shouting: 'Hello Åsa Goose-girl! Hello Little Mats!'

The instant Nils had caught sight of the two children he had completely forgotten where he was! The crows, the burning cottage, talking animals – all that vanished from his mind and he was walking once more in a stubble field in Västra Vemmenhög tending a flock of geese while those two Småland children were looking after their geese in the field alongside. And every time he had met them he had jumped up onto the stone wall and shouted: 'Hello Åsa Goose-girl! Hello Little Mats!'

But now, when the two children saw this tiny little fellow coming towards them with his hand outstretched, they grabbed hold of one another, took a few steps back and looked frightened to death.

On seeing their fear Nils came to himself and remembered who he was now. And he could think of nothing worse than being seen by those two children while he was under the power of the elf's spell. Overcome by shame and sorrow at no longer being a human being, he turned and fled. Where he was going from there, he just did not know.

But there was a very welcome sight awaiting him when he came out on the heath. There in the heather he caught a glimpse of a flash of white and coming towards him he saw the white gander accompanied by Finedown. When the gander saw Nils running towards him at such a speed, he assumed that dangerous enemies must be pursuing him, so he hastily threw the boy up onto his back and carried him off.

XVII

THE OLD PEASANT WOMAN

Thursday, 14 April

It was late evening and three weary travellers were seeking somewhere to spend the night. They were travelling through a poor and desolate part of northern Småland and, not being weaklings who demanded soft beds and well-furnished rooms, they should have been able to find the kind of resting place they needed.

'If just one of these long ridges had a top steep and high enough to stop a fox climbing it, it would be a good place for us to sleep,' one of them said.

'If just one of these great bogs was not frozen but so wet and swampy that a fox would not dare to walk on it, it would be a really good place to spend the night,' another of them said.

'If the ice on just one of these frozen lakes we are passing stopped short of the shore so a fox could not get out onto it, we would have found just what we are looking for,' the third traveller said.

The worst thing was that once the sun had gone down two of the travellers became so sleepy that they were about to crash into the ground at any moment. The third of them, the one who was able to stay awake, became more and more uneasy as night approached. 'It's very unfortunate,' he thought, 'that we've come to a district where the lakes and mosses are frozen and a fox can walk all over them. The ice has thawed in other places but here we are right in the coldest part of Småland and spring hasn't reached here yet. I don't know what to do to find us a good sleeping place. Unless I can find somewhere well-protected, we'll have Smirre on our backs before morning.'

He peered around in all directions but nowhere could he see a place they could shelter for the night. And it was a dark and chilly evening, with a strong wind and drizzling rain. Things were becoming grimmer and more unpleasant by the minute.

It might appear strange that the travellers were reluctant to ask for lodgings at a farm and that they had already travelled past many villages without knocking on a single door. Nor had they paid any attention to those little cabins that every poor traveller is happy to come across tucked away in the edge of the forest. It is tempting to suggest that they deserved their discomfort since they did not ask for help where it was available.

But eventually, when it had grown so dark that there was hardly a glimmer of daylight left in the sky and the two sleepy ones were travelling half-asleep, they came to an isolated farm, far from all its neighbours. Not only was it very isolated, it looked as if it was completely uninhabited. There was no smoke rising from the chimney, no light shining from the windows, and not a soul moving around the yard. When the only one of the three who could stay awake saw the place, he thought: 'However things turn out, we shall have to try this farm. We are not likely to find anything better.'

A moment later all three of them were standing in the farmyard. Two of them fell asleep as soon as they were allowed to stop but the third looked round to see if there was any way of getting a roof over their heads. It was by no means a small farm. Apart from the farmhouse, the stable and the cowshed, there were long rows of barns and storehouses and sheds and tool-sheds, but everything looked in a hopelessly poor and dilapidated state. The walls of the buildings were grey, mossy and leaning – they looked ready to collapse. There were gaping holes in the roofs and the doors hung crookedly on broken hinges. It was obvious that it was a very long time since anyone had bothered to knock in a nail at this place.

In the meantime, however, the one of the three who was still awake had worked out which building was the cowshed. He shook his travelling companions awake and led them to the door of the cowshed. Fortunately this was only held shut by a hook and he had no trouble pushing it up with a piece of stick. He gave a sigh of relief at the thought that they would soon be in safety. But when the door swung open with a piercing squeak he heard a cow begin mooing: 'Here you are at last, mistress. I thought you weren't going to feed me tonight.'

The one of the three who was still awake came to a halt in the doorway, frightened out of his wits when he heard that the cowshed was not empty. But as soon as he saw that there was only one cow and three or four hens, he regained his courage.

'We are three poor travellers who would like to take shelter in a place where a fox cannot attack us and no human beings will find us,' he said. 'We wondered whether this might be a good place for us?'

'I can't imagine why it shouldn't be,' the cow answered. 'The walls are in a pretty poor condition but no fox has got through them yet. And there is no one else living here apart from an old woman who definitely isn't up to taking anyone prisoner. But tell me about all of you,' she continued, turning round in her stall to take a look at the newcomers.

'Well, I'm Nils Holgersson from Västra Vemmenhög and I've been turned into an elf,' he answered. 'And with me I've got a greylag goose and the tame goose I usually ride on.'

'I've never had such nice visitors in my residence before,' the cow said. 'And you are very welcome – although I would have preferred it if you were my mistress coming to give me my supper.'

The boy then led the geese into the cowshed, which was quite big, and put them in an empty stall, where they immediately fell asleep. He scraped together a little bed of straw for himself and thought that he too would fall asleep at once.

But nothing came of that idea because the poor cow, who had not had her supper, could not keep still for a moment. She shook the chain around her neck, moved round in her stall and complained about how hungry she was. The boy simply could not get off to sleep and lay there going through everything that had happened to him in the last few days.

He thought of Åsa Goose-girl and Little Mats whom he had met so unexpectedly and he worked out that the little cottage he had accidentally set alight must be their old home in Småland. He recalled hearing them talk of a cottage just like that one and of the great heathery heath below it. They had obviously come to look at their old home and had found it in flames when they reached it! There could be no doubt about the grief he had caused them and it pained him greatly. If he ever became human again he would try to make up for all the damage he had done.

Then his thoughts went to the crows, and when he remembered Fumble-Bumble who had saved him and then met his death so soon after being chosen as chieftain, he felt so sad that tears came to his eyes.

The last few days had been a hard time for him and he had been lucky that Finedown and the gander had managed to find him.

The gander had told him that as soon as the wild geese noticed that Thummitot was missing they asked all the small creatures in the forest whether they had seen him. They soon learnt that a flock of crows from Småland had abducted him. But the crows had already vanished and no one could say which direction they had taken. In order to try to find the boy as quickly as possible, Akka had ordered the geese to set off in pairs in different directions to look for him. After two days searching, whether they had found him or not, they were all to meet in north-western Småland on the Taberg, a high mountain that resembles a chopped-off tower. Once Akka had described how to find the Taberg and given them the best waymarks, they had all gone off in their different directions.

The white gander had chosen Finedown as his travelling

companion and, deeply concerned about what had happened to Thummitot, they had flown in one direction after another. During their wanderings they had heard a thrush in the top of a tree making a fuss because he had been made fun of by someone who called himself Kidnapped-by-Crows. They talked to the thrush and he pointed out the direction in which Kidnapped-by-Crows had been travelling. After that they met in turn a wood pigeon, a starling and a mallard, all of whom complained about a mischief-maker who had interrupted their songs and called himself Abducted-by-Crows or Captured-by-Crows or Stolen-by-Crows. In this way they had been able to track Thummitot all the way to the heath in Sunnerbo.

As soon as the gander and Finedown had collected Thummitot they had set off north towards the Taberg, but it had been a long journey and darkness had overtaken them before they sighted the peak. 'As long as we get there tomorrow all our troubles will be at an end,' the boy thought, burrowing deeper into the straw to get warm.

Meanwhile the cow had been restless in her stall all the time. Then she suddenly began talking to the boy. 'I thought one of you who came in said he was an elf. If that's the case, he should know how to look after a cow.'

'What is it that's the matter with you?' the boy asked.

'Anything and everything you can think of is the matter with me,' the cow said. 'I've neither been milked nor groomed. No one has put my night's fodder in the crib and no one has given me any bedstraw. My mistress came here to tend to me at dusk as she usually does but she felt so ill she had to go straight back to the house and she hasn't come back.'

'It's a pity that I'm so small and weak,' the boy said. 'I don't think there is anything I can do to help.'

'Don't assume you are weak just because you are small,' said the cow. 'All the elves I have heard of have been strong enough to pull a cartload of hay and to kill a cow with a single punch.'

The boy could not help laughing. 'They must have been a

different kind of elf to me, then,' he said. 'But I can undo your chain and open the door so that you can go out and drink from one of the puddles in the yard. And I'll try to climb up to the hayloft and throw some hay down into your crib.'

'That would certainly be some help,' the cow said.

The boy did what he said and when the cow had a full crib in front of her he thought that he might at last get some sleep. But no sooner had he crept back into his bed than she began talking to him again.

'You'll be sick and tired of me if I ask you to do just one more thing,' the cow said.

'No I won't,' the boy said, 'as long as it's in my power to do it.'

'In which case I'd like to ask you to go over to the house opposite and see how my mistress is. I'm afraid she may have had an accident.'

'No, I can't do that,' the boy answered. 'I can't risk showing myself to people.'

'You surely can't be afraid of a sick old woman,' the cow said. 'And you don't need to go in – just stand outside the door and look in through the crack.'

'Well, if that's all you're asking of me, I can certainly do it,' the boy said.

And with that he opened the door of the cowshed and went out into the yard. It was a dreadful night to be outside. Neither moon nor stars shone in the sky, the wind was howling and the rain pouring down. The worst thing of all was that seven big owls were sitting in a row along the roof-ridge of the house. Just listening to them sitting there complaining about the weather was terrifying enough, but it was even worse to think that it would be the end of him if a single one of them caught sight of him.

'Pity the one who is small!' the boy said as he went out into the yard. And he had good reason for saying it. He was blown over twice before he reached the house and on one occasion the wind swept him into a puddle so deep that he came close to drowning. But he got there at last.

He climbed up a couple of steps, scrambled over the threshold and entered the porch. The front door was shut but a piece had been cut out of the bottom corner to allow the cat to go in and out, so the boy had no difficulty in seeing how things were in the house.

He had scarcely poked his head in and taken a quick glance before he recoiled and withdrew his head. An grey-haired old woman was lying outstretched on the floor. She was neither moving nor moaning and her face was a strange white colour as if an invisible moon was shining its pale light on her.

The boy remembered that when his grandfather had died his face, too, had been that strange white and he realised that the old woman lying on the floor must be dead. Death must have come to her so quickly that she had not even had time to go and lie on her bed.

On realising that he was alone with a dead person in the dark of the night, the boy was terribly afraid. He threw himself headlong down the steps and hurried back to the cowshed.

When he told the cow what he had seen in the house, she stopped eating. 'Ah well, so my mistress is dead,' she said. 'In which case my time will soon be up, too.'

'Surely there will be someone to look after you?' the boy comforted her.

'What you don't know,' the cow said, 'is that I'm already twice as old as cows normally are when they are sent off to be slaughtered. Anyway, I'm not bothered about living any longer if my mistress can't come and make a fuss of me.'

She said nothing else for a while though the boy knew that she was neither asleep nor eating. But it was not long before she started talking again.

'Is she lying on the bare floorboards?' she asked.

'Yes, she is,' the boy answered.

'She used to come out here to the cowshed,' the cow said, 'and talk about everything that was worrying her. I could understand what she was saying though I couldn't answer. For the last few days she's been talking about being frightened that there would be no one with her when she died. She was anxious that there would be no one to close her eyes or to cross her arms over her breast when she was dead. Perhaps you would go and do those things?'

The boy was hesitant. He remembered that when his grandfather had died his mother had taken great care to lay him out properly and he knew that it was something that had to be done. But he also knew that, on a dreadful night like this, he did not dare to go in to the dead woman. He did not say anything but nor did he make a move in the direction of the cowshed door.

The old cow remained silent for a moment or two, as if waiting for an answer. When the boy said nothing, she did not repeat her request. Instead, she started telling him about her mistress.

There was much to tell. First and foremost there were all the children she had brought up. They had come to the cowshed every day and during the summer they had herded the cattle out on the moss and in the wooded pastures, so the old cow knew all about them. They had been fine children, all of them, happy and hard-working. A cow knew well enough whether a cowherd was good or bad.

And there was a great deal to be said about the farm, too. It had not always been as poor as it was now. It was very large, though most of it consisted of boggy land and stony pastures. There was little by way of arable land but there was excellent grazing everywhere. There had been a time when there was a cow in every stall in the cowshed and the ox stalls, which were now empty, had been full of oxen. Happiness and joy had ruled in the house and in the barns in those days and the mistress had always been humming and singing when she opened the cowshed door. All the cows had lowed with joy when they heard her coming.

But the farmer had died while the children were still too small to be of any help and the mistress had to take over the farm and all the work and all the responsibility. She had been as strong as a man and she had both ploughed and reaped. Sometimes when she came into the cowshed to do the evening milking she was so weary that she wept. But when she thought of her children she was happy again. Then she would shake her head to jerk the tears from her eyes and say: 'It doesn't matter. I shall have good times again, I shall, once the children are grown up. Yes, once the children are grown up.'

As soon as the children had grown up, however, they were afflicted by a strange kind of longing. They no longer wanted to stay at home, they wanted to travel off to foreign lands. Their mother never did receive any help from them. A couple of her children had married before they left and they left their own small children behind. And now these children followed the mistress into the cowshed just as her own children had done. They herded the cows and they were good and fine children. In the evenings when the mistress was so weary that she might fall asleep in the middle of the milking, she would wake with new courage at the thought of them. 'I shall have good times again, I shall, once they are grown up,' she said, shaking herself awake.

But when these children grew up they went off to join their parents in a foreign land. None of them came back, none of them stayed at home. The old woman was left all alone back on the farm.

And, of course, she never asked them to stay at home with her. 'You don't think I should have asked them to stay here with me, do you Rödlinna, when they could go out in the world and have a good life?' she used to say when she stood in the stall with the old cow. 'After all, poverty is all that's in store for them here in Småland.'

When the last of the grandchildren had gone, life had gone out of the mistress. All at once she became bent and grey and she tottered as she walked as if she no longer had the strength to move properly. And she stopped working. She did not want to look after the farm and she let everything go to pieces. She stopped repairing the buildings and she sold the oxen and the cows. The only one she kept was the old cow who was now talking to Thummitot, and she let her live because all of the children had herded her.

She could perhaps have employed maids and farm-hands to help her with the work but she could not bear seeing strangers around her when her own flesh and blood had left her. And she perhaps found some satisfaction in letting the farm go to rack and ruin when none of the children would take it over. She did not care that she was becoming poor by not looking after what was hers to look after. But she took great care that her children never learnt how bad things were. 'As long as the children don't find out! As long as the children don't find out!' she would sigh as she tottered round the cowshed.

The children wrote to her and constantly asked her to come and join them, but she did not want to. She did not want to see the country that had taken them away from her. She was angry with it. 'I've no doubt it's stupid of me,' she would say, 'not to like the country that has been so good to them. But I don't want to see it.'

She never thought of anything but the children and the fact that they had been forced to leave. When summer came she led the cow out to graze on the great moss. She herself sat for days on end on the edge of the moss with her hands in her lap. As they walked home she would say: 'They wouldn't have had to leave, you know Rödlinna, if there had been big fertile fields here instead of this barren moss.'

She could become really angry with the moss for lying there so big and so useless, and she would sit there saying that it was the moss's fault that the children had left her.

That last evening she had been weaker and shakier than ever before. She had not even managed the milking. She had leant on the stall and told the cow that two farmers had come to see her and offered to buy the moss. They were going to drain it and cultivate it. This had made her both anxious and happy. 'Listen now, Rödlinna, listen now,' she had said. 'They said they could grow rye on the moss. I'm going to write to the children and tell them to come home. They don't need to stay away any longer. They will be able to make a living at home now.'

And she had gone into the house to write to them ...

The boy did not wait to hear any more of the old cow's story. He opened the door of the cowshed, crossed the yard and went in to the dead woman who had seemed so frightening just a little while before.

First of all he stood still for a while and looked around.

It was not as poor in there as he had expected. There were many of the kind of things that are found in the homes of people who have family in America. There was an American rocking chair in one corner, a colourful plush cloth lay on the table by the window, a pretty cover was spread on the bed, photographs of the absent children and grandchildren hung on the walls in nicely carved frames and a pair of candlesticks with thick spiral candles stood on the chest of drawers alongside some tall vases.

The boy looked for a matchbox and lighted the candles, not because he needed to see better but because he thought it was a way of honouring the dead woman.

Then he went over to the woman, closed her eyes, laid her hands in a cross on her breast and stroked her thin grey hair back from her face.

He no longer gave any thought to being afraid of her. He felt a profound grief that she had to live through her old age in loneliness and longing and he meant to keep watch over her body for this one night at least.

He looked round and found the hymn book and sat down to read some hymns half aloud, but in the middle of his reading he came to a stop because he had begun to think of his own mother and father.

So parents can feel that much yearning for their children, can they? He had never known that. So life can come to an end for them, so to speak, when their children go away! What if his parents at home were longing for him in the same way as the old woman had been longing for her children?

The thought filled him with happiness, though he did not dare believe it. The way he had been, no one could possibly be longing for him.

But perhaps he could become something he had not been before?

All round him he saw the portraits of those who had emigrated. They were big strong men and women, their faces serious. There were brides wearing long veils and men in fine clothes and children with crimped hair and beautiful white dresses. And he thought they were all staring blindly out into space, as if they did not want to see.

'Poor you!' the boy said to the portraits. 'Your mother is dead. You can never make up for the fact that you left her. But my mother is still alive.'

He broke off at this point, nodded and smiled quietly to himself. 'My mother is still alive,' he said. 'Both my father and my mother are still alive.'

XVIII

FROM TABERG TO HUSKVARNA

Friday, 15 April

The boy stayed awake almost all night but towards morning he fell asleep and dreamt of his father and mother. He could hardly recognise them. Both of them had grey hair and their faces were old and wrinkled. He asked what had happened and they told him they had aged like this because they had missed him so much. He was both surprised and moved because he had always believed that they would be happy to be rid of him.

When the boy woke, morning had arrived bringing clear and beautiful weather with it. First of all he ate a piece of bread he found, then he provided morning fodder for the geese and the cow and opened the door of the cowshed so that the cow could go to the nearest farm. When the cow arrived alone, the neighbours would be bound to understand that something had happened to her mistress. They would hasten to the deserted farm to see how the old woman was, find her body and bury her.

Very soon after the boy and the geese had taken off they caught sight of a high mountain with almost vertical walls and a sliced-off top. They knew that this must be the Taberg, and Akka with Yksi and Kaksi, Kolme and Neljä, Viisi and Kuusi and all six goslings were standing on top waiting for them. It is impossible to describe the joy and the cackling and the flapping and the calling when they saw that the gander and Finedown had managed to find Thummitot.

Trees grew quite far up the sides of the Taberg but the topmost peak was bare and from there it was possible to see a long distance in every direction. Looking to the east, to the south and to the west there was very little to be seen but poor highlands with dark spruce forests, brown mosses, ice-covered lakes and blue ridges. The boy could not help feeling that it was true that whoever had created this landscape had not taken very much trouble with his work and simply carved it out in a hurry. But it was a very different story if you looked to the north: the landscape there looked as if it had been formed with great love and care. In that direction there was nothing but pretty hills, gentle valleys and rivers wending their way towards the great lake, Vättern, which lay there ice-free and wonderfully clear, shining as if it was filled with blue light rather than water.

It was Vättern that made the view to the north so beautiful. It looked as if there was a blue shimmer rising from the lake and spreading across the landscape. Hills and woods and the spires and roofs of the town of Jönköping, which was just visible on the shore of Vättern, lay veiled in a pale blue light so gentle that it caressed the eye. If there are countries in heaven, the boy thought, they would be just that shade of blue, and he felt he had been given a glimpse of what paradise must look like.

When the geese continued their migration later that day, they flew up along the blue valley. They were in the very best of spirits, calling and shouting so that no one with ears to hear could fail to notice them.

This happened to be the first really beautiful spring day the people of this district had enjoyed. Up to now spring had been going about its work in rain and storm, but now that the weather had suddenly turned fine everyone was so overwhelmed by a yearning for green woods and the warmth of summer that they found it hard to go about their daily business. And as the wild geese flew past, happy and free and far above the earth, everyone stopped whatever they were doing and gazed up at them.

The first people to see the wild geese that day were the miners on the Taberg, who were digging for iron ore on the mountain. When they heard the geese honking, they stopped drilling dynamite holes and one of them shouted up to the birds: 'Where are you going? Where are you going?'

The geese could not understand what he was saying but the boy leant over from the gander's back and answered for them: 'We're going where there are neither picks nor hammers!' And when the miners heard those words they thought it was their own deep desires that had made the cackling of the geese sound like human speech.

'Let us come with you! Let us come with you!' the miners shouted.

'Not this year!' the boy shouted. 'Not this year!'

Still making the same noise, the wild geese followed the River Taberg down to Munksjön where, on the narrow strip of land between the two lakes, Munksjön and Vättern, lay the town of Jönköping with its great factories. First of all the wild geese flew over the Munksjö paper-mill. The midday break was just coming to an end and a great crowd of workers was streaming towards the factory gates. When they heard the wild geese they stopped for a moment to listen to them.

'Where are you going? Where are you going?' a worker shouted up to them.

The geese could not understand what he was saying but the boy answered for them: 'We're going where there are neither machines nor steam boilers.' And when the workers heard those words they thought it was their own deep desires that had made the cackling of the geese sound like human speech.

'Let us come with you! Let us come with you!' many of them shouted.

'Not this year!' the boy answered. 'Not this year!'

Next the geese flew over the famous match factory that lies on the shore of Vättern – it was as big as a castle and had chimneys reaching high into the sky. There was no one moving around the yards but in a large hall young women were sitting filling matchboxes. Because of the good weather they had opened a window and the call of the wild geese reached them through it. The girl sitting closest to the window leant out with a matchbox in her hand and shouted: 'Where are you going? Where are you going?'

'To the land where neither matches nor candles are needed,' the boy said. And the girl thought that all she had heard was the cackling of geese, but she also felt she had picked out a few words, so she answered them: 'Let me come with you! Let me come with you!'

'Not this year!' the boy answered. 'Not this year!'

To the east of the factories, Jönköping occupies the most magnificent site any town could wish for. Vättern is a narrow lake with high and steep sandy shores on its eastern and western sides, but at the southern end these walls open up to make room for a great gateway through which the lake may be reached. Right in the middle of this gateway, with hills to the right and hills to the left, with Munksjön behind and with Vättern in front, sits Jönköping.

The geese flew on over the long narrow town making the same noise and fuss as they had made out in the country. But no one in the town answered them – townspeople cannot be expected to stand on the street and call up to wild geese.

Their journey continued along the shore of Vättern and after a while the geese came to Sanna Nursing Home. Some of the patients had come out onto the veranda to enjoy the spring air and they, too, heard the cackling of the geese.

'Where are you going? Where are you going?' one of them asked in a voice so weak it could scarcely be heard.

'To the land where there is neither sorrow nor sickness,' the boy answered.

'Let us come with you,' the patients asked.

'Not this year!' the boy answered. 'Not this year!'

When they had flown on a little farther they came to the town of Huskvarna. It lay in a valley surrounded by fine steep hills from which a river descended in long narrow falls. Great factories and workshops lay at the foot of these hills and the valley floor was filled with workers' houses and their little gardens. Right in the middle were the school buildings and just as the wild geese were passing over, a bell rang and a host of children marched out row by row. There were so many of them that they filled the schoolyard.

'Where are you going? Where are you going?' the children shouted when they heard the geese.

'To where there are neither books nor lessons,' the boy answered.

'Take us with you!' the children yelled. 'Take us with you!'

'Not this year but next,' the boy shouted. 'Not this year but next.'

XIX

THE GREAT BIRD LAKE

JARRO THE MALLARD

On the eastern shore of Vättern lies a hill called the Omberg; east of the Omberg lies a moss called Dagsmosse and east of Dagsmosse lies a lake called Tåkern. The great flat plain of the province of Östergötland spreads out around Tåkern.

Tåkern is a fairly large lake and is reckoned to have been even bigger in the old days. But then people took it into their heads that the lake covered far too much of the fertile plain and they tried to drain the water out of it in order to dry out the bottom of the lake and cultivate it. They probably intended to drain the whole lake but they failed and consequently the lake still covers a good deal of ground. But since it was drained the lake has become so shallow that it is hardly ever deeper than six or seven feet at any point.* The shores have turned into wet and sludgy marsh-meadows and small muddy islands poke up all over the surface of the lake.

Now there is one plant, anyway, that is fond of standing with its feet in the water as long as it can keep its body and head up in the air – and that plant is the reed. There is nowhere that reeds thrive more than around the small muddy islands and along the shores of Tåkern, where the water is shallow a long way out. The reeds grow so well there that they become taller than a man and so dense that it is almost impossible to push a boat through them. They form such a wide green hedge around the whole lake that it is only accessible at the few places where people have removed the reeds.

The reeds may shut people out but they give protection and shelter to many other things. In among the reeds there are numerous small pools and channels of still green water where duckweed and pondweed flourish and where innumerable hosts of mosquito larvae and fish-spawn and tadpoles hatch out. And round the edges of these small pools and channels there are numerous well-hidden places where waterfowl can hatch their eggs and feed their young without being disturbed either by enemies or food worries.

So there is an incredible number of birds living in the Tåkern reed-beds, and more and more come with every passing year as the word spreads as to what a wonderful place it is. The first to settle there were the mallards and they still live there in their thousands. But they do not own the whole lake any longer and now they have to share the space with swans, grebes, coots, divers, shovelers and many others.

Tåkern is without doubt the biggest and finest bird lake in the country and the birds will consider themselves fortunate as long as they are able to occupy a refuge like this. But it is not certain that they will be allowed to hang on to these reed-beds and muddy shores much longer, for human beings simply cannot forget that the lake covers a wide expanse of good and fertile earth. Time after time people have brought forward proposals to drain the lake, and if these proposals ever became reality, many thousands of waterfowl would be forced to leave the area.

At the time Nils Holgersson was travelling with the wild geese, there was a mallard called Jarro living on Tåkern. He was a young bird who had only lived one summer, one autumn and one winter. And now it was his first spring. He had recently returned home from North Africa and had reached Tåkern in such good time that there was still ice on the lake.

One evening, when he and the other young drakes were enjoying themselves flying back and forth across the lake, a hunter fired off a couple of shots at them and Jarro was hit in the breast. He thought he was going to die but in order not to fall into the hands of the man who had shot him he carried on flying as far as he could. He did not think about where he was going, he was simply struggling to get as far away as possible.

When his strength failed and he could not fly any farther, he discovered that he was no longer over the lake. He had flown a little way in over the land and come down in front of the entrance of one of the large farms that lie on the shores of Tåkern.

A little while later a young farmhand was crossing the yard when he caught sight of Jarro and came and picked him up. Jarro, however, wanted only to be left to die in peace. He gathered what strength he had left and pecked the farmhand's finger hard to make him let go.

Jarro did not manage to escape but one good thing about pecking the man was that the farmhand realised that the bird was still alive. He carried him carefully indoors and showed him to his mistress, a young woman with a kind face. She immediately took Jarro from the farmhand, stroked his back and wiped off the blood that was still oozing through the feathers on his neck. She examined him very carefully and when she saw how beautiful he was with his shining dark-green head, his white neckband, his reddish brown back and blue speculum, she no doubt thought it would be a real pity if he were to die. She quickly arranged a basket and bedded the bird down in it.

Meanwhile Jarro spent the whole time flapping and fighting to get free, but as soon as he understood that the people had no intention of killing him he settled down comfortably in the basket. It was only then that he realised how exhausted the pain and the loss of blood had made him. The woman carried the basket across the room to put it in the corner by the stove and Jarro had already closed his eyes and fallen asleep before she put it down.

A little while later Jarro was woken by someone prodding him gently. When he opened his eyes, he was so terrified that he almost fainted. Now he really was lost because standing in front of him was something much more dangerous than either people or birds of prey: it was none other Caesar, the long-haired setter, who was poking him inquisitively with his nose.

When Jarro had been a little yellow chick the summer before, he had been pathetically terrified whenever he heard the reed-beds resound to the cry: 'Caesar's coming! Caesar's coming!' And when he had actually seen the brown and white dog, his jaws bristling with teeth, come wading through the reeds, he had thought he was seeing a vision of Death himself. He had always hoped that the time would never come when he met Caesar face to face.

Now, however, it had been his misfortune to land on the very farm where Caesar lived, and now the dog stood looming over him. 'Who are you?' he growled. 'How did you get in here? Don't you belong out in the reed-beds?'

Jarro could scarcely find the courage to answer. 'Don't be angry with me for coming into the house, Caesar!' he said. 'It wasn't my fault. I've been shot and wounded and it was people who put me in this basket.'

'So it was people who put you in that basket, was it?' Caesar said. 'In which case they must be intending to nurse you, although personally I think they would be wiser to eat you while they have the chance. Anyway, you're off limits to me now. You don't have to look so frightened – we're not down on Tåkern now.'

After saying this, Caesar went and lay down to sleep in front of the blazing open fire, and as soon as Jarro realised that the dreadful danger was past, he was overcome by weariness and went back to sleep.

The next time Jarro woke he saw a dish with groats and water in front of him. He was still very ill but was so hungry that he began to eat anyway. When the woman saw he was eating, she looked happy and came over and stroked him. Then he fell asleep again and for several days did nothing but eat and sleep.

One morning, however, Jarro felt well enough to leave the basket and walk across the floor. He had not gone far before he collapsed and simply lay there. Along came Caesar, opened his huge jaws and took hold of him. Jarro, of course, thought the dog was going to bite him to death but Caesar carried him back to the basket without harming him. After this, Jarro trusted Caesar so much that, on his next trip out of the basket, he went over to the dog and lay down beside him. So Caesar and Jarro became good friends and every day Jarro would spend several hours lying asleep between Caesar's paws.

Jarro was even more devoted to the mistress of the house than he was to Caesar. He felt no fear of her at all and would rub his head against her hand when she came to feed him. He would give a sigh of sorrow whenever she left the room and a cry of welcome in his own language when she came back.

In fact, Jarro completely forgot how afraid he had been of people and dogs in the past. Now he thought they were mild and kind and he loved them. He wanted to be healthy again so that he could fly down to Tåkern and tell the mallards that their old enemies were not in the least bit dangerous and that there was no need to be frightened of them.

He had noticed that both Caesar and the human beings had calm eyes that were good to look into. The only one in the house whose eyes he did not like to meet was Klorina, the cat. She, like the others, did him no harm but he never felt he could trust her. She was, moreover, constantly nettling him about his love for the people. 'You believe they are caring for you because they like you,' Klorina would say. 'Just you wait until you're fat enough and then they'll wring your neck. I know what they're like, I do!'

Like all birds, Jarro had a tender and affectionate heart and became inexpressibly sad on hearing this. He could not conceive that the mistress might want to wring his neck, nor could he believe it of her son, a little boy who sat for hours by his basket burbling and babbling. He was certain that both of them felt the same love for him as he felt for them.

One day when Jarro and Caesar were lying in their usual place in front of the fireplace, Klorina sat up on the hearth and began to annoy the mallard.

'I wonder what you mallards are going to do next year, Jarro, when Tåkern has been drained and turned into fields,' Klorina said.

'What's that you are saying, Klorina?' Jarro shouted and leapt up in horror.

'I always forget, Jarro, that unlike Caesar and me you don't understand human language,' the cat answered. 'Otherwise you would have heard those men who came to the house yesterday talking about draining all the water from Tåkern so that by next year the bottom of the lake would be as dry as a cottage floor. I was just wondering where all you mallards will go then.'

When Jarro heard this he was so angry that he hissed like a grass snake. 'You're as nasty as a coot!' he yelled at Klorina. 'You are just trying to stir me up against human beings, but I don't believe they intend to do anything of the sort. Surely they know that Tåkern belongs to the mallards – and why would people want to make so many birds homeless and unhappy? You have made all this up in order to frighten me. I wish Gorgo the eagle would rip you to pieces! I wish mistress would cut off your whiskers!'

But Jarro's outburst failed to silence Klorina: 'You think I'm lying, don't you? Ask Caesar, then. He was in the house last night, too. And Caesar never lies.'

'Caesar,' Jarro said, 'you understand human speech much better than Klorina. Tell me that she heard wrong! Just imagine what it would be like if people drained Tåkern and turned the bottom of the lake into fields! There wouldn't be any pondweed or duckweed for the adult ducks and no fish fry nor tadpoles nor mosquito larvae for the ducklings. And the reed-beds would disappear, too, which is where the ducklings hide until they can fly. All the ducks would be forced to move and find somewhere else to live, but where would they ever find a refuge like Tåkern? Caesar, say that Klorina did not hear right!'

Caesar's behaviour during this conversation was quite remarkable to see. He had been wide awake up to the point when Jarro turned to him, but then he yawned, laid his long snout on his front paws and was sound asleep in an instant.

The cat looked down at Caesar with a sly smile. 'I do believe that Caesar doesn't care to answer you,' she said to Jarro. 'He's just like all the other dogs – none of them will ever admit that human beings can do any wrong. But you can rely on what I'm saying in any case, and I'll tell you why they are going to drain the lake just now. While you mallards were still in control of Tåkern people did not want to drain it because they had some use for you. But now that grebes and coots and other birds which are no good as food have invaded all the reed-beds, people can't see any point in keeping the lake for their sake.'

Jarro did not bother to answer Klorina but he raised his head and shouted in Caesar's ear: 'Caesar! You know that there are still so many ducks on Tåkern that they fill the sky like clouds. Say it isn't true that people are thinking of making them all homeless!'

At this, Caesar leapt up and lost his temper with Klorina so violently that she had to take refuge up on a shelf. 'I'll teach you to keep quiet when I want to sleep,' he roared. 'Of course I know they are intending to drain all the water out of the lake this year, but they have talked about it many times before without anything coming of it. And I certainly don't approve of draining it. What's going to happen to the hunting if Tåkern is dried out? You are a complete idiot to be pleased at the thought. What would you and I have to entertain us if there were no birds left on Tåkern?'

THE DECOY DUCK   Sunday, 17 April

A couple of days later Jarro had recovered enough to be able to fly all around the house. The woman stroked and caressed him and the little boy ran out into the farmyard and picked the first blades of fresh grass for him. And when the woman stroked him Jarro knew that, although he was now strong enough to fly down to Tåkern at any time, he did not want to be parted from the human beings. He would have no objection to remaining with them for the whole of his life.

But early one morning the woman put a halter on Jarro that prevented him from using his wings and then she handed him over to the farmhand who had found him in the yard.

The farmhand tucked him under his arm and went down to Tåkern.

The ice had melted while Jarro's wounds had been healing. Last year's dry old reeds still stood along the shore and around the islands but all the water plants had started to send out shoots down in the depths and their green tops had just reached the surface. Almost all of the migratory birds had now returned and the curved beaks of the curlews were visible among the reeds, the grebes were gliding around with new frills around their necks and the snipe were collecting dry grass for their nests.

The farmhand went down to a skiff, laid Jarro in the bottom of the boat and began to pole the punt out on the lake. Jarro, who had become accustomed to nothing but kindness from human beings, said to Caesar, who was also with them, that he was very grateful to the farmhand for taking him out on the lake but there was no need for the man to keep him so tightly pinioned since he had no intention of flying away. Caesar did not answer him – he was, in fact, being very taciturn that morning.

The only thing that seemed a little strange to Jarro was that the farmhand had taken a gun with him. He could not believe that any of the kind people on the farm would want to shoot birds and Caesar had told him that people did not hunt at this time of year. 'It's the close season,' he said, 'though that does not apply to me, of course.'

Meanwhile the farmhand poled them out to one of the small reed-enclosed islands of mud where he got out of the boat, dragged together a big pile of old reeds and lay down behind it. Jarro, still wearing the halter over his wings and now tethered to the boat on a long line, was allowed to potter about out in the shallow water.

Suddenly Jarro caught sight of some of the young drakes in whose company he had formerly patrolled back and forth across the lake. They were a long way off but Jarro gave a couple of loud calls to attract them. They answered him and a large and beautiful flock approached. Even before they came close, Jarro had started telling them about the wonderful way he had been saved and about the kindness of human beings. But then two shots sounded behind him, three ducks fell dead among the reeds and Caesar splashed out to collect them.

At last Jarro understood. The human beings had saved him so that they could use him as a decoy duck. And it had worked. Three ducks had died because of him. He wanted to die of shame. He felt that even his friend Caesar was looking at him scornfully and when they returned to the house, Jarro did not dare lie down and go to sleep by the dog.

The following morning Jarro was once again taken out into the shallows and once again he soon caught sight of other ducks. But the moment he noticed that they were flying towards him he shouted: 'Go away, go away! Watch out! Take a different direction! There is a hunter hidden behind this pile of reeds. I am just a decoy.' And he prevented them from coming within range of the gun.

Jarro was so busy keeping watch that he hardly had time to eat a blade of grass. As soon as a bird approached, he shouted out a warning and he even warned the grebes, although he detested them because they were crowding the ducks out of the best hiding places. He simply did not want any of the birds to meet with misfortune because of him. And thanks to Jarro's vigilance the farmhand had to go home without firing a single shot.

In spite of this, Caesar seemed less displeased than the day before and in the evening he took Jarro in his mouth, carried him over to the fireplace and let him sleep between his front paws.

But Jarro was no longer happy in the house – indeed, he was deeply unhappy. His heart was pained by the thought that the people had never really loved him and when the mistress and the little boy came over to stroke him, he stuck his head under his wing and pretended to be asleep.

Jarro continued his melancholy guard duty for several days and he was already known across the whole of Tåkern. Then one morning as he was shouting his usual 'Watch out, birds!

Don't come near me, I'm just a decoy!' a grebe's nest came floating towards the shallows in which he was tethered. There was nothing very peculiar about this – it was a nest from last year and since grebes' nests are built to float on water like boats, it often happens that they drift around the lake. Jarro nevertheless found himself standing and staring at the nest because it was coming so directly towards him that it looked as if someone was steering it across the water.

As the nest came nearer Jarro saw that there was a little person, the smallest he had ever seen, sitting in the nest and rowing it with a couple of sticks. And this little person shouted to him: 'Go as close to the water as you can, Jarro, and get ready to fly! You will soon be free!'

A few seconds later the grebe's nest reached the shore, but the little oarsman did not leave it, he sat still, crouching in the twigs and straw. Jarro also remained almost motionless, paralysed by fear that his rescuer might be discovered.

What happened next was that a flock of wild geese came flying along. Jarro came to his senses and called loudly to warn them but they flew back and forth over the water several times. They stayed so high up that they were out of gunshot, in spite of which the farmhand could not resist firing off a couple of shots at them. No sooner had these shots been fired than the tiny fellow jumped ashore, drew a small knife from its sheath and cut Jarro's halter with a couple of quick strokes. 'Fly away now, Jarro, before he has time to reload his gun!' he shouted, jumping back into the grebe's nest and pushing off from the shore.

The hunter had been watching the geese and had not noticed that Jarro had been set free. Caesar, however, had been keeping a closer eye on what was happening and just as Jarro was opening his wings Caesar leapt forward and grabbed him by the nape of the neck.

Jarro screamed pitifully but the little creature who had freed him spoke calmly to Caesar: 'If you are as honourable as you look, you surely don't want to compel a decent bird to sit here decoying others into disaster?'

On hearing these words Caesar pulled his upper lip back in a sneer, but after a moment he released Jarro. 'Fly away, Jarro!' he said. 'You are truly too good a bird to be a decoy. And that wasn't why I wanted to keep you here anyway – I wanted to keep you because the house is going to be empty without you.'

THE LOWERING OF THE LAKE   Wednesday, 20 April

It really was very empty around the house once Jarro had gone. Time passed slowly for the dog and the cat now that they no longer had Jarro to quarrel about, and the mistress missed the happy quacking that had greeted her whenever she came in. But the one who pined most for Jarro was the little boy, Per Ola. He was just three years old and an only child and he had never had a playmate like Jarro in all his life. He could not get used to the idea that Jarro had returned to the other ducks on Tåkern and he spent all his time thinking about how he could get him back.

Per Ola had spent a lot of time talking to Jarro while the duck was lying quietly in his basket and the boy was sure that the duck understood him. Now he asked his mother to take him down to the lake so that he could meet Jarro and convince him to come back to them. His mother paid no attention to this but the child would not give up his plan.

The day after Jarro's disappearance Per Ola was running around in the yard. As usual he was playing on his own, but Caesar was lying on the steps and when his mother let the boy out she had said: 'Look after Per Ola now, Caesar!'

If everything had been as usual, Caesar would have obeyed the command and the boy would have been well looked after and not in the slightest danger. But Caesar was just not himself these days. He knew that the farmers living around Tåkern were having frequent discussions about lowering the level of the lake and they had more or less decided to do so. The ducks would leave and Caesar would never again enjoy a decent hunt. He was so preoccupied thinking about this misfortune that he did not remember to keep an eye on Per

Ola.

No sooner had the child been left alone in the yard than he realised that this was just the right moment for him to go down to Tåkern and talk to Jarro. He opened the gate and, taking the narrow path across the water meadows, he walked down towards the lake. As long as he was still visible from the house, he walked slowly, after which he speeded up. He was afraid that his mother or one of the others would shout and say he was not allowed to go there. He did not want to do anything naughty, he only wanted to convince Jarro to come back, but he sensed that the others would not have approved of his undertaking.

When Per Ola arrived at the shore of the lake he shouted for Jarro several times and then he stood and waited for a long time but there was no sign of Jarro. He saw some other birds that resembled the mallard but they flew past without paying any attention to him so he realised that none of them could be the right bird.

When Jarro did not come to him, the little boy thought it would probably be easier to find him if he went out on the lake. There were several good boats on the bank but they were all firmly tied up. The only one that was untied and available was a rotting old skiff in such bad condition that no one ever thought of using it. Without worrying that the bottom of the skiff was full of water, Per Ola scrambled aboard. He was not strong enough to use the oars so, instead, he began to rock and sway in the skiff. It is very unlikely that any big person would have succeeded in moving the skiff out on to Tåkern in that way, but when water-levels are high and misfortune just round the corner, small children have a peculiar ability to get out on the water. Per Ola was soon drifting around Tåkern shouting for Jarro.

As the old skiff rocked around the lake, the cracks in it opened wider and the water really poured in. Quite unconcerned by this, Per Ola sat on a little seat in the prow shouting at every bird he saw and wondering why Jarro did not show himself.

At last Jarro caught sight of Per Ola. He heard someone shouting the name that he had among the human beings and he realised that the little boy had come out on Tåkern looking for him. Jarro was unspeakably happy to discover that one of the human beings really did love him and he shot down like an arrow, sat down beside Per Ola and allowed him to stroke him. Both of them were very happy to see each other again.

Suddenly, however, Jarro saw what was happening to the skiff. It was half full of water and on the point of sinking. Jarro tried to tell Per Ola that since he could neither fly nor swim he must try to get ashore, but Per Ola could not understand. Then, without a moment's delay, Jarro hurried away to fetch help.

A little while later Jarro returned and on his back he was carrying a tiny little fellow, much smaller than Per Ola. If the little fellow had not been able to move and to talk, Per Ola would have taken him for a doll. The little fellow at once ordered Per Ola to pick up a long thin pole lying in the bottom of the skiff and to try to pole them to one of the small reedy islands. Per Ola obeyed and he and the little fellow helped each other to move the skiff. With just a couple of pushes they reached a small island surrounded by reeds where Per Ola was told to step ashore. No sooner had he set foot on land than the skiff filled with water and sank to the bottom.

When the little boy saw this, he felt certain that his mother and father were going to be very angry with him and he would have started to cry if he had not immediately been given something else to think about. A flock of big grey birds came and landed on the island and the little elf led Per Ola over to them and told him what they were called and what they were saying. This was so much fun that Per Ola forgot everything else.

By now the people on the farm had noticed that the boy was missing and started looking for him. They searched all the outbuildings, looked down the well and checked the cellar. Then they moved out on to the roads and paths and walked to the neighbouring farm to see if he had wandered there.

Finally they also looked for him down by Tåkern, but however much they searched they failed to find him.

Caesar knew perfectly well that the whole household was hunting for Per Ola but he did nothing to put them on the right track. Instead, he just lay there quietly as if the whole thing had nothing to do with him.

Later in the day they found Per Ola's footprints down by the landing place for the boats and then they noticed that the rotting old skiff was no longer lying on the bank. Now they began to understand the course of events.

The farmer and his farmhands set out in the boats to look for the boy. They rowed around Tåkern until late evening without seeing any sign of him at all. They were left with no choice but to believe that the old skiff had sunk and that the little boy was lying at the bottom of the lake.

In the evening Per Ola's mother wandered around the shores of the lake. All the others were convinced that the boy had drowned but she could not bring herself to accept it and carried on looking for him. She searched among the reeds and sedge, walked and walked on the boggy ground without giving a thought to how deep her feet sank or how wet she became. She was filled with despair and her heart was breaking. She did not weep but she wrung her hands and called her child's name in a loud plaintive voice.

All around she could hear the cries of swans and ducks and curlews and she thought they were following her and that they, too, were wailing and lamenting. 'They must also have sorrows,' she thought, 'since they are wailing so.' But then she remembered that what she was hearing were only birds – and surely they could not have any worries?

It was strange that they did not fall silent after sunset, but even then she could still hear all the innumerable flocks of birds around Tåkern screaming and screaming. Some of them followed her wherever she walked, others flashed past on quick wings, and the air was filled with the sound of wailing and lamentation.

The anguish she was feeling opened her heart and she

no longer thought that she was as distinct from all other living creatures as human beings usually feel they are. She understood better than ever what things were like for the birds. Like her, they were constantly worried about their homes and their children. There really was not such a great difference between her and them as she had always thought.

Then it occurred to her that the decision that all these thousands of swans and ducks and divers were to lose their home on Tåkern was as good as made. 'Things will certainly be difficult for them,' she thought. 'Where are they going to bring up their young?'

She stood there wondering about this. It seemed a good and sensible piece of work to turn a lake into fields and meadows, but it would have to be some other lake rather than Tåkern, some other lake that was not home to so many thousands of animals.

She remembered that the decision about lowering the level of the lake was to be taken the next day and she wondered if that was why her little boy had gone missing today. Could it be that God intended sorrow to open her heart to mercy on this day of all days and before it was too late to avert the cruel deed?

She walked quickly back to the farm and began to talk to her husband about all this. She talked about the lake and about the birds and she said to him that she thought Per Ola's death came as a punishment from God. And she saw that he shared her view.

They already owned a large farm. If the lowering of the level of the lake took place, such a large part of the bed of the lake would become theirs that the size of their property would almost double. This explains why they had been keener on the project than any of the other landowners, who had been anxious about the expense and worried that the draining would be no more successful than the last time it was done. Per Ola's father was well aware that he was the one who had convinced them to go along with the project. He had used all his powers of persuasion so that he could leave his son twice as big a farm as his father had left him.

Now he stood and wondered whether it was the will of God that had led to Tåkern taking his son the day before he was intending to sign the contract to drain the lake. His wife did not need to say much to him before he answered: 'It may well be that God does not wish us to upset his order. I shall talk to the others in the morning and I think we'll decide that everything should stay as it is.'

While the farmer's family was talking about this, Caesar was lying in front of the fireplace. He had lifted his head and had listened very carefully. When he thought he could be sure of things, he went over to his mistress, took hold of her skirt and pulled her to the door. 'Caesar, what are you doing?' she said and tried to break free. Then she suddenly exclaimed: 'Do you know where Per Ola is?' Caesar barked joyfully and threw himself at the door. She opened it and Caesar rushed off towards Tåkern. His mistress was so certain that he knew where Per Ola was that she simply ran after him. No sooner had they reached the shore of the lake than they heard a child crying out on the lake.

Together with Thummitot and the birds Per Ola had enjoyed the happiest day of his life, but now he had started crying because he was hungry and afraid of the dark. So he was happy when mother and father and Caesar came and fetched him home.

XX

THE PROPHECY

Friday, 22 April

One night when the boy was lying asleep on an island on Tåkern he was wakened by the beat of oars. He had no sooner opened his eyes than a bright light shone in them and made him blink.

At first he could not work out what was shining so brightly out on the lake but he soon saw that there was a skiff floating at the edge of the reeds and it had a big burning torch fixed on an iron spike at the stern. The red flame from the torch was reflected clearly in the nocturnal darkness of the lake and the brilliant gleam must have been attractive to fish for there were many dark shapes continually moving and changing places around the reflection of the flame down in the deep waters.

There were two old men sitting in the skiff. One of them was sitting at the oars and the other was standing aft and holding a short and heavily barbed spear in his hand. The man rowing seemed to be a poor fisherman. He was small, wizened and weather-beaten and he was wearing a thin threadbare coat. It was clear that he was so used to being out in all weathers that the cold did not bother him. The other was well-fed, well-dressed and looked like a haughty and self-confident farmer.

'Hold steady now!' the farmer said when they were right opposite the island where the boy was. Then he suddenly jabbed the spear down into the water and when he lifted it out he brought a fine long eel from the depths.

'Look at that!' he said, taking the eel off the fishing-spear. 'Nothing the matter with that one! I think we've caught enough now and can go home.'

His companion did not lift the oars, he just sat there looking around. 'It's beautiful out here on the lake tonight,' he said. And indeed it was. The calm was so complete that all the surface of the water lay unruffled except for the strip where the boat had passed, which lay and shone like a golden pathway in the firelight. The sky was clear and deep blue and densely studded with stars. The shores of the lake were concealed by islands of reeds, except to the west where the Omberg shot up dark and high, seeming to be a much more massive hill than usual as it cut a great triangular segment from the vault of the heavens.

The second man turned his head to avoid the firelight shining in his eyes as he looked around. 'Yes, it is beautiful here in Östergötland,' he said, 'but the best thing about the province is not its beauty.'

'What is the best thing, then?' the oarsman asked.

'The fact that it is a province that has always been respected and honoured.'

'That might well be true, I suppose.'

'And then, of course, that we know that it will always be like that.'

'How on earth can we possibly know that?' the man sitting at the oars asked.

The farmer drew himself up to his full height and leant on his fishing-spear. 'There is an old story that has been passed from father to son in my family and from it we can learn what will happen to Östergötland in the future.'

'You can tell me the story, can't you?' the oarsman said.

'We're not in the habit of telling it to any Tom, Dick and Harry, but I won't keep a secret from an old friend.'

He began his story and from the tone of his voice you could tell he was talking about something that he had heard from others and learnt off by heart. 'Many years ago at Ulvåsa here in Östergötland there lived a woman who had the gift of being able to see into the future and tell people what was going to happen to them as certainly and accurately as if it had already happened. Her reputation spread far because of this and it's easy to see why people came from far and wide to visit her and find out what they were going to have to endure – whether it was good or bad.*

'One day when the Ulvåsa woman was sitting spinning in her hall – as was the custom in the old days – a poor peasant came into the hall and sat on the bench right down by the door.

'After a while the peasant said: "I wonder what it is you are thinking about as you sit there, dear lady."

'"I am sitting here thinking of matters both sacred and solemn," she answered.

'"In that case it wouldn't be right for me to ask you something that lies close to my heart," the peasant said.

'"I don't suppose you have anything much close to your heart apart from how to harvest as much corn as you can from your field. Usually I have the emperor asking me questions about the future of his crown or the pope asking about his keys to the kingdom of Heaven."

'"Yes well, I don't suppose there are easy answers to things like that," the peasant said. "I've also heard that everyone leaves here dissatisfied with what they have heard."

'When the peasant said this he saw that the Ulvåsa woman bit her lip and sat up higher on her bench. "So that's what you've heard about me, is it?" she said. "In which case you may as well tempt fate and ask me whatever it is you want to know and let's see if I can answer it in a way that makes you satisfied."

'On hearing this, the peasant did not hesitate any longer. He said he had come to ask what the future held for Östergötland. Nothing in the world was so dear to him as his home province and he felt that if the answer to that question was good he would be happy to his dying day.

'"If that is the only thing you want," the wise woman said, "I think you will be satisfied. Because true as I sit here now, I can tell you that in the future Östergötland is always going to have something more to boast about than other provinces have."

'"That is certainly a good answer, dear lady," the peasant said, "and I would be completely satisfied if I could only understand how that could possibly come to pass."

'"Why shouldn't it?" the Ulvåsa woman said. "You must be aware that Östergötland is already renowned? Do you think any other province in Sweden can boast of having two abbeys like Alvastra and Vreta and a cathedral as beautiful as the one in Linköping?"

'"That may well be so," the peasant said, "but I am an old man and I know that the mind of man is changeable. I'm afraid that the time will come when we shan't be honoured for Alvastra and Vreta nor, indeed, for our cathedral."

'"You may be right," the Ulvåsa woman said, "but you don't need to doubt my prophecy just because of that. I shall have a new abbey founded at Vadstena and it will become more famous than any other in Scandinavia. Both the high-born and the lowly will make pilgrimages to it and everyone will praise the province for possessing such a holy site within its borders."

'The peasant answered that he was very glad to hear that. But knowing that everything in this world is transient, he wondered what the reputation of the province would depend on should Vadstena Abbey ever fall into disrepute.

'"You are not an easy man to satisfy, are you," the Ulvåsa woman said, "but I can see far enough into the future to tell you that, before Vadstena Abbey loses its glory, a great castle – the most magnificent of its time – will be built close by. Kings and princes will stay there and the possession of such a jewel will bring honour to the whole province."

'"Well I'm very glad to hear that, too," the peasant said. "But I'm an old man and I know the fate that tends to afflict the splendours of this world. So, should this castle go to rack and ruin, I wonder what there will then be to draw people's eyes to our province."

'"You certainly want to know a lot," the Ulvåsa woman said, "but I can see far enough into the future to see life and activity up in the forests around Finspång. I can see foundries and smithies being built and I believe that the iron being produced there will bring honour to the whole province."

'The peasant did not deny that he was particularly pleased to hear this. But if things were to go from bad to worse and even the ironworks at Finspång were to lose their reputation, it would surely be impossible for anything new to arise and provide Östergötland with something to boast about?

'"You really are difficult to satisfy," the Ulvåsa woman said, "but I can see far enough into the future to see manor houses being built on the shores of our lakes – manor houses as big as castles, built by men who have fought wars in foreign countries. And I do believe that these manor houses will bring as much honour to the province as any of the other things I have mentioned."

'"But what if there comes a time when no one praises these great manor houses any more?" the peasant insisted stubbornly.

'"There is no reason for you to worry even then," the Ulvåsa woman said. "I can see the waters bubbling up from health-giving springs on the meadows at Medevi close to the shores of Lake Vättern. I believe the springs at Medevi will bring the province as much praise as you could wish for."

'"It's really good to hear that," the peasant said. "But what if there comes a time when people seek health at other spas?"

'"You have nothing to worry about on that account," the Ulvåsa woman answered. "I can see an army of people working from Motala to Mem, digging a canal right across the country – and that will bring the name and fame of Östergötland to everyone's lips again."

'But the peasant was still looking concerned.

'"I can see the rapids in the Motala river driving wheels," the Ulvåsa woman said and two red patches appeared on her cheeks because she was beginning to lose patience. "I can hear the pounding of hammers in Motala and the rattle of looms in Norrköping."

'"That's good to know," the peasant said, "but everything is transient and I fear that this, too, will also be gone and forgotten."

'But, since the peasant was still not satisfied, the woman's patience ran out. "You said that everything is transient," she said, "but let me tell you one thing that will always stay the same, which is that until the very end of time this province will be full of stubborn and arrogant peasants like you!"

'No sooner had the Ulvåsa woman said this than the peasant got up happy and satisfied and thanked her for the good news. Now, he said, he could be at peace at last.

'"Ah, now I don't understand what you mean," the Ulvåsa woman said.

'"What I mean, dear lady," said the peasant, "is that everything built by kings and monks and nuns and noblemen and merchants only survives for a few years. But when you tell me that there will always be ambitious and tenacious peasants in Östergötland, then I know that the province will retain its ancient renown. For it is only those who are bent by their eternal labour with the soil who can sustain the welfare and repute of this province from one age to the next."'

XXI

HOMESPUN CLOTH

Saturday, 23 April

The boy was travelling high in the sky. He had the great plain of Östergötland below him and he was counting all the white churches that poked up from the small clusters of trees surrounding them. It did not take him long to reach fifty, after which confusion set in and he could not keep track of the number.

Almost all the farms had big white-painted farmhouses of such a grand appearance that the boy could only marvel at them. 'There can't be any farmers in this province,' he said to himself, 'because I can't see any farms!'

Then all the wild geese yelled at once: 'The farmers here live like lords! The farmers here live like lords!'

All the ice and snow had disappeared from the plain and the work of spring had begun. 'What on earth are those long crabs creeping across the fields?' the boy asked after a while. 'Ploughs and oxen! Ploughs and oxen!' all the wild geese replied.

The oxen's progress across the fields was so slow that it was impossible to see whether they had moved at all and the geese shouted to them: 'You won't get there until next year. You won't get there until next year.' But the oxen were not short of an answer. They raised their muzzles in the air and bellowed: 'We do more good in an hour than the likes of you do in the whole of your lives.'

In some places the ploughs were pulled by horses, which moved much more quickly and vigorously than the oxen, but the geese could not resist annoying them, too. 'Aren't you ashamed of doing ox-work?' they shouted at the horses. 'Aren't you ashamed of doing ox-work?'

'Aren't you ashamed of being a lazybones?' the horses neighed back.

While the horses and the oxen were out working, the stud ram was strolling around the farmyard. Newly shorn and touchy, he butted small boys and knocked them over, drove the dog back into his kennel and marched round showing off as if he alone was in charge of the farm.

'Baa, baa, ram, ram, have you any wool?' the geese asked as they passed overhead. 'I've sent it to Drag's Mill in Norrköping,' the ram answered with a long baa.

'Baa, baa, ram, ram, have you any horns?' the geese asked. But to his great sorrow the ram had never had any horns and nothing upset him more than someone asking about them. He became so angry that he spent a long time running around butting the air.

Along the highway came a man driving a herd of Skåne pigs which were no more than a couple of weeks old and were to be sold up-country. Small as they were, they were trotting along bravely but sticking close to one another as if for protection. 'Nurf, nurf, nurf, we've left our parents too soon. Nurf, nurf, nurf, what's going to happen to us, poor children that we are?'

But not even the wild geese had the heart to tease these poor little souls. 'Things will be better than you can ever imagine,' they called as they passed the piglets.

The wild geese were never in a better humour than when travelling over a plain. They did not hurry, they simply flew from farm to farm and joked with the farm animals.

While the boy was riding over the plain, a tale he had heard a long time ago came into his mind. He could not remember it properly but it was something about a skirt which was made half of velvet woven with gold thread and half of grey homespun. But the owner of the skirt decorated the homespun part with so many pearls and precious stones that it shone brighter and was more precious than the part with the gold thread.

What made him remember the story about the homespun cloth when he looked down at Östergötland was that the countryside below consisted of a large plain enclosed by two hilly forested areas, one to the north and one to the south. Both of the tree-covered ranges of hills lay there a beautiful blue colour in the morning light and shimmered as if they were cloaked in golden veils whereas the plain, which consisted of nothing but one bare field after another, was no prettier to behold than grey homespun.

But because the plain was generous and kind, there is no doubt that human beings had thrived there and they had tried to decorate it as well as they could. As the boy passed high overhead he thought that the towns and farms, churches and factories, castles and railway stations looked like big and little trinkets scattered across the plain. The tiled roofs shone and the window-panes glittered like jewels. Yellow country roads, shining railway tracks and blue canals ran from one place to another like ribbons of embroidered silk. Linköping lay around its cathedral like the pearl setting for a precious stone, and the farms in the countryside were like small brooches and buttons. There was not much order to the pattern, but there was a splendour that the eye never tired of.

The geese had left the area around the Omberg and were travelling east following the Göta Canal. That, too, was getting itself in order for summer and workmen were mending the canal banks and painting the great lock-gates with tar.

Indeed, there was work going on everywhere, even in the towns, in order to give spring a good reception. Painters and bricklayers stood on scaffolding as they put the houses in order, servant girls climbed up, opened the windows and washed the glass. The sailing boats and steam vessels down in the harbour were being spruced up.

At Norrköping the wild geese left the plain and flew up towards Kolmården. For some time they had been following a hilly old country road that wound its way along ravines and under rocky walls when the boy suddenly gave a shout. He had been swinging his foot back and forth as he sat there and now one of his clogs had slipped off.

'Gander, gander, I've dropped my shoe!' the boy yelled.

The gander turned and flew down towards the ground, but then the boy saw that two children who were walking along the road had picked up his shoe.

'Gander, gander,' the boy shouted hastily, 'go back up! It's too late. I can't get my shoe back.'

But down on the road Åsa Goose-girl and her brother Little Mats stood looking at a tiny wooden shoe that had fallen from the sky.

'It was the wild geese who dropped it,' Little Mats said.

Åsa Goose-girl remained silent for a long time as she pondered over their find. At last she spoke slowly and thoughtfully: 'Do you remember, Little Mats, that when we were passing Övedskloster we heard them say that the people on a farm had seen an elf dressed in leather breeches and wearing clogs just like any other working man? And do you remember how when we reached Vittskövle a girl told us she had seen an elf wearing clogs and that he had flown away on the back of a goose? And when we went home to our cottage, Little Mats, we saw a little midget dressed in the same way – and he climbed up on a goose and flew away too. Perhaps it is the same one who was riding along up there on a goose when he dropped his wooden shoe?'

'Yes, that's what must have happened,' Little Mats said.

They turned the clog this way and that and studied it closely, for it is not every day that you find an elf's clog lying on a country road.

'Wait a minute, Little Mats, there is something written on one side,' said Åsa Goose-girl.

'Yes, there is, but the letters are so small.'

'Let me see! Yes, it says – it says: Nils Holgersson, V. Vemmenhög.'

'That's the strangest thing I've ever heard,' Little Mats said.

XXII

THE SAGA OF KARR AND GREYFUR

KOLMÅRDEN

North of Bråviken, where the border between Östergötland and Sörmland runs, there is a hill many miles long and seven or eight miles wide. If its height corresponded to its length and breadth, it would be one of the most impressive hills that exists, but it does not.

We sometimes encounter a building that is so over-ambitious from the start that the owner has never managed to finish it. Everyone who approaches it can see the solid foundations, strong arches and deep cellars, but the walls and roof are missing and the whole thing does not rise more than a couple of feet above the ground. Anyone approaching this hill on the border between Östergötland and Sörmland may well be reminded of an abandoned building of that kind, because it does not really look like a finished job, it looks like the foundations of a hill. It rises from the plain with steep walls and there are bold piles of rocks everywhere – they look as if they are designed to support high, enormous halls of rock. Everything is mighty and wild and on a grand scale, but nothing ever reaches up to any real height or elevation. The builder wearied of it and left his work before he had got round to erecting those long and precipitous slopes and sharp peaks and ridges which usually form the walls and roof of finished mountains.

As if to compensate for its lack of peaks and summits, this great hilly zone has always been cloaked in tall and mighty trees. Oaks and lime trees grow around the fringes and in the valleys, birch and alder around the lakes, pines up on the steeper slopes, and spruce wherever it has been able to find a handful of soil to take root. Taken together, all of these trees formed the great forest of Kolmården, a place which used to be so terrifying that anyone who had to travel through it would pray to God and prepare themselves for their final hour.

The origins of the forest of Kolmården are so long ago that it is impossible now to say how it became what it was. Given the bare rocky nature of the ground it must have had a hard time at the start, and it was made tough and tenacious by having to find a foothold among hard slabs of rock and drawing sustenance from meagre gravelly streams. Things went as they often do among those who have a hard struggle in their youth but who go on to become vigorous and strong in their mature years. When the forest was full-grown it had trees that measured twenty feet in circumference, trees whose branches were plaited into an impenetrable tangle, and the ground beneath these trees was a network of hard, slippery roots. It became the perfect refuge for wild animals and for robbers who knew how to creep and crawl and scramble in order to make progress. But the forest had little to attract anyone else. It was dark and bleak, trackless and confusing, scrubby and prickly – and the old trees looked like trolls as they stood there with beards of lichen on their branches and moss on their trunks.

When human beings first moved into Sörmland and Östergötland those provinces were almost completely cloaked in forest, but the settlers soon cleared it from the plains and from the fertile valleys. But no one bothered to fell Kolmården, which was growing on poor rocky soil, and the longer it was left there undisturbed, the mightier it became. It was like a fortress, the walls of which grew thicker with the passing of time, and anyone wanting to penetrate these dense forest walls needed an axe to help them.

Other forests have reason to be afraid of people, but in the case of Kolmården it was the people who were afraid. It was so dark and dense that hunters and wood-gatherers were forever going astray and coming close to perishing before they managed to find a way out of the thick woods. And for travellers who had to make the journey between Östergötland and Sörmland, the forest was no less than life-threatening. They had to find their way along narrow paths made by animals because the people of the border area had not even been able to maintain a cleared track through the forest. Nor were there any bridges across the rivers or ferries across the lakes or boards laid across the bogs. There was not a single hut inhabited by decent people in the whole forest but there were plenty of lairs for wild beasts and hide-outs for robbers. Not many people emerged from the forest unharmed, whereas any number of them fell over precipices or rode into bogs or were plundered by robbers or hunted by wild animals. Even the people living just outside the forest, who had no thought nor desire to enter it, suffered because of the bears and wolves that were forever emerging from the trees and savaging their cattle. And since the dense forest offered such good hiding places, it was impossible to root out the wild animals.

There can be no doubt that the people of Östergötland and the people of Sörmland would have been glad to be rid of the Kolmården forest, but as long as there was land to cultivate elsewhere, there was no great hurry to do much about it. Gradually, however, it was brought under some sort of control and farms and parishes grew up on the hilly slopes around the fringes of the great forest itself. A few roads were built and at Krokek, right in the middle of the wilderness, monks built a monastery to provide travellers with a safe sanctuary.

But the forest continued to be an overpowering and dangerous place until the day came when a traveller, who had penetrated far into its depths, discovered that there was iron ore in the rock beneath. As soon as this became known mining engineers and miners hurried to the forest to assess its riches.

What happened next broke the power of the ancient forest. People dug mines and built foundries and ironworks which, in itself, would not have done any serious damage if it had not been for the incredible quantities of wood and charcoal required to process the iron ore. Charcoal burners and woodcutters went into the mysterious primeval forest and almost put an end to it. All around every ironworks the land was clear-felled and the ground laid out as fields. Settlers moved in and soon new parishes with their churches and manses sprang up on ground where only the lairs of bears had existed a short time before.

Even in places where the forest was not clear-felled, ancient trees were taken down and dense thickets cleared. Roads were pushed through in all directions and the wild animals and robbers chased out. And once people had won control of the forest, they treated it disgracefully: chopping and firing and charcoal burning without limit. They had not forgotten their old hatred of the place and they seemed determined to destroy it.

Fortunately for the forest there was not a great deal of ore in the Kolmården mines and mining and iron-working declined. Charcoal burning also came to a halt and that gave the forest a small breathing space. Many of the people who had settled in the Kolmården parishes became unemployed and found it hard to survive, but the forest itself began to grow and spread again, surrounding farms and ironworks so that they lay there like islands in the sea. The people of Kolmården tried their hand at agriculture but without any great success. The soil of the old forest floor preferred to support giant oaks and great pines rather than turnips and wheat.

People cast dark and gloomy looks at the forest, which seemed to be flourishing more and more as they themselves became poorer, but at last it occurred to them that there might be some good in it after all. Might it not be possible to make a living out of the forest itself? It was worth finding out what the possibilities were, anyway.

So they began harvesting trees and timber from the forest and selling them to the people living out on the plain, where the forests had already been used up. They soon noticed that if they went about it in a sensible way they could earn a living from the forest just as well as from fields or mines. And they began to see the forest in a new light. They learnt to value it and love it. They completely forgot the enmity they had felt in the past and began to think of the forest as their best friend.

KARR

About twelve years before Nils Holgersson started travelling with the geese, an ironmaster in Kolmården wanted to put down one of his hunting dogs. He sent for his gamekeeper, told him it was impossible to keep the dog since no one had managed to train him out of chasing all the sheep and hens he caught sight of, and so the keeper was to take the dog into the forest and shoot him.

The keeper put the dog on a lead to walk him out to the place in the forest where all the worn-out dogs on the estate were taken to be shot and buried. He was not an unkind man but he was quite happy to shoot this dog because he knew that in addition to chasing sheep and hens, he would quite often go to the forest and steal a hare or a young blackcock.

The dog was small and black and had a buff bib and buff front legs. His name was Karr and he was so clever he could understand what people were saying. He knew perfectly well what was in store for him when the keeper led him off into the forest, but no one would have known that from his behaviour. He neither hung his head, nor did his tail droop, he looked just as carefree as usual.

It was precisely because they were walking through a forest that the dog was so careful not to show any anxiety. All around the old ironworks lay a great expanse of forest that was famous among animals and human beings because its owners had taken such care of it that they had even been loth to fell trees for firewood. Nor had they had the heart to thin it out or discipline it. The forest had been allowed to go its own way and do as it pleased. Naturally enough, a forest that was so well protected became a favourite place for forest animals and they lived there in very large numbers. Between themselves they called it Sanctuary Wood and reckoned it to be the best refuge they had in the whole country.

As the dog was being led through the forest he thought about what a scourge he had been to all the small animals who lived there. 'Well Karr,' he thought, 'they'd be really glad in their hiding places if they knew what you had to look forward to.' And he wagged his tail and gave a happy bark so that no one would think he was worried or downhearted.

'What would have been the fun of living if I hadn't chased things now and again?' he said. 'Others may have their regrets but that's not my style.'

No sooner had the dog said this than a strange change came over him. He raised his head and stretched his neck as if he wanted to howl and instead of trotting along beside the keeper, he hung back. It was obvious that something unpleasant had come into his mind.

Now all this was happening at the start of summer. The cow elk had just given birth to their calves and the previous evening the dog had managed to separate a calf, which could not have been more than five days old, from his mother and driven him out into a bog. There he had chased him back and forth among the tussocks, not so much to catch him as to enjoy seeing his terror. The cow elk knew that the bog would be a bottomless morass so soon after the thaw and would not yet bear the weight of an animal her size, so she stayed on firm ground for a long time. But when Karr chased the calf farther and farther away, the cow suddenly went out into the bog, drove away the dog and turned back towards firm ground again. Elk are more skilful than other animals when it comes to moving on boggy and dangerous terrain and it looked as if she would make it back to safety. But when she was almost on firm ground again, a tussock that she stepped on sank right down into the bog and she went down into the depths with it. She attempted to get out but could not find any firm footing and so she sank deeper and deeper. Karr stood and watched, hardly daring to breathe, but when he saw that the elk could not save herself he ran away as quickly as he could. He had suddenly remembered the thrashing he would get if anyone were to find out that he was the one who had caused the elk's misfortune. He was so frightened that he did not dare stop until he reached home.

This was the incident that had come into the dog's mind and it troubled him in a very different way to all the other bad things he had done. Perhaps this was because he had not wanted to kill the cow elk or her calf but, unintentionally, he had done so anyway.

'Perhaps they are still alive,' the dog thought suddenly. 'They weren't dead when I ran away. Perhaps they have managed to save themselves.'

He was seized by an irresistible urge to find out – while he still had time to find anything out! Seeing that the keeper was not holding the lead very tight, he quickly jumped sideways and broke free. Then he rushed off through the forest towards the bog at such a speed that the keeper had no time to raise and sight his gun before the dog was out of sight.

The gamekeeper had no choice but to hurry after him and when he reached the bog he saw the dog standing and howling with all his might out on a tussock in the bog some yards from safe ground. The man thought he had better find out what this was all about, put down his gun and crept out on the bog on all fours. He had not gone very far before he caught sight of a cow elk lying dead in the sludge, and tucked close beside her was a little calf. The calf was still alive but so exhausted that it could not move. Beside the calf stood Karr, who bent down and licked it every now and again and sometimes howled at the top of his voice to call for help.

The gamekeeper lifted up the calf and began pulling it out of the bog. The dog was beside himself with joy when he realised the calf would be saved and he jumped up at the keeper, licking his hands and whining in pleasure.

The keeper carried the calf home and shut it in a pen in the cowshed. Then he called for help to pull the dead elk out of the bog and only when all that was finished did he remember he was supposed to shoot Karr. He called Karr to him – the dog had been following him the whole time anyway – and set off again into the forest.

For a start the keeper walked straight towards the dogs' grave but as he walked he seemed to be having a change of heart, and then, out of the blue, he turned and began walking towards the manor house.

Karr had been following him calmly but when he saw that the keeper was going towards his old home he became worried. The gamekeeper must have worked out that it was Karr who had caused the death of the cow elk and they were on their way up to the manor for him to be punished before he died.

Getting a beating was the worst thing in the world and, with the thought of that in mind, Karr found it impossible to keep his spirits up. He walked along with his head hanging low and when they reached the manor house he did not look up and pretended not to recognise anyone.

The estate owner was standing out on the front steps when the keeper walked up. 'What dog is that you've brought along, for Heaven's sake?' the owner said. 'It surely can't be Karr? He's supposed to be dead and gone by now!'

The gamekeeper began to tell him about the elk and Karr, meanwhile, made himself as small as possible, crouching behind the keeper's legs to hide. But the keeper did not tell the story in the way the dog had expected him to tell it: he had nothing but praise for Karr, saying that it was obvious that Karr knew that the elk were in distress and had wanted to save them. 'You must do as you will, master,' the keeper said in conclusion, 'but I can't shoot the dog now.'

The dog stood up and pricked up his ears. He could hardly believe that he had heard properly. Although he really did not want to show how worried he had been, he could not help whining a little. Was it possible that his life was about to be spared just because he had shown some concern for the elk?

The master also thought that Karr had behaved well, but since he did not want him back anyway, he was not sure what to decide. 'Well, if you are willing to take him and be responsible for him being better behaved than in the past, he can live,' the master said after a while. Yes, the keeper was willing to do that, which is how Karr came to move in to the keeper's cottage.

GREYFUR'S FLIGHT

From the day Karr moved in with the gamekeeper he completely gave up his unlawful hunting in the forest. This was not just because he had been given a real fright but probably also because he did not want the gamekeeper to have any reason to be angry with him. Since the keeper had saved his life, Karr loved him more than anyone else and his only thought was to follow him around and to guard him. Whenever the keeper left home, Karr would run in front and check the road and when the keeper was sitting at home, Karr lay outside the door and kept an eye on everyone who came or went.

When everything was quiet at the keeper's cottage, when no footsteps could be heard along the road and when the keeper was busy with the small saplings he cultivated in his garden, Karr spent his time playing with the elk calf.

In the beginning Karr had no desire to have anything to do with him. But since the dog went everywhere with his master, that also meant he accompanied him to the cowshed when he went to give the calf milk. Karr would sit outside the pen and watch. The keeper called the calf Greyfur because he did not really think he was worthy of a prettier name, and Karr could only agree with him. Every time he looked at the calf he thought he had never seen anything so ugly and so badly designed. He had long gangly legs that were attached under his body like loose stilts. His head was big and old and wrinkly and it always hung to one side. His skin was all folds and furrows, as if he was wearing a fur-coat that had been made for someone else. He looked sad and despondent the whole time but, strangely enough, he always stood up quickly whenever he saw Karr outside his pen, as if he was glad to see him.

But the elk calf grew weaker from day to day. He did not grow at all and eventually was unable to stand up even when he saw Karr. The dog then jumped into the pen with him, and all at once a glimmer came to the poor weak animal's eyes as if to reveal that his deepest desires were being fulfilled. From then on Karr used to visit the calf every day and spend hours with him, licking his fur, playing and frolicking with him and teaching him a little of everything a forest animal needs to be aware of.

It was quite remarkable how, once Karr had taken to climbing into the pen, the calf had begun to grow and thrive. And once he had started he grew so much in a couple of weeks that there was no longer space for him in the pen and he had to be moved out to an enclosure. After he had been in the enclosure for a few months his legs were long enough for him to step over the fence whenever he wanted to, so the gamekeeper asked permission from the owner to erect a high fence. Here the elk lived for several years and grew into a big and splendid animal. Karr kept him company whenever he could, but it was no longer just a case of sympathy but because a strong bond of friendship had developed between the two animals. The elk was still melancholy and seemed both lazy and lacking in enterprise but Karr had the knack of making him playful and happy.

Greyfur had been living at the keeper's cottage for five summers when the estate owner received a letter from a foreign zoo asking to buy the elk. The owner favoured the proposal and although the keeper was sad he did not have the authority to refuse. So it was decided that the elk would be sold. Karr soon got to know what was being planned and he hurried to tell the elk that they were intending to send him away. The dog was extremely upset to be losing him but the elk took it calmly and seemed neither happy nor sad.

'Are you going to let them take you away without putting up any resistance?' Karr asked him.

'What would be the point of resisting?' Greyfur said. 'I would rather stay where I am but if I am sold I shall have to leave.'

Karr stood and looked at Greyfur, measuring him up with his eyes. It was obvious that the elk was not yet full grown. His horns were not so broad, his hump was not so high and his mane was not so full as those of a fully-grown bull elk, but he certainly had enough strength to fight for his freedom. 'It's very obvious that he has been a prisoner all his life,' Karr thought, but he said nothing.

Karr did not return to the elk's enclosure until after midnight, by which time he knew that Greyfur would be fully rested and eating his first meal. 'You're probably doing the right thing, Greyfur, letting them take you away,' Karr said, appearing to be quite happy with the idea. 'You'll be kept prisoner in a big garden and you'll be able to lead a life free of trouble. But I do think it's a pity that you'll have to leave here without having seen the forest. You know that your kin have a saying, which states that the elk and the forest are one. But you haven't even been into a forest.'

Greyfur looked up from the clover he was chewing and said in his usual lethargic way: 'I'd certainly like to see the forest but how am I supposed to get over the fence?'

'Yes, I don't suppose that would be possible for someone with legs as short as yours!' Karr said.

The elk gave Karr – who, small as he was, jumped over the fence several times a day – a sly look, went over to the fence, jumped it and was out of his enclosure almost without knowing how it had happened.

Karr and Greyfur then set off into the forest. It was a beautiful moonlight night at the end of summer but it was dark beneath the trees and the elk went quite slowly. 'Perhaps we'd better turn back,' Karr said. 'Never having been out in the wild forest before, you could easily break a leg.' Greyfur immediately began walking faster and less nervously.

Karr led the elk to a part of the wood where enormous spruce trees grew so densely that even the wind could not penetrate. 'This is where your kin take refuge from the cold and the storm,' Karr said. 'They have to stay out under the open sky right through the winter. I'm sure things will be much better for you where you are going. You'll have a roof over your head and you'll be stabled like an ox.'

Greyfur said nothing, he just stood there breathing in the strong scent of pine-needles. 'Do you have any more to show me or have I seen the whole forest now?' he asked.

Karr then took him to a great moss and showed him the tussocks and the quagmire. 'Elk can usually flee across a moss like this when they are in danger,' Karr said. 'I don't know how they do it but, big and heavy as they are, they get across without sinking. I doubt whether you'd be able to stay on the surface of such dangerous ground, but then you won't need to because you are never going to be chased by hunters.'

Greyfur did not answer but with one long bound he was out in the moss. He was happy to feel the tussocks swaying beneath him as he ran right across the moss before returning to Karr without falling down into a single boggy hole. 'Have we seen the whole forest now?' he asked. 'No, not yet,' Karr answered.

Next he led the elk to the edge of the forest where fine deciduous trees grew – oak and aspen and lime. 'This is where your kinsfolk eat leaves and bark,' Karr said. 'They consider it the very finest food but no doubt you will get better abroad.'

Greyfur was amazed by the mighty trees which spread their green vault over him. He tasted both oak leaves and aspen bark. 'This tastes sharp and good,' he said. 'It's better than clover.'

'It's good you've had the chance to taste them at least once, then,' the dog said.

After that he took the elk to a little forest tarn. It lay there shining and still, reflecting its banks which were lightly veiled in thin mist. When Greyfur saw it he stood absolutely motionless. 'What is it, Karr?' he asked, it being the first time he had seen a lake. 'It's a big stretch of water, it's a lake,' Karr said. 'Your kin usually swim across it from shore to shore. It would be too much to expect you to do it, but you ought at least go down and have a bath.' Karr himself went into the water and started swimming. Greyfur remained on land for quite some time but finally he followed Karr. He was breathless with pleasure when the water crept soft and cool all round his body. He wanted it on his back as well and went out farther; he felt the water supporting him and he began to swim. He swam around Karr and felt completely at home in the water. Once they were standing on the bank again the dog asked whether it was time for them to go home. 'It's still a long time until morning. We can walk around the forest for a while yet,' Greyfur said.

They went back in among the fir trees and soon they came to a small open space where, in the bright light of the moon, the grass and flowers were sparkling with dew. In the middle of this small meadow there were some large animals grazing. There was a bull elk, several cow elk and some heifers and calves. When Greyfur caught sight of them he came to a sudden halt. He scarcely paid any attention to the cows and the young animals but he stared at the old bull with his wide, spade-like antlers with many points, the high hump on his shoulders and the long hairy pouch hanging from his throat.

'What kind of animal is that?' Greyfur asked, his voice trembling in amazement.

'He's called Horncrown,' Karr said, 'and he's one of your kin. One day you too will have broad antlers like that and a mane like that – and if you stayed in the forest you would no doubt also have a herd to lead.'

'If he's my kin I'd like to go closer and take a look at him,' Greyfur said. 'I'd never have believed that an animal could be so magnificent.'

Greyfur went up to the elk but returned almost immediately to Karr, who had been waiting at the edge of the trees.

'You didn't get a good reception, I imagine,' Karr said.

'I told him that this was the first time I had met kinsfolk and I asked if I might join them on the meadow but he told me to go away and he threatened me with his antlers.'

'You were right to back away,' Karr said. 'A young bull who only has antlers with small tines should beware of fighting an old elk. Anyone else would have got a bad name if they had backed off without putting up some resistance, but you don't need to worry about things like that since you will be going abroad.'

Karr had scarcely finished speaking before Greyfur turned and went back to the meadow. The old elk came towards him and they immediately started fighting. Their antlers joined and the two animals heaved and Greyfur was pushed backwards right across the meadow. He did not seem to understand how to use his strength. But when they came to the edge of the trees, he dug his feet deeper into the ground, pushed powerfully with his antlers and began to drive Horncrown back. Greyfur fought in silence but Horncrown panted and snorted and the old bull was now, in his turn, pushed back across the clearing. Suddenly there was a loud crack and one of the points in the old bull's antlers snapped. He jerked himself violently free from Greyfur and ran into the forest.

Karr was still standing at the edge of the clearing when Greyfur approached him. 'You have seen what there is to see in the forest,' Karr said. 'Do you want to come home with me now?'

'Yes, it's about time now,' the elk said.

Both of them were silent on the way home. Karr sighed a few times as though he had miscalculated something but Greyfur strode on with his head held high and seemed pleased with the whole adventure. He walked on without any hesitation until he came to the fence and there he stopped. He looked in and saw the confined space in which he had lived until then, saw the trampled earth, the withered fodder, the small trough from which he had drunk his water, and the dark shed in which he had slept. 'The elk and the forest are one!' he roared, throwing his head right back and storming off in full flight into the forest.

HELPLESS
Every year in August in a cluster of spruce trees in the very

deepest depths of Sanctuary Wood a few greyish-white moths would appear. They were small and few in number, of a kind called nun moths, and hardly anyone paid any attention to them. After fluttering around in the deep forest for a couple of nights, they would lay several thousand eggs on the tree-trunks and shortly afterwards sink lifeless to the ground.

With the arrival of spring the small speckled larvae would creep out and began to eat the needles of the tree. They had a good appetite but they never did the trees any serious harm because they were vigorously hunted by birds. There were rarely more than a couple of hundred larvae who escaped their persecutors.

The poor larvae that did manage to survive crawled up on the branches, wound themselves tightly in white thread and remained there immobile for some weeks as pupae. More than half of them were usually gobbled up during this time. If a hundred or so nun moths emerged with wings and ready to fly in August, it could be counted a good year for them.

Nun moths led that sort of obscure and uncertain existence in Sanctuary Wood for many years. There was no other species of insect in the whole district that existed in such small numbers and they would have continued to be weak and unthreatening if they had not, quite unexpectedly, got a helper.

The fact that nun moths found a helper was connected with Greyfur moving away from the keeper's cottage. Following his flight Greyfur had spent the whole of the following day going round the forest in order to make himself feel at home there. In the afternoon he happened to push through some tight tangles of bushes and behind them found an open space where the ground was nothing but mud and soft sludge. There was a pool of black water in the middle and all round it were tall spruce trees that had lost most of their needles because of age and a poor environment. Greyfur disliked the place and would have left it at once if he had not caught sight of the bright green leaves of bog arum growing beside the pool.

As he lowered his head to eat the bog arum he chanced to wake a big black snake that was sleeping under the leaves. The elk had heard Karr talk of the poisonous adders that lived in the forest and when the snake raised its head, stuck out its forked tongue and hissed at him, he believed he had met a dreadfully dangerous animal. Utterly terrified, he raised his foot, kicked out with his hoof and crushed the snake's head. Then he fled in a wild panic.

As soon as Greyfur had gone, another snake emerged from the pool. It was as long and black as the first and it slithered over to the dead snake and ran its tongue over its crushed head.

'Are you really dead, old Harmless?' the snake hissed. 'The two of us have lived together for so many years! We've been so happy with each other and thrived so well in this marsh that we've lived longer than all the other grass snakes in the forest. No greater sorrow could have befallen me.'

The grass snake was so distressed that his long body writhed as if he too had been wounded. Even the frogs, who normally lived in constant fear of him, felt sorry for him.

'Oh, how evil he must be, to kill a poor grass snake who could not defend herself!' the snake hissed. 'He deserves to be punished severely.' The snake lay there for a while writhing in sorrow but then he raised his head: 'As sure as my name is Helpless and I am the oldest grass snake in the forest, I will take revenge for this. I shall not rest until that elk lies as dead on the ground as my dear mate.'

Once the snake had made this promise he coiled himself into a circle and lay there thinking. It is hard to think of anything more difficult for a poor grass snake than to take revenge on a big strong elk and old Helpless spent days and nights pondering without finding a solution.

But one night as the grass snake lay there thinking his thoughts of revenge and unable to sleep, he heard a slight rustling above his head. He looked up and caught sight of some pale nun moths playing between the trees. For a long time he followed their movements and then he began to hiss aloud to himself, but finally he fell asleep and seemed to be pleased with the idea that had come to him.

The following morning the grass snake set off to visit Crawler, an adder who lived in a stony upland part of Sanctuary Wood. He told him of the death of his old mate and asked him to take over the duty of revenge since his bite was so dangerous. But Crawler was not inclined to declare war on elks. 'If I attacked an elk,' he said, 'he would kill me immediately. Old Harmless is dead and we cannot bring her back to life. Why should I hurl myself headlong into misfortune for her sake?'

When the grass snake heard this answer, he raised his head a good foot above the ground and began hissing vehemently. 'Visch, vasch! Visch, vasch!' he said. 'It's a great shame that you have been given such weapons and yet you are so cowardly that you don't dare use them!'

On hearing these words the adder, too, became angry. 'Time for you to crawl away, old Helpless,' he hissed. 'The poison is running into my fangs but I'd rather not use it on someone who is supposed to be my kin.'

The grass snake did not budge and for a long time the two snakes lay there hissing abuse at one another. But when Crawler became so angry that he could no longer hiss and just flicked his tongue back and forth, the grass snake quickly changed tack and started talking in a very different tone.

'I actually have another errand as well,' he said, dropping his voice to a gentle whisper, 'but I've probably annoyed you so much that you won't want to help me.'

'I'm quite prepared to be of service as long as you don't ask me to do something completely mad.'

'There is a species of moth that lives in the spruce trees around my marsh,' the grass snake said, 'and they fly around at night in late summer.'

'I know the ones you mean,' the adder said. 'What's the matter with them?'

'They are the least numerous of all the insect families in the forest,' Helpless said, 'and the least damaging since the larvae eat nothing but spruce needles.'

'I know that,' Crawler said.

'I'm afraid that species will be completely wiped out,' the grass snake said. 'There are so many animals picking off the larvae in spring.'

Now Crawler assumed, of course, that the grass snake wanted to keep the larvae for himself and he answered in a friendly tone: 'Do you want me to tell the owls to leave the caterpillars alone?'

'Yes, since your word carries some weight in this forest it would be good if you would undertake to do that,' Helpless said.

'Perhaps I should also have a word with the thrushes, too?' the adder said. 'As I said, I'm happy to be of service as long as you're not asking something unreasonable.'

'That's a fine promise you've given me,' Helpless said. 'I'm glad that I came here to see you.'

THE NUNS

One morning some years after this, Karr was lying asleep on the porch step. It was early summer, the time of short nights, and it was full daylight even though the sun was not up yet. Karr was woken by someone calling his name. 'Was that you, Greyfur?' Karr asked, for he was used to the elk coming to visit him almost every night. There was no answer, but he heard someone calling him once again. He thought he recognised Greyfur's voice so he hurried off in the direction it came from.

Karr could hear the elk running ahead of him but he could not catch him up. The elk was charging through thickets into the densest part of the spruce forest, following neither tracks nor paths, and Karr found it very hard not to lose track of him. 'Karr! Karr!' came the shout and the voice was that of Greyfur although there was a ring to it the dog had never heard before. 'I'm coming, I'm coming! But where are you?' the dog answered. 'Karr, Karr, don't you see how it's all falling, falling, falling?' Greyfur asked. And then Karr noticed that the needles were falling from the branches ceaselessly, falling like light rain. 'Yes, I see how it's falling,' the dog called, and set off at once into the forest to find the elk.

Greyfur rushed on in front, right through thickets so that Karr once again almost lost track. 'Karr, Karr!' Greyfur shouted, really roaring now. 'Can you smell it? Can you smell the forest?'

Karr stopped and sniffed the air. He had not thought of it before but now he noticed that the scent coming from the spruce trees was much stronger than usual. 'Yes, I can smell it,' he said, but rather than stop to find out what it was he hurried on after Greyfur.

The elk continued running at such a speed that the dog still could not catch up. 'Karr, Karr,' he shouted after a while. 'Can you hear the clicking in the spruces?' The elk's voice was now sad enough to draw tears from the rocks and stones. Karr stopped to listen and he could hear a faint but definite clicking sound up in the trees. It sounded like the ticking of a clock.

'Yes, I can hear the clicking,' Karr shouted, and he stopped running. He realised that the elk did not so much want him to follow as to make him pay attention to something that was happening to the forest.

Karr stood under a spruce tree with bushy sloping branches and coarse dark-green needles. He looked closely at the tree and the needles seemed to be moving. When he approached closer he discovered a great host of greyish-white larvae making their way along the branches and eating the needles. Every branch was full of them and they were all gnawing and eating. All the trees were ticking and clicking with the sound of their small jaws working. A constant shower of chewed-off needles was falling to the ground and the poor trees were emitting such a powerful scent that it really troubled the dog.

'That spruce certainly won't be keeping many of its needles,' he thought, his eyes moving on to the next tree. That, too, was a tall stately tree but it was in the same state as the first one. 'What can it be?' Karr wondered. 'It's a pity for all these lovely trees – they won't have much beauty left.' He went from tree to tree, trying to find out what was happening to them. 'That's a pine tree. Perhaps they'll have left that one alone,' he thought, but they had also attacked the pine. 'And there's a birch – and they are there, too. The keeper's not going to be pleased about this,' Karr thought.

He ran deeper into the forest to see how far the devastation spread and wherever he went he could hear the same ticking, smell the same smell and see the same rain of falling needles. He did not even have to stop and look in order to recognise what was happening. The small larvae were everywhere and the whole forest was being stripped bare by them.

All of a sudden he reached an area where there was no scent and where everything was silent and still. 'Ah, this is the end of their domain,' he thought, stopping and looking round. But it was even worse here, for the larvae had finished their work and the trees were stripped of their needles. They looked as if they were dead and the only covering left was the web of tangled threads the larvae had spun to use as bridges and roads between the trees.

Greyfur was standing waiting for Karr in among the dying trees. He was not alone; beside him stood four old elk, the most respected in the forest. Karr knew them. There was Crookback, a small elk who had a bigger hump than any of the others; Horncrown, the most magnificent of the elk; Stiffmane, who had thick fur; and an old, long-legged elk called Headstrong, who had been extremely hot-tempered and combative until he had received a bullet in the thigh during the last hunt of the autumn.

'What on earth's happening to the forest?' Karr asked when he reached the elk, who were standing there looking thoughtful, their heads hanging low and their top lips pouting.

'No one can say,' Greyfur answered. 'This particular family of insects has always been the least powerful in the forest and has never done any damage before, but in the last few years their numbers have grown very quickly and now it looks as if they are about to destroy the whole forest.'

'Yes, it looks bad,' Karr said, 'but I see that the wisest animals in the forest have come together to take counsel – perhaps you have already come up with a remedy?'

When the dog said this, Crookback lifted his heavy head solemnly, flipped his long ears and said: 'We've called you here, Karr, to find out whether the human beings are aware of this devastation.'

'No,' Karr said, 'they are not. No human being ever ventures this far into the densest part of the forest, except during the hunting season of course. They know nothing about this disaster.'

'Those of us who are old in the forest,' Horncrown said, 'do not believe that we animals can deal with this insect population on our own.'

'And that in itself will be a misfortune almost as great as this,' Stiffmane said. 'There's not likely to be any peace in the forest from now on.'

'But we cannot let the whole forest be ruined,' Headstrong said. 'We don't have a choice.'

Karr realised that the elk were finding it difficult to come out with what they really wanted to say so he tried to help them. 'Perhaps you want me to let the human beings know what is going on?'

All the old animals started to nod their heads: 'It's a dreadful piece of bad luck to have to ask human beings for help but there is no other way.'

A little while later Karr was on his way home. As he was hurrying along deeply concerned about everything he had discovered, a big black grass snake came towards him.

'Nice to see you in the forest!' the snake hissed.

'Nice to see you too!' Karr snapped and hurried on past without stopping. But the snake turned and tried to stop him. 'Perhaps he's worried about the forest too,' Karr thought and came to a halt.

The snake immediately started talking about the great devastation. 'I'm sure it will mean the end of any peace and quiet in the forest if human beings are called in,' he said.

'I share your fears,' Karr said, 'but the forest elders must know what they are doing.'

'I think I could come up with better counsel,' the grass snake said, 'as long as I was given the reward I desire.'

'Aren't you the one they call Helpless?' the dog said scornfully.

'I am old in the forest,' the grass snake said, 'and I know how to get rid of pests of this kind.'

'If you can get rid of this one,' Karr said, 'I don't think anyone is going to deny you anything you want.'

When Karr said this the snake slid in under the root of a tree and found a well-protected position in a narrow hole before continuing the conversation. 'Tell Greyfur this, then,' he said, 'that if he will leave Sanctuary Wood and not stop until he gets so far north that there are no oaks growing in the forest, and if he never returns as long as Helpless the grass snake is alive, I will spread disease and death among all the insects who are infesting and gnawing away at the spruce trees.'

'What are you saying?' Karr asked, the hair on his back beginning to bristle. 'What harm has Greyfur ever done you?'

'He killed the one I held most dear,' the snake said, 'and I want my revenge.'

Even before the grass snake had finished, Karr leapt at him but the snake lay in an unreachable position under the root of the tree. 'You can lie where you are for as long as you like,' Karr said at last. 'We'll drive these caterpillars away somehow without any help from you.'

The following day the estate owner and his gamekeeper were walking along a track in the forest. Karr was running alongside them at first but after a while he disappeared and just a little later loud barking could be heard in the forest.

'Karr must have put something up and be chasing it,' the estate owner said.

The gamekeeper did not want to believe it. 'Karr hasn't done any illegal hunting for many years,' he said and ran into the forest to find the dog that was making all the noise. The estate owner followed him.

They followed the barking all the way into the densest part of the forest, where it suddenly fell silent. They stopped to listen and then, in the silence, they could hear the noise of the larvae's jaws, see the rain of falling needles and smell the strong smell. And they noticed that all the trees were covered with the larvae of nun moths, those small but devastating pests capable of destroying mile after mile of forest.*

THE GREAT NUN MOTH WAR

The following spring Karr came running through the forest one morning. 'Karr! Karr!' someone shouted to him. Karr turned round. He had not misheard, an old fox was standing outside his den and calling him.

'Is it true that human beings are doing something to save the forest?'

'They are indeed!' Karr said. 'They are working on it as hard as they can.'

'They have killed all my kin, and they are going to kill me as well,' the fox said. 'But they can be forgiven for all that as long as they help the forest.'

Whenever Karr ran through the forest that year someone would ask him whether human beings could help the forest. It was not an easy question for Karr to answer, for even the human beings did not know whether they would succeed in defeating the nun moths.

When we remember how feared and hated Kolmården had been in the old days, it was more than a little amazing to see over a hundred men in the forest every day, working to save it from destruction. Where the damage was worst they felled the forest, cleared away the undergrowth and removed the lowest branches so that it was more difficult for the larvae to spread from tree to tree. They chopped out wide breaks around the affected parts of the forest and erected limed fences to shut the larvae in and prevent them moving to new ground. When they had done this they began painting lime rings around the trunks of the trees. The idea was to prevent the larvae climbing down from a tree once they had stripped it bare: it would force them to stay where they were and starve to death.

The human beings continued this work far into the spring. They were full of hope and waited almost impatiently for the larvae to emerge from the eggs. They were certain they had fenced them in so well that by far the most of them would die of hunger.

Then, at the beginning of the summer, the larvae emerged and their number had multiplied and was many, many times greater than the year before. But that did not matter, of course, as long as they were fenced in and unable to find enough to eat.

Things did not go exactly as planned, however. There were indeed larvae that stuck on the limed fences, and the lime rings prevented hordes of them from coming down from the trees, but no one could claim that the larvae were enclosed. They were outside the fence and they were inside it. They were everywhere. They crawled along the country roads, along fences and up the walls of the cottages. And they moved out of Sanctuary Wood and into other parts of Kolmården.

'They are not going to stop until the whole of our forest is destroyed,' people said and, in their utter despair, they could not go into the forest without tears coming to their eyes.

Karr was so sickened by everything that crawled and gnawed that he could hardly bring himself to go outdoors. One day, however, he felt he should go and see how things were with Greyfur. He took the most direct route towards Greyfur's territory and hurried along with his nose to the ground. When he came to the tree root where he had met Helpless the year before, the snake was lying there again and called to him: 'Have you told Greyfur what I said to you the last time we met?' Karr just snapped at the snake and tried to get at him. 'You had better do it,' the snake hissed. 'You can see now, can't you, that the human beings have no remedy for the devastation.'

'And nor do you,' Karr answered before running on.

Karr found Greyfur but the elk was in such a gloomy mood that he scarcely said hello. He started talking about the forest immediately. 'I don't know what I wouldn't do to bring this misery to an end,' he said.

'In that case I'll tell you that it's been suggested that you could save the forest,' Karr said and passed on the grass snake's message.

'If it was anyone but Helpless making that promise I would immediately go into exile,' the elk said. 'But how could a poor grass snake possibly have such power?'

'He's just boasting, of course,' Karr said. 'Grass snakes always like to pretend they know more than other animals.'

When it was time for Karr to go home, Greyfur kept him company on the way. Then Karr heard a thrush sitting in the top of a spruce begin to call: 'There goes Greyfur, the one who destroyed the forest! There goes Greyfur, the one who destroyed the forest!'

Karr thought he had misheard the bird but a little while later a hare came scurrying across the path. When the hare saw them, he stopped, flipped his ears and shouted: 'Here comes Greyfur, the one who destroyed the forest!' Then he scuttled off as fast as he could.

'What do they mean by that?' Karr asked.

'I don't rightly know,' Greyfur said. 'I think the little creatures in the forest are upset with me because I was the one who counselled us to seek help from human beings. With all the undergrowth being cleared away, they have had their homes and hiding places destroyed.'

They walked along together for a while and Karr could hear the same call coming from every side: 'There goes Greyfur, the one who destroyed the forest!' Greyfur pretended not to hear it but Karr thought he knew now why his friend was so despondent.

'Greyfur,' Karr asked quickly, 'what is the grass snake talking about when he says you are supposed to have killed the one he loved best?'

'How should I know?' Greyfur said. 'You know that I'm not

in the habit of killing things.'

A little later they met the four old elk: Crookback, Horncrown, Stiffmane and Headstrong. They were walking slowly, one behind the other and deep in thought.

'Forest greetings to you!' Greyfur shouted to them.

'Greetings to you too,' the elk answered. 'You are just the one we wanted to meet so we could have a talk about the forest.'

'It's like this,' Crookback said, 'we have learnt that a crime was committed in the forest and because it has gone unpunished the whole forest is being destroyed.'

'What sort of crime?'

'Someone killed a harmless animal, but did not kill it for food. That counts as a crime in Sanctuary Wood.'

'Who could have committed such a dreadful deed?' Greyfur said.

'They say it was an elk and we wanted to ask if you know who it might be.'

'No,' said Greyfur, 'I've never heard of an elk killing a harmless animal.'

Greyfur left the elders and walked on with Karr. He had become even more silent and his head hung low as he walked. They happened to walk past Crawler the adder, who was lying on his rock. 'There goes Greyfur, the one who destroyed the forest!' the adder hissed, joining in with all the others. But this time Greyfur lost patience and he went over to the snake and raised his front foot.

'So you're intending to kill me just like you killed the old grass snake, are you?' the adder said.

'Did I kill a grass snake?' Greyfur asked.

'Yes, the very first day you came into the forest, you killed the wife of Helpless the grass snake,' Crawler said.

Greyfur quickly left Crawler and carried on walking alongside Karr. Suddenly he came to a stop. 'Karr, I'm the one who committed the crime. I'm the one who killed a harmless animal. It's because of me that the forest is being destroyed.'

'What are you saying?' Karr broke in.

'You can tell the grass snake Helpless that Greyfur will go into exile this very night!'

'I'll tell him nothing of the kind!' Karr said. 'It's a dangerous country for elk up in the north.'

'Do you really think I want to stay here after causing such devastation?' Greyfur said.

'Don't be too hasty. Wait until tomorrow before doing anything!'

'You are the one who taught me that the elk and the forest are one,' Greyfur said, after which he parted from Karr.

Karr went home but this conversation had made him anxious and the very next day he went out into the forest again to find Greyfur. But Greyfur was nowhere to be found and the dog did not spend too long searching for him. He knew that Greyfur had taken the snake at his word and gone into exile.

On the way home Karr's mood was bad beyond description. He could not understand why Greyfur would let that wretched grass snake fool him into going into exile. He had never heard anything so stupid. What kind of power did that snake, that Helpless, actually have?

As Karr walked along with these thoughts in his mind, he caught sight of the gamekeeper, who was standing and pointing up a tree. 'What is it you are looking at?' a man with him asked. 'There is a disease beginning to spread among the larvae,' the keeper said.

Karr was totally amazed but, even more than that perhaps, he was angry that the grass snake had the power to keep his word. Now Greyfur would be forced to stay away for a very long time because that grass snake was probably never going to die.

While Karr was feeling at his most miserable, a thought came into his mind and gave him some comfort. 'Perhaps the grass snake won't grow that old after all,' he thought. 'He can't always lie in the protection of the roots of a tree. And I know someone who will be only too happy to bite him to death once he has rid us of all the larvae!'

A disease really had broken out among the larvae, though it did not have time to become widespread that first summer because shortly after it had flared up the time came for the larvae to become pupae. Millions of moths hatched out of these pupae and they flew like spindrift between the trees at night and laid an incalculable number of eggs. Even greater devastation was to be expected the following year.

Devastation came, not only to the forest but to the larvae, too. The disease spread rapidly from one part of the forest to another and the sick larvae stopped eating, crawled up to the tops of the trees and died there. Seeing them die brought great joy to the human beings and even more joy to the animals of the forest.

Karr the dog went around every day with a sense of grim satisfaction, thinking of the moment it would be safe to bite and kill Helpless.

But the larvae had spread for tens of miles through neighbouring forests and the disease did not reach all of them that summer either, so that many still survived to become pupae and moths.

Migrating birds brought Karr greetings from Greyfur, saying that he was alive and that things were going well. But the birds confided in Karr that Greyfur had been hunted by poachers several times and it was only with the greatest difficulty that he had escaped with his life.

Karr's life was one of sorrow and longing and anxiety, and he still had to wait two more summers before the larvae were wiped out.

No sooner had Karr heard the keeper say that the forest was no longer in danger than he set off to hunt Helpless. But when he reached the dense parts of the forest he discovered something dreadful – he could no longer hunt, he could no longer run, he could no longer track his enemy, he could not even see. During his long wait, old age had crept up on Karr. He had grown old without noticing it. He was no longer fit enough even to kill a grass snake. He was incapable of freeing his friend Greyfur from the clutches of his enemy.

REVENGE
Akka from Kebnekaise and her flock landed one afternoon on the banks of a tarn in the forest. They were still in Kolmården but no longer in the province of Östergötland – they had crossed over to the district of Jönåker in Sörmland.

Spring was late as it often is in hilly country and ice still covered the whole lake apart from a rim of open water along the shore. The geese immediately rushed into the water to bathe and to search for food but Nils Holgersson had lost one of his clogs that morning and he went off into the alders and birches growing on the bank to look for anything he could tie on his foot and use as a shoe.

The boy had to go quite a long way before he found anything suitable and he kept looking round nervously because he really did not like the forest. 'Give me a plain or a lake,' he thought, 'because then you can see what lies in front of you. It would be all right if it was a beech wood, where the ground is almost bare, but I don't understand how people can be doing with wild and trackless woods of birch and spruce like this. If I owned it, I would chop it all down.'

At last he caught sight of a piece of birch bark and was in the process of fitting it to his foot when he heard rustling behind him. He turned round and saw a snake shooting through the undergrowth towards him. It was unusually long and thick but, quickly noting that it had a white patch on each cheek, the boy remained where he was. 'It's only a grass snake after all,' he thought. 'It surely can't do me any harm.'

The very next moment, however, the snake struck him such a powerful blow to the chest that he fell over. He scrambled back to his feet as fast as possible and ran away, pursued by the snake. The ground was scrubby and stony so that the boy could not make a rapid escape and the snake was close on his heels.

All of a sudden the boy saw a large boulder with steep sides in front of him and he hurried to climb up onto it. 'I doubt if the grass snake can follow me up here,' he thought, but the moment he was up and turned round to look, he saw that the snake was trying to follow him.

On top of the boulder, close beside the boy, lay a stone, almost round and the size of a man's head. It was lying there loose on a narrow ledge and it was hard to see how it could have lodged there. As the snake came closer, the boy jumped in behind the round stone and pushed it hard. It rolled right down onto the snake, pushing the animal back down to the ground and landing on its head.

'That made a good job of it,' the boy thought, taking a deep breath as he saw the snake twitch violently a couple of times before lying still. 'I don't think I've been in more danger than that on this journey so far.'

He had hardly had time to gather his thoughts before he heard something swish over his head and he saw a bird land on the ground right beside the snake. It resembled a crow in size and shape but it was garbed in beautiful black plumage that gleamed like metal. The boy carefully hid himself in a cleft in the boulder. Being abducted by the crows was still fresh in his memory and he was not keen on letting himself be seen if he could help it.

With long strides the black bird strode back and forth the length of the snake's body before turning it over with his beak. After that he flapped his wings and shrieked in a voice so piercing that it hurt the ears of a listener. 'There can be no doubt that this is Helpless the grass snake lying here dead.' The bird walked the length of the snake once more, before standing deep in thought and scratching the back of his neck with his claw. 'There couldn't possibly be two snakes that big in the forest. I'm absolutely certain it's him.'

He seemed to be on the point of driving his beak into the snake but suddenly stopped himself. 'Don't be such an idiot, Bataki,' he said. 'You surely can't be thinking of eating the snake before you go and fetch Karr. He won't dare believe that Helpless is dead unless he sees it for himself.'

Nils was trying to stay quiet but, given the solemn way

the bird strode around talking to himself, he could not help laughing.

The bird heard him and with a single flap of his wings he was up on the boulder. The boy stood up quickly and walked towards him. 'Aren't you the raven called Bataki, who is a good friend of Akka from Kebnekaise?' the boy asked. The bird studied him carefully and then nodded his head three times.

'You surely aren't the boy called Thummitot who's flying with the wild geese, are you?'

'I surely am!' the boy said.

'Well, it's good that I've met you. Now perhaps you can tell me who killed this grass snake?'

'It was that stone,' the boy said. 'I rolled it down on him and it killed him.' And he told the raven all that had happened.

'That was very clever for someone as small as you,' the raven said. 'I've a friend who lives in this part of the country and he will be happy that the snake has been killed. Now I'd like to do something for you in return.'

'Tell me why you are so happy that the grass snake is dead!' the boy said.

'Oh, it's a long story,' the raven said. 'You won't have the patience to listen to all of it.'

But the boy insisted that he definitely would have enough patience and so the raven told him the whole story of Karr and Greyfur and the grass snake Helpless. When the bird had finished, the boy sat silent for a while, staring straight ahead. 'I must thank you,' the boy said. 'It's as if I understand the forest better since hearing that story. I wonder if there is anything left of the great Sanctuary Wood nowadays?'

'Most of it has been completely destroyed,' Bataki said. 'The trees look as if a fire has swept through them. They are having to be felled and it will be many years before this forest once again becomes what it was.'

'The snake deserved to die, then,' the boy said, 'but I wonder whether it's really possible that he was clever enough to be able to send a plague among the larvae?'

'Perhaps he just knew that the larvae were likely to catch

that sort of disease,' Bataki said.

'Yes, that may be it. But I have to say that he was a pretty clever animal anyway.'

The boy fell silent. The raven was no longer listening, his head was turned away and his attention was elsewhere. 'Listen!' he said. 'Karr is nearby. He will be happy when he sees that Helpless is dead.'

The boy turned his head in the direction the sound was coming from and said: 'He is talking to the wild geese.'

'Yes, he has probably dragged himself down to the tarn to hear news of Greyfur.'

Both the boy and the raven jumped down from the boulder and hurried down to the shore. All the geese had come out of the water and were standing talking to an old dog, who was so frail and weak he looked as if he might fall down dead at any moment.

'That's Karr,' Bataki said to the boy. 'Let him listen to what the geese have to tell him first and then we'll tell him that the grass snake is dead.'

They soon heard what Akka was saying to Karr. 'It was when we were making our spring journey last year,' the lead goose said. 'We had flown one morning – Yksi and Kaksi and me – from Lake Siljan in Dalarna and out over the great border forests between the provinces of Dalarna and Hälsingland. Below us we could see nothing but dark-green pine forests. The snow still lay deep among the trees, the rivers were frozen apart from one or two black holes in the ice, but the river banks were partly clear of snow. We scarcely saw any villages or farms, just grey wooden shielings that were deserted during the winter. Narrow twisting forest roads ran here and there in places where people had been extracting logs during the winter, and large stacks of logs were piled up by the riversides.

'As we were flying along we saw three hunters making their way through the forest. They were travelling on skis, with their dogs on leashes and knives in their belts, but with no guns. There was a hard crust on the snow so they were skiing straight ahead as the crow flies and not bothering about the winding forest roads. And they looked as if they knew where they needed to go to find what they were looking for.

'We wild geese were flying very high and the whole forest was visible below. Once we had seen the hunters, we wanted to find out what game they were after and we started flying back and forth and spying between the trees. Then, in a dense thicket, we saw what looked like big moss-covered rocks. But they couldn't be rocks, of course, because there was no snow lying on them.

'We descended quickly and landed in the middle of the thicket. Then the three blocks of stone moved and turned out to be three elk – a bull and two cows – lying there in the darkness of the forest. When we landed the bull stood up and came over to us. He was one of the biggest and finest animals we had ever seen. But when he saw that it was only a couple of poor wild geese that had woken him, he lay down again.

'"No, no, Father Elk, I said to him, don't go back to sleep! Flee as quickly as you can. There are hunters out in the forest and they are heading straight for you and your cows."

'"Thank you for telling me, Mother Goose," the elk said, looking as if he was about to fall asleep even as he spoke. "But surely you know that elk are protected at this time of year. Those hunters must be out hunting for foxes."

'"The forest was full of fox tracks but the hunters were paying no attention to them. Believe me, they know you are lying here, Father Elk, and they are coming to kill you. They are coming without guns, just with spears and knives, because they can't risk firing their guns in the forest in the close season."

'The bull elk just lay there calmly but the cows were becoming anxious. "Perhaps the geese are right in what they say," they said and began to rise. "Just lie still where you are," the bull said. "No hunters are going to come to this thicket, you can be sure of that."

'There was nothing more to be done about it and we wild geese took off again. But we continued to fly over the same spot because we wanted to see what would happen to the elk.

'We had hardly reached the height we usually fly at before we saw the bull elk leaving the thicket. He sniffed the air and then set off straight towards the hunters. As he strode on, he stepped hard on dry twigs so that they snapped with a loud crack. A big barren moss lay on his route. He went there and took up a stance in the middle of the open moss with nothing to hide him.

'The bull stood there until the hunters appeared at the edge of the trees, then he turned and fled in a different direction to the one he had come from. The hunters loosed their dogs and then skied after him as fast as their skis would carry them.

'With his head thrown right back, the elk ran as fast as he possibly could. He kicked up the snow so that it whirled around him like spindrift and both the dogs and the hunters were left far behind. Then he stopped as if to wait for them, and when they came into view again, he stormed off once more. We realised that he was intending to draw the hunters away from the place where the cows lay. We thought it was brave of him to put himself in danger so that those who belonged to him could be left in peace. We could not bring ourselves to leave the spot until we had seen how all this came to an end.

'The hunt went on in this way for several hours. We wondered why the hunters were taking the trouble to follow the elk since they were not armed with guns. They surely could not imagine that they would succeed in tiring out such a fine runner.

'But then we noticed that the elk was no longer fleeing as fast as before. He was placing his feet more carefully, and when he lifted them, there were traces of blood to be seen in the snow.

'Then we understood why the hunters were being so tenacious. They were reckoning on the help of the snow. The elk was heavy and with every step he took he sank to the bottom of the drifts so that the hard crust on the snow scraped and tore his legs. It had scraped away the fur and ripped holes in his hide so that he was in agony every time he set down his foot.

'The hunters and their dogs, who were light enough not to break through the crust, were still on his track. He ran and he continued to run but his steps became more and more faltering and unsure. His breath was coming in heavy gasps, and not only was he suffering great pain, but all the wading through the deep snow was exhausting him.

'Finally he lost patience. He stopped to allow the hunters and their dogs to come to close quarters and fight. While he stood waiting, he cast his eyes upwards and when he saw the wild geese above him, he called: "Stay here until it is all over, wild geese! And next time you pass over Kolmården, seek out Karr the dog and tell him his friend Greyfur had a good death!"'

When Akka had reached this point, the old dog got to his feet and went a couple of steps closer to her. 'Greyfur has had a good life,' he said. 'He knows me. He knows that I am a brave dog and that I will be happy to hear that he had a good death. Tell me how …'

He raised his tail and lifted his head as if to give himself a bold and proud bearing, but then he sank down again.

'Karr! Karr!' a human voice called from somewhere in the forest.

The old dog stood up quickly. 'It's my master calling me,' he said, 'and I shan't hesitate to go with him. I saw him loading his gun and the two of us will go into the forest together for the last time. I am grateful to you, wild geese. Now I know everything I need to know to go to a happy death.'

XXIII

THE BEAUTIFUL PARADISE GARDEN

Sunday, 24 April

The following day the wild geese flew north over Södermanland. The boy looked down at the ground beneath and thought it was quite unlike any of the provinces he had seen before. There were no great plains as there are in Skåne and Östergötland, no great unbroken stretches of forest as in Småland, but there was a mixture of all kinds of things. Seeing nothing but small valleys and small lakes and small hills and small woods, the boy thought: 'What they've done here is to take a big lake and a big river and a big forest and a big hill, chopped them up into pieces, mixed them all together and spread them out on the earth in no particular order.' Nothing was permitted to spread too far. The moment a piece of flat country began to grow too big, along came a little hill and got in the way – and should that hill get too big for its boots and try to become a ridge, the flat country would take over again. As soon as a lake became so big that it began to make something of itself, it would narrow down and become a river, but the river would not be allowed to flow any great distance before it widened out into a lake. The wild geese were flying close enough to the coast for the boy to be able to see out to sea and he could see that even the sea was not allowed to spread in any really expansive way. Instead, it was broken up by a myriad islands, which in turn were not permitted to get too big before the sea took over again. Everything was in a permanent state of change. Pine woods alternated with deciduous woods, fields with mosses, mansions with farm cottages.

There was no sign of people working in the fields since they were all making their way along the roads and paths. They came, dressed in black clothes with the book and a handkerchief in their hands, from all the small forest holdings on the slopes of Kolmården. 'Today is Sunday, of course,' the boy thought and sat looking down at the people going to church. Once or twice he saw bridal couples driving to church accompanied by large parties of people; on another occasion a funeral party was moving slowly along the road. He saw the great carriages of the nobility and the gigs of the humble farmers and he saw boats on the lake – all on their way to church.

The boy flew over the Björkvik church and over Bettna and Blacksta and Vadsbro churches, and from there on towards Sköldinge and Floda. Everywhere he could hear the bells ringing. There was something wondrous and beautiful about the sound of the bells at this height. It was as if the air itself in all its clarity had been transformed into sounds and tones.

'Well, one thing is certain,' the boy said, 'which is that wherever I go in this country I shall meet the ringing of bells.' And that thought made him feel safe for, although he was presently in a different world, it was as if he could never really go astray as long as the mighty voices of the church bells could call him back.

They had gone quite a distance into Sörmland when a black dot moving on the ground beneath them caught the boy's eye. He thought at first it was a dog, in which case he would have given no more thought to the fact that it seemed to be trying to follow the same course as the wild geese. It was rushing across open ground and through clumps of trees, leaping over ditches and jumping fences and not letting anything stop it.

'It looks rather as if Smirre Fox is out and about again,' the boy said. 'But I've no doubt we'll soon fly away from him anyway.'

The wild geese immediately began flying as fast as ever

they could and they kept it up for as long as the fox was in sight. And when he could no longer see them, they turned and travelled in a great wide sweep to the west and south almost as if they were intending to fly back to Östergötland. 'It really must have been Smirre,' the boy thought, 'since Akka is curving off to the side and taking a different route.'

As the day moved towards evening, the wild geese flew over an old Sörmland estate called Stora Djulö. The great white mansion house lay there, a leafy parkland behind it and the lake with its headlands and hilly shores in front. It looked both old-fashioned and inviting and Nils could not help sighing and wondering how it would feel to enter the doors of such a place at the end of the day's journey rather than having to make do with a boggy swamp or a cold crust of ice.

But this was, of course, beyond the realms of possibility. Instead, when the wild geese did land, it was in a grassy forest clearing so inundated with water that only the occasional tussock stuck up here and there. It came close to being the worst night's lodging the boy had endured on the whole journey.

He stayed where he was on the gander's back for a while, not knowing what to do for the best. Then he set off in a series of great bounds from one tussock to the next until he reached firm ground, when he hurried in the direction of the old manor house.

Now it just happened that that very evening some people were sitting talking by the fireside in a croft that belonged to the Stora Djulö estate. They had been discussing the sermon and the tasks that spring brought and the weather, and when they began to run out of things to talk about, they asked the crofter's old mother to tell them some ghost stories.

It is a well-known fact that nowhere else in the country has as many mansion houses and as many ghost stories as Sörmland. In her younger days the old woman had been a servant in many of the big houses and she knew so many strange things that she could go on storytelling until dawn. She talked so well and so convincingly that her listeners were tempted to take everything she said as the truth. They would jump nervously when the old woman broke off now and again to ask if they could hear something rustling. 'I'm surprised you can't hear that there is something creeping around in here!' she would say. But the others could hear nothing.

After the old woman had told them stories about Eriksberg and Vibyholm and Julita and Lagmansö and many other places, someone asked whether strange things like that had ever happened at Stora Djulö. 'Indeed they have, we haven't exactly been spared!' the old woman said, and all of them immediately wanted to hear what sort of stories there were about their own estate.

Then the old woman told them that once upon a time there was said to have been a castle on a hill north of Stora Djulö, in a place where there was now nothing but forest, and there was said to have been a beautiful paradise garden in front of this castle. It so happened that a man called Lord Karl, who ruled the whole of Sörmland at that time, came travelling to this castle.* When he had eaten and drunk, he went out into the paradise garden and stood there for a long time, looking out over the lake and its beautiful shores. But while he was standing there rejoicing in all he saw and thinking that there was no more beautiful place in all the world than Sörmland, he heard someone behind him breathe a deep sigh. This made him turn round and he saw an old labourer bent over his spade.

'Is it you who is sighing so deeply?' Lord Karl asked. 'What do you have to sigh about?'

'I have every reason to sigh, working here on the land day in and day out as I do,' the labourer answered.

Now Lord Karl had a violent temper and he did not like people complaining. 'Is that all you have to complain about?' he shouted. 'Let me tell you that I should be quite happy to be allowed to spend all my days digging the soil of Sörmland.'

'May your Grace's wishes come to pass, just as you desire,' the labourer said.

As a result of that speech, so people said, Lord Karl had no peace in his grave after his death and every night he used to come to Stora Djulö to dig in the paradise garden. Now, of course, there is neither a castle nor a paradise garden there, just an ordinary wooded hill where they were said to have been. But if people walk through the forest on a dark night, they might well see the paradise garden.

At this point the old woman broke off and looked over to a dark corner of the cottage. 'Wasn't that something moving over there?' she asked.

'No, no, mother! Just get on with the story,' her daughter-in-law said. 'I noticed yesterday that the rats have made a big hole over in that corner and I forgot to block it up. But can't you tell us whether anyone has actually seen the paradise garden?'

'Well, I can tell you,' the old woman said, 'that my own father saw it on one occasion. He was walking through the forest one summer's night and he suddenly saw a high garden wall beside him and over the top of the wall he caught a glimpse of the most exquisite trees, so heavily weighed down with flowers and fruits that their branches hung right out over the wall. Father was walking slowly along wondering where the garden had come from when a door in the wall suddenly opened and a gardener came out and asked whether he would like to see the paradise garden. The man was carrying a spade and wearing a big apron just like any other gardener and father was just about to follow him when he happened to catch sight of his face. Father immediately recognised the pointed forelock and the Vandyke beard – it was Lord Karl, exactly as father had seen him depicted on portraits at all the great houses where father …'

Here came another break in the story, this time caused by the fire flaring up and spitting so that sparks and coals shot out onto the floor. All the dark corners in the cottage were momentarily lit up and the old woman thought she caught a glimpse of a tiny little elf who was sitting by the rat hole and listening to the story but who quickly hid himself away.

The old woman's daughter-in-law fetched a brush and

shovel, swept up the coals and sat down again. 'You can carry on again now, mother,' she said. But the old woman did not want to. 'That's enough for one night,' she said, and her voice sounded strange. The others all wanted to hear more but her daughter-in-law noticed that the old woman had gone pale and that her hands were trembling. 'No, mother is tired now and it's time she was in her bed,' she said.

A little while later the boy set off back to the wild geese in the forest. As he walked along he was chewing on a carrot he had found outside the cellar and which he thought made a really splendid supper. He was happy to have spent several hours in the warm cottage. 'Now, if only I can find somewhere good to sleep,' he thought.

Then it struck him that the best thing would be to make a sleeping platform in a bushy spruce tree at the edge of the road. He swung up into the tree and plaited together some small twigs to make a bed to lie on.

He lay there for a while pondering on what he had heard in the cottage and thinking in particular of the Lord Karl who was supposed to be somewhere in the forest here at Stora Djulö. But he soon fell asleep and would probably have slept right through until the morning if he had not been woken by the creaking sound of a set of iron gates being opened directly below him.

The boy woke in a trice, rubbed the sleep from his eyes and looked around. Right alongside him was a wall the height of a man and over the wall could be seen trees that were bowed down by the weight of their fruit.

At first he thought it was all very strange. There had been no fruit trees there when he went to sleep. But after a few seconds everything came back to him and he understood which garden this was.

The strangest thing of all, perhaps, was that he did not feel in the least afraid – quite the opposite; in fact, he had an irresistible desire to enter the garden. It was dark and bleak up in the spruce tree but in the garden it was light and he thought he could see fruit and roses shining in the bright sunlight. After all the time spent out in the rain and cold, it would be so good to enjoy some of the warmth of summer.

It did not appear to be particularly difficult to get into the garden. There was a gateway in the high wall very close to the tree in which the boy was lying and an old gardener had just pushed open the big iron gates. He was standing in the gateway now, looking out into the forest as if expecting someone.

The boy was down from the tree in a flash. With his cap in his hand he went up to the gardener, bowed and asked if he may be permitted to see the garden.

'Yes, you may!' the gardener answered in a rather gruff voice. 'Just come on in!'

The gardener closed the gates behind them and locked them with a heavy key, which he stuck in his belt. The boy, meanwhile, stood and studied him. He had a stern face and a generous moustache, a pointed goatee beard and a sharp nose. Had it not been for the blue gardener's apron he was wearing and the heavy spade in his hand, the boy would have taken him for an old soldier.

The gardener strode into the garden, taking such great steps that the boy had to run to keep up with him. They walked along a narrow path and the boy happened to step on the grass – he was immediately reprimanded and told not to walk on the grass, after which he continued trotting along behind his leader.

The boy sensed that the gardener felt he was far too good to be showing the garden to a mere changeling and he did not dare ask about anything. So he just ran along behind the gardener, who every now and then tossed a remark in his direction. There was a dense hedge just inside the wall and after they had gone through it the gardener told him that he called the hedge Kolmården. 'It's certainly big enough to do justice to the name,' the boy answered, though the gardener was making no effort at all to listen to anything he said.

Once they were through the bushes the boy had a view over much of the garden. He noticed at once that it was not particularly extensive, no more than a couple of acres. The high wall protected it on the south and west sides and there was no need for a fence on the north and east because it was bordered by water.

The gardener stopped to tie up a vine, giving the boy time to look around. He had not seen very many gardens in his life but he was in no doubt that this one was different from all the rest. It must have been laid out according to some old-fashioned design because all these busy clusters of small mounds, small flowerbeds, small hedges, small lawns and small bowers are simply not seen these days. Nor do we see all the small ponds and winding canals that were visible on every side here.

The proudest of trees and the loveliest of flowers were growing on every side and the water in the little canals lay deep-green and as clear as a mirror. To the boy, everything seemed like paradise and he clapped his hands and exclaimed: 'I have never seen anything so beautiful! What kind of garden can it be?'

He shouted this quite loudly and the gardener immediately turned to him and said in a stern voice: 'The name of this garden is Sörmland. What kind of person are you if you don't know that? It has always been reckoned to be one of the finest gardens in the kingdom.'

This answer made the boy rather thoughtful, but there was so much to look at that he had no time to wonder what the gardener meant. And as beautiful as it all was with its flowers and its winding watercourses, there was something that gave him even greater pleasure, and that was all the small play-houses and summer-houses that had been erected in all parts of the garden. They were everywhere, but particularly along the sides of the small ponds and canals. They were not proper houses, they were small, as if built for people no bigger than him, but they were unbelievably neat and tidy. And they were of every kind imaginable: some were like castles with towers and wings, others looked like churches, and others again like mills or farm cottages.

They were so beautiful that the boy would have liked to stay and take a closer look at every one of them but he was afraid to do other than follow the gardener. Soon they reached a building that was bigger and more magnificent than anything they had come across before. It was three storeys high, with a frontispiece and projecting wings. It stood on a mound surrounded by flower beds and the drive that led up to it crossed one canal after another over elegant little bridges.

The only thing the boy dared do was to hang hard on the heels of the gardener, but when his stern guide heard him sighing deeply at having to go past, he came to a halt and said: 'We call this place Eriksberg. You can go inside if you like but beware of the Pintorp Wifie!'*

Nils did not need to be asked twice! He ran along the tree-lined avenue, over the little bridges, up through the flowerbeds and in through the door. Everything seemed designed for someone of exactly his size. The steps were just the right height and he could reach all the latches. But he could never have imagined that he would see so many beautiful things. The oak floors had been polished until they gleamed; the ceilings were plastered and covered with painted pictures; the walls were lined with painting after painting; the sofas and chairs were upholstered in silk and their arms and backs gilded; he saw rooms where the walls were lined with books and rooms where the tables and cupboards were laden with treasures.

However much he hurried, he did not have time to see even half of the house before the gardener called him, and when the boy emerged the old man was standing there chewing his moustache impatiently.

'Well, how did you get on?' the gardener asked. 'Did you see the Pintorp Wifie?' But the boy had not seen a living soul and when the gardener heard this, he screwed up his face and said: 'So that Pintorp woman has been allowed to go to her rest, but I cannot!' The boy would never have believed that a human voice could be so tremulous with despair.

Then the gardener strode on again with long steps and the

boy ran behind him, still trying to see as many of the wonders as possible. They walked round a pond that was a little bigger than the others. Long white pavilions like manor houses rose among the shrubberies and flowerbeds. The gardener did not stop but as he walked he made the occasional comment: 'I call this pond here Yngaren. This manor is Danbyholm. And this one is Hagbyberga. That one is Hovsta, and that one Åkerö.'

Next, after taking a couple of enormous steps, the gardener reached another little pond, which he said was called Båven, and there he stopped again on hearing the boy gasp in surprise. The boy had stopped and was standing in front of a little bridge that led out to a manor house on an island in the pond.

'You can run over to Vibyholm and have a look round if you want to,' the gardener said. 'But watch out for the Woman in White!'*

Nils was not slow to take up the offer. There were so many portraits on the walls in the house that the place reminded him of a big picture-book. He had so much fun there that he would have liked to stay all night, but it was not long before he heard the gardener calling him.

'Come on! Come on! I've got other things to do than to stand here waiting for you, you young rascal!'

As Nils was running back over the bridge, the gardener shouted to him: 'Well, how was it? Did you see the Woman in White?'

But the boy had not seen a living soul, as he told the gardener. With his spade, the old man struck a stone with such force that the stone split in two. Then, in a voice that emerged from the deepest pits of despond, he said: 'So the Woman in White at Vibyholm has been allowed to go to her rest, but I cannot!'

Up until then they had been walking in the southern part of the garden but now the gardener moved over to the west. Here the design was of a different kind. The ground had been levelled into large grass areas broken up by strawberry beds, cabbage patches and berry bushes. There were little summer-houses here, too, but they were mainly painted red to resemble farm cottages and they were surrounded by hop gardens and clumps of cherry trees.

The gardener stopped here for a moment and threw a few words in the boy's direction: 'This is the area I call Vingåker.'

Immediately afterwards he pointed to a building of much simpler design than all the rest – most of all it resembled a smithy. 'This is a large mechanical workshop,' he said. 'I call it Eskilstuna. You can go in and have a look round if you like.'

The boy went in and saw an enormous number of wheels spinning round, hammers pounding and lathes turning. There was so much to look at that he could have stayed all night if the gardener had not called him.

After that they walked along the lake on the north side of the garden. The shore swung in and out, headland following bay, bay following headland, for the whole length of the garden. Offshore and close to the headlands there were small islands cut off from the shore by narrow strips of water. These small islands also belonged to the garden and they had been cultivated with the same care as everything else.

The boy walked past one beautiful place after another but did not stop until he reached a splendid red church, large and impressive, on a headland shaded by fertile fruit trees. The gardener, as usual, wanted to walk past but the boy plucked up courage and asked for permission to go in. 'Oh, all right, go in then!' he answered. 'But watch out for Bishop Rogge! It's quite possible that he is still in Strängnäs today.'*

So the boy ran into the church and looked at old memorial stones and beautiful altar screens. But more than anything else he admired a knight in gilded armour that he found in a room beside the porch. There was so much to see here, too, that he could have spent the whole night but he had to leave in order not to keep the gardener waiting.

When he came out again he saw that the gardener was watching an owl hunting a redstart up in the sky. The old man whistled to the redstart, which came and settled safely on his shoulder, and when the owl, its hunting spirit aroused, flew after it, he chased her away with his spade. 'His bark is worse than his bite,' the boy thought when he saw how tenderly the old man protected the poor song-bird.

As soon as the gardener saw the boy returning he asked if he had seen Bishop Rogge. And when the boy answered no, he said in a voice echoing with the most profound grief: 'So Bishop Rogge has been allowed to go to his rest, but I cannot.'

Shortly afterwards they came to the most imposing of the many dolls' houses. It was a fortress built of brick, consisting of three sturdy round towers linked by long walls of high buildings.

'Go in and look round if you want to!' the gardener said. 'This is Gripsholm Castle and here you need to watch out that you don't bump into King Erik.'*

The boy went in through a deep arched gateway and entered a three-cornered yard surrounded by low buildings. They did not look particularly distinguished so he did not bother to go in – instead he leapfrogged several times over a pair of long cannon which were standing there and then ran on. He passed through yet another arched gateway into another courtyard, this time surrounded by splendid buildings. Then he went inside and found himself in big old-fashioned rooms with beams on the ceilings and walls covered by tall dark paintings depicting earnest-looking ladies and gentlemen in peculiar stiff clothing.

One floor up he found rooms that were lighter and more cheerful. Now he could really tell he was in a royal castle because all he could see on the walls were fine portraits of kings and queens. One floor up again was the top floor, which was extensive and contained rooms of many kinds. There were light rooms with beautiful white furniture and there was a little theatre, next door to which there was a real prison cell with bare stone walls and barred windows and a floor worn by the heavy tread of the prisoners.

There was so much to see that the boy would have liked to spend many days there but once again the gardener called him and he dared not disobey.

'Did you see King Erik?' he asked when the boy emerged. But the boy had not seen anyone and then, as before but now even more despairingly, the gardener said: 'So King Erik has been allowed to go to his rest, but I cannot.'

Then they walked over to the eastern part of the garden, passing on the way a bath-house that the gardener called Södertälje and an old castle he called Hörningsholm. Apart from that there was not much to see. There were rocks and skerries everywhere, all of which become barer and more desolate the farther out they lay.

Then they turned south and the boy recognised the hedge called Kolmården and realised that they were approaching the way out of the garden.

He was happy to have been able to see all this and as they approached the great iron gates he wanted to thank the gardener. But the old man was not paying any attention to him and was just walking straight towards the gate. There he turned to the boy and handed him his spade: 'Here, hold on to this while I unlock the gate!'

But the boy was already concerned about all the trouble he had put the gruff old man to and he wanted to spare him any further work. 'You don't need to open the heavy gate on my behalf,' he said, slipping quickly through the bars without any difficulty at all since he was so small.

He did this with the best of intentions and was taken completely by surprise when he heard the gardener utter an angry roar behind him, stamp his foot on the ground and shake the barred gate violently.

'What's the matter? What's the matter?' the boy said. 'I just wanted to save you any trouble. Why are you so angry?'

'I have every reason to be angry,' the old man said. 'All you needed to do was to take my spade and then you would have had to stay here and tend the garden and I would have been released. Now I've no idea how long I shall have to stay here.'

He stood there rattling the gate and looking dreadfully angry and the boy could not help feeling sorry for him and wanting to console him.

'You mustn't be sad about it, Lord Karl of Södermanland,' the boy said, 'for there is no one who could look after your paradise garden as well as you do.'

The gardener fell silent when the boy said this and the boy thought the old man's harsh features brightened up a little. But he could not see clearly for the whole figure was now starting to fade and disappear like mist. Not only the gardener but the whole garden faded away and disappeared, along with its flowers and fruits and sunshine, and the only thing left in its place was the wild and poor forest.

XXIV

IN NÄRKE

YSÄTTER KAJSA

Back in the old days in the province of Närke there existed something that quite simply did not exist elsewhere – that something was a troll called Ysätter Kajsa.

She had been given the name Kajsa because she had a great deal to do with storms and winds, and Kajsa was the name often given to wind-trolls. She had been given her other name because she was supposed to have come from Ysätter Marsh in the parish of Asker.

It does seems that her home really was in Asker, although she also showed up in other places, and there was nowhere in the whole of Närke that you could be guaranteed not to meet her.

She was certainly not a dark and gloomy troll, she was actually jolly and cheerful, and what she liked best of all was a good gale. As soon as there was enough wind, out she would go to dance around the plain of Närke.

Närke, in fact, consists of nothing but a plain surrounded on all sides by forested hills. It is only in the north-eastern corner, where a lake called Hjälmaren crosses the border of the province, that there is a gap in this long boundary fence of hills.

In the morning, once the wind has gathered strength out in the Baltic Sea and set off inland, it passes more or less unhindered through the Sörmland hills and slips without any great trouble into Närke up in the region around Hjälmaren. From there it charges across the Närke plain until, right over in the west, it bumps into the high wall of the Kilsbergen hills and is thrown back. Then the wind turns like a snake and travels south. But there it meets the forest of Tiveden, which gives it a nudge that sends it rushing off eastwards. But, of course, the forest of Tylöskog lies to the east and that turns the wind northwards up towards the forested ridge called Käglan – from where it is bounced back to Kilsbergen, Tiveden and Tylöskog again. Then the wind begins to go round in ever smaller circles until at last it stands still like a spinning top right in the middle of the plain and just spins round. On days like that, with whirlwinds spinning across the plain, Ysätter Kajsa enjoyed herself. She would stand in the middle of the spiralling wind and spin, her long hair streaming out among the clouds in the sky, the train of her dress sweeping the earth like a dust-cloud, and the whole plain lying beneath her like a dance-floor.

Ysätter Kajsa's mornings were spent sitting up in a tall pine tree on the crest of a steep slope looking out over the plain. If it was winter and the snow was in good enough condition for there to be many travellers out on the roads, she would hasten to blow up a blizzard and pile up drifts so deep that people had trouble getting home by nightfall. If it was summer and good harvesting weather, Ysätter Kajsa would sit quietly until the first hay-wains had been fully loaded and then she would come along with a couple of torrential downpours that would put an end to work for the day.

The plain truth of it is that she rarely if ever thought about anything apart from causing mischief. The charcoal burners up in the Kilsbergen hills hardly dared take a nap because as soon as she saw an unwatched kiln she would come creeping along and puff on it until it began to burn with a high flame. And if the iron ore carters from Laxå and Svartå mines were out late, she would swathe the road and the countryside in mists so dark and dense that both men and horses would lose their way and their heavy sledges would end up in bogs and marshes. If the dean's wife at Glanshammar set her coffee table out in the garden on a Sunday in summer and along came a gust of wind that lifted the cloth from the table and knocked over all the cups and plates, everyone knew who lay behind the practical joke. If the mayor of Örebro's hat blew off and he had to chase it across the square, if the people on the island of Vinön out in Hjälmaren ran aground in the skiffs taking their vegetables to market, if clothes hanging out to dry blew away and got covered in dust, if smoke blew back into the cottages in the evening and seemed incapable of finding its way up the chimney – in all of these cases it was not difficult to guess who was out and about and having some fun.

Although Ysätter Kajsa liked to get up to all sorts of annoying pranks, there was nothing really bad about her. It was noticeable that she behaved worst to mean, nasty and quarrelsome people whereas she often took care of decent people and poor little children. And old people tell the story that when Asker church was on fire, along came Ysätter Kajsa, swooped down on the roof amidst all the fire and smoke and averted the danger.

There were, however, many occasions on which the people of Närke became more than a little sick of Ysätter Kajsa whereas she, for her part, never tired of stirring things up among them. When she sat up there on the edge of a cloud and looked down at Närke lying prosperous and friendly below her, with all its fine farms out on the plain and its rich mines and ironworks up in the hills, with its slow-moving river Svartån and its shallow lowland lakes full of fish, with the good town of Örebro spread out around its staid old castle with sturdy towers at the corners, she must certainly have thought: 'If it wasn't for me, everything would be just too good for the people here. They would become dull and boring. There has to be someone like me here, someone to stir them up and keep them in good spirits.'

Then she would laugh in the same wild and mocking way as a magpie before whirling off to dance and spin from one corner of the plain to the other. And when the people of Närke saw her dragging her train of dust across the plain, they could not help smiling. Tiresome and annoying she may be, but she was also good-humoured. It was as refreshing for the farmers to have to deal with Ysätter Kajsa as it was for the flat plain to be lashed by storm winds.

These days there are people who claim that Ysätter Kajsa is dead and gone, just like all the other trolls. But it is almost impossible to believe that. In fact, it is not unlike someone coming along and stating that the air must stand still over the plain from now on, that the wind will never again dance across it with the swish and roar of fresh air and sudden showers.

Anyway, anyone who believes that Ysätter Kajsa is dead and gone should listen to what happened in Närke the year that Nils Holgersson passed over the province. After that they can say what they think.

THE EVENING BEFORE MARKET DAY   Wednesday, 27 April
It was the day before the big cattle market in Örebro and the rain was lashing down. It was the kind of rain that is impossible to cope with. It came streaming down from the clouds and there were many people who thought to themselves, 'This is just like it was in Ysätter Kajsa's day. She always got up to some mischief at markets, more than at any other time. It would be just like her to have sent this kind of torrential rain on the eve of the market.'

The day wore on and the rain grew worse. Towards evening there were several real cloudbursts that turned the roads into bottomless quagmires. People who had set out from home with their animals in order to arrive in Örebro in good time the following morning were in a bad way. Cows and oxen were so exhausted they could scarcely put one foot in front of another and many of the poor beasts lay down in the middle of the road to show that they did not have the energy to go any farther. People living along the road had to open their houses and make room as best they could for those on their way to market, and barns and stables as well as houses were soon full to overflowing.

Those who could tried to struggle on until they reached an inn but when they arrived there they rather regretted they had not stopped at a cottage along the road. All the stalls in the cowshed and all the cribs in the barn were already taken. They had no choice but to leave their horses and cattle standing out in the rain – indeed, it was touch and go as to whether the owners would get a roof over their own heads.

The farmyards were wet, filthy and crowded. Things were so dreadful that some animals could find nowhere to lie down and were simply standing in deep puddles. There were some farmers, of course, who managed to find straw for their beasts to lie on and covers to go over them, but there were others who just sat in a tavern drinking, playing cards and not giving a thought to the animals they should be caring for.

That evening the boy and the wild geese had arrived on an island in Hjälmaren. It was separated from the shore by no more than a narrow and shallow strip of water and it was obvious that it would be possible to cross dry-shod when the water was low.

Out on the island it was raining just as mercilessly as everywhere else and the boy could not sleep for the raindrops that kept dripping on him. In the end he began walking round the island, thinking that he felt the rain less when he was on the move.

He had only just walked around the island when he heard splashing from the stretch of water that cut the island off from the shore and immediately afterwards he saw a solitary horse coming through the bushes. It was an ancient horse, so worn-out and wretched that he had never seen anything like it. It was broken-winded and stiff-legged and so skinny that every bone showed through its hide. It was wearing neither a saddle nor a harness, just an old halter with a half-rotten piece of rope attached – it could not have had any difficulty in pulling itself free.

The horse walked straight towards the place where the geese were standing asleep and the boy was afraid he would trample on them.

'Where are you going?' the boy shouted. 'Watch out!'

'Ah, there you are,' the horse said and walked towards the

boy. 'I've walked half a dozen miles to meet you.'

'Have you heard of me?' the boy asked in surprise.

'I may be old but I've still got ears, I have. There's a lot of talk about you going round these days.'

The horse had lowered his head in order to see better while he was talking and the boy noticed that he had a small head with beautiful eyes and a fine soft muzzle. 'He has clearly been a good horse in his day,' he thought, 'though he's fallen on bad times in his old age.'

'I'd like you to come with me and help me with something,' the horse said. The boy thought it would be risky to go anywhere with such a wretched-looking animal and he made an excuse about the bad weather.

'Sitting on my back won't be any worse for you than lying here,' the horse said. 'Or is it just that you are afraid to come with an old wreck like me?'

'Oh, I'm certainly not afraid of that,' the boy said.

'Wake up the geese, then, so that we can arrange where they should come to pick you up tomorrow morning,' the horse said.

In no time at all the boy was up on the horse's back. The old horse trotted along better than the boy had thought him capable of, but it was still a long journey through the night and foul weather before they stopped at a large inn. It looked an extremely unpleasant place. The wheel-tracks in the road were so deep that the boy was sure he would drown if he went down into them. Thirty or forty horses and cows were tied to the fence without any protection at all from the weather and in the yard there were carts with high-sided divisions full of sheep and calves and pigs and hens.

The horse walked over and stood by the fence. The boy remained on his back and thanks to his good night vision he was able to see clearly how harsh the conditions were for the animals.

'Why are you all standing out in the rain?' he asked.

'We are on our way to market in Örebro but we had to stop here because of the rain. This is an inn, but so many travellers have arrived that there is no room for us in any of the buildings.'

The boy did not answer, he just sat there silently looking round. Not many of the animals were asleep and he could hear moans and complaints from all sides. And they had every reason to complain, for the weather had become even worse than earlier in the day. An icy cold wind had begun to blow and the rain, which was now lashing down painfully, was mixed with snow. It was not hard to see what the horse wanted the boy to help with.

'Do you see that fine farm standing right across the road from the inn?' the horse asked.

'Yes,' said the boy, 'I can see it and I can't understand why they haven't asked for room for you there. Or is it full already, too?'

'No, there are no outsiders there at all,' the horse said. 'The people who live at that farm are so mean and unhelpful that there is no point in anyone asking them for room.'

'Ah, I see, so that's the way of it! In that case, you will just have to stay where you are.'

'But I was born and brought up on that farm,' the horse said. 'I know that there is a big stable and a large cowshed with many empty cribs and stalls and I wondered whether you could somehow arrange things so that we could get in.'

'I don't think I can risk trying that,' the boy said. But then he felt so sorry for all the animals that he thought he would try anyway.

He ran across to the farm and saw at once that all the outhouses were locked and the keys removed. He stood there perplexed and helpless for a moment but then help came from an unexpected quarter. A gust of wind came roaring along at a fearful pace and hurled open the door of a large barn right in front of him. The boy, of course, wasted no time at all getting back to the horse.

'It won't be possible to get into the stables or the cowshed,' he said, 'but there is a big empty hay-barn that they have forgotten to lock up and I can take you there.'

'Thank you!' the horse said. 'It will be nice to sleep in the old place again. It's the only pleasure I've got left in life.'

The people in the wealthy farm opposite the inn had, however, stayed up much later than they usually did.

The farmer was a man of thirty-five. He was a tall fine-looking man with a handsome but very melancholy face. He had been out in the rain during the day and, like everyone else, got soaked. When suppertime came he asked his old mother, who was still the mistress of the farm, to light a fire in the stove so that he could dry his clothes. His mother had proceeded to light a small and feeble fire because they were not in the habit of being generous with the firewood in that house and the farmer had then hung his coat on a chair and placed it in front of the fire. Then he put one foot up on the hearth, rested his elbow on his knee and stood there looking into the fire. He remained in that position for a couple of hours, not moving at all except to throw a piece of wood into the fire every now and then.

The mistress of the house cleared away the supper, made up his bed and then went to sit in her bedroom. Now and again she came to the door and, with a puzzled look, gazed at him standing there by the fire and not going to bed. 'It's nothing, mother,' he said. 'I'm just thinking about something from the old days.'

What had happened was this: as the farmer had been walking past the inn a little earlier, a horse-coper had approached him and asked if he wanted to buy a horse. The man had then shown him an ancient wreck of a horse that was in such a bad way that the farmer had asked the dealer whether he was mad, trying to palm him off with defective goods of that kind.

'Not at all,' the horse-coper had answered. 'It's just that I thought that since you used to own this horse, you might want to provide it with a peaceful old age – and it certainly needs one.'

When the farmer had looked at the horse, he recognised it. It was a horse he himself had bred and broken in, but it did not occur to him to buy an old and worthless beast just because of that. Oh no! He was not the man to throw his money around!

But just seeing the horse had stirred many memories and it was the memories that were keeping him awake and stopping him going to bed.

Oh Lord, what a fine and handsome animal that horse had been, and his father had let him look after it right from the start. He was the one who had broken it in and he had been fonder of it than of anything in the world. Father had complained that he fed it too well and many was the time he had crept quietly to the stable to give it some oats.

While he owned that horse he had never wanted to walk to church, he had always driven – just to show off with the young horse. He himself might be wearing home-spun and home-sewn clothes, and the cart might be plain and unpainted, but the horse was more handsome than any of the others that came to church.

On one occasion he had plucked up the courage to ask his father whether he could buy clothes and paint the cart. It was as if his father had been turned to stone – indeed, the young man thought the old man might have a stroke. He had tried to make his father understand that, since he had such a fine-looking horse to pull him along, he should try to look decent himself.

His father had not answered him, but a couple of days later he took the horse into Örebro and sold it.

It was a cruel thing to do but it was clear that his father feared that the horse would lead the young man into vanity and extravagance and now, all this time later, he had to admit that his father had been right. A horse like that would certainly have been a temptation. But in the beginning his grief had been dreadful. He had sometimes gone into Örebro just to stand on a street corner and see the horse driven past. Or he would slip into the stable and smuggle him a bit of sugar.

'If father dies and I take over the farm,' he had thought, 'the first thing I shall do is to buy my horse back.'

Now his father was dead and he had been running the farm for a couple of years but he had made no effort at all to buy back the horse. Until tonight, he had not thought of him for ages.

It was strange that he had been able to forget the horse so completely. But his father had been a very authoritative and strong-willed man and when the son became an adult and the two of them constantly worked side by side, his father had great power over him. The younger man had come to believe that his father was right in everything he did. Once he had taken over the farm himself, he simply tried to do everything in the way his father would have done it.

He was well aware that people said that his father was miserly but it was surely sensible to keep a tight grip on your purse and not throw money around unnecessarily. The benefits a man was allotted should not be allowed to go to waste. Better to have a farm free of debt and be called miserly than to struggle to pay off big loans like other farmers.

He had reached that point in his thinking when a strange sound made him jump. It was as if a shrill and mocking voice had repeated what he had just been thinking: 'It's best to keep a tight grip on your purse. Better to have a farm free of debt and be called miserly than have to struggle to pay off big loans like other farmers.'

It sounded as though someone was mocking his wisdom and he was on the point of losing his temper until he realised that he was mistaken. The wind had started blowing and he had become so sleepy while standing there that he had taken the howling of the wind in the chimney for someone speaking.

He turned and looked at the kitchen clock just as it struck eleven ponderous strokes. It really was very late. 'Time you went to bed,' he thought. But then he remembered that he had not yet gone round the farm as he did every night to check that all the doors and shutters were closed and all the lights were out. It was a job he had never neglected since becoming master of the farm, so he threw on his coat and went out into the storm.

He found everything as it should be except that the wind had blown the door of the empty hay-barn open. He went back to fetch the key, locked the barn and put the key in his coat pocket. Then he returned to the house, took off his coat and hung it in front of the fire. But he still did not go to bed and he started to walk back and forth across the room instead. The weather outside was dreadful, with a bitingly cold wind and rain mixed with snow. And his old horse was standing outside in this storm without as much as a blanket for protection. He really should have given his old friend a roof over his head now he was back in the district.

Over at the inn, the boy heard an old and squeaky kitchen clock strike eleven just as he was untying the beasts to lead them over to the farmer's barn. It took some time to wake them all up and get them organised but eventually they were ready and, led by the boy, they processed in a long line over to the miserly farmer's yard.

During the time it had taken the boy to do all this, the farmer had gone round the farm and locked the hay-barn so that when the animals came marching over they found that the door was locked. The boy stood there utterly dismayed. No, he was not going to just leave the animals standing there! He would have to go into the house and get hold of the key.

'Keep them all calm while I go and fetch the key!' he said to the old horse before he ran off to do so.

He stopped in the middle of the farmyard to work out how he could get into the house. While he was standing there he saw two small figures walking along the road and stopping outside the inn.

The boy quickly saw that they were two small girls and he ran towards them, thinking that they might be able to assist him.

'There, there now, Britta Maja,' one girl said. 'You don't have to cry any more. We have reached the inn and I'm sure we'll be able to get in.'

No sooner had the girl said this than the boy shouted

to her: 'Don't even try to get into the inn, it's completely impossible. But they don't have any guests at this farm. You should try here instead.'

The girls could hear the words clearly but they could not see who was talking to them. But they did not spend too long thinking about it - the night, after all, was as black as coal. The bigger of the two girls answered at once: 'We don't want to go to that farm because the people who live there are mean and nasty. It's because of them that the two of us are out on the road begging.'

'That may be so,' the boy said, 'but you should go there anyway. Things will turn out well, you'll see.'

'Well, I suppose we can try but I doubt if we'll be let in,' the girl said, and the two of them went up to the house and knocked on the door.

The farmer was still standing in front of the fire thinking about the horse when he heard the knock. He went to see what was happening, thinking at the same time that he was not about to let himself be cajoled into taking in travellers. Just as he turned the latch, however, the wind was ready and waiting and snatched the door from his hands and hurled it wide-open back against the wall. He had to go out onto the porch steps in order to catch hold of the door and pull it closed and by the time he stepped back into the house the two little girls were already inside.

They were two poor beggar girls, ragged and hungry and dirty, a couple of little lasses bent beneath the weight of bags as big as they were.

'Who on earth are you, wandering about so late at night?' the farmer asked in an unfriendly way.

The two children did not answer him at once. First of all they put down their bags and then they went up to him and held out their little hands to shake his. 'We are Anna and Britta Maja from Engärdet,' the elder of the two said, 'and we would like somewhere to stay for the night.'

The farmer did not take their outstretched hands and was on the point of throwing out the young beggars when another memory came into his mind. Engärdet, wasn't that the little cottage where a poor widow and her five children had lived? The widow had been in debt to his father to the tune of a few hundred crowns and in order to get his money back his father had forced the sale of her cottage. The widow and her oldest children had then travelled up to Norrland looking for work, but the two youngest children had fallen on the parish.

The memory made him feel bitter. He knew how much his father had been criticised for demanding that money, even though it was rightfully his.

'What are you doing these days?' he said to the children in a stern tone. 'Doesn't the Poor Law Board look after you? Why are you wandering around begging?'

'It's not our fault,' the bigger girl replied. 'The people we are living with have sent us out begging.'

'Well, you can't complain,' the farmer said. 'I see your bags are full. You'd better take out whatever you have in them and eat your fill because you won't get any food here. All the womenfolk have already gone to bed. Then you can lie down in the corner by the stove so you won't freeze.'

He waved his hands as if dismissing the children and a harsh glint came into his eyes. He had every reason to be grateful that his own father had been careful with what he owned, otherwise he could easily have ended up like these children, forced to roam the high road as beggars.

No sooner did this thought pass through his mind than the shrill mocking voice he had heard already that evening repeated it word for word. He listened and immediately realised that it was nothing, just the wind whistling in the chimney. But the thing was that when the wind played his thoughts back to him like that, in some strange way they seemed to be foolish, harsh and false.

Meanwhile, however, the children had stretched out side by side on the hard floor. But they were not silent, they were lying there mumbling.

'Will you just be quiet!' he said. He was in such a foul-tempered mood that he felt like hitting them.

But the mumbling continued and again he shouted at them to be quiet.

'When my mother left me,' a clear little voice answered him, 'she made me promise that I would say my prayers every evening. So I have to say them – and so does Britta Maja. Once we've finished saying "God who holds all children dear," we shall be quiet.'

The farmer sat very still and listened to the small children saying their prayers. Then he began to stride up and down the room with long steps, wringing his hands as if afflicted by profound distress.

The horse had been sent away from the farm and ruined, and these two children had been turned into beggars and vagrants! Both of these things were his father's doing! Perhaps he had not been so right in everything he did after all.

The farmer sat down on a chair and put his head in his hands. Suddenly his face began to tremble and shake and his eyes filled with tears that he quickly brushed away. But more tears came and he hurried to wipe them away too. It was no help, for the tears came again.

The farmer's mother opened the door from her bedroom and he quickly turned his chair so that his back was to her. But she must have noticed something unusual because she stood quietly behind him for a long time as if waiting for him to say something to her. Then she remembered how difficult men always find it to talk about the things that lie closest to their hearts. She was obviously going to have to help him.

From her bedroom she had seen everything that had gone on in the room so there was no need for her to ask any questions. She just went quietly over to the two sleeping children, lifted them up and carried them through to her own bed. Then she went back to her son.

'Lars,' she said, pretending not to see that he was crying, 'you have to let me keep these children.'

'What, mother?' he said, trying to hold back his tears.

'I have been suffering because of them for many years –

ever since your father took the cottage from their mother. And you have been suffering too.'

'Yes, but ...'

'I want to keep them here and make good people of them. They are too good to go round begging.'

He was unable to answer her for his tears were flowing uncontrollably, but he took his old mother's wrinkled hand and patted it.

But then he jumped up as if something had frightened him.

'What would father say about this?' he said.

'Father had his days in charge,' his mother said, 'and now it is your time. As long as he lived he had to be obeyed, but now it is time for you to show what kind of man you are.'

Her son was so surprised by these words that he stopped crying. 'I am showing the kind of man I am, aren't I?' he said.

'No, you are not,' his mother said. 'You are just trying to be like your father. Father lived through hard times, which made him afraid of being poor. He believed he had to think of himself first and foremost. But you have never had to endure the kind of harsh things that make people hard. You own more than you need, which means that it is quite unnatural not to think of others.'

When the little girls entered the house, Nils had crept in behind them and been hiding in a dark corner ever since. It did not take him long to locate the key to the barn, which was sticking out of the farmer's coat pocket. 'As soon as he throws the children out, I'll take the key and run,' was what he had intended to do.

But the children were not being thrown out and Nils was still sitting in the corner, not at all sure what he should do.

The woman talked to her son for a long time and as she talked his weeping fell silent and an expression of such beauty came to his face that he looked like a different person. And all the time he was stroking her wrinkled old hand.

'Well, now it's time for us to go to bed,' the old woman said when she saw he had become calm.

'No,' he said, standing up quickly. 'I can't go to bed yet.

There is one more stranger I must provide with house room tonight.'

That was all he said before quickly putting on his coat, lighting a lantern and going out. It was still just as cold and just as windy but when he was up on the porch steps he began to hum to himself. He wondered whether the horse would recognise him and whether he would enjoy coming back to his old stable.

As he crossed the farmyard he heard a door banging and slamming in the wind. 'That barn door has blown open again,' he thought and went to close it.

A moment or so later, when he reached the barn and was about to shut the door, he thought he heard a rattling noise inside.

The noise was caused by the boy, who had seized the opportunity to leave the house at the same time as the farmer and immediately run to the barn where he had left the animals. But they were no longer standing outside in the rain. A strong gust of wind had thrown open the barn door some time before and allowed the animals to go in and take shelter. The noise the farmer had heard was the boy running into the barn.

The farmer now shone his lantern into the barn and saw animals sleeping all over the floor. Not a sign of a human being anywhere. The animals were not tethered, they were just lying scattered here and there on the straw.

This intrusion angered him and he started shouting and yelling to wake the sleeping animals and drive them out. The animals lay still, with no intention of letting anything disturb them. The only one to move was an old horse, which walked very slowly towards him.

Suddenly the farmer fell completely silent. He recognised the horse from his gait alone. He raised his lantern towards him and the horse came up and laid his head on his shoulder.

And the farmer began to stroke him. 'O my dear horse, my dear horse!' he said. 'What have they done to you? I shall buy you back and you will never have to leave this farm again. You will be able to do anything you like. All these others you have brought with you, they can stay here, but you must come to the stable with me. Now I can give you all the oats you can eat without having to smuggle them to you. And you haven't been completely ruined. You will be the most handsome horse in the parish again, just as you were before. Yes, you will, you will.'

XXV

THE ICE BREAKS UP

Thursday, 28 April

The weather the following day was bright and beautiful. It is true that there was still quite a strong wind blowing from the west, but there was every reason to be grateful for it because it dried out the roads that had been drenched by the very heavy rains of the day before.

Early in the morning Åsa Goose-girl and Little Mats, the two Småland children, were walking along the highroad that led from Sörmland into Närke. The road ran along the southern shore of Hjälmaren and the children were looking at the ice which still covered most of the lake. The morning sun shone its clear light down on the ice which, far from looking dark and unpleasant as spring ice usually does, gleamed white and inviting. For as far as they could see out over it, it lay there firm and dry. The rainwater had already run down through holes or cracks or been absorbed into the ice itself and all the ice they could see seemed to be in the very best condition.

Åsa Goose-girl and Little Mats were travelling north and they could not help thinking of how much walking would be saved if they could go straight across the big lake rather than walk round it. They knew, of course, that spring ice is dangerous but this ice looked absolutely safe and they could see that it was several inches thick close to the shore. They saw a route they could follow and the other shore of the lake looked so close that they felt they ought to be able to reach it in an hour.

'Come on, let's try!' Little Mats said. 'As long as we keep our eyes open so that we don't fall down any holes in the ice, we shall be fine.'

And so they set out across the lake. The ice was not particularly smooth or slippery and it was very pleasant to walk on. There was, however, more water lying on it than they had noticed and here and there the ice was porous and water bubbled up and down. They had to watch out for places like that, but that was not difficult in bright sunlight in the middle of the day.

The children's progress was quick and easy and the only thing they talked about was how clever they had been to take to the ice rather than carry on walking along the road, which was rutted and slushy after all the rain.

After walking for a while they came close to the island of Vinön, where an old woman caught sight of them from her window. She ran out of her cottage waving her arms at them and shouting something they could not hear. They understood very well that she was warning them against continuing their walk but they, after all, were the ones out on the ice and they could see that there was no danger. It would have been silly to leave the ice when everything was going so splendidly.

So they walked on past Vinön and now there was a stretch of six or seven miles of ice out in front of them. Out here the water on the ice had collected in large pools and the children were forced to make long detours around them, but they thought it was fun and they held competitions to see who could find where the ice was best. They were neither tired nor hungry and they had the whole day in front of them so they just laughed when they met new obstacles.

Now and again they cast a glance over at the far shore and it still seemed a long way off even though they had been walking for a good hour. They were a little surprised at how wide the lake was. 'It's almost as if that shore keeps on moving away from us,' Little Mats said.

There was no shelter from the west wind out here and it was growing stronger with every passing minute, pressing their clothes against them so hard that they found it difficult to move. The cold wind was the first really unpleasant thing they had met since they started their journey. What surprised them was that the wind was making such a loud roar, as if it was carrying the sound from a great mill or from a noisy factory, although such places obviously could not exist out here on the expanse of ice.

They passed west of the big island of Valen and were beginning to feel they were getting close to the northern shore. But the wind was becoming more and more troublesome and the loud roar that accompanied it was increasing so much that they began to feel uneasy.

And then, suddenly, it dawned on them that the roar they could hear was the sound of waves breaking and crashing against the shore. But that was impossible, surely, since the lake was still covered in ice.

In any case, they stopped and looked around and then they noticed, far away to the west, down towards the island of Björnön and the Göksholm peninsula, a white wall running right across the lake. At first they thought it was a rim of snow along a road, but then they realised it was the foam made by waves breaking against the ice.

As soon as they saw this, they took one another by the hand and, without saying a word, began to run. Out to the west of them the ice on the lake had opened up and that rim of foaming water seemed to be rapidly moving east. They did not know whether the ice would break up everywhere or what was going to happen, but they felt that they were in danger.

All of a sudden it felt as if the ice on which they were running rose … rose … and then sank back again as if someone had been pushing it up from below. Then they heard the ice make a dull cracking noise, which was followed by cracks appearing in every direction. The children could see the cracks shooting out across the sheet of ice.

Now everything went silent for a little while, and then the lifting and sinking could be felt once more. The cracks in the ice began to widen out into splits through which they could see water bubbling up. And then almost at once the splits became fissures and the ice began to divide up into big floes.

'Åsa,' Little Mats said, 'this must be the ice breaking up.'

'Yes, it is, Little Mats,' Åsa said, 'but we can still reach land. Come on! Run!'

In fact, the wind and the waves still had much to do before the lake would be clear of ice. The hardest part at the start, no doubt, was to break the ice sheet into pieces, but all of those pieces had to be broken up again and hurled against one another until they were shattered, ground down and dissolved. There was still a good deal of hard, firm ice forming large and as yet undamaged expanses.

The greatest danger for the children, though, was that they could not look down upon the ice from above; they could not see where the fissures were so wide that there was no chance of crossing them; they did not know where the large ice-floes were, the ones that could carry their weight. And so they wandered back and forth, hither and thither on the breaking ice, getting farther out onto the lake rather than closer to the shore, until they became so terrified and confused that they just stood still and wept.

But then, swinging in above them, came a skein of wild geese in rapid flight. The calls of the geese sounded loud and strong and the strange thing was that amidst all the cackling the children could hear the words: 'You must go to the right, to the right, to the right!'

The children set off at once to follow that advice but it was not long before they came to another wide crack and halted in confusion once again.

And once again they could hear the geese calling overhead and amidst all the cackling they could pick out a few words: 'Stay where you are! Stay where you are!'

The children did not say a word to each other about what they were hearing, but they obeyed the words and stayed still. Soon the ice-floes drifted together so that they could step across the gap. Taking each other by the hand, they jumped, though they were worried not just by the danger they were in

but also by the help they were receiving.

Soon they came to another place where they hesitated and once more they heard the voice calling down to them: 'Straight on! Straight on! Straight on!'

All this went on for half an hour until they reached the long headland at Lungersudden where they were able to leave the ice and wade ashore. It was easy to see how frightened they had been because once they were on dry land they did not even stop to look back at the lake, where the waves had now begun to overturn the blocks of ice more and more violently. But once they had climbed a little way up the headland, Åsa suddenly stopped. 'Wait here, Little Mats!' she said. 'There is something I have forgotten.'

Åsa Goose-girl went back down to the shore. There she began digging around in her bag until at last she found a tiny wooden shoe, which she put down on a stone where it was clearly visible. Then she walked back to Little Mats without looking back at all.

But no sooner had she turned her back than a big white gander hurtled down from the sky, snatched up the wooden shoe and rose back up into the air just as swiftly.

NOTES

p. 41   *Yksi, Kaksi, Kolme, Neljä, Viisi, Kuusi*: the names of the geese are the Finnish numerals 1-6.

p. 92   *Kullamannen's Cavern*: Kullamannen was a legendary figure with prophetic gifts supposedly resident on the Kullaberg.

p. 128   *Maglesten boulder*: an enormous erratic boulder near Kristianstad; according to Linnaeus it is approximately 30ft long by 24ft wide by 20ft high.

p. 132   *Karl XI*: (1655-1697), King of Sweden from 1660 until his death.

p. 134   *Chapman*: Fredrik Henrik af Chapman (1721-1808), Swedish shipbuilder and naval architect, son of an English naval officer. The floating youth hostel in Stockholm is named after him. *Puke*: Johan af Puke (1751-1816), Swedish admiral. *Trolle*: Henrik af Trolle (1730-1784), Swedish admiral. *Hogland*: indecisive naval battle between Swedish and Russian fleets in 1788. *Svensksund*: Swedish naval victory over the Russians in 1790.

p. 153   *Great Alvar*: (Swedish: Stora Alvaret), a limestone plateau of c.100 square miles on Öland. The whole of southern Öland is a World Heritage Site.

p. 171   *Blåkulla*: the place to which witches traditionally went to celebrate the witches' sabbath with the devil.

p. 180   *Vineta*: a town, possibly legendary, on the coast of the Baltic Sea in the area of the current Polish-German border. While there is no hard evidence that Vineta ever existed, there are a number of medieval references to a great port.

p. 192 *Götaland*: generic name for the southern provinces of Sweden, roughly equivalent to the areas south of (and including) the great lakes Vänern and Vättern.

p. 208 *Caspar, Melchior, Balthasar*: the 'three kings' or the 'three wise men' who brought gifts to the infant Jesus. Painted wall hangings depicting religious themes and stories were popular items of folk art, particularly in the southern provinces of Sweden in the period 1750-1850.

p. 229 *Tåkern*: a shallow lake in Östergötland, east of Lake Vättern. Tåkern is one of the most important European bird lakes. Its water level was lowered in the 1840s and it has an average depth of only 2.6 feet.

p. 247 *Ulvåsa woman*: St Birgitta (1303-1373) and her husband Ulf Gudmarsson lived at Ulvåsa in Östergötland.

p. 279 *nun moths*: there was a major plague of nun moths (Lymantria monacha) in Sweden between 1898 and 1902. Kolmården was so badly afflicted that a railway was built to transport out all the timber felled as part of the effort to control the plague.

p. 295 *Lord Karl*: Karl (1550-1611), Duke of Södermanland and later King Karl IX.

p. 300 *Pintorp Wifie*: up until the seventeenth century the site of the Eriksberg manor house was known as Pintorp and was reputed to have been the home of an evil lady of the manor who took pleasure in tormenting her peasantry.

p. 301 *The Woman in White*: a ghost reputed to haunt the manor house at Vibyholm.

p. 302 *Bishop Rogge*: Kort Rogge (1425-1501), Bishop of Strängnäs who rebuilt and extended the cathedral there as well as building an impressive bishop's palace.

p. 303 *King Erik*: King Erik XIV (1533-1577) imprisoned his brother Johan III in Gripsholm Castle and, after he was deposed, was himself imprisoned there.

TRANSLATOR'S AFTERWORD

The two volumes of *Nils Holgerssons underbara resa genom Sverige* (*Nils Holgersson's Wonderful Journey through Sweden*) were first published in November 1906 and December 1907. In 1901 Selma Lagerlöf had been approached by Sveriges Allmänna Folkskollärareförening to write a geography reader suitable for use with nine-year-olds in elementary school. After stipulating a number of conditions, among which were that she alone would be responsible for writing the text and that her approach would be literary/storybook rather than textbook, Lagerlöf took on the commission. The literary approach to school readers she was proposing was very different indeed from the original proposal put to her and her ideas were to bear fruit in a number of other classics of Swedish literature that followed in the same series of readers: Verner von Heidenstam's *Svenskarna och deras hövdingar* (*The Swedes and their Leaders*, 1910) and Sven Hedin's *Från pol till pol* (*From Pole to Pole*, 1911) were later to join *Nils Holgersson* in the series. The original timescale envisaged for the task soon proved hopelessly optimistic and over the following years, in addition to a variety of other literary projects that included the completion of *Jerusalem* and the writing of *Herr Arnes penningar* (*Lord Arne's Silver*), Lagerlöf spent much time researching and gathering the background material necessary to a geography reader, a great deal of which was sent to her by a varied and expert body of informants which included many elementary school teachers. She also made a number of journeys to visit parts of Sweden she was unfamiliar with, including notably a six-week tour of the far north in the summer of 1904.

With much of the factual material to hand, years passing and a rather impatient committee of teachers exerting a certain amount of pressure, Selma Lagerlöf still found herself unable to decide how to tell her story. Initially her intention had been to structure her narrative around local legends and folk tales but she had been unable to make any progress that way. In the spring of 1905, however, the way forward suddenly became clear to her and she described it in a later letter (June 1906) to Alfred Dalin, one of the two leading spirits of the reader project, the other being Fridtjuv Berg.

'While I was trying to find a way of making descriptions of streams and mosses and coasts and hills palatable to nine-year-olds the animal books written by the English author Kipling came to my mind. … it was his example that encouraged me to try to make the country come alive by peopling it with animals. In the old animal stories (the fables) the animals behave very strangely in that they thresh and sow and are identical to people. Kipling makes them talk and be very shrewd but in other respects they retain their animal ways. And that is what I have now done. I have tried to be as faithful to nature and the truth as it is possible to be, so that the book will provide a genuine depiction of the animal life of our country. As with everything that is told in story form, a deal of what actually happens is invented, but all the underpinnings are as correct as I could make them on the basis of the research of my sources.'

From that point onwards the writing of the text proceeded rapidly, the intention being that the book as a whole should be ready for publication by the Christmas of 1906. The decision to issue it in two volumes was not taken until the autumn of that year and was mainly a result of problems with the illustrations. The leading wildlife and nature artist Bruno Liljefors had been approached to provide illustrations but had turned the offer down. John Bauer was approached instead, but Selma Lagerlöf was horrified by his preliminary sketches, describing them as 'atrocious' – only two of his illustrations were eventually used, the rest of the volume being illustrated with rather drab photographs. In fact the illustrations in the first edition underline the school reader origins of the book and most of them depict worthy architectural or landscape subjects; it was only in later editions, as the storybook status of the text became more established, that more imaginative illustrations became the norm.

Nor were the illustrations the only difficulties at this stage since the project committee felt the need to require a substantial number of editorial changes, many of which were trivial and most of which Selma Lagerlöf resisted. Given that the aim of the revisions sometimes seemed to be to ensure that only appropriately orderly behaviour by pupils and teachers in the classroom and playground was described, it is difficult not to smile at some of the emendations requested. In her original description of the flight of the geese over the elementary school in Huskvarna (Alfred Dalin's own school), for instance, Lagerlöf had written that 'a crowd of children rushed out of the school building'. At Dalin's request – he pointed out that it was at least thirty years since any rushing had gone on in his school – she changed this to read: 'A crowd of children marched out rank by rank'.

The production of any new school reader is, of course, a matter to be taken seriously and that was all the more so in the case of *Nils Holgersson*. Given its unparalleled later status as a story, it is easy to overlook quite how radical an initiative it was at the time. The members of the teachers' organisation that lay behind the project were educational reformers with a mission to provide an alternative reader to the official *Läsebok för folkskolan* (*Elementary School Reader*) first published in 1868, which they considered to be not only out-dated and boring but also backward-looking. What should be expected of a school reader was a matter of debate in the years around the turn of the century and no less a figure than Ellen Key had joined the debate with an essay, 'Patriotism and School Readers', in 1898. Lagerlöf herself had written expressing her support for Key's views, and we should remember that

Selma Lagerlöf, having spent a decade as a teacher, had direct knowledge and experience of the reader issue. How important she considered it to be becomes apparent in a letter to Dalin in 1909 in which she wrote: 'With the help of good readers we should really be able to introduce into the schools a level of public education so considerable that current distinctions of social class are significantly diminished'. *Nils Holgersson*, then, is part of the democratically reformist development in the late nineteenth and early twentieth century that created modern Sweden.

*

The idea of putting a boy on the back of a gander and flying him from one end of the country to the other and back now seems an obvious one. But that is now and, anyway, that is just the starting point of the story. It is, of course, a story on multiple levels. On one level it is the story of Sweden, of the geography and the geology of the country, of its climate and vegetation and natural resources, and of the creatures (human and non-human) whose lives depend on using those resources. The great and the grand, lords and ladies, make their appearances but are notable for the rarity of their presence and, instead, the focus – in keeping with the democratically progressive spirit of the book's inception – is on farmers and fishers, goose-herds and Sami, miners and loggers, and on the animals – rats and eagles and elk, foxes and geese, cows, bears, horses and sheep. Plants as well as animals, trees in particular, mark our climatic march to the north, spurred on by the 'Onwards!' call of the smiling sun before we are driven back south by the great Ice Troll. Hills and mountains are created by primeval giants hurling rocks, valleys are carved out by personified rivers, Öland is a calcified butterfly too heavy to fly above the water, Uppland a beggar who becomes rich and successful on pickings from others. Every province has its story and out of the many fantasies a country emerges, a country in which the core values are perhaps best symbolised by the resolute and patient toil and solidarity of the many watercourses that join the Dalälven River in cutting a way through to the sea.

As any school reader should, *Nils Holgersson* delineates the identity of the country and celebrates its virtues, but it does so without glorification. Just as radical as the use of fable and fantasy in the context of a school reader is the way Lagerlöf weaves in social issues. The northwards route of Nils and the geese is paralleled by the journey of Åsa Goose-girl and Little Mats in search of their father, but their journey is set in motion by the scourge of the tuberculosis that has wiped out their family and driven their father to despair. The lonely death of the old peasant woman on her dilapidated farm in Småland reveals the sadness of those left behind by the great nineteenth-century emigration. The small children made homeless and sent out to beg on the roads in Närke implicitly question both the attitude of affluent farmers and the poor laws. Nor are the animals forgotten – both bears and birds plead for space to be left for them.

Nils himself has multiple roles to play. He is, of course, the main character, the unkind and naughty boy who develops and changes in the course of the journey and who returns home at last as a responsible citizen, having learnt virtue from the geese he travelled with and from observing their interplay with people and animals. He is also the intermediary between the reader and the animal world, making it possible for us to understand the language of that world. And in a narrative sense he is both an agent of change and our eyes and ears in the story. It is Nils who plays the part of the Pied Piper and leads the rats from Glimmingehus, and it is through the small concealed listener and watcher that we share the life story of Kersti from Dalarna or the history of the mythical town of Vineta.

Inevitably, there were conservative voices keen to point out that *Nils Holgersson* was not how a proper school reader should be. How could children be expected to distinguish between fantasy and fact? Worse, perhaps, was the danger that it might lead the young to expect all their learning to be entertaining and imaginative, thus encouraging superficiality and even promoting a morally deleterious desire to read for pleasure! Rather more serious was the critic (Professor Einar Lönnberg) who drew attention to quite a few, though frequently trivial, inaccuracies of natural historical detail – the snipe on Lake Tåkern hatch too early, red deer do not rut in the spring and so on: Lönnberg, though correct on such points, rather reveals his true colours when he concludes that inaccuracies of this kind may cause children to develop 'a deplorable contempt for the truth which could have unfortunate consequences for them in the future'. (The timing of the publication of his article – the day before Selma Lagerlöf was to receive an honorary doctorate from Uppsala University – highlights just how radical *Nils Holgersson* was perceived to be and how the opposition was prepared to fight dirty.) Fortunately, however, even at the start there were far more supportive voices than there were disapproving ones. The radical new approach, that reflected an equally radical new understanding of the world of childhood, won favour and *Nils Holgersson* was quickly on its way to becoming much more than a school reader.

*

There was something just a little daunting about setting out to translate *Nils Holgersson's Wonderful Journey through Sweden*. It is six hundred pages long, has already been translated into close to fifty languages (in some cases several times), has been made into animated films (Sweden 1939 and the Soviet Union 1955), a 52-part animé television series (Japan 1980 and sold on to twenty-five countries), a film (Sweden 1962) and a two-part television drama (Germany 2011). A 1997 poll in Sweden voted *Nils Holgersson* the fifth best Swedish book of the century and a further poll in 1998 voted it the sixth most important Swedish book of the century; a poll in the French newspaper *Le Monde* found it to be the sixty-eighth best book of the twentieth century worldwide. Nils and/or his goose companions have appeared on postage stamps (Sweden and Germany) and on banknotes (Sweden). Schools have been named after him, as many in Germany as in Sweden, as have hotels and restaurants (including one in Hungary), ships and aircraft. Nils has been the subject of jigsaws and plastic figures, as well as the inspiration for several fine statues (Skurup and Karlskrona). He is frequently dramatised, particularly for summer theatres, and he is also commemorated by the Nils Holgersson-plakett, a prize awarded annually to the author of the year's best Swedish book for children or young people. Least expected, perhaps, though quite logical once thought about, is the use of the name in the Nils Holgersson-rapport, an annual comparative cost-of-living survey that covers all the local authorities in Sweden.

All of that makes the fact that the present volume is the first full English translation of *Nils Holgersson* rather surprising. The book was translated into English very soon after its Swedish publication: the American translator Velma Swanston Howard, who was to be Selma Lagerlöf's main English-language translator, produced *The Wonderful Adventures of Nils* in 1907 and followed it with *Further Adventures of Nils* in 1911, both volumes being published in London and New York. Howard's translations are, however, far from complete. She notes in her short translator's introduction to *Further Adventures* that: 'Some of the purely geographical matter in the Swedish original ... has been eliminated from the English version. The author has rendered valuable assistance in cutting certain chapters and abridging others. Also, with the author's approval, cuts have been made where the descriptive matter was merely of local interest. But the story itself is intact.' The excisions are, in fact, rather more substantial than this modest statement suggests, including whole chapters where it is difficult to see 'local' or 'geographical' justification for the cuts. Nevertheless, both in Britain and the United States, Howard's translations have to all intents and purposes come to represent *Nils Holgersson* in English during the century since they first appeared and virtually all of the many adaptations, abridgments, revisions, simplified versions and picture books that have appeared since have been based directly on Velma Swanston Howard's work with little or no reference to the original Swedish. The solitary exception to this appears to be Joan Tate's translation, published in 1992 by the Edinburgh publisher Floris, of the very abbreviated (88 pp.) picture book version of *Nils Holgersson*, edited by Rebecca Alsberg, illustrated by Lars Klinting and published in Stockholm by Bonniers juniorförlag (1989).

The present translation was made using the following two editions: Selma Lagerlöf, *Nils Holgerssons underbara resa genom Sverige*, Volume 1 (1907) and Volume 2 (1909), Läseböcker för Sveriges barndomsskolor utgivna av Alfr. Dalin och Fridtjuv Berg, Stockholm: Albert Bonniers förlag; and Selma Lagerlöf, *Nils Holgerssons underbara resa genom Sverige*, illustrated by Bertil Lybeck, Stockholm: Bonniers Juniorförlag, 1981. The sole textual difference between those editions is that the 1907/1909 edition still makes use of plural verb forms whereas the 1981 edition does not. It should be noted that, for practical reasons of size, the present translation does not split the volumes at the same point as the 1907/1909 Swedish edition.

*

In the century of his existence *Nils Holgersson* has not been given the critical attention in English he deserves. In the last decade or so, however, a number of scholars have set about rectifying that omission and I list here a selection of recent articles in English.

Beckett, Sandra L. "*The Wonderful Adventures of Nils*: the 'perfect' text for which Michel Tournier strives". *Selma Lagerlöf seen from abroad. Selma Lagerlöf i utlandsperspektiv: ett symposium i Vitterhetsakademien den 11 och 12 september 1997.* Ed. Louise Vinge. Stockholm: Kungl. Vitterhets, historie och antikvitets akademien, 1998: 73-86.

Cabanel, Patrick. "Book, school and nation: Sweden in *The wonderful adventures of Nils*", *Nordic Historical Review* 3 (2007): 93-112.

Graves, Peter. "The reception of Selma Lagerlöf in Britain". *Selma Lagerlöf seen from abroad. Selma Lagerlöf i utlandsperspektiv: ett symposium i Vitterhetsakademien den 11 och 12 september 1997*. Ed. Louise Vinge. Stockholm: Kungl. Vitterhets, historie och antikvitets akademien, 1998: 9-18.

Oscarson, Christopher. "*Nils Holgersson*, empty maps and the entangled bird's-eye view of Sweden", *Edda* 109 (2009): 99-117.

Rahn, Suzanne. "Rediscovering Nils", *The Lion and the Unicorn* 10 (1986): 158-166.

Rahn, Suzanne. "The boy and the wild geese: Selma Lagerlöf's Nils", *Rediscoveries in children's literature*. Ed. Suzanne Rahn. New York and London: Garland Publishing Inc, 1995: 39-50.

Sundmark, Björn. "Lagerlöf's legacy: a hundred years of writing the nation", *Bookbird* 46 (3) (2003): 14-20.

Sundmark, Björn. "Of Nils and nation: Selma Lagerlöf's The wonderful adventures of Nils", *International Research in Children's Literature* 1 (2) (2008): 168-186.

Sundmark, Björn. "'But the story itself is intact'. Or is it?". *Northern Lights: translation in the Nordic countries*. Ed. Brett Epstein. Bern: Peter Lang, 2009: 167-180.

Sundmark, Björn. "Citizenship and children's identity in *The wonderful adventures of Nils* and *Scouting for boys*", *Children's Literature in Education* 40 (2) (2009): 109-119.

Thomsen, Bjarne Thorup. "Terra (In)cognita. Reflections on the Search for the Sacred Place in Selma Lagerlöf's *Jerusalem* and *Nils Holgerssons underbara resa genom Sverige*". *Selma Lagerlöf seen from abroad. Selma Lagerlöf i utlandsperspektiv: ett symposium i Vitterhetsakademien den 11 och 12 september 1997*. Ed. Louise Vinge. Stockholm: Kungl. Vitterhets, historie och antikvitets akademien, 1998: 131-142.

*

Finally it remains for me to thank friends and colleagues who have helped along the way: Gunilla Blom Thomsen for helpful suggestions and clarifications; Charlotte Berry for helping to steer a path through a tangle of editions; Janet Garton and Helena Forsås-Scott for detailed reading and many helpful suggestions; Elga Graves for patient encouragement; Elettra Carbone and Marita Fraser for good ideas and good design; Bea Bonafini for her wonderful illustrations. Anyone who has read my friend and colleague Bjarne Thorup Thomsen's fine book *Lagerlöfs litterære landvinding* (Amsterdam Contributions to Scandinavian Studies Volume 3, Amsterdam: Scandinavisch Instituut, 2007) will recognise that this Afterword owes it a considerable debt, as it also does to Gunnar Ahlström's *Den underbara resan* (Lund: Gleerups, 1942).

ILLUSTRATOR'S AFTERWORD

From the very first chapter of *Nils Holgersson's Wonderful Journey through Sweden*, I too hopped onto the back of a Swedish farm goose, finding myself swept away from reality and into Lagerlöf's tale, transported there by her creatures. As her stories unfolded beneath my eyes, I could not help but create and so began a collaboration with the author on this wonderful narrative. My aim is the visual enrichment of her textual creation, with illustrations that act as a fresh means of imaginative transportation and an exploration of her tale and beyond.

Consequently, I embarked on a creative process that spans seven months of Nils's life. The scenes that are illustrated were those that seemed to me to vibrate the most with visual splendour, either because they represented climactic moments in Nils's adventure, or because they seemed dense with magical power, often both.

My set of illustrations for this first complete English translation of *Nils Holgersson's Wonderful Journey through Sweden* comes after a long lineage of previously conceived visual interpretations of the book. Amongst these are the iconic image of Nils on the back of a goose printed on the reverse side of the Swedish twenty-kronor banknote, the Japanese animé adaptation for a television series circulated all over the world in 1980 by Studio Pierrot, and Ralf Borselius's sculpture of a tiny Nils sitting on a huge book in Karlskrona, (2006). My approach, however, has been so different from this visual history of interpretations that it dispensed with referencing other material; instead, I hope I have been able to present an experimental, inquisitive and curious new vision of Lagerlöf's story.

As this book sits comfortably on the border between a children's and an adult's read, my illustrations attempt to remain faithful to this dual role by incorporating aesthetic traits accessible to readers of all ages. In them, I have combined drawings with photographs of Sweden, as well as anatomically accurate depictions of animals alongside more stylised representations of humans. The creative process involves the hand-drawn silhouettes that are subsequently digitally processed: in a similar way to collage, the shapes are cut out to reveal the image beneath, which has been previously manipulated.

The duality of the aesthetic style of the illustrations initially allows you to perceive just the patterned silhouettes of the characters in action; only after this can you proceed to recognise the world beyond, contained within the forms of the characters (or vice versa). They therefore act as windows, often consisting of photographs of places faithful to the geographical location of the selected passage, or the scenery of the setting, or of an image that translates the feeling of the scene. It appears, therefore, that the represented characters have an internal energy and movement, as well as acting as windows on to Sweden.

The Boy, p. 29.
This first chapter takes hold of the reader in very much the same way as the goose carries Nils away; the latter, who had intended to grab hold of the goose to prevent his escape, and whose inability to do so resulted in a life-changing journey, is emblematic of the reader's own experience as she plunges into this long novel, aware of the instantaneous hold it has on her and yet unaware of what awaits her.

Multiple layers of meaning are expressed simultaneously as Nils hangs on to the goose. Firstly, he is lifted off the ground to a tremendous height, and comes to the realisation that what he experiences is an altered perception of the world, seen from a new perspective. Through one symbolic action, Lagerlöf speaks of the change that will occur in Nils from then on, as he finds himself in situations that force changes in his perspective on life, and which increase his understanding of the world whilst making him a better and wiser person. Secondly, this marks Nils's very first intimate contact with the gander, who will become his best friend. The necessity of staying with the gander makes Nils dependent on him, whilst forcing him to 'put himself in his shoes', or rather, experience life from the perspective of a goose.

Consequently, it was inevitable that my first illustration would be of this precise moment, so that those who are familiar with the book would be able to recognise it at first glance. The unusually small proportion of the petrified child hanging next to the flying gander is an immediate sign of the magical essence of the text, through which you can see an aerial view of the 'checked-cloth' landscape that forms beneath Nils's eyes.

Akka from Kebnekaise, p. 49.
After Nils spends a dangerous night with the geese, a malign character that disrupts the peace of their sleep and will continue to do so throughout their journey, Smirre Fox, is introduced. I chose this moment as it culminates in a situation where loyalty is reciprocated with loyalty, as in their turn the geese rescue Nils after the latter rescues the captured goose. The boy waits alone in a dark forest for the entire night, out of reach of the vigilant fox but unable to escape, and unaware that aid is on its way. It is a moment that tests his courage, patience and endurance – qualities he will resort to extensively further on. I therefore chose a dark, foggy Swedish forest to express this dramatic moment.

Glimmingehus, p. 87.
Nils's human qualities come to the fore in order to divert malign characters – the grey rats – from their evil deeds, through non-violent means. Lagerlöf adopts the well-known sixteenth-century story of a piper who uses his magic pipe to lure rats away, handing the pipe over to Nils, who plays

it in order to hypnotise the rats and lead them away. I was particularly affected by the sinister and creepy image of this tiny boy confronting the masses of rats (almost larger than himself) all on his own, creating order only through the use of a magical and mythical instrument, the event set in the architecturally unique Swedish castle Glimmingehus.

The Great Crane Dance on the Kullaberg, p. 99.
I was tempted to create a complex tapestry of the various species showing off the beauty for which they are most admired. Instead, what I chose to depict was the perfection of order, unison and harmony of co-ordination. Since Lagerlöf epitomises the flying cranes as the sight that held most power and beauty, I created an image where the elegance of the individual cranes transforms into an increasingly solid, unified shape.

The scene is located in the Kullaberg nature reserve in northwest Skåne, where the Swedish artist Lars Vilks had built Nimis in 1980. Details of this sculpture, which consists of driftwood assembled into tower-like constructions, allow the cranes to appear as if also made of wooden sticks, whilst remaining visually feather-like.

By Ronneby River, p. 119.
There is an inherent tension in this chapter that again presents the unsettled life of Nils and the geese. With the threatening presence of Smirre, who tracks down the geese wherever they go, Lagerlöf expresses the indispensability of Nils to the geese as their most trustworthy guardian against predators. I have depicted the cunning of Smirre which allows him to reach the geese even when he is incapable of attacking them himself. A photo of Swedish wild water provides the cliff and the animals themselves, so that the fast-paced water current expresses the energy of movement and agitation as the geese flee.

The Island of Lilla Karlsö, p. 165.
I presented the dramatic moment in which the three hunting foxes are taught a lesson by the combined strength of the ram and the intelligent guidance of the boy. The scene forms into a dynamic chain as the ram powerfully launches head-on into the approaching foxes, resulting in sequential somersaults. Nils is once again the mind behind the action that punishes the evil and grants safety and peace to the good. Due to the intensity of dynamism and energy in this sequence, I chose a detail of wispy sheep wool, from the sheep of this geographical area, as the most appropriate background.

Two Towns, p. 177.
The magical quality of a town's extraordinary appearance and disappearance is also an event in Nils's adventure where the boundary between dream and reality is blurred. It has an incredibly strong effect on the boy, as he is incapable of helping those in need. As a result, he carries with him a sense of guilt that haunts him as he envisions what could have been and what in reality is not, and ponders the fact that he has been the cause of the loss of such a beautiful and wealthy town. I chose an aerial view of waves in the Baltic Sea as the entity that swallows up the town. Its smoky quality is appropriate for this magical and ephemeral vision.

The Crows, p. 205.
In this sensational scene, Nils is captured and bullied by crows to carry out a deed arranged by Smirre. I depict the chaotic simultaneity of events, where we see the crow leader unintentionally killed by Nils moments before, and the curious appearance of a hand from within a pot; coins are thrown that are instantaneously snatched away by the uproar of disorderly crows. Nils is now on a big heath in the province of Småland, known at the time for its expanses of heather. As these are characteristic of the location, I chose an expanse of heather from the geographical area to flesh out the characters.

The Saga of Karr and Greyfur, p. 275.
This image pictures the strong bond of friendship between Greyfur the elk and Karr the hunting dog, as they reunite in this moment of need where they seek each other's support. It is a troubled moment where the tragic destruction of the forest affects an overwhelming number of creatures, and the collective effort to save the forest unites people and animals in a struggle for survival. In my image, the elk and the dog helplessly look up at the disintegrating trees in an attempt to understand the disaster. The image I chose is of a Swedish forest in wintertime, where the lack of leaves provokes a feeling of complete desolation.

The Ice Breaks Up, p. 327.
Possibly my favourite image, I chose this tragic moment for its visual power, as well as for how poignantly Lagerlöf depicts the race for survival of the brother and sister. I imagined the aerial view of the running children, seen from the perspective of the gander and the boy as they direct the children out of the maze of cracking ice. The image evokes the precarious balance between life and death as the children try to avoid running into dead ends while making their way across. It is the first inverted image I use, where the picture of the iced lake fills a negative space, causing an initial sense of disorientation appropriate to the nature of the image.

PHOTOGRAPHIC CREDITS

Credits for the photographs adapted by the Illustrator in the creation of the illustrations for this book.

The Boy, p. 29.
Bea Bonafini

Akka from Kebnekaise, p. 49.
Sara Ingman / www.imagebank.sweden.se

Glimmingehus, p. 87.
Tristanf / www.flickr.com

The Great Crane Dance on the Kullaberg, p. 99.
Jens Rydén / www.imagebank.sweden.se
Karen Chan / www.flickr.com

By Ronneby River, p. 119.
Fredrik Broman / www.imagebank.sweden.se

The Island of Lilla Karlsö, p. 165.
AnnaKika / www.flickr.com

Two Towns, p. 177.
Rayandbee / www.flickr.com

The Crows, p. 205.
Melker Dahlstrand / www.imagebank.sweden.se

The Saga of Karr and Greyfur, p. 275.
Hans Kylberg / www.flickr.com

The Ice Breaks Up, p. 327.
Marcus Hansson / www.flickr.com

SELMA LAGERLÖF

Lord Arne's Silver

(translated by Sarah Death)

An economical and haunting tale, published in book form in 1904 and set in the sixteenth century on the snowbound west coast of Sweden, *Lord Arne's Silver* is a classic from the pen of an author consummately skilled in the deployment of narrative power and ambivalence. A story of robbery and murder, retribution, love and betrayal plays out against the backdrop of the stalwart fishing community of the archipelago. Young Elsalill, sole survivor of the mass killing in the home of rich cleric Lord Arne, becomes a pawn in dangerous games both earthly and supernatural. As the deep-frozen sea stops the murderers escaping, sacrifice and atonement are the price that has to be paid.

ISBN 9781870041904
UK £9.95
(Paperback, 102 pages)

SELMA LAGERLÖF

The Phantom Carriage

(translated by Peter Graves)

Written in 1912, Selma Lagerlöf's *The Phantom Carriage* is a powerful combination of ghost story and social realism, partly played out among the slums and partly in the transitional sphere between life and death. The vengeful and alcoholic David Holm is led to atonement and salvation by the love of a dying Salvation Army slum sister under the guidance of the driver of the death-cart that gathers in the souls of the dying poor. Inspired by Charles Dickens's *A Christmas Carol*, *The Phantom Carriage* remained one of Lagerlöf's own favourites, and Victor Sjöström's 1920 film version of the story is one of the greatest achievements of the Swedish silent cinema.

ISBN 9781870041911
UK £11.95
(Paperback, 126 pages)

SELMA LAGERLÖF

The Löwensköld Ring

(translated by Linda Schenck)

The *Löwensköld Ring* (1925) is the first volume of the trilogy considered to have been Selma Lagerlöf's last work of prose fiction. Set in the Swedish province of Värmland in the eighteenth century, the narrative traces the consequences of the theft of General Löwensköld's ring from his coffin, and develops into a disturbing tale of revenge from beyond the grave. It is also a tale about decisive women. The narrative twists and the foregrounding of alternative interpretations confront the reader with a pervasive sense of ambiguity. Along with the narrative technique, the spell of the ring extends into the two subsequent volumes, *Charlotte Löwensköld* (1925) and *Anna Svärd* (1928).

ISBN 9781870041928
UK £9.95
(Paperback, 120 pages)

AUGUST STRINDBERG

Strindberg's One-Act Plays: A Selection

Simoom, Facing Death, The Outlaw, The Bond

(translated by Agnes Broome, Anna Holmwood,
John K Mitchinson, Mathelinda Nabugodi,
Nichola Smalley and Anna Tebelius)

To most English-language readers and theatregoers, Strindberg is mainly known for naturalistic plays such as *Miss Julie* and *The Father*, but the dramatic output of Sweden's national playwright is infinitely richer and more extensive than these would suggest. This volume presents four of Strindberg's lesser-known one-act plays, *The Bond*, *Facing Death*, *The Outlaw* and *Simoom*, written between 1871 and 1892, which showcase Strindberg's remarkable range. *The Bond* and *Facing Death*, which fall at the end of the time span, are familiarly naturalistic plays set in contemporary European settings and demonstrate Strindberg's provocative engagement with contentious issues of his day. The early experiment *The Outlaw*, however, takes place in the bleak landscapes of the Viking north, drawing heavily on the style of Icelandic sagas. In *Simoom*, written in 1889, a practically gothic narrative transports us to the scorching deserts of French-colonial Algeria, allowing us to observe the beginnings of Strindberg's experimental, mystical phase which culminated in *A Dream Play*. Different as the four plays are, however, when read together they form a thematic unity, revealing the beating heart of Strindberg's creativity, the issue at the core of his writing: love as a war eternally waged between man and woman, husband and wife, children and parents, and individuals and society.

ISBN 9781870041935
UK £9.95
(Paperback, 128 pages)

JONAS LIE
The Family at Gilje
(translated by Marie Wells)

Captain Jæger is the well-meaning but temperamental head of a rural family living in straitened circumstances in 1840s Norway. The novel focuses on the fates of the women of the family: the heroic Ma, who struggles unremittingly to keep up appearances and make ends meet, and their eldest daughter Thinka, forced to renounce the love of her life and marry an older and wealthier suitor. Then there is the younger daughter, the talented and beautiful Inger-Johanna, destined to make a splendid match – but will the captain with the brilliant diplomatic career ahead of him make her happy? With great empathy and affection for each member of the family Lie evokes the tragedy of hopes dashed by the harsh social and economic realities of the day, and the influence of one person who dares to think differently. Both in the landscape and in the characters the wildness of nature is played out against the constraints of culture.

ISBN 9781870041942
UK £14.95
(Paperback, 210 pages)

Lightning Source UK Ltd.
Milton Keynes UK
UKOW042114110213

206113UK00005B/34/P